Published by Font Publications, London, UK.
All enquiries to info@ornaross.com.

ISBN EBOOK: 978-1-909888-23-4
ISBN PBOOK POD: 978-1-909888-22-7
ISBN TRADE PBOOK: 978-1-909888-24-1

Cover Art: Jane Dixon Smith
Cover Design: JD Smith Design
Editorial: Joni Rodgers. Jerusha Rodgers. Helen Baggot. Anna Farano.
Formatting & Interior Design: Amie McCracken

Her Secret Rose

Orna Ross

About the Author

Orna Ross inspires people to "go creative", through her novels and poetry; her work for the Alliance of Independent Authors (ALLi), which has seen her named one of the 100 most influential people in publishing, by *The Bookseller* magazine; and her writings about conscious creation and creative living. She was born and raised in Ireland and now lives in London.

For Ross.
"Irish poets, learn your trade." WB Yeats.

Table of Contents

Part One:
1889–1891

A Burning Cloud

WHAT YOU have to understand is that they were like gods to us. That was how they put themselves across, as if two people of the *Shee* had come to earth amongst us, and that was how some of us took them up.

Their height alone was a wonder, especially in her. This was a time when most of Ireland and England went half-hungry, and the average person did well to reach five-foot-four. If you didn't see your ribs when you looked down at yourself naked, if you had a few decent rags to pull about your person, you were well got. If you'd two meals a day and a winter coat, you were on the pig's back.

Then along would come those two, striding the full length of their legs down Grafton Street or Piccadilly, she in her Parisian finery, with a hat atop her great height, one of those elevated concoctions they loved back then. Oftentimes too, she'd have her Great Dane stepping out in front of them, a slavering beast of a thing, tall as a donkey and as imperious as his mistress. And WB, not rich like her, but costumed too, with every stitch, from the flowing tie to the black clerical cloak, from the eyeglass on a ribbon to the pointy black boots, chosen to announce the presence of a poet.

You'd have to stop and stare at them. Even those who disdained them would be brought to stopping and staring.

He was always delighted to be seen with her, that was the other thing you'd notice. Though he'd be stuck into whatever he was talking about, head bent, all intense, two hands fluttering like captured birds in front of his chest, still you could see that awareness sitting on him: *Look at me, walking down the highway with Maud Gonne.*

Everything you've heard about her beauty is true. Never listen to those who say otherwise, they're being pure political. And don't mind the photographs, they don't do her justice. You had to be in her presence to feel it, and see how it drew every man in the room, whether he was for the cause of Ireland or against.

Oh yes, they were a queer pair, Mr. Yeats and Madame Gonne, Miss Maud and Master Willie. You may already have heard all sorts about them. Don't believe the half of it, the quarter of it, even. Much of it comes from the scholars, and too many of them are too intellectual, too protected in their choice of life, to understand what went on between those two wild, bewildered souls.

I saw it all for myself, for I lived in Dublin and in London in the old days, and in Paris too, the last years of the old century, along with many other Irish in exile. We were a small crew and I knew everyone on our side who knew them. And I read everything they ever wrote, their memoirs and books, and the diaries and articles and letters in the libraries, hundreds of thousands of words between them.

They were famous among us. What they did thrilled us and sometimes threw us, but when I went deep looking for them, to find the real people behind the wonder and thrills, they did not disappoint. They were more magnificent and foolish than even our overheated talk about them.

Call me curious but I had to find the truth about them and, having found it, had to tell. For, bedazzled and distracted, the world has once again forgotten what it most needs to know and their story says it all.

You'll be wanting to know my name, I suppose, if you're to trust me with this tale. You can call me Rosie but you won't mind, I hope, if I tell you as little as necessary about myself.

WB said, "words alone are certain good." Well... sometimes, I'll give him that, but in my book, the most certain good is the opposite. The space between the words. The nothingness between the things. You can trust in nothing. It's always there, holding all, and never a bit of blather out of it.

We Irish do love to blather and none more than our friend,

WB. But oh, what exquisite blather he gave us. Yes, I'm Irish, if you haven't guessed already from how I talk. My name is Rosie Cross, and I was born in Ireland 101 years ago, and I gave the first half of my life over to the cause of Irish freedom, in the days when it was dangerous to do so.

Already now, your mind is setting itself around that information and, the thing is, I don't want it to. You have a notion of me now you didn't have a minute ago, but none of that matters one jot to the story I'm telling and anyhow, by the time you get to reading this, I'll most likely be gone. They've been telling me for years it's all up for me, and one of these days, they'll be right.

When you get to my stage of life, you realize it never mattered what you were called, or where you came from. All that is only the smallest part of who you are. My own grandmother was the first to tell me so. "You can call me anything you like," she used to say, "so long as you don't call me too early in the morning."

For my preference, call me nothing. No one. Only the teller of the tale.

~

We'll begin on 3rd of January 1889, in Bedford Park in London, which the scholars—going on WB's word—accept as the where and the when of the first meeting. And didn't he write it up so nicely, how she came spinning in to the family abode and knocked them all—especially him—sideways, with her great stature and her bronze hair and her Valkyrie features and her luminous complexion and, most of all, her passionate energy with its lacing of tragic vulnerability?

A combination guaranteed to lance straight to the heart—and nether regions—of a *fin de siècle* poet.

WB. Double-You-Be: that's what I call him. It has a nice pun to it, I think, for a man who was so divided on himself. He was, as he always insisted, the last of the romantics, and in the month Maud Gonne came calling, he'd just published a long poem full of mists and caverns and castles and, of course, a young and handsome hero compelled to gallop after an exotic seductress.

A maid, on a swift brown steed
Whose hooves the top of the surges grazed,
Hurried away, and over her raised
An apple of gold in her tossing hand;
And following her at a headlong speed
Was a beautiful youth from an unknown land...

Oh yes, he had himself well-primed for instant infatuation.

Maud Gonne always insisted they met earlier and much more prosaically, at the house of John O'Leary, when WB was still an art student, in Dublin. O'Leary, one of the last of the old Fenians, was mentor to them both, to all the young people of that time who were taking the cause of Irish freedom as their own. WB had carried her books from Mr. O'Leary's house to her hotel, she said.

She said, he said, they said...

Here's something you'd better hold in your head as you read their sayings: that there were two Maud Gonnes, and two WB Yeats. The living, breathing woman and man, what he called "the bundle of accident and incoherence that sits down to breakfast". And the creations they made, separate and together, to feed the newspapers and stalk the history books.

For him, their great love affair started on the day she came calling to his father's house in London, and like most else that passed between them, his has become the accepted account. But in this story, we'll be weighing male and female, outer and inner, public and private, in equal measure.

When looked at from the woman's side of the bedsheet, most tales take a turning, and this one more than most.

~

So: London in the year of 1889, on the early afternoon of Wednesday, 30th of January. Here, buttoned and bonneted, comes twenty-two-year-old Maud Gonne, banging the hall door of her uncle's Belgravia home behind her, half-running down the pathway.

She's spent the morning chattering with her sister and cousin, Kathleen and May, who are always delighted when she whirls in from France in a flurry of animals and birds, holding out presents for all, her generosity and impetuosity giving the English aunts and uncles a shake-up. All three young ladies have new beaus and so, a lot to discuss and Maud is now, as so often, running late, pulling on her gloves as she goes.

The cab at the curb is a hansom, where the driver sits low in front, close to the horse. One of the new speedy ones, so she might just yet be on time. "Bedford Park, please," she says, sitting in.

The driver flicks the reins—"Right away, Miss."—and the horse begins its trot.

She picks up on the accent and leans forward to say, "You are Irish?"

"Indeed and I am."

Maud Gonne always liked to talk to cabbies or servants or peasants, those of us she called "The People". She thought us purer of heart than those of her own class and held that opinion all her life, through all evidence to the contrary. It was one of the reasons her uncle William lately gave for saying she was not fit to be let out of the house. But she is now of age, and Uncle William can no longer keep her locked down.

"How very interesting," she says. "I have just returned from Ireland."

"And whereabouts were you?"

"County Donegal. Falcarragh. Do you know it?"

"I don't, Miss, but I hear tell it's beautiful in them parts."

"It ought to be. Alas, there is much distress."

She leans further forward to share the full drama of what she witnessed in Donegal: a woman who threw herself screaming up on the back of one of the bailiffs sent to evict her and her children clinging to each other by their rags, terrified of starvation or the workhouse.

"You're a rare one, Miss," the cabbie said. "A lady like yourself to care a bit about the like."

"I care a great deal, Mr...?"

"O'Driscoll, Miss. The Tipperary O'Driscolls. If you're ever in Borrisoleigh, you can enquire after the family. Just tell them

Michael sent you, and they'll organize anything for you. Anything you need doing. Anything at all."

He turns around and screws up his face at her in what she guesses is intended to be a smile. The conversation lapses, and Maud Gonne relaxes back. From Ebury Street, the journey takes them through the newly fashionable suburbs of Kensington, and then into the countryside and riverscapes around the new station of Hammersmith. her mind is on what lies ahead.

For a time now, since her father died and she met her ally, Lucien Millevoye, she has been collecting Irish nationalist contacts and that's what's brought her into this cab today, to taking this trip out to west London. She wants to meet the young poet who's making a name for himself, having recently issued two important, uniquely Irish, books.

Mr. O'Leary passed them to her on their publication and she read them with pleasure and increasing admiration. Both have already affected her profoundly. The first is a book of folklore, tales of old Ireland she can't get out of her mind. The second, even more indelible, a volume of poems called *The Wanderings of Oisin*, a Gaelic name pronounced, Mr. O'Leary said, as "Usheen".

The folklore is fascinating and strange but the poems have lines so hauntingly beautiful and redolent of old Ireland that they have been circumambulating her mind since she read them, behind all her sleeping and eating and talking.

> ...[They]... came to the cairn-heaped grassy hill
> Where passionate Maeve is stony still;
> And found on the dove-grey edge of the sea
> A pearl-pale, high-born lady.

A pearl-pale, high-born lady, who... rode... something. How did it go again? She couldn't quite remember now, but there were already lines she knew she would never forget:

> ...Her eyes were soft as dewdrops hanging
> Upon the grass-blades' bending tips
> And like a sunset were her lips
> A stormy sunset o'er doomed ships...

She thinks this young Mr Yeats might have genius. Mr. O'Leary believes so, and his sister Ellen organized for her the letter of introduction to their friend, the poet's father. Mr. Yeats senior, Mr John Butler, JB, Yeats is a portrait painter, quite bohemian they say, overflowing with Irish conviviality. After the poet come three younger offspring, two sisters and a brother: Lily and Lolly and Jack.

It's not just at the O'Learys' house but everywhere that the Yeats family is spoken of as a slip of old Ireland in the branches of London's suburbs. A light of artistic dedication among the murk of materialism. Willie and Lily and Lolly and Jack. Such names! She is keen to meet them, but yes, she is nervous. That's why she's talking too much to the cabbie. Intellectuals always make her nervous, more than any other class of people.

She hopes the O'Leary recommendation will carry her, that they are not anti-female, or inclined to think her an English spy. One could never tell in advance who would be an ally. In Dublin, Mr. Oldham, middle-aged and bluff, had seemed unpromising, yet he had loved taking her to the Contemporary Club and throwing open the door and booming: "Maud Gonne wants to meet John O'Leary. I thought you'd all like to meet Maud Gonne."

With the Yeats family, she would do as she had done that day, when she'd felt so very shy. Mustering her courage, she had said, "Mr. O'Leary, I have heard so much about you. You are a leader of revolutionary Ireland, and I want to work for Ireland. Can you show me how?"

He'd liked this direct talk; the frown had vanished from his ancient, cagey eyes, and he led her to a sofa, while Mr. Oldham busied himself, making tea.

"You must read," he'd told her. "Read the history of our country, I shall make you a list and lend you books."

A citron color gloomed in her hair
But down to her feet white vesture flowed,
And with the glimmering crimson glowed...

The clip-clop, clip-clop of the horse's hooves beat the rhythm of the beautiful, romance-soaked lines. It must be marvelous to be able to express one's feelings in words like that. She sits back, closes her eyes to the London through which they pass.

London is no longer the city made famous by Dickens, where rich and poor, healthy and afflicted, co-mingled public and private on thronged and tiny streets. Now the center and the east side teem with the under-fed and under-clothed poor, while the middle-classes are expanding the city out in this direction, west, and north. Roads upon roads of housing are being heaped upon each other, in long strips along the river and the passenger railways.

She fancies if she were to take flight up out of the carriage and look down, she would actually see London ravenously advancing over the fields, its concrete army of houses felling hedges and trees, curling in around farms and fields, gobbling up villages and towns. She lies back into Mr. Yeats's wondrous words instead:

...And it was bound with a pearl-pale shell
That waved like the summer streams,
As her soft bosom rose and fell...

The cab pulls up in front of No. 3 Blenheim Road and Maud Gonne lingers a moment to take a good look. A quiet and tree-lined road; the attractive house appears roomy, with Dutch gables, white casement windows and a porch with decorative tiling.

"You can wait," she says to O'Driscoll. "I shouldn't be too long."

She knows she shall be at least an hour, but she would keep the fare running for his sake, so Mrs. O'Driscoll and the little O'Driscolls, of whom there is doubtless a surfeit, might have a good week.

His profuse Irish thanks—"Thanks a million to you now, Miss, and a million times more"—follow her out of the carriage, through the little gate, and up the pathway as she consciously pulls herself up, and steps towards the front door with what she hopes is calm dignity.

For a time, Maud Gonne had thought she might be an actress, had taken some training to annoy Uncle William. She was young then, and half-crazed in those days after their dear father, Tommy, had departed and she and Kathleen had whispered through many bedroom nights about going to live in Paris with their great-aunt Mary, the Comtesse de la Sizeranne, who had said she would help Kathleen find a husband and Maud to become famous courtesan. Either girls' beauty, said Great-aunt Mary, could net a monarch.

It was Millevoye, Maud Gonne's Parisian friend, who had disabused her of this ambition. "An *actrice!*" he'd snorted, in his French manner. "*Pshaw!* You underestimate your own power, my dear. An actrice—even one as great as Sarah Bernhardt, who is truly the greatest—even she only portrays the life of another. Where is the glory in that?"

They had agreed that instead she should make Ireland her stage and now, on Ireland's behalf, she draws on her acting training to make her entrance to the Yeats's abode. Suppressing a shiver, though it is not cold, not for January, she rings the door-bell with a sense of significance. She feels like the bell is ringing down through the future, striking into being the spiritual and political work she and the poet are to do together, which might be a kind of poetry too.

She's not wrong. What she and WB create over the next de-cade will make them both famous, down through time and has me talking about them here now, fifty years on. Together, they will alter the history of two nations and it is with just such an intention, vague and un-clarified as yet, that she has come here, to his house, today.

So when the serving girl answers the door, she speaks to her slowly, with a sense of import. "I am Miss Gonne," she says. "Miss Maud Gonne, lately come from Ireland."

The Troubling Of His Life

INSIDE THE Yeats house, timings have all gone awry. WB blames Lolly, his younger sister, as he likes to do. Our poet is unsure of much, desperately, reluctantly unsure, but not of this: that his sister is an irritant beyond all bearing, sent to try him and remind him of what is least attractive in his own nature, but with added flaws of which he—for all his self-acknowledged inadequacies—is not guilty. Jealousy, for one.

He has no doubt it was she who chose now—*now?*—as the time to bring Mama downstairs. The pretext is some female cleaning task but he is not fooled. Knowing that Miss Gonne—the English heiress who has descended from her ascendancy position to take up the cause of Ireland—is arriving to the house this afternoon; and knowing that Miss Gonne is really coming to see *him*, not Papa (and certainly not the girls); and knowing that he has won this attention, this compliment, this esteem from the celebrated beauty by his recent publications, his sister wishes, in her envious and cantankerous way, to embarrass him.

She has been like this since they first got news of his books' success. When she heard he was to be published, she asked only how much the books would bring in, never once acknowledging the achievement that makes Papa and Lily so proud. Well, he shall not oblige her by being vexed. No. He shall take up his position in the drawing room as usual, and if, when their guest arrives, Mama should still be sitting there, dumb and distant disturbed, so be it. He shall be... disinterested.

Yes. He shall convey to Miss Gonne his detachment from this impossible family of his, that he is remaking himself in accordance with a different philosophy.

That his life is to be an experiment in dedication to beauty, to the life beyond life, is something, in any case, that their guest may not understand. O'Leary believes she may be of use in furthering the cause of Ireland, but if she is a dogmatist or worse, a do-gooder, he shall most surely leave her to make polite talk with his family, and absent himself. For *he* is a *poet*.

This is how WB's thoughts turn at this time in his life, strings of I-shoulds and most-surely-I-shalls that he holds to as he circles, endlessly, round twin maypoles of self he has internally erected. He's greatly conscious of how exhausting he finds it all and no notion of how fortunate he is to have space in his head for such musings, of what a luxury it is to be able to believe that the everyday—the quotidian, he'd no doubt call it, if he stopped to pay it any attention—is beneath him.

For him, and for Maud Gonne, liberated by her money, life is about national affairs and poetic movements and the turning of time through eons and ages... not who's going to get the dinner, do we have enough fuel in for the fire, and hadn't we better get Mama's room cleaned out today, as Lily has just heard that she has to go to work tomorrow, after all.

Such considerations—and not any sabotaging notions of Lolly's—are why his sisters have had to take their mother out of her room and downstairs. They are just about to dispatch Rose up to do the work; only just as she is crossing the hall, the doorbell rings, and she answers it before anyone has time to tell her not to. Next thing, Maud Gonne is stepping into the hall and meeting, head on, face to face, up close, the troubled form of Mrs. Yeats.

All are brought to stillness by awkwardness and surprise. The only movement is the blood rushing to Lolly's cheeks (which would have gratified her brother, were he there to see it) and Rose's backward retreat towards the kitchen. The rest of them stand, unsure how to proceed, as if in a tableau of youthful, vigorous beauty meeting aged decrepitude and disintegration.

Through their embarrassment, the Yeats girls register that their visitor is six feet tall and lovely almost beyond belief, with figure and deportment just short of haughty. She's added to her great height with a hat in the most advanced style, with a cornucopia of dried, exotic fruits on one side topped off by a stuffed, yellow canary. Beneath the hat that looks so ridiculous to us now but was then the height of style, shines a fringe of auburn hair, glistening gold against a cool and delicate complexion.

Years later, their brother will write a line about Maud Gonne standing in a railway station looking like the Greek goddess of wisdom and justice: "Pallas Athena in that straight back and arrogant head." And she has the quality about her already, at the age of twenty-two.

The Yeats sisters perceive it immediately and Lolly can't stand it, especially when caught like this with their mother, whom even her devoted daughters must admit, is startlingly, shockingly, *un*lovely.

What Maud Gonne finds before her is a middle-aged woman, heavy of chin and slack of jaw, with a melancholic scowl. Her eyes are each a different color, one blue, one brown, and even more disconcerting is how they travel, wayward as if unfixed in their sockets, shrouded and unseeing.

Something is wrong with Mrs. Yeats, something more than the mutism resulting from apoplexy, something that was in place many years before and has, together with the stroke, left her with a condition the doctors have dubbed "General Paralysis of the Insane".

None of the Yeats family ever allows that diagnosis to be repeated. Indeed, they don't believe in it. Mama does not suffer delusions, unless thinking herself sometimes in her beloved Sligo and not here, in this hated concrete suburb, is a delusion.

How dismayed the Yeats sisters would be to know that Maud Gonne heard all about their mother already. And heard of how her own family, the Polloxfens of Sligo, blame her husband for her condition. When they married, he was a barrister with good prospects in Dublin, but he determined instead to be an artist, and brought the family to live in bohemian penury in

London, a city which she, a West of Ireland girl, detested from the moment she set foot here.

Could this be true, Maud Gonne wonders now. Could marital disagreement and social dislocation really account for the condition of the woman she sees before her? If every woman disappointed by her husband were to collapse into such, the world would cease to turn. When life disappoints, one must apply one's will, not crumple.

She moves to smooth the embarrassment. "Good afternoon," she says brightly.

"Ah Miss Gonne, do come in. We've been expecting you," says Lily, who can English-talk with the best if she has to.

Lolly picks up the cue. "Our mother is a trifle indisposed and just on her way to her room, Miss Gonne."

"I'm sorry to hear it, Ma'am." Maud bows to Mrs. Yeats, without a quiver of fear or recoiling. "But pleased, even so briefly, to make your acquaintance."

Susan Yeats doesn't so much as lift an eyebrow. Her eyes revolve around some point in the far distance, above a scowl that suggests a demon of especially evil intent is headed her way.

"And to be able to congratulate you on your clever son and his publication. Such beautiful books, you must be very proud."

Again, no response.

"Thank you, Miss Gonne," Lily says, knowing her mother doesn't even realize that Willie writes poetry. "It's most kind of you to say so."

Maud bows, delicately, as demanded by the stacked hat. "Please, ladies, don't let me detain you a moment longer."

Lolly takes her mother's arm and leads her upstairs while Lily ushers Maud into the drawing room, where the fire is lit and Willie and their father are waiting. Papa Yeats jumps up to warmly take her hand, while his son stands at the side of the fireplace, elbow crooked on the mantle, pince-nez glinting in the afternoon light from the window and his little navy book of poems is laid on the side-table, as if casually, but in pride of place.

He is pale and unfeasibly thin, with a raven lock falling across

his forehead and a pointed beard that makes him look a little diabolic. In contrast to his father, he moves with minimum motion
to offer his hand, affecting a careless attitude that, contrary to its
intention, only highlights how he is, at the age of twenty-three, a
lost boy living at home.

They take their seats, facing the mock-Adams fireplace with
its fruit-and-flowered white mantelpiece. Maud Gonne has no
idea that the sods of turf burning so cheerily in her honor mean
the family will forgo meat tomorrow. She smiles about her.

"Your suburb here is quite delightful. I do so love the red
brick of the housing."

"Oh, we do not think of Bedford Park as a suburb," says JB. His
voice is laced with the Irish vowels despised by many English,
but not Maud. "It is more of a village. Or a colony, perhaps. At any
rate, it resists the mechanizing spirit of our age."

"I'm told many interesting people live about. And you lived
here before, did you not?"

"We had happy times here ten years ago, before we went
back to live in Ireland for a time. On our return to London two
years ago, we were first in Earls Court, close to the Exhibition
Centre. *That* rather made us appreciate Bedford Park."

"It was noisy, I suppose?"

"My son had to ponder his poems of ancient Ireland with the
sound of the steam organs blaring."

"And," the poet says, in an affected drawl. "Buffalo Bill making the crowd whoop like Indians and pretend-shoot each other
with a finger." He shudders, theatrically, and they all laugh.

He is handsome beneath the beard, but his face is shadowed
and so thin that there's hardly room for his misty black eyes. He
has a look, she thinks, of the woman she just met in the hall.

"*The Wanderings of Oisin* have brought you a long way from
Buffalo Bill, Mr. Yeats," she says when the laughter subsides.
"What a remarkable book."

Willie tilts his head, trying to hide his gratification.

"I cried at the Island of Statues section. And how I hated
Nachina. Can you explain to me the symbolism of the three islands—the Island of Dancing, the Island of Victories, the Island
of Forgetfulness?"

"They are the three incompatible things man is always seeking: vain gaiety, vain battle, vain repose."

"Condemned to a hundred years in each... and all in vain?" The question is wistful, she does not quite understand.

"I liked it better when it was finished than when I was writing it," he says. "Now that it's published, I begin to dislike it again."

Lolly comes in and takes the empty seat behind Lily, who has been following the conversation but not contributing. Then Rose arrives, pushing a trolley.

"Ah," says JB. "Tea!"

Over bread-and-butter, they learn that Maud Gonne was born in England, she and her sister, to a colonel father and a mother whose family traded in linens and wines. The mother died in 1871, when Maud was only two, and the father's regiment was sent to Ireland, to curb the Fenian uprisings. They'd lived happily there, "like perfect little savages," she tells them, with one of her tinkling laughs, until her father was called to India, when the mother's English relations had them brought back to London to be civilized.

When she was sixteen, her father was again sent to Ireland, and she served as his companion until Thomas Gonne—she called him Tommy—contracted typhoid fever in the winter of 1886. She and Kathleen, now orphans, were again taken in by the English relatives who, she said, only wanted to get at their inheritance. Her uncle William told them their father had left them nothing and that they would have to be adopted by one of their aunts. Instead, they determined to earn their own living. Kathleen decided to become a nurse, and she, an actress.

"That must have pleased Uncle William," JB says, drily.

"Oh quite!" Maud says, with another laugh, leaving no doubt as to how she enjoyed her rebellion.

Neither she nor her sister succeeded in their career plans but the attempt kept them busy while their father's will was being probated, on completion of which they found Uncle William had lied. With the greedy relatives left behind, she returned to Paris, to Tommy's aunt instead, the Comtesse de la Sizeranne.

And, on coming of age, set herself up in her own apartment. "I found myself free to choose what I should do with my life," she declares brightly. And what she had chosen was Ireland.

Ireland is her nation now, and the Irish people her concern, and she turns the talk to the latest news from there. Yesterday, William O'Brien was arrested in Manchester for Land League agitation and she is keen to know what Mr. Yeats makes of it all.

The Land League has been a popular movement in Ireland for a decade, organizing farmers and peasants against high rents and unfair landlords. Many leaders of the movement, including the "Chief", Charles Stewart Parnell, have been jailed, and though the Irish Parliamentary Party now gives the matter less attention, evictions and resistance continue. And continue to stir emotion.

JB gives his opinion, balancing teacup and bread-and-butter plate on his knee. "These outrages against landlords are so unintelligent. They go against all the work that has been done to build relationships in Westminster."

Which is clearly not the reply Maud Gonne hoped for. "But Mr. Yeats, you do not support Mr. Parnell's 'union of hearts' with the Liberal Party, surely?"

JB is discomfited to be addressed in this manner by one so young. A young woman, at that.

"Political overtures to Mr. Gladstone do nothing to alleviate the distress," she says.

"Political overtures are more complex and far-reaching than they might appear on the surface, my dear."

"I have just been to Ireland, Mr. Yeats. The evictions are causing such dreadful distress."

"We have a parliamentary party and a judiciary to resolve such matters."

"In Ireland I met priests and many others I respect, who are wary of both politicians and judges, who believe that both exploit the people."

"The Irish Parliamentary Party exploits the Irish people? How so, pray?"

"The people are encouraged to refuse to pay unfair rent,

which gets them evicted, but we do nothing to help them. We tell them to wait for politicians to solve the trouble, but they are homeless, helpless. What are they to do?"

"What would you have them do? Shoot the landlord?"

"It would be hard to blame them if they did."

"My dear girl, I really think—"

"A robber won't stop robbing for the asking."

Lolly looks at Lily, a little alarmed. They always feel out of it when the men gather to talk, yet here is this young woman, no older than themselves, haranguing and interrupting their father. She has her face turned from them, towards the men, but they can see the side of her self-possessed smile and hear her imperious voice. And they don't think much either of her sharing so many personal details.

JB asks, "Do you think any means justified, then, in the service of your desired ends?"

The question is loaded but Maud Gonne either doesn't notice or doesn't care.

"Such is England's treatment of Ireland that whatever an Irishman may do in retaliation should not be considered a crime. It may suit England to call Irish protests outrages, but in truth, they are justified acts of war."

"Miss Gonne, I really think you..."

"Oh I hate war and am by nature a pacifist, but the English are forcing war on us."

Lily wishes Willie would speak up, but he just sits there, enthralled and useless. Maybe even, Lily suspects, pleased to see Papa challenged.

What WB is actually thinking is: why all this attention to those on the field of battle or politics? A man may show as reckless a courage in entering into the abyss of himself. But he's too shy to say this aloud. And yes, he sees his two sisters glancing at each other, and Lolly making one of her faces but, in truth, if Maud Gonne said the world was flat or the moon an old caubeen tossed up into the sky, he'd be proud to be of her party. Her beauty answers every argument for him.

Maud Gonne goes on: "The first principle of war, Mr. Yeats,

is to kill the enemy. Unfortunately, the English have been more successful in killing than we have... So far."

JB endeavors to steer the conversation to more comfortable territory, by giving one of his speeches, as freshly delivered as if he had just baked it up, directed away from politics but delivered in a tone that makes it seem to answer the questions raised.

"The typical Irish family is poor, ambitious, and intellectual," he says, "but all have the national habit of conversation. When there is a dull boy in an Irish family, we send him to England and put him into business, but the Irish love the valor of the free intellect."

JB is also staking territory. It took me a time before I understood this about the Yeatses and the other Protestants of Ireland. We thought of them as English but they thought of themselves as Irish. Everyone they associated with in Sligo would look down on the likes of me and mine but were as prejudiced, in a different way, against England. To them, the English ate dogfish, put marmalade in their porridge, kissed at railway stations and discussed their affairs with strangers.

And of course I know they were Irish, having being born and reared there, and their families having lived there for centuries, yet even now, b'times, it's hard for me to think of them as such.

"Oh, and the Irish approve of amusement," says JB, drawing another of his distinctions, for if ever there was a people who didn't approve of amusement, it was the Protestant English. "To do so is an Irish tradition unbroken from the days before St. Patrick."

Maud takes the hint and drops the political talk. They move to literature. WB recommends that she should read Carleton. "He has the most Celtic eyes that ever gazed from under the brows of story-teller."

"What about Miss Edgeworth? I found *Castle Rackrent* most amusing."

"She has judgment," says JB. "Serenity and balance too. Though they say her books are written by her father."

Maud opens her mouth, as if to argue, but this time Willie does interject. "Carleton's art is unconscious," he says, "while hers is conscious. Living a half-blind, groping sort of life, drinking and borrowing, he has outdone her by the sheer force of his nature."

"Have you read him, Miss Gonne?" JB asks. "You will find him full of violent emotion and brooding melancholy."

And he begins a long discourse on Irish literature to which they all listen politely, interjecting only with words that meet his wishes. For the rest of the visit, the love-struck youth, the silent sisters, the glamorous visitor all play their part in soothing the ego of the older man. Yet, even as they move to appease, there's a sense that the visit is winding up, that Miss Gonne has accomplished what she came for, and will soon be off.

As she takes her leave, she shakes hands with them all, first the father, then the two girls, leaving the poet till last, and has the satisfaction of feeling his fingers tremble in her glove. She says, half sotto voce but loud enough for all to hear: "You must meet my sister, Mr. Yeats. She should greatly love to hear you read some of your poetry. And my cousin May Gonne is very well connected. I am sure she would be able to arrange something for you. Would you dine with us this evening?"

"Willie, see Miss Gonne to her cab," JB says, giving them reluctant blessing to make the arrangement.

~

They stand at the gate, a little removed from the hansom, so the cabbie might not hear. "I think I rather frightened your father."

"His income has been affected by the Land Acts. But it is more that he abhors physical violence."

"As do so many of his generation."

"But ours is the time that is coming."

She smiles at him. "Precisely, Mr. Yeats. Precisely."

"When I was younger, I thought my father the wisest of men. Until I read Ruskin's *Unto This Last* and AP Sinnott's book on esoteric Buddhism. Have you read these?"

"I should dearly like to."

"I shall lend them to you. They have made my father's doubt wearing to me. Doubt is a douser, it would put out sun and moon."

He does not tell her, not yet, that their quarrel over Ruskin came to such a height that his father, pushing him out the door, broke the glass in a picture with the back of his head.

"Yet you must appreciate still having him."

He flushes alarmingly again, the blood seems to swell into every pore of his visage. Then she realizes he thinks she means in comparison to his mother. She rushes to clarify. "My own father... I still miss him every day."

"Ah yes." Then awkwardly: "I am sorry for your trouble."

It's inappropriate, her father being dead now more than two years, but again Maud Gonne picks up for them. "That is what the Irish country people say, is it not? I have always thought it such a beautiful phrase. Tell me, Mr. Yeats, what do you think of Mr. Parnell? I know that in Ireland he is much loved."

Instead of answering, for he is unsure of what she would like him to say, Willie quotes Parnell's famous dictum: "No man has the right to fix the boundary of a nation... No man has the right to say to his country, 'Thus far shalt thou go and no further.'"

"Yes, yes, we are all with him on this. But do you not think him a little too pale, too political? A little too constitutional? In France our hero is Général Boulanger. Now there is a hero. Oh, how the people adore him, *le brave général.* You can wash with Boulanger soap, suck Boulanger sweets, eat food off Boulanger plates... We need such a man in Ireland."

"Or such a woman?"

"Oh Mr. Yeats, do you think the world is ready for such? I should dearly love to be Ireland's Joan of Arc."

"Or her Queen Maeve? The old Irish tales are full of female heroes."

"Truly?"

"In ancient Ireland women had equality with men, the power to raise armies, hold property, act as lawyers and judges. At the top of Knocknarea, the mountain that overlooks the town where my mother's people come from, is a heap of stones said to be Maeve's cairn."

"Ah yes. You mention it in your poem: *the cairn-heaped grassy hill, where passionate Maeve is stony still.*"

So she *has* read it, and read it well. He falls another inch in love.

She asks: "What did Queen Maeve do to be so remembered?"

"She is said to have had five husbands and thirteen children."

"Thirteen children!" Maud Gonne laughs. "That's a common enough achievement in Ireland."

"She was a warrior queen. With her beauty and presence, she made her armies invincible."

"I don't know if today's Ireland can approve of the five husbands! Joan of Arc may be a better model than your pagan queen. After all, Joan was a Roman Catholic. And she went to war against the English..."

"But not a..."

"Oh, Mr. Yeats, I had really better leave you, the cab has been waiting an hour. But we shall continue this delightful conversation this evening, no? You simply must dine with us. Are you free? I so want my sister and cousin to meet you. They shall have their beaus with them, both of whom are far too English for my liking, so you can help me add balance. Would you be so kind as to oblige me?"

She places her gloved hand on his wrist, scandalizing the sisters, who are watching from the window.

He agrees, of course, and then she is off, hopping into the hansom, waving him "*adieu, adieu,*" for a little French goes a long way, Maud Gonne knows, in impressing impressionable young men.

On the way back in the cab, she doesn't speak to O'Driscoll; she prefers her thoughts. They are a delightful family. She has heard they huddle round a single lamp at night to do their work and have no credit at the butchers, yet they are gay and artistic, devoted to a more noble way.

Back at her uncle's house, she has trouble extricating herself from O'Driscoll's thanks and urgings for her to visit County Tipperary on her next visit to Ireland. "Thank you, Mr. O'Driscoll, I'll remember it. And if I do meet any of your people, I shall tell them how well you have done for yourself. I know how the London men like to keep the cabbie jobs for themselves."

"Oh the family all knows I done well, Miss. 'Tis money from the auld cab that keeps 'em going over there."

Which leads her to give him a higher tip, as he intended. He takes it straight to Kavanagh's public house. Not a penny of it finds its way across to Ireland, for O'Driscoll has more of a handle on Maud's type than she, as yet, has on his.

~

After she's gone, WB stands for a long time at the gate. The emptiness left behind by her departure is like the eerie calm that follows when a whirlwind has blown itself out. The air holds something of her presence long after she's left.

He had never thought to see in a living woman such beauty. It's not just her features but her movements, so worthy of her form, that hold him transfixed. Virgil's line "She walks like a goddess" seems meant for her alone. Now he understands why the poets of antiquity, where a modern person would speak of face and form, sing of how their lady paces.

Her face, and her body, have the lineament that Blake called the highest beauty, because it changes least from youth to age. It belongs to famous pictures, to poetry, to some legendary past, and at eighty, she would still have that bearing. And that jawline. Her independent nature seems very Irish, in the old way. She is like Meredith's Diana of The Crossways or, yes, the warrior Queen Maeve.

He sighs, turns reluctantly back up the pathway. His father's house somehow seems less, not more, bearable for the thought that tonight's dinner with her is but a few hours away. In the novel WB has begun to write, he has made his hero, John Sherman, an only child. No father, no siblings, only a devoted—and fully cognizant—mother.

In the drawing room, he finds his sisters, as he knew he would, still talking about Maud Gonne. They had noticed that she was apparently wearing slippers. Lolly is saying: "We're not important enough, I suppose, to change shoes first."

"Perhaps," Lily says, with an eye to him, "she forgot."

Actually, Maud's footwear is not carpet slippers as WB's serviceable-boot-wearing siblings think, but the most advanced style from Paris. Neither sister is à la mode, and the new flimsy shoes like Maud's are wearable only by those who travel by horse and carriage.

"What did you make of her, Willie?" Lily asks. "She is very handsome."

"I don't know how you could tell," Lolly says. "She had her face turned from us the whole time, towards the men. For myself, I can never endure that sort of royal smile."

He would not sully his fervor by discussing her with them. He would take his images and impressions to his room, until it is time to leave.

"And where do you think you're going?" Lolly says, as he turns.

"Come to the kitchen, Willie,' Lily says. "You can take up Mama's tea."

"I fear I have—"

"You may fear nothing," says Lolly, "except what will be done to you if you refuse this simple request."

She points the way down the passageway, towards the kitch-en and he is forced to follow, dragging his long legs after him.

Eternal Beauty Wandering

ON ARRIVAL that evening at Maud Gonne's uncle's house, WB is shown into the drawing room, a far finer affair than theirs at Bedford Park. Rich furnishings to sit on, elegant draperies to admire, ceilings with intricate plasterwork to elevate the eyes. He had feared her uncles or aunts might be present, but just four in addition to herself were there, and all of them young: her cousin May and sister Kathleen, who sit one on either side of her, and their two sweethearts standing at the window.

WB is glad to see neither of them is in a dinner suit. This may be at her tactful behest; they all seem the sort to dress for dinner. His velvet smoking jacket would not impress, he knows, but he has tied his tie in a poet's knot, his pocket handkerchief overflows his top pocket and his father's old Inverness cape completes what he hopes is a bohemian picture. The Irish bohemian card is the only card he has to play.

Her dress is green, cinched tight at the waist with a high ruched collar and a long string of pearls. She smiles brightly to see him but does not move. A wave of her hand towards her lap explains why she must remain seated. "Forgive me, I cannot disturb Macha."

Then he sees the black Persian, curled up in her lap, apparently asleep.

"Macha!" laughs one of the men. "The cat's name was Jefferson until she paid you a visit this afternoon."

Macha is the Celtic goddess of war. And, he thinks, sex? He

blushes, the embarrassment immediately followed by a wave of self-loathing.

"Mr. Yeats," she says, doing the introductions. "This is Captain Thomas Pilcher, my sister's fiancé." Her voice is perfectly polite, but something in her manner manages to convey to him that, although the Captain shares the first name and profession of her beloved father, this ruddy faced fellow, bluff and conceited, the very picture of an English army officer on the rise, is *not* a man she would have chosen for her beloved sister.

This house is not far from where he dined at Christmas with Oscar Wilde, a fact he injects quickly into the conversation. Wilde is not yet the dramatist who will dazzle all London but is already known for flamboyant dress and glittering conversation.

It is his best suit, and he had meant to hold it for later, but she quickly caps it, saying: "Kathleen and I met Mr. Wilde in Paris."

"He said Maud was the very picture of a European sophisticate," Kathleen says, in a voice softer and lower than her sister's.

"She was fending off an American and an Italian Count," laughs her cousin, May. "Both at once."

"The American had brought a wonderful armful of flowers," says Maud Gonne. "And the Italian a large bag of chocolates that had grown sticky in the heat. Mr. Wilde was most amused. Afterwards he told me the American had a wife in Chicago."

Is she swearing him off, letting him know she is used to the admiration of all sorts of dashing men? She need not trouble herself, he already knows it. Or has he been brought along tonight so she can play with him, in front of her friends? Can she be, contrary to her noble exterior, one of those girls who collects admirers to feed her vanity?

"Oscar Wilde!" says Captain Pilcher, dismissively. "That phony."

"Whatever do you mean, Tom? You don't find Mr. Wilde phony, do you, Mr. Yeats?"

"He has created himself in a style to match his literary style," WB says. "People may call this posing. It is really the putting on of a mask."

"Posing, yes, that's the word. Damn right, yes. A poseur."

"The mask is a necessity for the true artist, Captain Pilcher."

The curl of the Captain's lip makes it clear that he thinks that remark phony too.

"I believe," WB says, pulling past his shyness, determined not to be beaten in this, his own field, "the impression of artificiality may have come from Mr. Wilde's perfect rounding of sentences. I never before heard a man talking so, as if he had labored over them all night, yet all spontaneous."

Maud says, "I think him a disappointment."

WB plummets to despair at this. So it is true, he thinks. She's brought him here as a bit of diversion, to encourage him and then argue, to lead him on then slap him down, all for the amusement of her friends. He eyes the door wondering whether escape might be possible. Only then he'd miss the dinner.

"I had expected," she is saying, as emotional humiliation fights it out with physical hunger in the Yeats belly, "that being the son of Speranza, the poetess who did so much good work for Ireland in the '40s, that he might be Ireland's literary savior. But," she announces to the room, "Mr. O'Leary and I have decided that honor is to go to Mr. Yeats."

He flushes again, and she launches into a dissertation on the merits of his work and he begins to feel better. She compliments his family and compares their artistic life to that of the Brontës.

And then reaches for a cigarette.

"Oh, are you shocked, Mr. Yeats? Please say you aren't shocked. Kathleen, pass Mr. Yeats the cigarettes."

He is a little shocked, deliciously so, and excited by her movements as she places the cigarette between her lips, draws and exhales the smoke. He is handed a cigarette and a drink and ushered to a chair opposite her, where conversation continues until they are called in for dinner.

At the meal, Maud Gonne spends much of the time baiting her brother-in-law-to-be, who distrusts the French, likes the Germans and adores the English, the direct opposite of her own leanings in matters Continental. WB relaxes, as course follows course: pastries, soup, chicken, beef, cake, wine and afterwards, whiskey. Her needling is more general than personal, he sees. Her much-vaunted hatred of England is really a hatred of mechanism and materialism. England, for her, is a symbol for dominance and avarice. They can be kindred in that.

~

The night is soon over, and as the servant brings his hat and coat, he arranges, through a head spinning with an overflow of culinary and sensual delight, to meet her again next day. He is to take her to the British Library and show her how to access the Irish collection.

The occasion can be deemed a success, he decides, as he steps out into night air that cools his heated face. He created no insurmountable awkwardness. Tonight, even the crowd jostling down the steps of the railway station feels bearable. Natural, even, like a flock of birds moving in unison.

As he changes trains at Hammersmith station, he sees a woman of the town walking up and down the empty railway platform. In the pent-up frustration that is his daily companion, now elevated by his new infatuation and a full stomach, he thinks of offering himself to her. Yes, that's how he frames it in his mind, as if she were the consumer, as if he were the one who would be consumed.

His friends all have mistresses of one kind or another. Most of them, if they feel the need, go home with a harlot, but he, since childhood, has never kissed a woman's lips. And none too often back then either. His mother, even before she retreated into the dark recesses of her mind, was never one for shows of affection. He does not remember ever receiving a kiss from her as a child.

Oh, childhood! Children live a fantastic life. They weep, like geniuses, tears upon tears for some dead Orpheus of whom they have dreamt, and passing with wondering indifference—yes, like geniuses—among the sorrows of their own household. He has begun a short poem on the theme. It is as yet shadowy, but one stanza is set:

Come way, o human child/ to the waters and the wild/, with a faery hand-in-hand,/ for the world's more full of weeping/ than you can understand.

To his horror, the harlot makes eye contact, smiles her smile of invitation. He slides his eyes from hers. Now he has a reason, beyond instinctive terror, to pull back and he takes it to his bosom and grasps it, tight, as he turns and clicks his way down the stairs. No, he says to himself, suppressing the lust that has also risen in the encounter. No. And neither shall he, when he reaches his bed, succumb to lone temptation. For now he loves the most beautiful woman in the world.

And, like Sir Lancelot, he shall love her exceedingly well.

~

She meets with him again the next day. He takes her around the British Museum and Library, showing her how to borrow a book and where the draught-free seats are. The day following, she asks him to accompany her to the visitor's gallery at the House of Commons, where they hear Tim Healy defending the Irish Party with what Maud Gonne calls good earth power, the elemental Irish quality.

Next, he takes her to meet Madame Blavatsky, founder of the Theosophical Society, at her home. By this time, WB has been a follower for years and relishes telling Maud Gonne about the old Russian lady's life of international "gypsyhood", marital misfortune and—or so her followers were required to believe— religious initiation at the hands of occult masters in Tibet.

"Seriously, Mr. Yeats, is it not true that your Madame Blavatsky has been denounced as an imposter? I seem to remember her staff exposed her experiments as fake."

Not so, says WB. It was a vicious attack by the jealous and small minded. Her theories have been tested and verified by generations of Seers. Madame seeks to offer the world a new presentation of that age-old wisdom, that body of Truth, that tree of Life of which religions, great and small, are but branches. Her task—and his, as he has also taken it on in his life and work—is to challenge on the one hand the entrenched beliefs and dogmas of Christian theology and on the other the equally dogmatic materialistic view of the sciences with Truth. Revealed Truth.

Maud Gonne says she looks like an old Irish peasant woman.

"Maybe," he says. "But with more of an air of humor. And of audacious power."

"More than her followers, certainly."

Maud Gonne looks around at the people in the room, making it clear she finds them drab and nondescript. WB insists there are interesting people among them.

The room is lit by gas chandelier, and there is clearly water or air in the pipes, for it flickers, badly. "Spooks in the room!" cries Madame Blavatsky to the assemblage.

She beckons over WB and Maud Gonne, making room on the long chair and patting its seat beside her, for Maud to sit. "They are all looking for a miracle," she whispers in Maud's ear, continuing to play cards—some form of patience?—dealing out mechanically onto the green card table as she talks.

"Have you a question for me, dear?"

Maud tells her that Unionist members in the Dublin branch of the Theosophical Society object to her Land League work for Ireland.

"My dear child," says Madame, "what you do in politics has nothing to do with Theosophy. If a man, for instance, cuts off a cow's tail,"—the British papers were full of such alleged Irish atrocities—"that will injure his own karma, but it would not prevent him being a member of the Theosophical Society."

Maud Gonne is reassured, and WB is happy he brought her.

Afterwards, they have a long and most interesting talk about esoterics and philosophy. She is not looking for a new religion or a miracle, but investigating any means that might enable her to focus her power. Emboldened, he tells her a little of the secret lore hidden in his poems. "Under disguise of symbolism, I have said several things to which I only have the key."

"But why disguised?"

"I must appease my father who is all for realism."

She raises an eyebrow.

"Oh but vehemently so. I tried to walk away from him the other evening after an argument about Ruskin, but he followed me upstairs, into the bedroom I share with my small brother, and squared up to me, and wanted me to box him for the winning of the argument."

She smiles. She can so easily imagine them, all three.

"Whatever did you do?"

"I just said: 'I cannot fight my own father.' He said: 'I don't see why you should not.'"

"So did you?"

"Jack, who shares my room, started up in the bed and, in a violent passion, began to scream at both of us to shut up and to get out. Father fled, taking his fury with him, and Jack held me, saying 'Not a word to him now until he apologizes'."

She laughs, as she is meant to, though at one level it is hardly funny.

He is gratified. And surprised by how easy she is to speak to. "You seem to have had great affection for your own father," he says.

"We were very close, Tommy and I. People who did not know us often mistook us for husband and wife. He looked very young for his age and I was an exceptionally tall child, five foot ten at the age of fourteen. I persuaded Nurse to lengthen my skirts and let me put up my hair so I could accompany him."

"And this he permitted?"

"Welcomed."

"An unconventional father."

"He did try sometimes to be conventional but it did not become him." A memory breaks a smile in her. "Once, after a visit to Rome, he became disturbed by the arrival of numerous letters to me with an Italian postmark, and he thought he should confiscate and read them. So I told my correspondent to write to me with milk on the edges of fashionable papers that Tommy would unsuspectingly hand over. This he did. When I received one of these dispatches, I sat Tommy down and showed him what we had done, held the paper to the flame and showed him the love letter emerging in brown letters. 'This, Tommy, is what you have just handed over,' I said, 'Don't you realize how absurd this inspection of correspondence is? In four years, I shall be of age and able to marry this young man, and you won't be able to prevent me. If he goes on writing like this, I certainly shall not want to marry him so please, stop making him interesting by opening his letters.'"

How did he write, WB wonders. How might one write in such a way that *would* make her want to marry?

"Tommy was far more interesting to me than the writer of these letters, and his education more important than the attentions of a beau."

Later, back home in the bedroom he shares with his young brother, WB questions why she is giving him so much time, whether it might possibly mean that she returns his feelings. He poses the question to friends in Dublin who also know her, answering his own question before they have time to reply. He thinks it is probably nothing beyond kindliness and friendship. But does it not say much of her generosity that it seems so natural for her to give her hours in such overflowing abundance?

~

On her last day in London for now, Maud Gonne's train is due to leave at 10 am. WB rises early to get across to Belgravia in time to help her transfer her luggage. The enormous trunk and two suitcases are easily managed, the challenge is the animals and birds: Macha the cat, a parrot, cages full of canaries and finches. The menagerie is a kind of surrogate family for the girl who lost her mother so young, who was shunted from relative to relative in the absence of a father, who never stayed long enough in one place to keep any friend, except her sister and cousins.

At ease with WB now, she has confided all: the sorrows and joys of her lonely childhood in Ireland and England and traveling the continent, some of her reckless escapades on fortune's flying wheel and, most movingly, the painful loss of mother and father. Especially her guilt about her mother.

While her mother lay dying, Maud had found a broken holly branch in the snow and ran back into the house with her treasure. Her mother, thinking it a gift, took it from her, but the little girl snatched it back, saying, "It isn't for you. Tommy says it will melt by the fire. I want to see."

"She looked so disappointed," Maud Gonne told him, as she shared this story. "I had not thought of her as I danced in the snow with Tommy. Because of that, I always see her eyes with a sad look in them."

Such revelations bind him to her more tightly than the gay abandon that is more often in evidence, that is in evidence now, as they make their way through the crowds under the great steel arches of Victoria station. How people stare at her in her swinging beaver coat, her glinting hair behind in the veil she always wears when traveling, and the railway porters following with her animals and birdcages, hurrying to keep up.

WB settles her into her carriage, the cages obstructing the rack and cushions, no matter how he arranges them. He fears what fellow travelers will say. A woman looks in the window with intent but seeing the animals and cages, passes on. He would be embarrassed, but Maud Gonne is blithe.

"Oh with any luck, my little friends shall keep others at bay too," she laughs. "Don't you find an empty carriage makes the tiresomeness of travel a little easier to bear?"

He tells her he should like to travel with her to Paris. Even the name makes him wistful. Paris is the center of art and poetry and nationalist exile but also the center of European occult activity. In Paris, unlike in London, the pride of the mage can naturally, and without ridicule, be added to the pride of the artist.

"This melancholy London," he says. "I sometimes imagine that the souls of the lost are compelled to walk through its streets in perpetuity. One sees them passing like a whiff of air."

He is discomfited when he sees her face. She looks like she might laugh, but instead she lays a gentle hand on his arm, as she did at the gate in Bedford Park, and smiles a sorrowful smile.

"Oh Mr. Yeats, I know exactly what you mean. I live *for* Ireland, but I can only live in Paris. In Paris, if a woman has personality, social circumstances permit her to make it felt."

"Not so Dublin."

"No. But we should arrange to be together in Dublin, Mr. Yeats. We can do a great deal more there together than in Paris."

"Perhaps we should beware of trying too hard," he says.

She looks puzzled. "Our enemies are strong, with vast resources."

He wants to say something original, to regain a little weight in their relationship, but also he needs her to understand. She is

devoted to the power of will, yet her real power is in her presence. "Perhaps even in politics," he says, "it will be enough in the
end to have lived and thought passionately—and have, like our
friend Mr. O'Leary, a head like a Roman coin."

"Perhaps," she says, but her voice is vague. In time, he trusts,
she will understand. Beauty like hers, so much like wisdom,
cannot be hiding a common heart.

"I should dearly love to visit Howth with you," she says.

They discovered in one of their late-night conversations a co-
incidence, that they both spent childhood years in the village of
Howth, outside Dublin, and share fond memories of that rocky
headland, its sea-crashed cliffs, and heathered outcrops. Paris is
beyond his financial reach, but he can travel to Ireland gratis on
the steamship run by his grandfather Pollexfen, Mama's father.
They agree to make it happen.

Then the whistle is sounding, and he has to leave. He goes
to stand on the platform, by her window, and she laughs and
waves at him through the glass as the *chug-chug-chug* starts up
and great billows of steam rise and waft over him as the carriage starts to slide. Laughing and waving, waving and laughing.
Then she is gone.

He stands, staring after her, as he had the first day in Bedford Park. He has been preparing his life and his poetry for just
such a woman, just such intermingling of beauty and sorrow
and mystery. But a woman like her will not settle into the role of
helpmeet or muse; she is too adventurous, too vital, too fond of
sensation. She will want to be, an ally. An equal. What can he, a
poor student of poetry, offer her? Only his words.

It may well be to his advantage that she is no respecter of
convention. Only such a woman—the kind he had thought to
meet only in books like *The Revolt of Islam*—only a woman wild,
and lawless, and childfree would ever accept a penniless suitor.

Another side of his mind, the side he dreads and fears and
spends a lot of time hiding from, is beginning to throw up dis-
comfiture and embarrassment, making him flinch as he recalls
some of the things he has said to her over the past days. He
dreads that she might laugh at him as he has heard her laugh at
other admirers. His worst fear is to be the butt of her laughter.

Does that mean that he is in love?

He turns towards home, a six-mile walk back but he cannot afford the tram. After ten days in her company, he is more indigent than ever. Yes, he realizes as he walks. Yes, he is in love, but being poor and unworthy, he can never speak of love.

As he walks back to his father's house, he lets the rhythm of the train drive the torments away, to settle some of his jagged thoughts into the consolation of verse. Murmuring as he passes startled faces he doesn't even see, he begins to turn a new poem in his mind.

Red Rose, proud Rose, sad Rose of all my days!
Come near me, while I sing the ancient ways...
...Come near, that no more blinded by man's fate,
I find under the boughs of love and hate,
In all poor foolish things that live a day,
Eternal beauty wandering on her way.

The crossing is rough, and Maud's ship is delayed above the two hours it usually takes to get from Dover to Calais. The English Channel is notorious for seasickness, even among hardy sailors, and all around her, people are imbibing preventatives: bicarbonate of soda or Mothersill's Seasick Remedy, powdered charcoal or cotton in the ears. Maud Gonne believes in Vichy water, cigarettes, brisk walks on the deck, and application of the will.

The air on deck is chilly, but she stays there for most of the journey, nose frozen, watching the hull cut through the water, the triangle of surf on both sides, the seagulls following. A hiatus. In many ways, the peripatetic life between Paris and London and Dublin that she has begun suits her but now, after a swirl of busy months, she is in need of the silence she senses in the large rolling ocean, underneath the flurried waves, and the two long ribbons of white the ship leaves behind in its wake. It is a balm, a nourishment, for her soul and she breathes it in, deeply.

So when on disembarkation at Calais, she is examined by a particularly disagreeable customs official, a fat harridan of a woman who enjoys torturing the more beautiful by prodding and poking and reaching under their stays, she easily disregards the indignities. And when, on the Paris train, in trying to use the single foot-warmer, she tramples the toes of the Frenchman sitting opposite and he scowls furiously over the edge of his newspaper, as if she had done it on purpose, she is able to smile a sweet apology, though he is obviously one of those men who disapproves of women traveling alone. Or perhaps, of her animals and birds. Probably both.

It's all rather tiresome but none of it can depress her. Her visit has been a triumph. She has made a number of contacts, among them the young poet who is such soothing company, the uncertainty of his character adding to his gentle kindness. Mr. Douglas Hyde had said he would bore her with blather, but she finds his talk rather wonderful. He has much to teach her about Ireland's history and the ancient Celtic beliefs and she has much to learn. In return, she can help seduce his indolent genius out of its shell of dreams.

And now, she returns to exciting times at home. France is about to have an election, in which Général Boulanger is almost certain to win his seat in the *Chambre des Députés* at last. The work her Boulangist friends have been doing is about to be rewarded, and she shall be at the very heart of the French government.

Oh, what a long way she has come since she met Millevoye, not even two years ago! Whatever might 1889 bring?

The train pulls into the *Gare du Nord*. As she exits into the concourse, she looks right and left, expectant and yes, there he is: Millevoye, Millevoye, her beloved Millevoye. A head and shoulder above the others on the platform, one of the very few men whose height tops her own.

"*Mon cher*," she says, striding towards him with graceful pride. "Oh, it is good—Oh it is oh so good—to see you."

They cannot embrace, not openly, but she takes his arm and squeezes it and he smiles down at her and she backs up and in the intimacy of their mutual appraisal is the knowledge of just how, as soon as they reach her apartment, they shall be together.

For yes, what her new friends in Ireland and London do not yet know is that Maud Gonne has a secret life, a secret love.

Best Lived In Love

WB ALWAYS said that Maud Gonne's life story was the stuff of Victorian fiction. Before she even got going on her career as British heiress turned Irish revolutionary, she had lined up all the requisites: a beautiful, dead mother; a dashing soldier father; a fiery Republican governess and a stern, patriarchal uncle who tried to make off with her money. To the list of those who made her what she was must be added her exotic and glamorous French great-aunt, Tommy's aunt Mary, the Comtesse de la Sizeranne.

Not long after Tommy died, Maud Gonne took ill, a lung hemorrhage brought on by grief, and the Comtesse prescribed a summer stay at Royat, a spa town in the fashionable Auvergne, for her and Kathleen. Great-aunt Mary had buried two husbands and now lived in Paris with her latest lover, Figlio, whom she claimed as her secretary, without convincing anyone, or much caring to. She had been a beauty in her youth and now always wore black velvet, not out of mourning but because black was the most flattering color against her pale, powdered, painstakingly-preserved complexion and snow-white hair.

The hair, too, was powdered and coiffed à la Marie Antoinette, a fashion still prevalent among the aging mistresses of the *fin de siècle* salons. Her hobby, as Maud Gonne described it in her book, was "launching professional beauties". I'd call it procuring good-looking girls for wealthy men. Yes, Great-aunt Mary was a pimp, though she insisted that she indulged her predilection for pure pleasure, not money.

That summer in Royat it was her pleasure to stroll her two young nieces, one eighteen, the other twenty, along the graveled paths, so they might be admired by passing straw-boater hat-ted men. One afternoon that was too humid for walking, as the three of them sat beneath a tree in the town square with friends, listening to military music from the bandstand, Maud Gonne was gripped by premonition.

"Something's going to happen," she whispered to her sister from behind her fan, but Kathleen said it was probably static from the ominous clouds overhead.

Millevoye approached with his friend Paul Déroulède, and from the moment she found him bending his exceedingly tall frame over her hand, pronouncing himself *enchanté*, she liked what she saw. One of the exceptional men taller than her own six feet. Thin long face, straight nose, small ears, distinguished countenance. Thinning hair (well, one can't have everything). More important were the fine eyes, protruding slightly from a lively face, within which she perceived concealed shadows. And the mouth. Something about it, barely visible under his handle-bar mustache, filled her with fear. Fear of a most delicious kind.

If not quite old enough to be her father, he was older by more than a decade. And behind the ostentatious admiration she sensed the same subdued sadness she used to sense in Tommy. Yes, he reminded her of Tommy, and she immediately wanted his admiration. Such men deserved to be gratified.

The talk was of how it would be too hot to play at the Ca-sino that night, unless the storm broke. Great-aunt Mary held forth on her great fear of thunderstorms, a fear she considered femininely becoming and Kathleen, more genuinely, concurred while Maud Gonne fought an alarming inclination to jump up and dance about. She forced herself to sit, twirling her parasol and her smile, the imposed stillness intensifying her strong, strange sense of déjà vu.

"Monsieur," she said directly to him. "I do believe we have met before?"

"*Mais non, Mademoiselle. C'est impossible.*" He smiled a meaning-ful smile. "If I had met you, I should not forget."

"I am sure we have met somewhere, sometime," she repeated. "But it is too hot to think."

The storm broke with flashes of lightning and crashing thunder and torrents of rain. They rushed back to the hotel where Great-aunt Mary asked the men to come in and wait until it abated.

She led the way to the drawing room upstairs and called the servant to draw the blinds and curtains and turn on the gaslight to keep out the sight of the storm and asked Figlio to play the piano to keep out the sound of thunder. He played well but Maud Gonne, as always, wanted to be where the drama was, outside. Without looking at Great-aunt Mary, or Millevoye, she slipped through the thick curtains, out onto the terrace.

The rosebushes in the garden below were being dashed to pieces by the driving rain, the petals sending up an intoxicatingly sweet aroma. She would have loved to go down into the garden amid the havoc of the flowers but contented herself with leaning forward from the covered terrace, stretching her bare arms into the rain.

He came to find her, as she expected he would but still his voice from behind made her jump. "Mademoiselle, your aunt has sent me to look for you, to tell you to come in."

"I cannot. How can one leave a storm like this?"

"You are not afraid?"

"Oh no, one must never be afraid of anything. Not even death."

This was Tommy's doctrine. He'd said those words to her when she was only four years old, too young to understand, but because he'd said them on the day her mother died, and because his voice was so strange and faraway as he spoke, she had never forgotten them.

"Death?" The Frenchman came to stand beside her. "What a thought in one so young."

"I have always been careless of death. I believe that's why I have survived so long."

"My dear girl, you are all of—what?—eighteen? You need hardly fear death just yet."

She didn't tell him of the lung disease that had been her trouble since childhood. Later, much later, she was to learn that he suffered from the same affliction.

"Oh I don't think of death at all," she said "I think only of life, of how life might best be lived."

"That is easily answered. Life is best lived in love."

"A pretty answer, Monsieur, but I am afraid love leads to marriage. And that is not how my life would be best lived."

He chuckled. "I thought all beautiful young ladies wished to marry."

"In December I shall be twenty-one, free at last from the bondage of my elders. Why

should I then choose to go into the bondage of a husband?"

"And what do your parents make of this unorthodox doctrine?"

"Both are dead, Monsieur Millevoye. Hence the freedom which will shortly come my way."

"Oh... My condolences, Mademoiselle."

"Thank you. My mother died many years ago and my father last November. The latter bereavement has left me, I will confess, a trifle raw. But also, soon, truly independent."

He closed in on her, so close that she could see the reflection of the terrace gas lamps in his eyes, streaks of orange amid the green.

"Where have we met before?" she whispered. "I have met you, try to remember."

Being a Frenchman, being Millevoye, he took this as an invitation and kissed the damp skin of her arm. His lips were hot and his mustache prickled her skin and she shivered.

"I am afraid you misunderstand me, Monsieur. We speak a different language. Let us go in, Great-aunt Mary will be anxious."

Neither that, nor the other rebuffs she dealt him over the coming days, deterred him. She did not intend that they should, and he did not intend to be rebuffed. He was an expert at the game of love and she no match, partly because she was less experienced, partly because she was so poorly chaperoned, but mainly because she was full of young and headstrong passion, pushing towards release.

WB, years later, was to describe the "wildness" that "set all her blood astir and glittered in her eyes", regretting it was not for him. How could she hold it back when what she most wanted was to set it free?

After that first afternoon, she met with Millevoye every day: at the springs, at the promenades, in the evening at the Casino. He wooed her with eloquence, but mostly with his demonstration of a different way to live. He was just the sort of person she wanted to be with, just the sort of person she wanted to be: the grandson of a poet, knowledgeable in the fine arts, skilled in the use of sword and pistol, deeply concerned for animals, and intensely political.

To Millevoye, the *Chambre* was a political club of swinging door ministries, with the same weak and incompetent members returned year after year, the same bribes given, the same big barrels of wine put up near the voting booths to swing the electorate. It had spectacularly failed to do anything about the principal political issue of their time: that, over in the east of what used to be France, the territories of Alsace and Lorraine had been annexed by the Prussians.

Like Maud Gonne, Millevoye suffered from pulmonary disease and was supposedly in Royat for a cure, but she soon learned that he was really there to be near Général George Boulanger, whom he dubbed "France's great hope". Boulanger had been removed from his position as Minister of War by enemies in government headed by the Prime Minister, Clemenceau, who had banished him to a post down the country, in Clermont-Ferrand. Millevoye, and his friend Paul Déroulède, were here to be with him, plotting to restore his power.

Boulanger had distinguished himself in Indo-China and in Algeria. He'd been wounded six times, looked good on a horse, and knew how to play the populace. He took the cavalry for regular jaunts down the Champs-Elysées, he welcomed new recruits with military music and the Marseillaise; he had all the sentry boxes painted red, white and blue. When representing France in the USA for the centennial of the British surrender, he refused to leave the ship on which he'd arrived until German flags flying in the harbor were taken down. These talents had taken him, at the age of forty-eight, to the head of the Republic's military division, all the while courting those who wanted the Republic destroyed.

Chief amongst those were Millevoye and his friends, especially Paul Déroulède who had formed an organization, the *Ligue des Patriotes*, which had over 180,000 members committed to sweeping out this present government, and the ramshackle edifice of democracy that created it, and sweeping in the simplicity of a popular president, who could choose his own parliament. Général Boulanger.

(Who would then, yes, *naturellement*, reward Déroulède and Millevoye and his other most ardent followers with posts in this new government.)

"Only Boulanger can turn the French army into a force capable of winning back our territories in Alsace-Lorraine," Millevoye told Maud Gonne. "Only he will instigate war again, if necessary."

This was the line presented by the new French newspapers that were rising up everywhere, fed by rightwing money, and delighting in the doings of Général George. Their *gros titres*, big headlines, made him a *chouchou*, one of the first celebrities of the mass media age. And like all celebrities, he was only a canvas on which they all projected their own desires.

So he managed to get votes from left-wingers, while getting money from Déroulède's *Ligue*, and support too from the monarchists. Oh, that French weakness for a strong man on a horse. It was exactly what Republican government sought to prevent: the sort of leader who rides in, like Napoleon III, like Boulanger, starting self-interested wars and repressing the people.

That's not how Millevoye saw it, though. As he lay with Maud Gonne in a cornfield or woodland by day, or walked with her under the high dome of a starry Auvergne sky by night, he would whisper to her the latest Boulangist scheme, or hum in her ear the Boulangist ditty that all France was singing that summer—Look at him over there/ he's smiling at us as he passes us by/he has just delivered us back/ La Lorraine et l'Alsace!

When she tells him of her plan to become an actress, he is scornful but not for the conventional reasons espoused by her London relatives.

"You underestimate your own power, my dear," he says. "An *actrice*, even one as great as Sarah Bernhardt—who is truly the greatest—even she only portrays the life of another. Why not devote yourself to a more noble aim? Free Ireland from England, as Joan of Arc freed France."

And then he makes her his great offer. They would form an alliance. He would help her to free Ireland if she would help him to regain Alsace-Lorraine for France.

"The Germans and the English are but one and the same," he says. "Saxons, Teutons. To hit one is to hit the other."

That was the day she told him that he did, after all, speak her language. They rode deep into the Clermont-Ferrand countryside. He brought a rug, some bread and cheese and a pitcher of red wine, and he orchestrated the afternoon, from the moment of flicking out the blue rug across the grass and bending over her reclining body, blocking out the sun.

~

The alliance did not please Great-aunt Mary. She had wanted a man more aristocratic, or more moneyed, or at least more famous, for her beautiful niece. This pontificating, politico-journalist did not impress.

"But his grandfather was the famous poet, Charles Millevoye," Maud Gonne protested.

Not famous enough.

"And he himself is contributing editor to *La Presse*, at only thirty-two. And likely to become a deputy in the general elections next year, on the Boulangist ticket."

Not enough. Perhaps if he owned *La Presse*. Or if he was Boulanger himself.

But Boulanger already had a mistress, a Mme Bonnemain. (Yes, Mme Goodhands! You couldn't make up some of the facts in this true story of ours.) Anyway, Maud Gonne was no more inclined to obey her maverick aunt than her conservative uncle.

"But," interjected mild and gentle Kathleen, who so very rarely interjected about anything, "surely what is most significant is that he is married."

Yes, Millevoye had a wife.

"Separated," said Maud Gonne.

As separated as a Roman Catholic Frenchman can be. Their son, Henri, kept him in touch.

"Marriage, separation, divorce: it is all irrelevant if the man has enough money or power," said Great-aunt Mary. "This Boulangist from Picardy does not have enough of either."

Maud Gonne didn't care about any of it, the money or the marriage. That he was said to be a philanderer did not trouble her either. From the moment of their meeting, she envisioned a life as his mistress and accomplice, a daring and dangerous life, dedicated to noble, nationalist ideals.

Vive la France! Eire abu!

When Millevoye gave her compliments or flattery, it stirred little in her, but when he ranted against the empty parliamentary debates, the endless, futile crises, the despicable corruption, and most especially when he spoke of his love for France and his determination her annexed territories must be returned, she squirmed with admiration and thrilled to his battle cry: *Retaliate! Reclaim! Revanche!*

She gave herself to him, that's how Maud Gonne always thought of it, to the end of her life. Gave herself willingly, first in the open air, under the gaze of the Puy de Dome and the other looming mountains of the Auvergne. Gave herself gladly, knowing that Kathleen and May and all their friends would think her wrong.

Other young women might be happy to wallow in cowardice and call it morality but not Maud Gonne. In her, action followed emotion as freely as Dagda, her dog, jumped into pursuit at the sight of a rabbit. Stop and think? Weigh and measure? Might as well ask Dagda to consider the sense of the chase.

For her, vacillation would have been the true dishonor. She loved; ergo, she would give her love. So she gave and gave again, and never regretted the decision she took that summer in Royat. What else could she have done, being who she was?

And now it is two years later, and she is returning to her Parisian lover with news of great gains, after her travels in London and Dublin and Donegal. A useful poet in the metropolis, an invaluable introduction to the men of The Contemporary Club in the Hibernian capital, and, most important to her, in the remotest, most northwesterly corner of Europe, the discovery of her life's purpose. Rallying and organizing the Irish people against their oppressors.

In Dublin at that time, many on our side thought Maud Gonne a dilettante. "A right notice-box," my friend Mary said, when she first told me about her. But there had been nothing easy about her work with the Donegal people. Days traipsing about the wilds in all weathers, in wind so severe it stopped her breathing. Nights of the hospitality of small smoking cabins with inhabitants who spoke no English, sometimes fighting off suffocation, aggravating her consumption until she coughed up blood.

She loved it. The casinos and crushes, soirees and balls of upper middle-class life bored her. Under the hulking bulk of Muckish mountain, in driving rain and piercing wind, she had discovered her skill in organizing and inspiring people. She had proven herself to the poorest of Ireland's people and in so doing, proven herself to herself.

She says none of this to Millevoye at first. Their talk, all the way from the station to her small apartment, is of the French campaign. She has never seen him so elevated. They've been working day and night, he tells her, but to great avail. The Paris to which she is returning is even more behind Général Boulanger than when she left. Victory in their by-election seems certain.

And then they are at the apartment, and she is turning the key, and they are hurrying towards the bedroom, and they do not even get that far before all is obliterated in the passion of long French kisses, and the unbuttoning of each other's boots and clothes, and the touch of long-missed hands.

Absence, contrast: these are Maud Gonne's keys to sensual pleasure at this time. What had begun, before she left for Ireland, to feel like a tiresome chore is now more than bearable. Quite delightful, in part. She loves the touch of skin on skin after long absence. She loves the adoration in his eyes and his need of her, mounting with each caress. She loves when he does something subtle, like spending a long time on the crook of her neck, or the creases between her toes. And she allows him some of his cruder approaches today.

As ever, there are some things, one thing in particular, that she can't and never will, allow but today, in the pleasure after long parting, it makes no matter that he tries, once again and she, once again, refuses. He quickly moves on and all is well between them, and soon it is over and they are in the period of lovemaking she most enjoys, the post-coital cigarette. That indolent smoky haze is the most delightful filter through which to view the world.

He tells her about their preparations for the by-election and when she has heard all, she then tells him of the little rooms she has taken in Dublin, over Morrow's bookshop in Naussau Street, near Trinity College, how she has added a low couch and decor in the same style as her Paris apartment, with many colored cushions, and comfortable armchairs, and tall vases for green branches.

These Dublin rooms are close to the new National Library, a very pleasant place for reading and writing, and she is making many friends who will help to further their Irish cause, most notably a Mr. Douglas Hyde whom he should meet, she says, when he visits Paris in spring. He is teaching her to speak Irish. It is still almost a crime to do so in Ireland. Children in the Gaelic-speaking districts are beaten for it and businesses are prosecuted for putting their names in Irish over their own shops.

She says little about WB. Most of what she has to tell centers on the people of Donegal. How the local curate, Father Stephens, took her to a court session where six mountain men and boys were being tried for stealing turf from land belonging to Col. Olpherts, the local landlord who was building up to a mass eviction. The previous week, the same court had sent down men for gathering seaweed on one of his deserted beaches. As the turf-cutters were sentenced to a fine of ten shillings or one month's imprisonment, Father Stephens had angrily whispered to Maud Gonne: "There is nothing free in Ireland, only the air."

She'd set up a station in the local hotel in Falcarragh, looking after as many of the sick as she could fit into her little bedroom. And she'd mobilized support for the people, in just the way Millevoye had taught her: writing energetic letters to the newspapers and enticing journalists to come to Donegal and tell the story of the evictions.

Readers were moved to hear of those howling, bewildered families, contorted with helplessness. And their old people, some bedridden and carried out on mattresses, clutching in claw-like hands a statue of the Blessed Virgin, or rosary beads, as the mattresses were dumped on the roadside, and their household goods pitched out after them. Their dogs and pet pigs, too. Under the law, every living thing had to be out of the house before an eviction was deemed complete.

"If I could only walk," one old lady had sobbed to her.

"Don't worry about needing to walk," Maud Gonne said. "We'll get you a car. But where are you going to go?"

"I don't know. Anyone who takes us in will be evicted themselves."

That was the fear. So Maud Gonne and her supporters persuaded Pat O'Brien—"Pat the Builder"—to come back to Donegal to start again the hut-building he used to do, back when the Land League was in the hands of women. That was when Parnell, the great leader whom the Irish called The Chief, and all the other leaders were imprisoned, and Mr Parnell's sisters took over.

When the women ran it, the League was a much stronger, much more practical force. They had huts built, only simple one- or two-room dwellings, but so much better than the workhouse where the little ones died like so many flies. And for some, better than the cabin the evicted family had called home.

The value of the Land League huts, though, went far beyond the physical. Putting up a hut asked for the cooperative work of the whole countryside. Boys and girls collected stones for the walls, strong farmers supplied straw for the thatch, carpenters and masons worked for the love of neighbor. And when one was finished, out would come some kind of food and drink and a local fiddler or two. Blazing turf torches would announce the celebration for miles.

What was killing the people now, killing their spirit, was fear. The shock of seeing and being with so much fear and dependency would never leave her, she tells Millevoye. She is a different person now to the woman who left for Ireland twelve weeks ago.

All she had been able to do was give them hope, enough heart to resist and delay. Delay was expensive for the landlord. He had to house and feed his "Emergency Men", the police he had to post about the doomed houses to ensure the deed was done. All the while Maud Gonne and the curate, and those with the heart to resist, did what they could to ensure it wasn't.

"But to what point?" Millevoye asks.

"I don't know, sometimes it felt so hopeless. But we must always do what we can, must we not? We must do what is right."

He looks unconvinced, and she knows he is holding back an opinion because he doesn't want to spoil their first day back together.

It's an ongoing argument between them. Her way is to follow impulses and inspirations and trust that God is in control of the pattern, that if she follows right, right will follow. His is to focus energy, which is always limited. To choose what one does wisely, and do what is most expedient.

Neither can convince the other, it's a matter of character, but Maud Gonne lives in hope. She moves in closer for another kiss.

Soon, Millevoye has to leave for a political meeting, which suits her very well. She's glad to have time alone to settle back in. It really is so lovely to be back among her own beautiful things. People are more important than things, and political advancement is more important than personal comfort, but oh, it's nice to be home all the same.

She shall call for some hot water, make up a bath, clean herself up. The leavings of the sex act disconcert her, and she has the dust of the journey under her fingernails. Yes, a bath.

She stretches her full length across the bed, languorous as Macha after a nap. Millevoye has had her today but he has not *had* her. No man ever shall. She spent much time with Tommy before he died, in the company of his officer friends and exposed to soldiers. She knows what men are like, how they speak of women when there are no women present.

She has no care. They can speak how they like so long as she keeps a vital part of herself intact, unavailable. She thinks about the London visit she made that she did not share with him, a visit she also kept secret from Mr. Yeats. Her visit to Mrs. Wilson's small flat on the Edgware Road.

Which reminds her... Before she prepares a bath, she must write to Mrs. Wilson. She goes to the little bureau by the window and takes out her writing paper, and fills her little inkwell. She likes to make a ritual of small moments, to do things with style, sometimes to impress others but also when alone, as an act of grounding herself. When one is busy, as she was in Donegal, life whistles by. One struggles to keep up with oneself. It is vital, when one slows down, to be conscious of small things, small moments. To take pains.

Pen, ink, blotting paper, writing paper: all ready, she begins to write to her father's mistress.

My dear Mrs. Wilson

It was so very gratifying to meet you on my recent visit to London and to see dear Eileen thriving. What a clever little girl she is. I shall send you soon that French toy I described, I think she will find it amusing. In the meantime, I hope the enclosed is useful to you, I had some English money left from my trip which is of no use to me here in France. I shall come to see you next time I am in London and hope to assist more formally with your affairs.

In the meantime.
With very kind regards
Maud Gonne

Friends Of Freedom

MRS. MARGARET Wilson first presented herself in Maud Gonne's life before she came into her money, while she was still living with her uncle William. Her uncle, like any Victorian patriarch, expected on return from work that tea would be poured for him in the drawing room, and by a female member of the family, not a servant. On the afternoon in question, Maud Gonne was hurrying, as ever almost late, to take her turn at the duty when she heard shouts from Uncle William through the drawing room door.

"I tell you, my good woman, I don't believe you."

Maud Gonne stopped, hand to the doorknob. Her uncle's voice was shaky with emotion, something she'd never seen. He was often forbidding, and had a gift of saying things incontestably true—"punctuality is most necessary in life"; "people generally eat too much"—which, when he said them, you wanted to contradict. But she had only ever seen him do feelings in two varieties: anger or irritation.

"I vow to you, Sir, that it is the truth I tell." The voice was middle-class but with a strong Irish brogue.

She peeped round the door. Her uncle was standing with his back to the fireplace, holding himself high and stern above a seated young woman in black, the onslaught of his anger raining down on her head. She had been crying and was now struggling to stop.

"This letter proves nothing," Uncle William said. "You must see how improper your presence is here? I must ask you to leave."

Maud Gonne walked in and the woman looked up, pale and rather beautiful even in her sorrow. Uncle William's fury rose another notch. "Maud, leave us. Come back in fifteen minutes."

Instead, she turned to the woman. "Are you Mrs. Wilson?" she asked, astonishing them both.

Uncle William said, "What the..." and stopped himself, re-membering he was in the presence of two women.

"Yes, yes I am," the woman said, recovering from her surprise to move on what she thought might be an opportunity. "And I wouldn't be troubling you, Miss, only I and the baby have no money at all."

Uncle William flinched at the word "baby" and turned his fury on her. "Maud, this is no affair of yours."

But it was. Maud Gonne had known immediately that this must be the woman to whom Tommy had written a check be-fore he died. It pains her to remember him at that time, so weak and delirious, with a thin and aged face that both was, but was not, his. He'd asked her plainly for his checkbook, and Nurse had said not to mind him, that he was only raving, but then he asked a second time, and Maud got it for him. He was too ill to hold the pen properly so she'd said, "Tell me what to write, and I will write it for you, Tommy."

He said the name Margaret Wilson and the amount, and she'd filled it in, and held his hand for the signature and put it in an envelope and sent it to the address he gave her.

The bank returned it, because the signature was illegible, but she'd given them permission to go ahead and cash it.

"Is it a boy or a girl?" she asked Mrs. Wilson now.

The woman looked at her, a half-hostile look, like a dog that fears you might take away its puppies.

"A girl," she said. "Eileen."

"Eileen," repeated Maud Gonne. "I should dearly love to see her."

"Enough," thundered Uncle William. "Maud, I insist that..."

"Oh Miss Gonne, I wouldn't ever have come at all, only I have no money to feed the child, no money at all, and I didn't know what to do."

"Of course you were right to come," Maud Gonne said. "Where are you staying?"

"Enough! This is most improper and must desist. Maud, this

woman is nothing to us. Please respect your father's memory, even if you have no sense for yourself."

"I am not one who tells lies. I want nothing from you, only enough to keep the child until I can get work. I never asked a penny from anyone and reared my son myself when my husband deserted us, and now the boy is grown."

Mrs. Wilson started to cry again, Maud Gonne could see she was a weeper.

"But I've been ill," she said, through her sniffs. "And so has the baby... And I can't get work... and I can't see the child starve, can I? The Colonel was a good man. He would never have left her unprovided for."

"I agree with you," said Maud Gonne.

"This talk can't go on," said Uncle William. "Madam, this is your final warning to leave voluntarily. I am now ringing for a servant to put you out." He goes across to the bell by the mantelpiece. "You must never come here again. Or try to see my niece. Do you hear?"

Maud Gonne pulled her uncle aside. She had no money of her own at that time, and indeed, Uncle William had lied to her, so she had, as yet, no idea that she was to come into a fortune at twenty-one. Knowing mercy wouldn't do it, she appealed to his sense of duty. She told him about Tommy sending the check and her conviction that he would have wanted them to help. After much persuasion and extraction of promises that Mrs. Wilson would never, ever darken their door, Uncle William relented, and handed over five sovereigns.

Next day, Maud Gonne went to see her at the address she'd given, a flat off the Edgware Road, and heard that Tommy had never seen the child, having died before she was born. And she paid another visit again when back in London, to give Mrs. Wilson some more money.

Her little half-sister was quite delightful, with a strong look of Tommy, and moving into the stage when children become delightful. And, unexpectedly, bouncing her up and down on her knee, playing "Horsey Horsey" with her, had given Maud Gonne an idea about how to deal with a problem that was becoming increasingly tiresome: her lover's wandering eye.

Yes, Millevoye had affairs, spent far too much time in the music halls of Montmartre, indulged in dalliances with coquettes. The discovery had come as rather a shock, especially as it was made in embarrassing circumstances, a snide remark at the salon of a vindictive *duchesse*. It could have been humiliating, except that Maud Gonne didn't care a farthing what the *duchesse* and her cronies thought of her, beyond the value they could be to her cause. And they hadn't proved much value at all. They were all talk: "Isn't it dreadful?" and "That's so interesting," but they became far more animated when boasting of their menfolk's exploits, or fretting over their offspring's bowel movements.

Their salons were a crashing bore; Maud Gonne had begun to mix with a new kind of woman, women who were beginning to earn money, to take jobs and pursue education, to work for social change. Women like Ghénia Glaisette, the author and journalist, who is eleven years older but becoming a friend. Ghénia has been minding Dagda while Maud Gonne was away, no easy task, for Dagda can crash ornaments to the floor with a swing of his tail, and eats enough meat in a day to keep a family for a week.

Maud Gonne has learned so much from Ghénia, who reminds her of her old governess, also a true Republican who saw merit in all people. Ghénia believes women should have a vote on the same conditions as men and has many other advanced opinions. She attends an annual meeting of Protestant women called the Conference of Versailles and is urging Maud Gonne to attend with her next year. Ghénia calls herself a *féministe*, and until she met her, Maud Gonne thought all such were man-hating and man-imitating shrews, fighting for rights that no real woman wanted. But Ghénia has a longtime lover, younger than her and handsome, who is always pestering her to marry. Napoleonic law has, since 1804, required married women to obey their husbands. Ghénia says that marriage is therefore impossible for her, unless French law changes.

This is Maud Gonne's type of woman, not the drawing room duchesses, who prefer gossip to work. So it was not as troubling as it might have been when the *duchesse* said: "Dear Monsieur Millevoye," in a tone that alerted all. Her lips curled back from her teeth like a dog, saliva in the corners, and she had a touch of hysteria in her eyes at her own malice, at the thought of break-ing another on the wheel of her words.

"He is so attentive to the poor people of Montmartre. Espe-cially the poor young girls."

One of her cronies tittered, and others began to take an ex-treme interest in the carpet or the ceiling, and Maud Gonne felt knowledge, plunging like a pail that has just had its rope cut, landing with a loud, hard clang. And as soon as it hit home, that part of her mind realized she had known all along. She had al-ways, almost since they met, been one of many, not the one to his one that the other part of her, the more trusting innocent part, had thought herself.

But why make a fuss, if she doesn't care about the clack-ing-tongued women—which she doesn't—and knowing that, without this siphon, Millevoye's expectations of her would be... how might she put this to herself? ...excessive. She knows this. She surrounds herself with beasts and birds because they can give the unconditional love that humans cannot. Especially, perhaps, men. Men always want something from her—and yes, most often that thing.

She refuses to give the sex act this undue prominence. It is not as if it is important to her. She and Tommy always laughed together over love affairs. That is the attitude to take: amused disdain.

What surprised her on visiting Mrs. Wilson this time was how the same instinct she always felt for birds and beasts was ignited by Eileen. Until that moment, children had seemed to her little more than a nuisance, the domain of those women who were her opposite, against whom she defined herself: women shy of public life, women over-satisfied with hearth and home.

But this child is her sister; this child is Tommy's. And such a marvelous little thing, now she is developing her own personal-ity: telling them both, Maud Gonne and her mother, what to do. Her favorite word is "No," little rebel. And when she got tired, she sat back in her mama's lap, one thumb in her mouth, the other soft, fat little hand brushing Mrs. Wilson's hair back from her face, adoration shining out of her as she gazed upwards, until her eyelids slowly closed, and she slipped into what Mr. Yeats would call the land of numberless dreams.

Maud Gonne can't get that picture, that adoring touch, out of her mind, and it has set her planning. Yes, to notice or discuss Millevoye's affairs would be beneath her; it would be foolish not to acknowledge that men—especially philandering men—can be fickle. She, and their alliance, might be enough to hold him now, but in a year or two? In five?

She needs something more, and what better than a child? Look at how he is with Mme Millevoye. Next to Clemenceau, the Prime Minister, nobody gets him more riled than his wife, but in any question concerning their son, Madame has his full support and attention.

If they, too, have a child together, he can wander where he wants, but she can be confident that he'll always find his way back.

~

January 1889 is a good month for the French side of their Franco-Irish alliance, vital and busy, as the people-pleasing popularity of *revanche* gives Général Boulanger his overwhelming victory. Maud Gonne shares Millevoye's triumph with Déroulède and their followers from *Ligue des Patriotes*, as they carry *le brave général* off to a celebration at their headquarters, Café Durand, with cries of "Vive la France!" and "Vive Boulanger!" and the drums of 'La Marseillaise', Europe's oldest marching anthem, playing all the way, and the words ringing out: *Aux armes, Citoyens/Formez vos battalions, Marchons, Marchons!*

As the Général's coterie orders champagne within, outside crowds throng the streets, spilling out into the boulevards as Déroulède and Millevoye and their closest associates circle round, urging him to seize the moment. Backed by the students of Paris, who are ever ready for a revolt, they can now lead the people—and more importantly, the army—onto the *Palais de l'Elysée* and stage a coup d'état.

They are ready to march. *Marchons, Marchons!*

The Général hesitates, perhaps remembering the fate of

Napoleon III. The only decision he is willing to make is that he is hungry.

Much to the disgust of Millevoye and Déroulède, he leaves them and goes to dinner with Mme Bonnemain who has been waiting for him in a private room upstairs. The restaurant is not far from the *Chambre des Députés*, it is right across the Seine. As they eat, the calls of the crowd for him to take action, to come out and greet his adorers, to cross the river and end this impotent republic, grow louder.

But he sits there (*en France, on mange quand-même*), listening to his mistress's thoughts on why it would be wiser to wait. Paris might well be behind him, but Paris is not France. In the autumn, there will be a general election. Why put himself in danger snatching power by illegal means now when in six months, he'll have the whole country behind him, the unanimous vote of all France?

Déroulède was just using him, just as he had used *Ligue des Patriotes*, for his own advancement. It was only after Déroulède lost the election in 1885 that he and Millevoye decided that the parliamentary system adopted from Britain had sapped France of its vitality and virtue, and should be replaced. So many of the *Ligue* have deserted him for using their non-political organization for political ends. Boulanger would do better to use the system that is there, rather than go against the might of the assembly to change it.

So he sits there, and he finishes his elaborate meal. And then he and Mme Bonnemain go home to bed—and the moment passes, unsealed.

While the Général hesitates, his enemies do not. They eliminate the parliamentary procedure that allowed him to be elected and put out a warrant for his arrest. He scuttles across the frontier to Belgium, to Madame's hometown of Brussels, and this, after all the grandiloquent speeches, makes him look considerably less dashing, considerably less brave. A French court is set up to try him in exile and finds him guilty. The same court outlaws *Ligue des Patriotes* as racist and anti-Semitic.

Instead of high stepping cavalry officers, anti-republican

Napoleonics, it is the forward push of modernism, new symbols of bourgeois materialism and prosperity like the Eiffel
Tower and the coming World Trade Fair, that seize the day.

~

Millevoye remains faithful to his hero and in the general election in July, he is elected deputy for Amiens, and so now, becomes part of the despised Chambre himself. His speeches are
a melange of superheated patriotic calls for unity and invective
against certain government officials.

And Maud Gonne, following her lover, continues to support
the reactionary movement in France. As a member of Parliament, Lucien can now do more for Ireland than before. And she
herself is coming to attention. WT Stead, the famous English
reformer and journalist whom she had met in Russia on her
first assignment from the Boulangists, had this to say in his new
newspaper, *The Review of Reviews*:

*The somewhat fantastic mission of Miss Maud Gonne in Paris has the
purpose of founding an alliance of "Friends of Irish Freedom" in France.
Miss Gonne is one of the most beautiful women in the world. She is an Irish
heroine, born Protestant, who became a Buddhist with theories of pre-exis-
tence, but who, in all her pilgrimages from shrine to shrine, has never ceased
to cherish a passionate devotion to the cause of Irish Independence.*

*She is for the Irish Republic and total separation, peacefully if possible,
but if necessary by the sword, that of France and Russia are not excepted. She
was at St. Petersburg in 1887, having travelled from Constantinople alone.
Everywhere her beauty and her enthusiasm naturally make an impression,
and although she is hardly likely to be successful where Wolfe Tone failed, her
pilgrimage of passion is at least a picturesque incident that relieves the gloom
of the political situation.*

Well yes, thank you Stead, Maud Gonne thinks, but the pilgrimage is more of politics than passion, and she intends to
create a great deal more than a picturesque incident. Always,
the beauty barricade. In St. Petersburg, Stead had written her
a very foolish amorous letter that got him into trouble with his
Russian girlfriend. He is a man with strong puritanical beliefs
that are constantly warring with an equally strong sensual
temperament. This induces a sex obsession in him; he can talk
of nothing else and sees it everywhere.

It made him rather repellent to her, who hates such talk, but he has done much good, especially in his newspaper crusade against prostitution. He went so far as to arrange the "purchase" of Eliza Armstrong, the thirteen-year-old daughter of a chimney sweep, so he could speak out. She hasn't seen him since they waved farewell in St. Petersburg, but he has promised to help her, if ever she needs him.

And Millevoye is helping her to write her first article under her own name. "*Un peuple opprimé*" they have called it, all about the evictions in Donegal. He has an editor at La Nouvelle Revue Internationale, who has agreed to publish. Gone are the days, however, when she had all his praise. When they met first, he was always saying things like "to hear a woman like you talking of going on the stage is infamous," or "If only you were French, together we could win back Alsace-Lorraine for France." Or "with the help of a woman like you, I could accomplish anything."

Now he helps their alliance, yes, but at the same time undermines the help with his sniggers and "ooooh"s.

Well, the help's the thing. She is planning a lecture tour for the following autumn. Around Valenciennes, Arras, Rouen, Bordeaux, Cognac, Perigueux, La Rochelle, maybe Luxembourg too. Her aim is to tear down the wall of silence that Britain has built up around Ireland. As soon as the baby permits, she will begin this tour.

Yes, the other part of her plan also proceeds well. She is almost certainly pregnant, though she hasn't told him yet. It has been nothing but lovemaking since she came back, and two months have now passed without menses.

She *feels* pregnant, and a dream she had that was more like a vision, of an old tree at the heart of a wood in which a young boy jumped from branch to branch, seems to confirm this feeling. If she is right, by the end of the year, she and Millevoye will have a son. Not just a son but a patriot son. All going well, they shall call him Georges, after *le brave général*.

Ever Flaming Time

MAUD GONNE is a scandal! So writes Miss Katherine Tynan to her friend, Willie Yeats, from Dublin, furnishing details of Miss Gonne traveling about in outside cars, quite alone—by which she means, without a male escort. And visiting prisoners. Is she sincere?

He writes back that she is, that he is proud to be associated with her. He has been planting out more articles in *The United Ireland* and *The Boston Pilot* and elsewhere, stressing her Irishness, praising her Celtic qualities, describing audiences of Parisian aristocrats reduced to tears by her oratory and helping along the image she wishes to cultivate as the Irish Joan of Arc.

And then, in October, comes news that rocks him. Indeed, it rocked the entire circle of Irish nationalists when we heard it. Miss Ellen O'Leary, sister to WB and Maud Gonne's mentor, John O'Leary, has died. As heroic a person to us as her brother, her kindness to us all, to each and every young person who trooped through their house visiting her brother, was legendary.

WB is devastated; they had no warning. She had always been so very kind to him, so motherly.

The day he hears the news, he also hears that Maud Gonne is in London, and he rushes to Hans Place to see her but when he arrives, she is already in the hall, fully coated and bonneted, and so very sorry, but it is impossible today to invite him in. She is just on her way out, in fact on her way back. Yes, to Paris. She is so dreadfully sorry she has not been in touch... She came across here to London to nurse her sister and had to come so suddenly, and Kathleen has been so awfully ill, that she hasn't had a free moment. And now must return home, urgently. She has been recalled. Boulangist business.

The doctors think Kathleen's condition is congestion of the liver, and certainly her sister's digestive system is affected, but she, herself, is certain beyond doubt that the real problem is her marriage to that boor. They plan their wedding for December and already, before they have even tied that commitment, she is ill. Oh, but it is a tragedy waiting to happen, and perhaps she should not be surprised. Had she ever told him about the ances-tor of theirs who was cursed by a witch for some foul deed done? The curse placed on him that none of his female descendants should have a happy marriage? Certainly Tommy's mother had not, and now this. For herself she intends never to marry.

This, she says lightly, as if the topic is not even a question between them.As of course it is not.

Oh how very upsetting to hear this news of Miss O'Leary. Impossible to imagine that they shall never see her gentle, no-ble face again. And who shall care for Mr. O'Leary now? How pleased she is that she persuaded Miss O'Leary to put her book of poems together. She had just completed the corrections. It must be one of the best things about being a writer, that one's work lives on? But of course all our work lives on, everything we do has an effect.

Yes, she knows he must think Miss O'Leary's poems too sim-ple but no influence in modern Ireland has been more ennobling than that of those two Fenians, brother and sister, and though her poems are not subtle, she was a balladeer, and ballads are not supposed to be subtle, are they? Or not usually.

Of course *his* are, most delightfully so. But though for Miss O'Leary the grass *was* simply green and the sea *was* simply blue, yet did not the nobility of her character give her work a purity?

And now she is dead. It is unbearable to contemplate, and yet the world goes on. Life is so strange...

Oh, she must leave, but she will be certain to see him next time, she wishes to talk more of the occult and its role in the Ireland that is coming. Mr. Russell told her something of his work with him when she was last in Dublin, and she is keen, most keen, to hear his thoughts on the matter, particularly on the Celtic aspect but now, alas, she simply must be gone.

She hustles him back out the door.

And she watches from the window, hand to her abdomen, him going back down the path and out the gate she had, so fortuitously, seen him come in and up. She feels sorry for him, but imagine if she hadn't seen him. She had only happened to be passing the window. A narrow escape.

This is another reason, as well as those she gave him, that she hopes to postpone, if not cancel altogether, her sister's impending nuptials. By December, she'll be at eight months, not six, and utterly unable to disguise her shape, even to an innocent such as him.

~

A scandal is a secret gone wide, so said one of the mistresses of the Prince of Wales. At the very end of the year, two poorly kept secrets become open scandals.

Just before Christmas, the Irish "Chief", Charles Stuart Parnell, overnights at Prime Minister Gladstone's home in Hawarden, Wales, to nail down negotiations on Irish Home Rule. From inmate at Kilmainham Gaol to intimate at Hawarden Hall in just over seven years is a quite a climb, but Mr. Parnell does not spend Christmas celebrating his achievement with his family.

For his beloved—his helpmeet and support, mother to three of his children, two still living, his darling Kitty—is married to another. A certain Captain O'Shea, an Irish MP, member of Parnell's own Irish Parliamentary Party. And on Christmas Eve, the Captain sues for divorce, citing Mr. Parnell as correspondent. Thus it is revealed, to those who did not already know, that Parnell has been the long-term lover of Mrs. O'Shea.

Maud Gonne has long been critical of Parnell, how he made the Irish Party cease agrarian agitation as a bribe to induce the Liberals to deliver reform. The "Union of Hearts" campaign, he called it. As if England had a heart! How ruthlessly he had cast aside his sisters' work and disbanded the Land League in favor of a new organization of his own, while pushing through a Parliamentary bill for Home Rule with his new Liberal friends. Women not welcome, though his sisters had kept the League going while he was in prison.

The new League, they say, is "an open organization in which the ladies will not take part," apparently without even seeing the contradiction in that statement. Neither does Mr. Parnell support the Irish political prisoners, whose actions offend his Liberal friends. He prefers hobnobbing with Gladstone. But all that appeasement has, as she predicted, come to naught in the end.

Seeing him fall victim to this English plot to destroy Home Rule, her only consolation is that at least she is back in Paris and spared having to witness the glee of her relatives and Captain Pilcher at the downfall.

For Maud Gonne failed to dissuade Kathleen to jilt her betrothed and so had returned to London for the wedding in December, carrying her swollen abdomen with high, haughty pride, to the utter consternation of her entire family—not just the elders and Kathleen's Pilcher in-laws but the Gonne and Cooke cousins too.

Only cousins May and Chotie and, of course, Kathleen were tolerant.

It was for Kathleen that Maud attended, it was for Maud that Kathleen accepted the attendance. For either sister, their mutual affection made one missing the wedding of the other unthinkable. Even more unthinkable than this complete flouting of convention.

It is the final breach for Maud Gonne's relatives. She has now irrevocably placed herself among the demi-monde of Paris, forever outside the pale of respectability.

Respectability's cruel code is not something Maud Gonne admires or aspires to live by, and she is confirmed in that when the Parnell scandal breaks that same month, with all its petty laughter at the bedroom farce that unfolded in court, Parnell and Mrs. O'Shea taking rooms under false names. Parnell, when Captain O'Shea turns up unexpectedly, escaping by the balcony and fire escape, and then a few minutes later coming round and presenting himself at the door as an ordinary visitor.

It is laughable and uncomfortably close to situations she herself has been in with Millevoye, which if subjected to public scrutiny, would expose them in just the same way.

Maud Gonne has plenty of time to consider such thoughts. Aside from the practical issues of moving apartment—she needs room for the coming baby and a nurse—she has now submitted to confinement. Dreadful word but not an unpleasant experience. She holes up with her sketchbook, a box of apples (she cannot get enough of that fruit since the first day of her pregnancy) and a consignment of novels from London. Proficient at reading in French, for relaxation she always prefers English.

And yes, it is time to relax, to settle in, to enjoy this last Christmas where she has only herself to think about and prepare for the dawn of 1890. A new year, a new decade and a new era for her and Millevoye, as parents.

Then comes the birth. She has made all the preparations, but as soon as it starts, waking her out of sleep in the middle of the night, she realizes nothing could have prepared her. At first, she grips the bedpost for a while. Lucien is beside her, snoring gently, but she is Maud Gonne, and not about to make a fuss. All who know most about these matters say first babies take their time in coming. When she begins to feel as if a giant elbow is being kneaded into her backbone and trying to break it, she touches his arm.

The snores continue. She squeezes, but nothing. "Millevoye!"

"Mmmmm."

"I think my time is here."

It takes him a while to climb out of sleep, and then out of bed. She hears the scratch of flint and steel. The tinder catches, and he lights the candle and the room comes into view. Her slippers, where she kicked out of them, one heel turned up. Millevoye's pipe. Her downturned, open book.

He looks at her, and she smiles an apology. "I think you must fetch Nurse."

"And Dr. Thibaut?"

"Not yet, not till morning, it is likely to take long."

Awake now, he begins to pull on his clothes, any old way, like a man who must make a quick getaway. As he's leaving, she calls him back.

"Millevoye...?"

"Yes?"

His long, strong, melancholic face is half lit by the candle. The handlebar mustache, ends uncurled. The shirt opens at the throat. Uncharacteristic dishevelment. "Before you go..."

"Yes?"

"Tell me that you love me, Millevoye."

He looks into her dark eyes, in surprise. He comes back to the bed, the last vestiges of sleep leaving him. She can see his alarm and simultaneous relief that her time is finally here and will soon be over. He just sees the clammy moisture on her face. Does he sense the worm of her fear? Perhaps. Does she want him to? Perhaps not.

He sets down the candle for a moment and looks at her, a different Maud Gonne from the jolly good fellow who caps his good stories and smokes like a train. He has never seen her help-less before. Her vulnerability makes her a little ashamed, and she sees something akin on his face.

"I love you, Maud," he says, kissing her without meeting her eyes. He goes across the landing to the drawing room, to pour her a glass of brandy. "Drink this," he says, coming back in.

He lights more candles but now she wishes him gone. He cannot help her, and he sees it. "I'll fetch Nurse," he says. "Then I'll be back."

"Don't come back. Tell Nurse and when light comes, tell the doctor. I'd rather you didn't see me like this."

"As you wish."

He takes one of the candles and rushes out. Hot grease run-ning over his hand in his hurry makes him swear: "*Merde!*"

Nurse comes first, then the dawn, then the doctor, then noon, then a different nurse to give the first one a break, then six o'clock, then the doctor back again after his dinner, then midnight, then another dawn and, finally, in the middle of the morning following, the baby.

She looks down at his coming as the contraction grips, as she pushes, to see if she can witness him being born. She tilts her head forward, to the maximum, and there he is, she sees him, his face, black shock of hair—she hadn't expected that—all red and wet with her blood. A look of rapt concentration, like a priest, eyes and mouth gently shut.

For the first time she understands what Willie Yeats means by terrible beauty. She pushes again, and on this one, Nurse catches him by the shoulders and pulls him up and out.

"It's a boy," she says. Well of course it is. Georges. Petit Georges. Her little Georgie.

Nurse hands him over, and Maud Gonne immediately adjusts her clothing and finds a place for him on her breast. "Hello, my beauty," she says. "Hello, hello." Georges: a most beautiful presence made incarnate. Her feelings for him, all her feelings, overspill. She is overcome, overjoyed, overflowing. Milk and blood, love and joy, ooze from her. More than anything, she is overawed.

This is the kingdom, this is the power, this is the glory that men try to annex with their anti-women laws and conventions and rules. Not having had her own mother, she hadn't understood. Now she knows.

She must tell Ghénia. Men are not overweeningly powerful, as they have always thought. They are jealous. They can never give birth.

Further Than The Morning Star

OUT IN WEST London, WB lies in his room, wishing she were closer. When she was before him, it seemed as though life trembled into stillness and silence, folded itself away on itself. Sometimes he wonders if he has chosen her beauty, which seems so unearthly to him, precisely because the individual woman is lost in its lines.

Women fill him with curiosity. He has long been a romantic, head full of the mysterious women of Rossetti and those hesitating faces of Burne-Jones who seem always anxious for a deity to come and avenge the wrongs of man.

Sometimes the barrier between himself and other people fills him with terror, his extreme shyness that keeps him from speaking his own thought. It is why he prefers the company of women. Women come more easily to that wisdom which ancient peoples, and all wild peoples even now, think the only wisdom.

He has in London various women friends on whom he can call towards five o'clock, mainly to discuss thoughts that he could not bring to a man without meeting some competing thought. (And because their tea and toast saves his pennies for the bus ride home.)

He still has the ambition, formed in Sligo in his teens, of living in imitation of Thoreau on Innisfree, a little island in Lough Gill. When walking through Fleet Street very homesick one day, he heard a little tinkle of water and saw in a shop window a fountain which balanced a little ball upon its jet and began to remember lake water. From the sudden remembrance came his poem "Innisfree", his first lyric with anything in its rhythm of his own music.

He has begun to use rhythm as an escape from rhetoric, and from that emotion of the crowd that rhetoric brings.

He wishes now to use more common syntax and now could not write that first line with its conventional archaism, "Arise and go." Nor the inversion of the last stanza. But his new forms are, he hopes only as yet, incoherent. He cannot make the words obey his impulse.

Apart from intimate exchanges of thought with women friends, he is timid and abashed. He stays in his room, imagining adventurous love stories with himself for hero, or at other times planning a life of lonely austerity.

He is tortured, tortured, as he has been for so many years, by sexual desire. For him, any kind of sexual contact, outside that permitted to a man and woman together in marriage, is moral pollution, including the self-contact that constantly calls. That way lies plain ruin, days of self-loathing, whenever he succumbs.

So today he refrains. He lies in bed and curdles in frustration, and dreams. Dreams of a heroic political victory, that wins freedom for Ireland and wins her favor. Dreams of the opposite, of refusing or failing in a public role and in the refusal or the failure, winning her understanding.

Mostly though, he just dreams of dying for her sake.

Wherever In The Wastes

Wherever in the wastes of wrinkling sand,
worn by the fan of ever-flaming time,
longing for human converse,
we have pitched a camp for musing in some seldom spot
of not unkindly nurture, and let loose
to roam and ponder those sad dromedaries,
our dreams, the Master of the pilgrimage cries,
"Nay—the caravan goes ever on.
The goal lies further than the morning star."

Nurse is quite wonderful with Georges, and it is high time for Maud Gonne to get back to work. Much as she dearly loves to spend time with her dear little Georgie, it also leaves her a teensy bit bored. She can never bring him to Ireland, but Tommy left her and Kathleen with nurses and governesses all their lives, without any great harm.

And her work will bring well-being to so many more children than just her own son. Ireland is the all-protecting mother who has to be released from the bondage of the foreigner, that she might be free to protect all her children.

She returns to Donegal, to protest the next round of evictions on the land of Col. Olphert, the same landlord who had the turf-cutters convicted.

She can get support for the Irish cause in France, but for her oratory to be effective, it has to be sincere. That means being there, seeing at first hand the hunger and evictions.

In any case, she always prefers action to talk. The speeches and the newspaper articles: for her, they are outcomes of the work, not—as she often feels they are for Millevoye, as they most certainly are for Willie Yeats—the work itself.

The Colonel wants his land cleared and has issued more than 150 eviction decrees. As she rides back into the village, she sees house after house with the chilling notice on its door: *On this day of _____ 1889, we hereby give notice of repossession, for non-payment of rent...* His plans will see more than 1,000 people homeless.

And, as he owns almost all the land around Facarragh, there's great difficulty in finding land on which to build huts for the evicted. The crisis has brought unusual visitors to Donegal: newspapermen, European agriculturalists and reformers, of course, the type Maud Gonne most dislikes, English do-gooders in serviceable boots, assuring her that when the Liberal Party is back in power, England will right all wrongs. They are piqued when she replies, "By clearing out of Ireland, I hope."

Maud Gonne settles in and gives herself over completely to the work: traveling back and forth from Donegal to Dublin to report to the leaders of the Plan of Campaign, writing letters to the press, fundraising, recruiting tenants and other supporters and doing all she can to alleviate misery. Again, she takes the homeless into her hotel room, she nurses the ill and dying, she does her best to rally morale with a positive and vigorous presence.

One wild and stormy night, a sudden clatter of hooves followed by shouts and cries breaks into the village. She looks out the window but, facing the back, can see nothing. The hubbub continues, and she pulls on her shawl to go downstairs, out into the night to investigate. It turns out to be two long police cars carrying prisoners, followed by a mounted escort of constabulary, drawing up to their little inn, and drawing a crowd of the curious. Maud Gonne makes her way to the cars through the women with shawls round their heads, beginning to set up a wailing.

Six prisoners are handcuffed together in pairs. Several only speak Irish, but she gathers, through the English speakers, that they were taken for defending their farms on the hills beyond Gweedore, from which the landlord was evicting them, and are now being sent to Derry Gaol. The priest comes up and speaks encouragement to the men, in Irish, but the police push him roughly aside. The people seem forlorn, dazed and helpless, and as the cart clatters away, Maud Gonne, mastering shyness as she always has to before speaking, waves her handkerchief and called for cheers.

"Well done to the Gweedore men!"

"*Eire Abu!*" cries Father Stephens, picking up on the need to foster morale. "Victory to Ireland."

Next day Maud Gonne makes enquiries and discovers there are others in gaol with life sentences, boys taken in round-ups after some bailiff, or emergency man, or landlord, or police inspector, has been given his due deserts. The sufferings of these long-sentenced men begins to obsess her. They must be helped; they must be free once more to walk the hills, the bogs and the rushes.

She makes the mental connection with other men, unconnected with the agrarian struggle, who are given the title of "Treason-Felony Prisoners." All are under life sentences, mostly in England. John O'Leary, the old Fenian chief, has himself spent many years in an English gaol, and many further years in exile, but he would never speak of his imprisonment. And contemptuously dismisses William O'Brien and others who demand the status of political prisoner and refuse to wear prison clothes.

Mr. O'Leary's reply to a prison-visiting Justice who asked if he had any complaints was, "I am not here to make complaints." This might be dignified, but it renders the gaolers' task too easy. Maud Gonne departs from her old mentor on this, as on the land question.

The plight of prisoners reminds her of the plight of women. To be a good woman is to be complicit in one's own oppression. Good prisoners get overlooked and written out of the record and are kept in place by silence. If they have long sentences, they become broken men, unfit for life. The government's own statistics tell that in Portland Gaol, five out of seventeen prisoners have lost their reason. No, thinks Maud Gonne, never be a good prisoner. Not unless you want to collude in your own imprisonment.

~

On one of her trips to Dublin, Willie introduces Maud Gonne to George Russell, AE, his old friend from the Dublin art school. He and Russell had bonded when young over their dislike of the School's teaching method, both believing it destroyed the only thing an art school exists to foster: creative enthusiasm. And they'd deepened the bond with shared mystical experiments and éances. They'd both joined the Theosophists together and tried various attempts to raise spirits, most useless, some—in their minds—successful.

Russell is a seer: visions of mythological peoples and gods, angels and faery folk appear before him, and it's his work, as he sees it, his life's purpose and mission, to capture these visions in sketches and paintings. For WB, the pictures express the inexpressible, the yearning in all men to go out into the Infinite. When you look at one of Russell's paintings, he says, you imagine yourself into its infinitudes and from there, moving into all things: earth, water, air, fire, æther. It was from the word æther, the substance between substances, that Russell took his pen name: AE.

Without this non-substance, the new men of science say, there would be no light. This, mystics and mages have always known.

Both Russell's and WB's father disapprove of the friendship. Mr. Russell, an accountant, deprecates young Yeats for luring his son away from Christianity; JB deprecates young Russell for luring his son away from secular realism.

It was Russell who made Willie realize his own gift was not for pictures but poetry. To him, his friend is a messenger. A God-send, sent to put him on his own true path, away from Papa's materialist, realist art. Together he and Russell try to know as Infinitude knows, to live as It lives, to be compassionate as It is compassionate. To equal their selves to It, that they might not so much understand It as become It.

It is thanks to Russell that WB is now able to say to Maud Gonne that he has been born into a faith he knows he shall live by, and die in. That his Christ is that Infinite, that unity of being which Dante compared to a perfectly proportioned human body, which Blake calls "Imagination," which the Upanishads name the "Self."

And for Maud Gonne, her conversations with Russell and WB help her understand the beliefs of the country people she is meeting and how she may draw on them to build a legend around herself, to have the Donegal people believe she is a woman of the Shee. The Shee is a halfway state between this world and the Infinite, the most vital location in Celtic art and story. Its inhabitants, also called the Shee, avoid our world, with its impurities. They are "The Lordly Ones," "The Good People," descendants of the people the ancient stories call the Tuatha de Danann.

"Christianity has pared the Shee down to leprechauns, banshees and the like, but they are not small or invisible," Russell says. "They are magical giants, tall and handsome, richly fed and dressed and they sometimes come to live among us."

~

One Donegal day, as Maud Gonne is visiting a Falcarragh family, a carriage pulls up outside their little cabin, and from the carriage a great fur rug unfolds itself and steps down and unpeels itself to reveal a portly, middle-aged man.

"Miss Gonne," he says, and he bows to her, as unseeing of the others as if they were flora or fauna, not people.

"Sir John! What on earth are you doing here?"

It is an elderly Liberal MP Maud met in London and tried to convert to the cause. He had proposed marriage to her, suggesting she could build a great Liberal salon as he would introduce her to men who could really make a difference. He is old and fat and grey and, anyway, English. She'd refused, telling him she could never look at an English man without seeing prison bars.

Now he has followed her here, apparently to prove his commitment to the Irish cause and is talking loudly in his upper-class English accent of how she is wasting her time on the bogs, and what great political influence she would gain as his wife in London. Maud Gonne doesn't know whether to laugh or scold, until he takes from his pocket a small box.

For a moment, she fears it might be an engagement ring, and when she opens it, she finds it almost as bad. An enormous diamond pendant. Did he really think she could be bribed with jewels?

She calls the woman of the house.

"This kind gentleman wishes to help the people of Donegal," Maud Gonne says, sweetly, handing over the pendant. "Please use this to raise some money for yourself or others."

That should teach him to insult her political integrity.

Sir John is furious and next day before returning to Dublin, retrieves the pendant for the exact sum of money he owes the landlady for a room for the night—and not a penny more. Such calculated meanness is typical of the English, Maud Gonne and the landlady agree.

And the old lady goes forth and tells the story of Miss Gonne's abilities and attitude. She is so tall and handsome, so richly fed and dressed and has the magic, able to conjure diamonds one minute, and shrug them off the next. She must surely be a woman of the Shee.

~

No sooner is one suitor dispatched than news comes of another, the only one who counts: Millevoye. She receives a letter telling her he is unwell, staying at a Dunfanaghy hotel having fallen ill while riding north from Derry towards her. This note is her first hearing of any such plan, and she does not like it, this disruption of their pattern. It puts her in danger.

She has explained to him how imperative it is to keep her Irish life and her French life separate, well apart. Mr. Parnell's divorce decree has been granted, and his two children placed in Captain O'Shea's custody, to great scandal. Mr. Gladstone has first regretfully requested, then demanded, a resignation, publishing a public letter. If Mr. Parnell insists on retaining the Irish Party leadership, he says, it will mean the loss of the next election, the end of their "Union of Hearts" alliance and the end of Home Rule for Ireland.

Maud Gonne is no great fan of Parnell but she admires this refusal to accept Gladstone's orders. And his self-possession in the face of all the bitterness and accusations and arguments, as he watches friends and foes fight out the most intimate details of his private life. It chills her to see and confirms that it is critical for her to keep her own affairs a secret. If the Irish nationalists are so unforgiving of Parnell, their Chief, how much more so would they be of her, a mere freelance. And a woman?

So yes, it is dangerous, and she is a little resentful as she goes to attend to Millevoye, bedridden with ague and high fever, apparently, in his primitive little hotel. She has increased in confidence, she realizes. Always, before, she felt his work to be more important than hers but her work with the people here is changing her.

Millevoye is unaware of any such change. He has come to take her back to France, he says, when she arrives. She is neglecting their alliance and it has gone on long enough. He is clearly unwell and she holds her tongue; this is no time to quarrel.

For a week, she nurses him, and when he is better, he speaks again of neglect and now, because he is stronger, she challenges him. "And what have you done for the Irish half of our alliance, Millevoye?"

"Slowing down a few evictions, nursing and tending the people... To what avail?"

"Will you help us here, now you are better?"

"Wasting your time on a handful of peasants."

"This is my work here."

"Any woman can do this work. You are Maud Gonne. You will achieve much more in France, speaking and writing to the influential."

She does not agree: she loves this more humble work among the people. She thinks of the hopeless families, sheltering in the bare mountains, of the joy of instating them in a home. She can allow nothing else to distract her. And she does not believe that his concern in this is for her as much as himself, and his own cause.

He is perturbed that she should think so of him. He must insist she come home. She is risking her health in this wet and inhospitable country and she is neglecting him and Georges.

"If not for me, then come home for Georges. Don't you think it's time you mothered your son?"

But Maud Gonne is not a woman to be told what to do by the man she loves or anyone else. Recovered, Lucien finds himself traveling back to France alone.

The very next day, Pat the Builder arrives to her door, looking very grave.

"Miss Gonne, I have come to take you away," he says. "There is a warrant out for your arrest. You must leave at once, and return to France."

He had heard in Dublin, through the IRB intelligence service, and taken the train to Donegal at once. He has all the arrangements made.

"Are there any other warrants signed?" she asks.

"As far as I have heard, there is only one, for you. They don't want to arrest the priests and call down trouble from the church."

Maud Gonne recalls the disdain that greeted Général Boulanger when he sidled off to Brussels.

"It's all arranged," says Pat, seeing her doubt. "You will be met at Larne and taken safe to Stranraer."

"I don't like to go off like this, Pat. The people need us."

"But we can't have our great lady taken to one of them hell holes."

It is true that one hears daily in the newspapers of the degrading hardships and personal indignities they are dealt by the government. In France, political prisoners are treated as such, by right, and have been for almost a century. The British use hard labor and, most recently, forcible stripping of political prisoners who refuse to wear convict garb.

What outrage there would be if they did any of that to a woman! To be the first woman imprisoned for the Irish cause: it would prove her sincerity to the doubters. It would make her famous.

And it isn't as if it would be forever.

"No I'm sorry Pat, let them do their worst. I won't be running away."

Yet, after he is gone, she has to admit to herself that she is afraid. Oh not of prison but of what Millevoye said. That he was right. That her work here is not useful.

Eighty-four of 116 estates have already reached agreement with the landlords. The struggle continues in only eighteen others. There's a legend growing around her, and she's helped to swell it but her work here has proven she is really only a freelance, trying to work the engine of what once was a great agrarian movement but now is stalled.

Out of steam.

Yet the legend itself has a value, inspiring hope and self-belief in the people. She cannot just run out on them.

Especially when the Irish movement is in such disarray. Mr. Parnell's divorce case continues to cause a sensation in England and Ireland. Apparently, he had had Captain O'Shea elected as an unpledged member back in '86, against opposition from his party, and he and Mrs. O'Shea have been trying to appease the Captain always. She had her own money, bequeathed by an aunt, and in such a way that her husband could not access it. The Captain asked for 20,000 pounds to keep silence, but she refused and it was this refusal to succumb to his blackmail that made him instigate the divorce.

The Irish Party has met in committee for a second time, and endured five days of wrangling. After a long discussion as to whether the man was more important than the cause, the party is split. Forty-four members have sided with Justin McCarthy, the vice-chairman, remaining in favor of the alliance with the Liberals. Only twenty-seven sided with Mr. Parnell.

He is no longer The Chief. But he refuses to accept this verdict against him. They say he intends to carry his campaign to Ireland in the new year, and fight in the upcoming by-election, and marry Mrs. O'Shea. For him, it is a "war to the death," through the indignities and bitterness, the mud-throwing and abuse.

He has all Maud Gonne's admiration now. He is not one to quit. And neither is she.

~

Less than a week later, Maud Gonne is on her way back to France. Pat the Builder returned with Father McFadden, and together they used all their persuasion. They've succeeded in delaying matters long enough against Olpherts, an election is now on the way, the evictions are saved for now. And how it would dishearten the people if she were taken.

She asks for twelve hours to think it over and what she thinks is that her lungs are, as Millevoye said, being affected by the harsh living. And gaol *would* make them a great deal worse. And she *does* want to work to see the prisoners released in Dublin. And she also wants to pick up the international fight against the British Empire again.

So she packs her bags, and Pat meets her, and together on a dark and wet evening, they are driven to a lonely place in the wild moorland, where the night train passes. There's no station, but the train slows and stops, and the guard gets out to help her into an empty carriage. And to give Pat their tickets, hers for Larne, his for Dublin.

"Goodbye, Miss Gonne, I'm so glad to have met you," Pat says as he leaves her. "From Stranraer to London and from there to Paris. Don't stop now, until you are in France. Wire me from there. Goodbye now and good luck."

She leaves Donegal believing she'll soon be back, but actually, she is not to return until the Irish movement she's helping to birth has taken itself all the way into a full-blown independence war, two decades hence. But there's where it began in earnest for her, I believe, where the seed of a desire for independence developed roots. If the speeches and the articles were the food and water, her experience with the people of Donegal was the soil itself.

The Rose of the World

Who dreamed that beauty passes like a dream?
For these red lips, with all their mournful pride,
Mournful that no new wonder may betide,
Troy passed away in one high funeral gleam,
And Usna's children died.

We and the labouring world are passing by:
Amid men's souls, that waver and give place
Like the pale waters in their wintry race,
Under the passing stars, foam of the sky,
Lives on this lonely face.

Bow down, archangels, in your dim abode:
Before you were, or any hearts to beat,
Weary and kind one lingered by His seat;
He made the world to be a grassy road
Before her wandering feet.

As soon as she gets back to France, she begins to spread word that she is a political exile. In truth, she is now pleased to be home. Little Georges has grown a good deal in her absence. He can walk now and sit; he is beginning to feed himself. How quickly babies change. At first he has no idea who she is and keeps running to Nurse, especially when tired.

She should try spending a little more time with him, Mille-voye says, when she mentions feeling a little hurt by this.

She resumes her speaking and writing. Vefour at the Palais Royal is the latest, most fashionable restaurant in Paris, and it is here, at the annual St. Patrick's Day banquet of *l'Association de Saint Patrick*, that she gives her first after-dinner speech.

The titled guests are descendants of those known in Ireland as "The Wild Geese", those families of old Irish descent who fled the country after defeat by English forces in 1601, followed by another wave after 1798. Men with queer Franco-Irish titles, like le Comte O'Neill de Tyrone and le Comte d'Alton O'Shea, and even queerer notions about their family trees. Or military men whose families led Irish Brigades in the French armies for generations, like Capitaine Patrice MacMahon. Or Celtic scholars like Comte d'Arbois de Joubainville, who take an advanced interest in Ireland.

Twenty years ago, Mr. O'Leary together with JP Leonard, a young Irelander and Professor of English at the Sorbonne, had inspired a few of these nostalgic noblemen to form an Association, only it has turned out more genealogical than political, and as anti-Republican as it is anti-English. Anti-feminist too, need I say. The association allows no women members, in the usual run of things, but makes an exception for the young and beautiful courtesan of the Bonapartist Lucien Millevoye.

So the lady who is positioning herself as Ireland's Joan of Arc is granted permission to speak to *l'Association* from the red-velvet-draped dais and raise money for her starving tenants and families of Fenian prisoners.

Though Maud Gonne notes that, like the parable of the old woman in the Bible, contributions from the Irish servant girls who go to Mass at Notre Dame des Victories are more generous, relatively speaking.

She sends an account of her performance to WB, who dutifully writes up what she said in an article for United Ireland: "*What a singular scene, this young girl of twenty-five addressing that audience of politicians, and moving them more than all the famous speakers, although she spoke in a language not her own.*" He compared her to Oscar Wilde's mother, who wrote about Ireland and Irish folklore under the pen name Speranza. "*What does it mean for Ireland? Surely that there is a new 'Speranza' who shall do with the voice all, or more than all, that the old 'Speranza' did with her pen.*"

He half believes his own publicity. The emotional temper of Maud Gonne's speeches is something marvelous to him, an appeal to something uncontrollable, he thinks, something that can't be coordinated. When speaking, she is the embodiment of a Celtic Druidess, her great dark eyes full of flame and he can vividly imagine her standing in front of her French audiences, like the one at the Catholic University of the Luxembourg, whom she recently thrilled with her description of the great famine of the 1840s.

Ireland was heroic in her suffering... men and women ate the dogs, the rats, and the grass of the field, and some even, when all the food was gone, ate the dead bodies...

Whole families when they had eaten their last and understood that they had to die, looked once more upon the sun and then closed up the doors of their cabins with stones, that none might look upon their last agony. Weeks afterwards, men would find their skeletons gathered around the extinguished hearth.

I do not exaggerate, gentlemen. I have added nothing to the mournful reality. If you come to my country every stone will repeat to you this tragic history. It was only fifty years ago. It still lives in thousands of memories. I have been told it by women who have heard the last cry of their children without being able to lessen their agony with one drop of milk.

It has seemed to me at evening on those mountains of Ireland, so full of savage majesty when the wind sighed over the pits of the famine where the thousands of dead enrich the harvests of the future, it has seemed to me that I heard an avenging voice calling down on our oppressors the execration of men and justice of God.

"Gentlemen, your great poet, Victor Hugo, has called hunger 'a public crime' and that crime England has carried out against Ireland by cold premeditation and calculation... You ask what we are seeking? I will tell you. We are three things—a race, a country, and democracy—and we wish to make of these three a nation."

She takes the show on the road. In drab lecture halls and council rooms all over France, he and Millevoye write in their respective outlets, audiences are fascinated by her presence and by the magic lantern she uses to show them her photographs of evictions, complete with battering rams and homeless peasants.

At La Rochelle her talk ignites a protest demonstration outside the British Consulate. In Bordeaux, more than 1,000 people gave her a standing ovation.

At the end of the tour, she is exhausted, and still carrying the cough she brought home from Donegal. She suggests to Millevoye that they take Georges for a sojourn. No not Samois, the little house she rents each year to escape the heat of Paris. Yes, she loves Samois but they should go somewhere new. To the south of France, the Riviera she has heard so much about. Not Cannes or St. Tropez, some simple, sunny place where they can be far away from everyone.

"There I can recuperate," she says. "We can spend some time together with Georges. And you and I can plan our next moves. It will do us all good to escape for a while."

A Dream Of A Life Before This One

IN 1891, St. Raphael was less lively than it is today: a sleepy small bit of a town, with two sleepy hotels overseeing a harbor half-full of fishing boats. But then, as now, the boatmen sold their fish in Place de la Republique, and the farmers their fruit and vegetables in Place Victor Hugo, and the forested hills clustered round the town, and a tall-domed sky of almost unnatural blue oversaw it all with intense clarity.

Each morning, as she opens the drapes of her hotel room, Maud Gonne delights to see another bright-blue day has arrived, as if freshly buffed overnight, without the smallest smudge of cloud to be seen. Such a steady, reliable climate, in comparison to Paris or London or rainy little Dublin.

She's brought her watercolors, and each day sees her sketching or painting in the hills overlooking the town, while on a rug beside her Millevoye plays with Georges. When she takes a break, the three of them search among the fallen needles for mushrooms, or wander back down to the beach to search for shells. And at night, after Georges has been put to bed, she works an embroidery while Millevoye reads. Or she and he read aloud to each other.

Such a simple life, revolving around their boy, now at eighteen months utterly adorable to them both. They carry him everywhere, or help him toddle on bandy legs set wide apart by the bulky couche Maud Gonne likes to remove when he's on the beach, so he can run naked. She would like to run naked

herself, only it would give Millevoye ideas. Their daily inti‑
macy is acute. For the first time ever, they live as a family, day
in, day out. Both are, if the truth is told, a little uncomfortable
in the novelty but they draw closer in it, all the same. Madame
Millevoye, Général Boulanger, the Parisian coquettes: all seem
very far away.

Maud Gonne loves being a mother. Pregnancy was a limbo
state, a non‑place in which she felt a lot like a clock that hadn't
been wound, running on a different time to the real world but
motherhood... Motherhood is a banquet of mutual adoration.
She had expected maternal emotion to be like the love she felt
for her dogs or cats or her little squirrel and yes, that is there,
but much else is there besides. She has never loved any person
or beast or bird more than she loves little Georges.

For him, each day is a parade of new words to share with
her—*bucket, belle, glace*—and a parade of new sensations to
explore together. At eighteen months, he is so sharp and so...
present. Yes, that is the word. Every passing thing gives him
such intense, pleasured interest, he makes her feel the whole
world anew too. The first time he experiences sand on his
bare feet, the first time she spoons him some vanilla *glace*: each
"first" is hers as much as his.

He has a way of smiling that juts forward his bottom teeth,
just like his father in miniature, which is adorable and all the
more so now that the smile reveals four tiny, baby teeth, through
a gurgle of happiness. Oh her darling, darling boy. He makes her
feel nostalgia for life, even while she's living it.

They take him to a local cobbler to buy him his first pair
of shoes, as fine a pair of bootees as ever graced a baby foot.
Dove‑grey, soft suede, fastening with a clasp he can manage
himself. They go for a walk in the woods, for the pleasure of
watching him walk in them, one of his hands in hers and one
in Millevoye's, lifting his knees high, so proud of his bootees,
lost in admiration of his feet in them.

As she and Millevoye exchange smiles above his head, Maud
Gonne notices how the evening sun is slanting through the
overlapping greenery of the trees, throwing a pattern of moving

flecks of sunshine across the faces and hands and hair of these two, boy and man, her most near and most dear. A surge of happiness almost sweeps her over. This is what she hoped for, when she conceived Georges.

At night, he sleeps in a cot beside them, face down, bottom aloft, like a little Muslim worshipper. Nurse is as good with him as ever, but he knows who his Mama is now, oh yes. And his Papa, too.

~

Paul Déroulède arrives, on his way back to Paris from Nice, he says. He looks more pretentious than ever in this simple place, with his silver-embroidered coat, and his ostentatious cross swinging on his breast. Maud Gonne has always disliked his hairstyle, the strict middle-parting and hair glued, either side, to his temples. In London, she translated his poetry for Mr. Yeats, who pronounced it bad. Full of vague words, he said, a sign of dangerous abstraction and unclear thought.

But he is Millevoye's closest friend and accomplice and his *Ligue des Patriotes* makes him very powerful. She tries hard with him.

The two men go for a walk, while she orders a simple lunch of bisque and grilled trout. Lucien asks that Georges should not be present for the meal. He would be a distraction, he says. From what, Maud Gonne wonders, if this is just a friends' luncheon? Why is Déroulède really here? He is a man who does nothing without motive.

Over their meal, a Count de Rochefort keeps arising in the talk, a new key to success, whom they need to cultivate. Maud Gonne has a vague memory of a small man in an overdressed waistcoat, but she resents this talk coming into their idyll and averts her attention, to observe the sea doing what the sea always does.

Derouledindon is how this man is known to their enemies in government: *Déroulède the ninny*. She had a dream where she saw him as a sheep, being prodded by the handle of a shepherd's crook. Mr. Yeats said it was a sure sign that he was untrustworthy. She feared, on hearing this, that Déroulède might betray them, accept

England as an ally, if he felt it furthered his anti-German agenda. Millevoye said no—"Déroulède knows as we do that the Saxon and the Teuton are one, and that to hit one is to hit the other." She wants to believe him.

It's so soothing, the sea's endless unfurling of itself. She wonders if she and Millevoye shouldn't just give it all up, the schemes and campaigns, and retire here and live a simple life of sun and sand and silence. She has a sudden longing for quiet, for the peace Willie Yeats wrote about in his "Inishfree" poem, the kind that comes "dropping slow... dropping from the veils of the morning..."

Could one live like that, always? The poet himself does not, for all his word conjurations of mood. Yet, it should be possible, should it not?

Her attention is plucked back by her name being called. "Madame Gonne?" Déroulède is looking at her expectantly. "I said, perhaps *you* can be of help?"

"Me?"

"Yes indeed. He is full of admiration for you. He saw you at the Association banquet, apparently. And heard you speak. He has expressed a wish to know you better."

She realizes he is talking about this man, this Count de Rochefort. "Should I organize a *salon*?"

"I believe his preference would be something more..." Déroulède glances quickly to, and away, from Millevoye, who is steadfastly staring where Maud Gonne was staring a moment ago, out the window, at the water. "more... intimate?"

The tip of his pink tongue flickers, snakelike, between his lips.

Maud Gonne is not a woman to cry, and certainly not in front of others, but when she realizes what is being suggested, a shock of tears stings up the back of her nose and throat. She looks to Millevoye but it is his turn now to be staring out the window, her eyes swing back to Déroulède but recoil, immediately, from his twisted, fanatical gaze, back to the man who last night, in passion, had told her she was magnificent.

"Millevoye...?"

Her call to him is imperious, a call for attention, for explanation, for refutation. She would expect him to call out his friend for this. Both are experienced duelists and certain insults cannot be allowed to pass, surely, even in these so-called civilized times. But Millevoye doesn't answer. Millevoye carries on looking out the window, at the scarf of golden-blistered sun on water.

Maud Gonne pushes back her chair, pulls herself to her full height, and walks out.

Her lover's voice, soft and sinuous and very, very gentle, stops her at the door. "A moment, *chérie.*"

Hand to the doorknob, she turns.

"Forgive us," he says.

Us? Us!

"It is a monumental request, we know that."

We. We is him and Déroulède, not him and her.

He is stroking his mustache and seems calm but as he finally turns his eyes to hers, she sees they are almost deranged with supplication.

"But it would not be asked if there were any other method, and if de Rochefort's contribution were not utterly essential to our cause."

More than once, she has saved him from despair, kept him from writing or saying or doing the wrong thing, helped steer him to victory. And he has helped her; always he helps with whatever she asks of him. But this....

"My dear girl, before you answer, do know that without de Rochefort, we are doomed. It is over for our party. Clemenceau and his cortège will see us utterly extinguished."

It is not these words about the Prime Minister that prevent her from crossing the threshold, but his eyes, his staring, yearning, needing eyes. "De Rochefort holds the key," he says. "His assistance will be our turning point."

Déroulède says: "He is dazzled by your charms, as indeed any man must..."

But Millevoye cuts off these compliments.

"Maud, no one else will know, but you will know. Yours will be the glory of having saved France. And Ireland too. For, as you know, to defeat Clemenceau will be to break his *entente cordiale* with England. With him gone, France can move again into its natural alliance with Ireland, and try again for the rebellion that failed a century ago."

She feels like she is swaying on a wall. He knows this is their dream, the foundation of their alliance.

"The glory days of 1798 will live again. England and Germany will fall, France and Ireland rise. It all hinges on you."

She comes back into the room, sits back down at the table.

~

In London, WB has also received an invitation. His brilliant old school-friend, Charley Johnston, another Theosophist, with whom he lived for a time in Dublin, has invited him to Ireland. Not to the old house they used to share in Ely Place, Johnston too has moved on from there, but to his father's home in Ballykilbeg, County Down.

WB has no money, not a farthing above his needs and them not met sometimes, but he begins to scheme as to how he might leave London. Thinking of the times he and Johnston had in that old Georgian house in the center of Dublin reminds him of how he loathes the metropolis.

What times. How he had relished living away from his family for the first time. He and Johnston shared the room upstairs and on the lower floor lived Althea Gyles, a strange red-haired girl, consumed by painting and poetry. Born into a Waterford "county" family, who were so haughty their neighbors called them The Royal Family, she had quarreled with her mad father, because she wanted to study art, and run away from home to Dublin. Their landlord had discovered her one day, half-starved, unable to afford even her usual bread and cocoa, some misfortune having robbed her of the penny a day she budgeted for food. The landlord, took pity on her, as he did on all artists, and gave her the room at a reduced rent. Johnston will be tickled to know Althea has moved to London, to Charlotte Street, still painting, and still living on a penny a day. As she will be tickled to hear that while they starve for their art, their old friend has been readying himself for a career in the Empire's civil service.

Now he's home in Ballykilbeg for the summer, on his final summer of freedom, and seeking company.

WB would love to go. To add to the inducement, Maud Gonne has also written to say she shall be in Ireland, soon. Back from her holiday in the south of France, she is now preparing to cross over, as she wishes to be in Dublin when the treason-felony prisoners are released.

And London is more abominable than ever this summer. He has been writing a book on Blake with his friend Edwin Ellis, but Ellis's wife has banned him from their house. She thinks he is casting spells on her husband and grows white with terror if she sees him appear.

Such willful ignorance. It is all around him in this detestable city. Last night when writing, he heard voices full of derision and looked up to see his neighbors, the stout woman who lives opposite and her family, standing in the window, mocking him. He has the habit of acting out what he writes and speaking it aloud without knowing; he'd been looking down over the back of a chair, talking into what he imagined an abyss, not knowing he was being observed.

Another day as he walked along the street, a woman had called him suddenly out of reverie, asking him for directions, and while he hesitated, a neighbor came by and said, "Ah don't mind him, he's a poet," which made his questioner turn contemptuously away.

"Ah well," said a policeman, also passing, attempting to soften but only adding the insult. "If it's only poetry."

Ignorance, ignorance.

In Ireland too, he is developing the reputation of a magician but how differently it is understood there. When he tells people in London that the Irish peasantry still believe in fairies, he is often doubted, but at Howth where he used to live, only ten miles from Dublin, there is a faery path, whereon a great colony of otherworld creatures travel nightly from the hill to the sea and home again.

A story is circulating among the Sligo people of his being carried five miles in the winking of an eye, and of him sending his cousin from her house at the First Rosses to the rocks of the Third, in a like eye-wink. He had indeed sent her there in a vision but in Sligo, any fear is commingled with respect. There, on one side of Ben Bulben a white square in the limestone is said to be the door to faeryland. It swings open at nightfall and lets pour through an unearthly troop of hurrying spirits. To those gifted to hear, the air will be full at such a moment with a sound like whistling.

Many have been carried away out of neighboring villages by this troop of riders, with brides and newborns in special danger, and peasant mothers sometimes, carried off to nurse the children of the faeries. At the end of seven years, they have a chance of returning but if they do not escape then, they are prisoners for always. A woman was taken from near Ballisodare and when she came home after seven years, she had no toes. She had danced them off.

The faery populace of hill and lake and woodland give a fanciful life to the dead hillsides, and surround the Irish peasant, as he ploughs and digs, with tender shadows of poetry. No wonder he can make up proverbs like this, from the old Gaelic: "The lake is not burdened by its swan, the steed by its bridle, or the man by the soul that is in him."

Oh yes, he must be away to Ireland.

The Lake Isle of Inishfree

I will arise and go now, and go to Innisfree,
And a small cabin build there, of clay and wattles made;
Nine bean-rows will I have there, a hive for the honey-bee,
And live alone in the bee-loud glade.

And I shall have some peace there, for peace comes dropping slow,
Dropping from the veils of the morning to where the cricket sings;
There midnight's all a glimmer, and noon a purple glow,
And evening full of the linnet's wings.

I will arise and go now, for always night and day
I hear lake water lapping with low sounds by the shore;
While I stand on the roadway, or on the pavements grey,
I hear it in the deep heart's core.

He is fortunate that he can, any time, cross from Clarence
Basin, Liverpool to Sligo Quay in the steamships owned by his
mother's family, the Pollexfens. The transportation will be free
but he must borrow money from John O'Leary, so he can see
Maud Gonne while there.

The crossing is smooth and as the voyage nears its end, the
passengers lounge about the deck in groups. WB sits on a pile
of cable looking out over the sea. It is just noon; the ship, having
passed by Tory and Rathlin, approaches the Donegal cliffs.

The cliffs are covered by a faint mist, which makes them loom
even more vast. Westward, the sun shines on a perfectly blue
sea. Seagulls come out of the mist and plunge into the sunlight,
and out of the sunlight and plunge into the mist.

Gannets strike, continually, and a porpoise shows now and
then, the arc of his fin and back gleaming in the sun.

WB is more perfectly happy than he has been for many a day,
and more ardently thinking. All nature seems full of a Divine fulfillment, everything fulfilling its law. Fulfillment that is peace,
whether it be for good or for evil, for evil also has its peace, the
peace of the birds of prey.

He looks from the sea to the ship and grows sad. On this thing,
crawling slowly along the sea, moves mournful and slouching
figures. Two cattle merchants are leaning over the rail, smoking,
looking like something between betting men and commercial
travelers.

For years they've slept only in steamers and trains.

A short distance from them a clerk from Liverpool, with a
consumptive cough, walks to and fro, a little child holding his
hand. Further forward, talking to one of the crew, is a man with
the red face and slightly unsteady step brought on by drink.
In the companion-house a governess, past her first youth, very
much afraid of seasickness, has her luggage heaped around her,
already ready for landing.

He looks from the sea to these and to himself, and his eyes fill with tears. On himself, on these moving figures, hope and memory feed, like flames. As he reverses his gaze, from ship to sea, his eyes gladden. Here he finds his present. He will live in his love and the day as it passes, he vows. He will live that his personal law might be fulfilled.

He feels himself fill with this truth. The saints on the one hand, the animals on the other, live in the moment as it passes. To this, his days have brought him. This is the one grain they have ground.

But to grind one such grain is enough for a lifetime.

In Dublin, and waits. As soon as he hears she has landed, down he goes to her hotel, but he has a shock waiting for him. Maud Gonne is not the woman she was. Her beauty is wasted, she looks ill and tired and so gaunt, the form of her bones shows through on face and body, and all life has gone from her manner.

Though it makes her less beautiful, to see her so vulnerable is attractive in a different way, and she seems very much more friendly than of late.

"Are you quite well?" he asks, after they have adjourned to the quietest corner of the hotel drawing-room, and ordered tea. She hints at some personal unhappiness, a profound disillusionment. Her old hard resonance is gone; she seems gentle, even indolent. It overwhelms him with emotion, an intoxication of pity for her that frightens him.

When he tells her of his intention to travel to his friend in County Down, she does not dissuade him, and a goodly part of him feels relief. He needs time to adjust to this new Maud Gonne.

So he travels the following day to Ballykilbeg and settles into a fine old time with Johnston and his brother, Charlie, exploring the old castles of County Down by day, and in the evenings making rice-paper fire balloons, with sponges soaked in alcohol. "Sky lanterns," Charlie calls them, and they set them off over the fields. One of their heroes, Shelley, launched such a balloon over London a hundred years before, to protest English rule in Ireland, with his version of the *Declaration of the Rights of Man* and *The Devil's Walk*, attached.

Each evening, as he and the Johnston brothers light the sponge beneath a new balloon, a line from that poem fires WB's mind: "unquenchable knowledge doomed to glow". They release the balloon and set off after it, as it fire-dances ahead of the wind, the three of them racing across the County Down countryside. The chase gets longer and longer each day, as they get better and better at making the balloons.

Afterwards, spent and happy, they lie around on sofas and talk. When they were boys at art college together, Johnston would often call to Papa's studio in the afternoons and he likes to recall those times, and believes many of the finer qualities of WB's mind and his own, were formed in that long room. WB had all but forgotten those walls of pale green, the frames and canvasses massed along; the sloping ceiling and skylights; the sofa and big armchairs; the stout iron stove and, filling the whole with his spirit, Papa.

Papa stepping forward along a strip of carpet to touch his work with tentative brush, then stepping back again. Always in movement, always meditating high themes and breaking into talk: on the second part of *Faust*, or the Hesperian apples, or the relation of villainy to genius. It is good to be reminded.

Yes, happy in this safe hiatus with his friend, WB finds it easy to love his father again, from a distance. To feel affection for them all, indeed, even Lolly. Yes, even his pitiful mother.

But being young men, it's not filial but conjugal love that takes up most of their talk. Johnston was always more daring than him in that department. At Theosophist meetings, he'd be swanking it up with Mme Blavatsky's niece, confidently speaking French and smoking cigarettes with her. Now, he tells him, that young woman has ruined his ambition to become a Mahatma, by making chastity an impossibility. He not only takes on adult work in the autumn, he is ready to make her his bride.

WB's Maud Gonne stories take rather longer to impart. He dissects the details of his recent meeting with her in Dublin, in particular how thin she was, quite gaunt, but seeming friendlier than ever... and yet to what avail? She can never be his. Johnston doesn't see why not, if the lady has money enough for them both, which launches WB into long hours of explanation of how his love is ill-omened, laced with a great many if-onlys, and maybe-perhapses, and who's-to-say-one-never-knows.

Then, into their boyish idyll comes a letter from said lady, touching on her sadness when she and he met so briefly in Dublin, and telling of a dream she just had, about a past life when they two were brother and sister, somewhere on the edge of the Arabian desert. She dreamt of them taking a long shared journey, traveling together across mile after mile of desert sand, then both of them being sold, together, into slavery.

It's a revelation of a spiritual association in another existence, he proposes to Johnston. His friend agrees it is a message, anyhow. A summons, you could say. Or as good as.

Tonight must be his last night chasing fire balloons. He must depart for Dublin at first light tomorrow.

~

It's so early when he sets out from Ballykilbeg that the stars and a honey-pale orb of a moon are still out, and the curlew and peewit are only beginning their cries across the dew-covered valley. In the distance, the sea sounds like a crooning mother, and the green leaves in the woodland seem to leap *"tossed in Love's robe, for he passes, and mad with Love's feet, for he flies."*

He arrives in Dublin early afternoon and goes straight to the Nassau Hotel to sit in the lobby and wait for her. Those who once were flattered by her descent among them have begun to criticize. Last time he met John O'Leary, he spoke of her attending a nationalist rally to show off her new bonnet. Another had a tale of her going to the Parnell Commission like a sentimental English or American sympathizer, in a green dress covered with shamrocks. A third had supposedly seen her at a tenant meeting, clapping her hands when someone shouted "shoot him!"

And Miss Purser, a painter of their mutual acquaintance, had said one day, "Maud Gonne talks politics in Paris, and literature to you, and at the Horse Show, she would talk of a clinking brood mare," following in with tales of how they'd lunched together in Paris and making repeated, arch references to a tall Frenchman.

Whenever he hears such bitterness, he murmurs to himself:

"All faces have Envy, sweet Mary, but thine..." From Blake's poem, "Mary" about another woman too beautiful to be borne by the weak and tame.

Maud Gonne lives entirely among literary and political men, a way of life that would excite some comment, even had she been plain and poor. Being rich and of the most surpassing beauty, she is followed about by a constant buzz of malice. She does not acknowledge it. She does not try to please people, she is happy to live surrounded by her dogs and birds. She is patient, far more than he, in handling birds or beast. Animals, the old, and the young have a special place in her life.

She has recently adopted a child, for example, a baby boy. Adoption is very much more common in France, she told him, when he questioned the move. Old women, and old men past work, also seek her out. This is her pilgrim soul, the side so few see. The poor know it, by nature, and love her for it and he will always defend her against those who fail to understand. He has begun a poem on the theme: one line, as is so often the way, is set from the start: *"Their children's children will say they lied."*

Here she comes.

Again, a shock.

Her face so pale and wasted. Where is her vitality, her animal good health? But he has had time, since first seeing her so to absorb the change, and now finds it more of a spur, not less.

She turns to him with eyes dark and soft and the world falls. She has dreamt it: a thousand years, cycles ago, they were brother and sister in an Arabian desert. Since then their love has been waiting. He is in love once more and now he means to speak. Oh, truth to tell he has never, since the day she first came calling to his father's house, been anything but in love, and he no longer wishes to fight it. Or think what kind of wife she would make.

Seeing her like this, he can think only of her need for protection and for peace. "Miss Gonne..."

"Oh Mr. Yeats, my dear friend. Thank you for coming."

It floods full into him, the knowledge that he entered the room, travelled from Ballykilbeg, with this purpose. Underneath not knowing, he had known. Since the moment he met her, he had known, but it all seems so different now, two years on.

Now he does not look at her, or think of her beauty. He addresses his eyes to her hand, so close to his on the little round table at which they sit, their backs to everyone, in the corner of the hotel drawing room, and thinks only of her need. Of how, through shared poetry and philosophy and love of Ireland, he might meet it.

That is the pathway. Only that way can she come to know, can they know together, the eternal rose.

The secret of the rose is that it is inner duty, not outer achievement, that wins peace. He will teach her that, if she will have him. He takes her hand. "I am as yet, Miss Gonne, only a poor student but... will you be my wife?"

Speaking of her internal beauty, and its great import for him, he gives her praise. It flows from him, for once without any motive or any thought of their work together: praise open and frank and directed only at the beauty of her character: her passionate heart, her pilgrim soul, her abundant spirit that overflows like a mountain spring, so pure and spontaneous.

Then he asks her again, simply and humbly, to give him her love, to become his wife. He can feel her nearness to him, feel her move towards consent. Or more accurately, assent. Everything is pure and passive. He ceases to speak. Outside, evening is falling over the cricket fields of Trinity College. He sits on, her hand in his, just being with her, his words alive in the smooth, still silence.

Part Two:
1891–1894

Were We Only White Birds

ONLY AS THEY sit, he becomes aware again, in the old way, of her beauty and the awareness ruffles the quiet and he starts to think of its power, and of the vow he wants them to take, to purify and exalt their spiritual natures, so that with Divine aid they might attain to become—at great length, of course; after great study, naturally—more than human.

She does not know it, but his intentions are based on the neophyte oath of the new magical order he has joined, the Order of The Golden Dawn. Though he cannot share their beliefs and rites with her, as yet, for he has taken a vow of secrecy, he knows marriage would strengthen their vows and their work. Together, they could tear rents in the veil that separates this world from the other.

As these thoughts solidify, she feels her grow distant from him, and she withdraws her hand. He begins to speak even more vehemently. He hardly knows what he says, the words issue from him in a torrent: "Miss Gonne, I am privy to some doctrines that are full of obscurity to the man of modern culture but that have never been difficult for simple people to understand. Peasants dreaming by their sheepfolds on the hills. Ascetics wrapped in skins. Women, like yourself, who cast aside the common way. We should pursue, together, these dim wisdoms, old and deep. In ancient Ireland the soul had but to stretch out its arms to fill them with beauty. Now all manner of ugliness besets the world... Ireland is awaiting those who will ignite its resurrection. It should be us. The fracturing of the nationalist movement around Parnell means the country is now ripe for an intellectual movement, it will be like soft wax for years to come. We have the opportunity to mold the wax. Popular feeling has abandoned the quarrelling politicians, and this leaves us a..."

He was going to say "an opening" but he can't go on. The squall has blown itself out.

"Oh Mr. Yeats." She sighs, touched not by what he said, he feels, but by whatever it is that has made her so profoundly sad. "I have suffered a great disillusionment with quarrelsome politicians. You save me from despair. Your thought is so... "

So what? But she seems too weary to go on.

"But I am sorry," she says, with grace, tender and pensive. "I cannot marry."

"Miss Gonne, I beseech you... Two nights ago, you had a dream. We were sold in slavery together. In such dreams begins responsibility."

She looks at him, eyes clouded with puzzlement.

"Your dream has spoken. It has told you. Cycles ago, you mingled your gaze with my gaze."

She shakes her head, very sad. "Mr. Yeats, I have told you of the curse on my family.... And there are other reasons too. I shall never marry."

So again, they are to be parted. Love is once again to pass him by, unheeding. He feels the sorrow of the ages falling on him; he envies the grass-covered dead. Yet still he says, knowing it is hopeless: "We who have seen the truth *will* reshape the world, and Ireland shall be our entrance to this world beyond words."

"Oh Mr. Yeats, I do wish to work with you, just as you say. Can we be each other's confidante and...?"

"Can we be friends?" he interrupts, bitterly. The most banal, most conventional, most pedestrian of refusals.

"Can we be soul mates?" she says, "in the true meaning of that word? Can we marry in a spiritual sense? You remember what you said about my becoming a Catholic, about the need to believe in my own way, not in some external will or imagination, however divine?"

She is turning his own words against him. One day, she had suggested that she might change her religion, to take her closer to the Irish people, and he had told her what he utterly believed: that for her, spiritual progress lay not in dependence upon a Christ outside herself but upon the Christ in her own breast, in the power of her own divine will and divine imagination.

"*Beloved, gaze in thine own heart, The holy tree is growing there...*" he mutters, a line from the poem he has begun to write for her.

"Well, yes. Precisely. And just as we would create our God not from the givens of the churches but from our own hearts and souls, can we not be spiritually married? Can our love for each other... Why do you look so surprised at that word? Our friendship is love, is it not? It is one of the most beautiful things in my life."

Is this hope? Confusion rends him, he no longer knows what he thinks, or should think.

"Oh Mr. Yeats, marriage is a convention. What we are creating is a connection *nonpareil*, something matchless and incomparable, as befits our connection in our past life. Can we not be grateful for this, which is so much more than a conventional marriage? Can we not be as the brother and sister of my dream? Can we not live as we did in the life before this one?"

~

The next day, they make their long planned visit to Howth, that heather-sprung headland of sea-crashed cliffs ten miles north of Dublin they both loved in childhood.

Maud Gonne's old nurse, Mary Ann Meredith—she calls her Bo—lives there still, in a cottage near the Baily Lighthouse, and she wants to visit her, to see if she might be willing to take in a child. Maud Gonne likes to adopt needy children from fallen or incapacitated women and put them to good homes, a consequence, perhaps, of her own orphaned childhood. And today, like all her emotions, funneled into quiet intensity.

This latest of her projects is a child of three, whom she has helped almost since its birth, and whose mother now has to find work, and can no longer afford to keep her at home. While "dear Bo" is so lonely and could do with a child to love. He delights in how such arrangements, advantageous to all, so delight her.

Howth, that perfect summer day, seems afloat on the blue of the sea, more turquoise even than the Mediterranean, Maud Gonne says. The little rock pools at the bottom of the high cliffs are very clear and full of colorful sea-life: blue and yellow anemones; white, green and bright buttercup yellow sea-snails; pink starfish and crabs, but they climb up to the top and settle on a grassy patch, away from the path, near the edge of the cliff.

She sits, plucking daisies, while he lies back and reads to her from the unfinished text of *The Countess Cathleen*, his new play of ancient Ireland in which two traders in souls work for the devil. Hunger is on the land and people must either starve or sell their souls to these emissaries of evil. To save her people, Cathleen sells them her pure, spotless, virginal soul, a priceless acquisition.

When he looks up from his reading, after a line of which he is particularly proud—"The joy of losing joy and ceasing all resistance"—he sees she is once again ashen, almost haggard.

"Mr. Yeats, sometimes I think everything you write is a test for me. A lesson in living." Her voice is faraway and strange.

"I must admit as I wrote I was thinking of your soul that seems so incapable of rest. Cathleen is a symbol of all souls who lose their peace, or any beauty of the spirit, in political service."

She starts, as if his words were pistol shots, and he is again locked down by his accursed timidity, and how it prevents him from knowing what to do next. After a long time, she says: "'The joy of losing joy and...' How does it go again?"

"'The joy of losing joy and ceasing all resistance.'"

"Ceasing all resistance." Something in the line moves her greatly. She looks as though she might weep. After another long pause in which WB inwardly squirms through outer paralysis, she says: "Can I share something with you, Mr. Yeats, something I've never told another?"

He puts down the manuscript.

"When I was a young girl, I longed more than anything for control over my own life. I read in one of Tommy's books of a man who sold his soul to the devil and so desperate was I to be free of the terrible restraints put upon me by my English relations that I told Satan he could have my soul, if I could have my freedom. I see I have shocked you, but I was very young, Mr. Yeats. The after-life seemed very far away, and what happened after my death seemed like a small price for freedom in this wonderful world. I wanted life."

"I am not shocked so much as troubled."

"As I made the pact, the clock struck twelve, and I felt of a sudden that my prayer had been heard and answered. But then, within..."

She falters, lifts her handkerchief to her eyes.

"Miss Gonne, you distress yourself. There is no need."

"But there is a need, Mr. Yeats. A great need. I must tell all." Her head drops, so she is speaking into lap, the handkerchief twisting between her fingers. "Then... within a fortnight... my dearly beloved father... dear, dear Tommy... was dead."

"Miss Gonne... Maud..."

Again, she checks him, gathers herself, goes on. "I was now an heiress, independently wealthy, free of my relatives as soon as I reached twenty-one. I had control of my life but... I had lost the person I loved most dear in all the world."

She turns her face up to him, and he has a sudden vision of how she will look when old. Gaunt and magnificent. "The re-morse, Mr. Yeats. The remorse."

If there is an opportunity of him here, he cannot take it. He thinks of his own mother, locked in her snare of disillusion and bewilderment. He cannot think of what he might do for Maud Gonne any more than for her. He is at a loss, out of his depth. He wishes he could rise out of his body and become vapor and feel nothing of this heavy passion that weighs them both. Gather in around her, touching her lightly, with impartiality, as does the air.

As he cannot, he does the only thing he knows how to do and reads her some more of his play.

As the sun reaches mid-day, they resume their journey to-wards the Bailey and her nurse's house. Maud Gonne says little as they walk, side by side, along the little winding pathway. When she does speak, her words are cryptic to him, all about the purity of child love and the wisdom of the old, especially old women.

He is silent too, thinking about his play. Her story has helped him perfect the ending of his own. The motive behind Cathleen Ni Houlihan's sale, the sacrifice done to save her people, is so perfect in its intention that it is declared null-and-void by God. The Satanic traders must lose in the end, she has helped him to see that.

Bo is delighted to see them, and she and Maud Gonne have much to discuss. He tries not to be jealous of their easy banter. Everyone who comes near her makes him jealous, but his envy is also for her easy ways. Not for her the strain of perplexed wooing. While they prepare food, he goes out to the garden, leaving them sitting companionably together, Maud Gonne shelling peas and soaking up comfort from this old, dear presence from her childhood.

Through the window, he hears the old lady ask Maud Gonne if she and he are engaged to be married. He cannot hear her answer but he knows it is not affirmative. The answer he wants can only come by him attaining mastery of words and deeds. He is not yet worthy of her.

Nurse agrees to take Maud Gonne's adopted daughter and after they have dined, they set out back over the headland, towards the train. It is one of those summer evenings in Ireland when night is held in suspension within fading light, unutterably beautiful in its gentle clinging to the day.

"Come up here," Maud Gonne says, leaping up a crag like a goat. "The heather grows so high up here. Kathleen and I used to make cubby houses in this heather and be entirely hidden and entirely warm, sheltered from the wind."

"I've slept out at night in friendly heather," WB says, wondering to himself whether they might spend the night together, here?

Might he propose it?

"Many a night in Sligo, I fell asleep on heather like this," he says, "and didn't wake until the call of the sea birds looking for breakfast broke my sleep. Heather is as springy as the finest spring mattress, if one chooses the place well."

They find a spot now and lie down on it, side by side. Below, at the bottom of the cliff, the sea beats its eternal drum and above them wheel crying seagulls, as the stars begin to emerge, one by one first, then in groups.

"One never knows a countryside until one knows it at night," he says.

But she does not accept the invitation, if she knows it to be such.

Instead, she jumps up and starts to worry about the last tram. On the way back, he takes her to see a thicket in the midst of the headland, between the three roads but a good distance from them all.

"That thicket gave me my first thought of what a long poem should be," he tells her. "Its unpeopled, life-filled stillness, its silence held by the crash of breaking waves below. I thought of a poem as a place into which one could wander, away from the cares of life. I realized its characters should be as unreal, and as utterly real, as the shadows that people this thicket."

"How beautiful. Thank you for sharing this with me."

"Dreamers are the realists, Miss Gonne. They see light at the end. Theorists see light along the way, but the end lies in darkness."

Two seagulls fly low, skimming over their heads, across the heather and out to sea. "Look at them, Mr. Yeats. Do you think they are carrying us a message? They seem to hold the secrets of the world."

"Blake said, 'To the eyes of the man of imagination, nature is imagination itself.'"

"God's imagination? Is that what you mean?"

"I have observed dreams and visions very carefully, and am now certain that the imagination has some way of lighting on the truth that the reason has not, and that its commandments, delivered when the body is still and the reason silent, are the most binding we can ever know."

She nods, emphatically agreeing. "You know, if you care about the foreign press, I can speak of your work in a revue which is very well known *La Société Nouvelle*, which is published in Brussels and for which I am asked to write some articles on Ireland."

As they walk back to Howth station, he tells her more. And then all. She seems to understand every subtlety now of his spiritual philosophy, and this sympathy seems to blend their two natures into one sphere.

As they are leaving, about to get onto the tram, she says: "If I were to have the choice of being any bird, I would choose to be a seagull. Wouldn't you?"

The White Birds

I would that we were, my beloved, white birds on the foam of the sea:
We tire of the flame of the meteor, before it can pass by and flee;
And the flame of the blue star of twilight, hung low on the rim of the sky,
Has awaked in our hearts, my beloved, a sadness that never may die.

A weariness comes from those dreamers, dew-dabbled, the lily and rose,
Ah, dream not of them, my beloved, the flame of the meteor that goes,
Or the flame of the blue star that lingers hung low in the fall of the dew:
For I would we were changed to white birds on the wandering foam—I and you.

I am haunted by numberless islands, and many a Danaan shore,
Where Time would surely forget us, and Sorrow come near us no more:
Soon far from the rose and the lily, the fret of the flames, would we be,
Were we only white birds, my beloved, buoyed out on the foam of the sea.

The Tumult Of Her Days

MY DEAR MR. YEATS

I write in haste. I am recalled to France, where our Boulangist friends need my help. I must leave at once, it is very urgent, and so cannot see you later, as arranged.
Thank you for your poem. It is very beautiful.

With kind regards
Very sincerely your friend
Maud Gonne

It was the existence and efforts of a great number of people that turned Willie Yeats the student boy into WB Yeats, the great poet. It takes a village to raise a child, they say, and it takes a community to raise a genius, no matter how singular the individual.

In addition to Maud Gonne, one of the many who bore him aloft was Douglas Hyde. How lucky WB was to begin writing as that gifted linguist and folklorist was bringing the tales and legends of old Ireland alive after centuries of suppression and neglect.

His writing was fragrant with turf smoke, WB said, and he praised it, profusely. It was Hyde who first had him see that Ireland could be a site of renewal, that a new nation might be brought to birth there through culture. Where he differed was with Hyde's call for the complete restoration of the Irish language throughout the island again.

Could they not build a national tradition, a national literature, which would be none the less Irish in spirit for being in the English language? Could they not keep the continuity of the nation's life not by reviving the Irish language, which Dr. Hyde himself pronounced practically impossible, but by translating or retelling in English, with that indefinable but unmistakable Irish quality of rhythm and style, all that was best of the ancient literature? These were questions he answered every day with his work.

Another important influence, but in England, was Samuel Liddell Mathers. WB first spotted this gaunt, resolute, red-haired man, in the Reading Room at the British Library, noticing his athletic body draped in a striking brown velveteen coat, and a powerfully visceral presence. Soon he was making the journey across London to Mathers' home in Forest Hill.

He is shown into a dim and dusty book lined room. Mathers closes the door and pulls across a tapestry curtain, covered in the blue and bronze of peacocks. As the curtain falls over the door, and shuts them in, WB feels, in a way he doesn't understand, that some singular and unexpected thing is about to happen.

He goes over to the mantelpiece, and finding amulets in disarray and a little chainless bronze censer has fallen on its side and poured out its contents, begins to gather it up, partly to collect his thoughts, and partly with that habitual reverence which seems to him due to things long connected with secret hopes and fears.

"I can show you an incense more precious than any you have ever seen," says Mathers and he speaks of how images welling before the mind's eye come from a deeper source than the conscious mind, or forgotten memory.

That is certainly how it feels, WB agrees, when one is writing a poem.

"I have read your books and I understand you better than you do yourself, for I have been with many dreamers at the same cross-ways."

It is not the individual memory, but the great, shared, race memory, the *anima mundi*, that is the source of symbol, Mathers says. Symbols provide a means to access and express the divine essence in the human. Symbols are the greatest of all mental powers, whether used consciously by the masters of magic, or half-consciously by the mage's successors: the poet, the musician, the artist.

Their talk grows very excited and after a time, Mather shakes some dust into the censer out of a small silk bag, and sets the censer on the floor and lights the dust which sends up a blue stream of smoke. He got it, he said, from an old man in Syria. It was made from the same flowers that laid their heavy purple petals on the hands and hair of Christ, in the Garden of Gethsemane.

No less.

The smoke spreads out over the ceiling, and flows downwards again until it is like Milton's banyan tree. WB is filled with a faint sleepiness. His new friend's eyes glitter through the haze as he hands him a cardboard with a symbol on it, over which he holds a mace of many colored squares, and repeats a form of words.

WB finds his imagination begins to move of itself and to bring before his closed eyes vivid images from somewhere beyond his control. A desert. A heap of ancient ruins. And a black Titan raising himself up by his two hands from the middle of the decay and disrepair.

"You have seen a being of the order of Salamanders," Mathers said, afterwards, when he told him what he had seen.

And he invited WB to attend a meeting of the Order Of the Golden Dawn, at the Temple of Isis Urania, on Charlotte Street.

"No, I cannot," says the poet.

"You must. You have shut away the world and gathered the gods about you, but if you do not throw yourself at their feet, you will be always full of lassitude, and wavering purpose."

"I cannot," WB repeats. And he tells Mathers of a seance he attended in Dublin. Some half-dozen people were at this seance, all known to each other, all interested in matters spiritual and theosophical. As soon as the lights were turned out, and they sat waiting in the dim light of a fire, he had found his shoulders beginning to twitch. And then his hands.

He felt he could easily have stopped the movement but he had never heard of such a thing, and was curious, so he let it proceed. But after a few minutes the movement became violent and he stopped it.

"I sat motionless for a while and then..." He closes his eyes, overcome by a great dread.

"Then...? Go on, man!"

"My whole body moved like a suddenly unrolled watch-spring. I was thrown backward against the wall. I again stilled the movement and sat back at the table. Everybody began to say I was a medium, and that if I would not resist some wonderful thing would happen.

"We were now holding each other's hands and presently my right hand banged the knuckles of the woman next to me upon the table. She laughed, and the medium, speaking for the first time, and with difficulty, out of his mesmeric sleep, said, 'Tell her there is great danger.' He stood up and began walking round me, making movements with his hands as though he were pushing something away. I was now struggling vainly with this force which compelled me to movements I had not willed, and my movements had become so violent that I broke the table.

"I tried to pray, and because I could not remember a prayer, I repeated in a loud voice: 'Of Man's first disobedience and the fruit of that forbidden tree whose mortal taste brought death into the world and all our woe... sing, heavenly muse.' My Catholic friend had left the table and was saying a 'Pater Noster' and 'Ave Maria' in the corner."

Mathers is listening, intently, a small, strange smile playing about his lips.

"Presently all became still and so dark that I could not see anybody. It was like going out of a noisy political meeting on to a quiet country road... The medium, in faint voice, said 'We are through the bad spirits'.

I said, 'Will they come again?'

'No, never again,' he said."

So now Mathers must understand. He banished the spirits in the end but he'd paid a terrible price. Dreadful. And he would never go to a seance or turn a table again.

His friend did not answer any of this. He shook the censer once, twice, thrice, releasing more smoke into the air.

"What was that violent impulse running through my nerves? Do you know? Was it a part of myself, something that will always be a danger in me?"

Silence.

"Or did it come from without?"

Mathers' wild red hair, fierce eyes, sensitive tremulous lips, and rough clothes make him look something between a *debauché*, a saint and a peasant. "Table tapping!" he says, spitting out the words with great contempt.

He murmurs something WB cannot hear, as though to someone invisible. Again he shakes the censer, three times. The room appears to darken, the light from the candles to dim. And also the little gleams of flame on the corners of picture frames, and the bronze divinities around the room.

Mathers leans forward and begins speaking with a rhythmical intonation, and as he speaks WB has to struggle again with the shadow, as of some older night than the night of the sun, which begin to turn the blue of the incense to a heavy purple and make the peacocks glimmer and glow as though each separate color were a living spirit. He feels himself fall into a profound, dream-like reverie, through which he hears Mathers continuing to speak, as if at great distance. He has stood up and begun to walk to and fro, and become in WB's waking dream like a shuttle weaving an immense purple web, whose folds have begun to fill the room.

The room seems to have become inexplicably silent, as though all but the web and the weaving were gone to the far ends of the world. "They have come to us; they have come to us," his friend's voice begins again, loud, insistent, declamatory. "All that have ever been in your reverie, all that you have met with in books. There is Lear, his head still wet with the thunderstorm, and he laughs because you thought yourself an existence who are but a shadow, and him a shadow who is an eternal god.

"And there is Beatrice, with her lips half parted in a smile, as though all the stars were about to pass away in a sigh of love.

"And there is the mother of the God of humility who cast so great a spell over men that they have tried to unpeople their hearts that he might reign alone, but she holds in her hand the rose whose every petal is a god.

"And there, O swiftly she comes! is Aphrodite under a twilight falling from the wings of numberless sparrows, and about her feet are the grey and white doves."

The voice fades. WB sees him hold out his left arm and pass his right hand over it as though he stroked the wings of doves, and he is mortally afraid.

He makes a violent effort which seems almost to tear him in two. "You would sweep me away into an indefinite world which fills me with terror," he shouts at Mathers, with forced determination. "I command you to leave me at once, for your ideas and phantasies are but the illusions that creep like maggots into civilizations when they begin to decline, and into minds when they begin to decay."

He is about to rise and strike him, it feels necessary for his own survival, when the peacocks on the door behind him appear to grow immense and he is drowned in a tide of green and blue and bronze feathers. As he struggles, hopelessly, against the glittering feathers that now cover him completely, he knows he has struggled for hundreds of years, and is conquered at last.

He is sinking into the depth when the green and blue and bronze becomes a sea of flame and sweeps him away, and as he is swirled along he hears a voice over his head cry, "The mirror is broken in two pieces," and another voice answer, "The mirror is broken in four pieces," and a more distant voice cry with an exultant cry, "The mirror is broken into numberless pieces".

Now a multitude of pale hands is reaching towards him and strange, gentle faces bending over him and half-wailing, half-caressing voices lifting him. He is being lifted out of the tide of flame, and feels his memories, his hopes, his thoughts, his will, everything he holds to be himself melting away, then he seems to rise through numberless companies of beings, each wrapped in his eternal moment, dreaming with dim eyes or half-closed eyelids.

And now he passes beyond these forms and passes into that Death which is Beauty herself, and into that Loneliness which all the multitudes desire without ceasing. All things that had ever lived seem to come and dwell in his heart, and he in theirs.

He feels he would never again have known mortality or tears, had he not suddenly fallen from the certainty of vision into the uncertainty of dream. He becomes a drop of molten gold falling with immense rapidity, through a night elaborate with stars, and all about him a melancholy exultant wailing.

He falls and falls and falls and then the wailing is but the wailing of the wind in the chimney, and he wakes to find himself leaning on the table, supporting his head with his hands. "I will go where you will," he said to Mathers, "and do whatever you bid me, for I have been with eternal things."

My dear Mr. Yeats

Thank you so much for your letters and poems. I have been meaning to write very often—but I have been rather ill—unable to leave the house. The reason I had to leave Ireland so very abruptly was not so much politics, as I said at the time. I had received the news that one of the children I adopted, a little boy, the tiny child I spoke of when we were last together, was taken ill. A disease not uncommon among children called meningitis.

As soon as I arrived back and went to him, I saw the death bird pecking at the nursery window. At sight of that bird, I brought doctor after doctor, but to no avail. He died a few days later. It has distressed me a great deal. He was like a son to me.

I'm afraid I cannot say when I will be back to Ireland. I find I cannot work. Indeed, I cannot go out, I need help to make me sleep. Please do not tell this to anybody else. In Howth, I talked to you far more freely than is my wont, and I must ask you very seriously to be careful not to mention even the seemingly unimportant things to anyone.

Once, a while ago, I found you had repeated a great deal of conversations

I had with you. Of course I did not tell you not to do so, and it really did not matter, but still I hate it. While I do not mind in the least the wild lies and calumnies people tell of me, it is very painful to me to find that the one or two people I speak freely to repeat my conversation.

I hope you will not be vexed at my writing to you like this. I am a little incoherent at the moment—again, please do not discuss this with anyone.

I feel wretched for the effect on the work we planned, especially as you are working so very hard, but I must—

He was such a dear little boy. We are all utterly devastated.

I'm sorry, I shall write again in due course.

Until then, I remain very sincerely Mr. Yeats,
Always your friend,
Maud Gonne

Life Out Of Death

KNOWING NOW that there is a tradition of belief older than any of the European Churches, WB stops reading any book that isn't a book of belief older than theirs. And his project becomes to trace belief back to its earliest evidence. He is convinced he'll find Ireland there, at the heart the experience of the world before the modern bias, and spends much time in the British Library Reading Room, playing detective.

At home, things are worse than ever. Lily, his older and frailer sister has been working for May Morris as an embroiderer for a few years now. It was supposed to be temporary, until their father found his financial feet but WB is beginning to realize this is not likely to happen too soon. It is not for a lack of talent, but with the dissipation of that talent in talk. His father got commissions but he has yet to complete a picture. Some form of peculiar self sabotage, only it's not merely himself who is sabotaged but the entire family.

None of them like Lily going out to work. Wage earning is not for women, and certainly not for women like Lily. Though it is an artistic occupation, one that his sister might well be doing at home anyway; and though it must be a pleasure to go to Kelmscott House, with its wooden furniture, some of it decorated by Morris himself, and its embroidered hangings, and its Pre-Raphaelite paintings (even though his sister quite failed to appreciate the sultry beauty of Rossetti's Jane Morris as Proserpine); and though Morris is such a great friend of Papa and the whole family, reminding them all of Grandfather Pollexfen, the same great build and great courage, great drive and great restless energy, the same poor wardrobe and great profusion of hair; and it is a privilege to be working in his business, WB doesn't like it and resented his father for it, especially now for Lily has come to hate the work and dislike Morris's daughter, May, who is deceiving her husband, having an ill-judged affair with the Irish writer, George Bernard Shaw. Lily is shocked, as any good woman must be, by the immorality and repulsed by the deceit and drama.

The embroidery department does seem to have moved a distance from the ideals with which Morris set it up, and the work is as mechanical and repetitive as machine work in a factory, Lily says. She would love nothing more than to stay home and look after her father and him, now Jack is gone.

Lolly, the keeper of the family accounts, is different. Lolly is slang for money in Ireland and his younger sister was always over-conscious of the halfpence and pence. She has taken up teaching, the refuge for ladies incapable of other work. But not at any ordinary school. She is assistant at Miss Jones's Froebel Kindergarten in Queen Anne's Gardens.

Froebel's theories, he must admit, are interesting: the child's capacity for growth needs only to be encouraged through pleasurable activity and play. Lolly has been taking his examinations, with much complaint about the burden of overwork, though all can see she likes being out of the house for a few hours every day.

When he said as much to her, she flung a quotation from GB Shaw, of all people, at him: "Home is the girl's prison and the woman's workhouse," the chronicler of the everyday is supposed to have said, and it does indeed sound like something he would say. It's the housework his sister wants to give up and she seems to be under some notion that he and Jack should share out her chores.

She complained so much that the family now has to take in a girl to help Rose, though that rather defeats the purpose of the extra money she brings in by working, does it not? And now she is talking about teaching painting to small groups of local children. The girl is impossible.

Her money and housekeeping inanities are more of a drain to good thought than any other kind of vexation. Except perhaps the news that his younger brother, Jack, at only twenty years, has met and won true love. And to a girl pretty and shy and utterly devoted, that none of them can dislike.

Making sure to underline his difference to Papa, Jack has announced his plans to make himself financially stable, able to support a wife, before he marries (though the girl has money herself). He has got himself a job as an illustrator for a Manchester newspaper. WB would never take such a job—he has known more poets and artists destroyed by the desire to have a wife and child and keep them in comfort than he has seen destroyed by drink and harlots—but it is galling nonetheless to see his brother, eight years younger than him, so well on his way to being established out of the house.

And Mama? Oh well, Mama is Mama...

So it is partly in search of a tradition, and partly to escape, that he heads over to Ireland again. He doesn't know it but this will be his last time to stay with his grandparents.

~

While in Sligo, WB spends much time with his uncle, the dour and hypochondriac George Pollexfen, his mother's brother, who is as interested as himself in studying the visions and thoughts of the country people, and whose housekeeper, Mary Battle, has second sight.

She tells him how, looking out of the window one day, she saw coming from Knocknarea, where Queen Maeve, according to local folklore, is buried under a great heap of stones, the finest woman you ever saw. Traveling right across from the mountains and straight to here, she was, looking very strong, but not wicked. It is striking how like Mary Battle's visions are to the symbols called up by Mathers. WB sees in this some kind of proof. He writes down all she has to say about this great lady.

"I have seen the Irish Giant too," she tells him. "And though he was a fine man he was nothing to her, for he was round and could not have stepped out so soldierly... She had no stomach on her but was slight and broad in the shoulders, and was handsomer than anyone you ever saw. She looked about thirty."

And when he asks if she has seen others like her, she says,

"Some of them have their hair down, but they look quite differ-ent, more like the sleepy-looking ladies one sees in the papers. Those with their hair up are like this one. The others have long white dresses, but those with their hair up have short dress-es, so that you can see their legs right up to the calf. The men are fine and dashing-looking, like the men one sees riding their horses in twos and threes on the slopes of the mountains with their swords swinging. There is no such race living now, none so finely proportioned ...

"When I think of her and the ladies now, they are like little children running about, not knowing how to put their clothes on right... Wild and free, why, I would not call them women at all."

Another friend of Uncle George, the Master Pilot at Rosses Point, tells him of meeting at night close to the Pilot House a procession of similar women, in what seemed the costume of another age. Were they really people of the past, revisiting, per-haps, the places where they lived, or must he explain them by some memory of the race, as distinct from individual memory?

Certainly these Spirits, the Shee as the country people called them, seemed full of personality: capricious, generous, spiteful, anxious, angry. Yet, did that prove them more than images and symbols?

If his images can affect Mary Battle's dreams, as she says they can, her folk-images can affect his in turn, for one night, lying between sleeping and waking in his uncle's house, he sees a strange long-bodied pair of dogs, one black and one white, that turn up afterwards in a country tale. In order to keep himself from the nightmares that troubled him so often, he had formed the habit of imagining four watch-dogs, one at each corner of his room, and, though he had not told his uncle or anybody, one day Uncle George said, "Here is a very curious thing; most nights now, when I lay my head upon the pillow, I hear a sound of dogs baying—the sound seems to come up out of the pillow."

How could one separate the dogs of the tale from those his uncle heard baying in his pillow?

WB is disappointed that, once the first excitement of their

experiments together and with Mary Battle is over, his spells have done nothing to rouse George from his gloom and thickening hypochondria. Neither has he himself found what he is looking for. He believes the truth he seeks will come to him like the subject of a poem, from some moment of passionate experience.

This is why he no longer reads contemporary books. If he fills his own exposition with other men's thought, other men's investigations, he would sink into all that multiplicity of interest and opinion. The passionate experience he seeks would never come, never can come until he has found the right image, or images.

He thinks of the image of Apollo, whose priesthood got that occasional power, described in the classical histories, of lifting great stones and snapping great branches. He thinks of Gemma Galgani who caused deep wounds to appear in her body by contemplating her crucifix. He thinks of the essay that Oscar Wilde read to him on that Christmas Day visit to his house, the line that has stayed with him: "What does the world owe to the imitation of Christ, what to the imitation of Caesar?"

And he thinks of his friend Mathers, painting little pictures combining the forms of men, animals and birds, and describing how citizens of ancient Egypt assumed, when in contemplation, the images of their gods.

Image calls up image in an endless procession, and he can't choose among them with any confidence. And when he does choose, the image loses its intensity, or changes into some other image. He is lost in that region warned about in a cabalistic manuscript shown to him by Mathers: astray upon *Hodos Camelionis*, the Path of the Chameleon.

Into this fuzz of imagist perplexity come the breaking news that none expected: Parnell has died, Parnell, the uncrowned king of Ireland, is dead.

~

WB is on his way to meet the boat at Kingstown. He and half the country it seems like, with buses, trams and trains all full, though it's not yet eight o'clock, and the recently risen sun invisible through curtains of thick, heavy rain, the sort that falls straight down, in sheets. Dublin rain.

WB is in shock, all Ireland is in shock, for Parnell is dead. Whatever way you took him—whether he was your chief, your uncrowned king, your hero or that adulterer, that unholy disgrace, that farcical failure—it's beyond mattering now. He is dead. Gone out with a whimper. After half a year of watching the rump of his once-great party lose by-election after by-election, he caught a cold campaigning in a heavy rainstorm and now, he is dead.

His remains are on the way back to Ireland from London to be buried in Glasnevin and Maud Gonne is returning on the same boat. No one is more in shock than her. She is still in mourning for the boy she adopted. He is surprised at how much this death distressed her—and continues to distress. For a while, she lost her ability to speak French, and she needed to take chloroform to sleep. She is worried she may now be addicted to opium.

This maternal side of her always surprises him. He sees it in her dealings with the treason-felony prisoners too. Children, the old, the vulnerable: they bring out a softer light in her. Parnell's death will raise the specter of her other loss, of all other losses, as bereavement always does.

~

When he arrives at the pier, there's already a substantial crowd, under a dark canopy of wet umbrellas, waiting in silence. The boat is in and Maud Gonne is one of the first off. She is dressed, head to foot, in black. She brings with her this time not one but two small dogs, one cat, the squirrel and the birdcages.

Some of the crowd nudge, some snigger, at her dress, her haggard look, thinking it theatrics for Parnell.

She pays attendants to take care of the animals, and they stand together, on the edge of the small somber crowd, awaiting the coffin.

"Oh Mr. Yeats, isn't it dreadful?" she whispers. "France seems to me to be alive with death at the moment."

"The child?"

"Oh please, don't speak of it. Never speak of it."

He is silenced.

After a time he thinks to ask, "May we speak of Général

Boulanger?" For the general too is dead. His mistress, Madame Bonnemain, who was more than a woman to him, more than a life partner, died first. Men who believe in beauty, who wear a beautiful woman as a badge, have the hardest time with illness, but lovely young bodies go the same way as the dumpy and decrepit. It's all the same to Mr. Death.

Watching his beloved die, the tide of life pulling out inch by inch, leaving unspeakable ugliness in its place, fever and pus and sores, was too much for *le brave général*. He went to her grave, threw himself upon it, and shot himself in the head.

"The Anarchists are placing bombs in industrialists' offices and police stations," says Maud Gonne. "They say the *Chambre des Députés* and the railway stations are next. And in Ireland, evictions and starvations continue. And now, Mr. Parnell. I drown in death."

Here comes the coffin. They watch, silent, without a sound, as the funeral attendants wheel it from the ship onto the Dublin train, and they board the train and go with it, on its short journey to Westland Row.

WB doesn't want to go to the Parnell funeral, pleading his hatred of crowds and what crowds imply. Maud Gonne is aghast, determined not to miss it, and though yes, the crowds are frightful, hundreds of thousands of people lining every street, and the rolling drumbeat of "The Dead March", and the keening wails from certain women in the crowd, she stands outside the old parliament building in College Green. The procession stops right there, and his famous speech to the Crown, made on the eve of his imprisonment back in the eighties, is read out: "No man has the right to fix the boundary of a nation. No man has the right to say to his country, This far shalt thou go and no further."

Maud Gonne is moved by the quiet dignity of the bowed heads, the silent prayers, the tears openly streaming down some people's faces. In his disgrace, Parnell has been returned to the people. No bishops, posing sorrow and salvation in purple and gold vestments, are here, as there would have been had he died before the divorce. Instead of damask, silk or brocade, are green banners, shrouded with black crepe, flapping clumsily in the wet wind. And the flags of the USA and France, the role models of freedom, and wreaths with inscriptions such as "Murdered by the Priests."

Those marching today march because they care about Ireland and a man who worked for its freedom, a man who was flawed like them, who gave himself to something greater than his flaws.

The coffin is borne aloft. Through the falling, silencing rain it floats, as if skating, across a waving lake of heads through Dublin town to St. Michan's church where the service is held, and from there onto City Hall, where he laid in state and eventually, after thousands have paid their respects, the coffin is placed on a gun carriage for its final journey across the city to Glasnevin Cemetery.

Dusk is falling before the last prayers are read, and the coffin is finally lowered. The sky seems to brighten with strange lights and flames, and just as the earth is thrown to land on the coffin with a thud, one big, bright celestial light plunges from the top of the heavens, down, down, down. A falling star, witnessed by thousands.

Life out of death, Maud Gonne says as she sees the star fall, trying to comfort herself with her old mantra. Life out of death, eternally.

~

WB sees that she is clearly very ill. She wants to meet Russell, AE, to ask him about reincarnation, so he organizes the meeting on Nassau Street. The tea in front of her grows cold as she asks question after question. How soon might somebody who has died be reborn? Can one influence it? Is it always centuries later? Could it be immediate? Is it always in another country? Are there different rules for adults and children? Might a child be reborn into the same family?

Russell gives answers that are at once vague and specific. There are no rules, only ways. He has had a vision of her in a past life, a shadowy grey figure, trapped through murderous actions to wander the earth, seeking appeasement. Souls are neither adult nor children and both. Only strong rituals and sex magic

can reincarnate a specific soul, and then only unreliably, but a
soul stands a good chance of reincarnation into the same family.

WB feels he ought to say: "The whole doctrine of the reincarnation of the soul is hypothetical. It is the most plausible of
the explanations of the world beyond this world but can we say
more than that?" Or some such sentence? But her anguish, and
the comfort she is drawing from the philosophy, makes speaking out impossible.

As they are leaving, he asks if he may see her, alone, in her
rooms next day. She agrees.

"Please ensure that nobody else is there," he says. "I have
something I believe will be of great help to you."

He has already told her about vellum notebook of poems he is
preparing for her. She thinks this is what he means, but he has
a gift more powerful, even, than poetry to offer. For all that he
tries to make verse that carries people out of everyday thought
behind the veil, poetry is the outcome, not the power itself.

He is not just poet now but mage. And he can use the ceremonial magic he is learning through his occult studies to offer her
protection.

The Hermetic Order
Of The Golden Dawn

As WELL AS offering him the spiritual comfort he craves, the Order is reinforcing WB's sense of special destiny. He is writing an article for United Ireland about an earlier Irish poet of nationhood, Clarence Mangan, about his doomed love affair. Poor Mangan had, in his mid-twenties, been led a dance by a fascinating coquette, who amused herself with his devotion, and then whistled him down the wind.

Sometimes he thinks his devotion, too, might as well be offered to an image in a milliner's shop, or to a statue in a museum. When a man's love affair goes bankrupt, romance makers say, a devil gets into the soles of his feet and makes him seek out some exciting activity, but for Mangan, as for himself, there was nothing but scrivening, scrivening. They could only watch their laboring quills traveling across ream after ream of paper. When such despair slides in, he reminds himself that the Order and its rituals are his great hope.

Spiritual power will give him symbols for poetry and draw Maud Gonne in, then together, like Nicholas Flamel and his wife, Pernella, they will unleash the oldest, deepest powers of their nation and of their kind. Such is worth waiting for, worth working for, worth withholding for. So he insists to himself needing, I suppose, some vindication of his ongoing virginity.

On his next visit to Maud Gonne, he takes along some paraphernalia and draws for her a symbol, according to the rites he's learned, and she is electrified. She sees, as if palpably present, a past personality of hers, seeking to be reunited. A female she comes to call her Grey Lady, a priestess of ancient Egypt who, under the influence of her lover, gave false articles to a priest, for money. Because of this wrongdoing, she was condemned to remain a shadowy spirit seeking a new life in which to make amends.

What Maud Gonne does not know is that Moina Bergson, Mathers' wife-to-be, has had a similar vision of her, not long ago. He must ask Mathers what it all means before he tells her this.

She is ecstatic from her vision, elevated as one always is by leaving this world for the world of spirit. Or imagination, if you prefer. Afterwards, they lie on her low couches drinking tea, and she tells him that she has always been psychic and shares various stories of premonitions and previsions, and he tells her that his sister Lily has similar gifts, as has Mary Battle, his uncle's housekeeper. Women come more easily than men, he thinks, to that wisdom which ancient peoples and wild peoples think the only wisdom. During their symbolical work this afternoon, he himself had only vague impressions.

This gratifies her. The work has bonded them, as he intended, and she seems more at peace than she has for a long time.

That night, to get himself to sleep, he creates the image of an Irish Celtic spiral slowly spinning, from the wide outer circle round and round growing ever smaller into a tiny center that becomes a tiny pin prick into which one can disappear. He dreams he is a child again, and one of the younger children has thrown a doll face down on the floor, and is crying and crying, wanting it back.

Mama is unmoved, can't be bothered to pick it up, so he bends to the task, to return it to the child whose crying is so annoying to him. He picks it up and finds it is himself, a live, squirming doll of him as a baby. He is also the crying child in the background as well as the older boy who is seeing the doll, and hearing the cries behind. Now he understands why his brother or sister self cries and cries. Half the doll's face is missing. Mama has taken a bite out of its head.

He wakes himself screaming.

For the first time, Mama has followed him to Ireland. He gets out of bed, sweating, and writes out the experience, and then half-shapes it into a poem, and determines he will work this image, until it is a perfect image of awe, and give it to Maud Gonne. In the morning, he tears it up.

Her Grey Lady shows herself to be very evil. He and Maud Gonne had thought her only sorrowful until one evening she appeared to Mrs. Rowley, a great friend of hers, a kindly and well-meaning lady, ardently Irish. The Grey Lady appeared to her while Maud Gonne was in a semi-trance. This time, she described herself as a murderess of children.

On another occasion, in the middle of Maud Gonne's vision, while he was invoking the names of the highest, most divine sephiroth angels and archangels, Mrs. Rowley suddenly screamed. She found herself amidst the fires of hell, she said, and for days afterwards, she found the smell of sulphur all about her. Even her towels smelled of it in the morning.

He thinks perhaps Maud Gonne has a strong subconscious conviction that her soul is lost. Her conscious mind repels all the accompanying symbols, but these can become visible in a mind in close accord with hers. Or perhaps there is an actual contest between two troops of spirits for control of her mind? Those who are pushing hard for God may have caused the other to take on a diabolic shape?

She is coming to have need of him, and he has no doubt that need would become love in time. He has even, as he watches it unfold, a sense of cruelty, as though he were a hunter taking captive some beautiful wild creature.

The Two Trees

BELOVED, gaze in thine own heart,
The holy tree is growing there;
From joy the holy branches start,
And all the trembling flowers they bear.
The changing colors of its fruit

Have dowered the stars with merry light;
The surety of its hidden root
Has planted quiet in the night;
The shaking of its leafy head
Has given the waves their melody,
And made my lips and music wed,
Murmuring a wizard song for thee.
There the Loves a circle go,
The flaming circle of our days,
Gyring, spiring to and fro
In those great ignorant leafy ways;
Remembering all that shaken hair
And how the wingèd sandals dart,
Thine eyes grow full of tender care:
Beloved, gaze in thine own heart.

Gaze no more in the bitter glass
The demons, with their subtle guile,
Lift up before us when they pass,
Or only gaze a little while;
For there a fatal image grows
That the stormy night receives,
Roots half hidden under snows,
Broken boughs and blackened leaves.
For all things turn to barrenness
In the dim glass the demons hold,
The glass of outer weariness,
Made when God slept in times of old.
There, through the broken branches, go
The ravens of unresting thought;
Flying, crying, to and fro,
Cruel claw and hungry throat,
Or else they stand and sniff the wind,
And shake their ragged wings; alas!
Thy tender eyes grow all unkind:
Gaze no more in the bitter glass.

Before she leaves Dublin, he confides in her, swearing her to secrecy.

"Why Mr. Yeats, you are being so mysterious!"

"Because I speak of the Great Mystery."

"Well yes, I promise, my lips are sealed."

"Last year I joined a great magical order, which teaches the science and art of creating changes in consciousness. And in entering into contact with intelligences that are beyond the human."

Now he has all her interest. He invites her to become a member of his Order, where she will learn esoteric philosophy, based on the Hermetic Kabbalah. She will find it most rewarding, he assures her, as she works through the four Classical Elements as well as the basics of astrology and geomancy. And the Tarot.

He himself is moving towards initiation into the Second, more advanced "Inner" Order, the *Rosae Rubeae et Aureae Crucis*, the Ruby Rose and Cross of Gold.

"And what are you learning there?"

"Full ceremonial magic. Skrying. Astral travel. Alchemy.

"So you are no longer with Madame Blavatsky?"

"No. When I returned from Theosophist meetings, I had no desire but for more thought, more discussion but after I have been moved by Golden Dawn rituals, I am full of plans for deeds of all kinds. I wish to return to Ireland and find there some public work."

She likes that, as he knew she would. He knows the access to this vast source of power will appeal to her, as will the Order's faith in the power of the will.

"Are there more orders?" she asks. "After the second?"

"Just one other. The Third Order is that of our Secret Chiefs. They direct the two lower orders by spirit communication."

"I am not sure that..."

"Pray, don't be frightened. Once it is visible to you, you will be able to understand it. What is unknown must first be brought into the light of knowing."

"The light of knowing," she says, wistfully.

"Light is the Order's prime symbol and illumination its purpose. But do not worry about any of this for now. All you need to know is that trained occultists can either call down a cosmic force from the greater universe or alternatively call up the same cosmic force from the depths of their own beings."

Now she is looking at him, rapt. He has never had the blazing stream of her energy focused on him like this before.

"Next comes the belief that, properly trained, the human will is capable of anything. Literally: anything, even acts that defy known physical laws."

"Tommy used to say that. The human will is a strange, incalculable force, he used to say. It could achieve anything. He could have been Pope if he willed it enough, he said."

"Our order uses many adjuncts of ceremonial magic. Special lights and colors and shapes and perfumes. All are aids to concentrate the will into a blazing stream of pure energy. Finally, we accept that man is but half way up the ladder of evolution, not at its top, and that there are planes other than the physical. Our rites and ceremonies forward our evolution to the Astral Light."

"Like Mme Blavatsky's Astral Plane?"

"Not quite. No. Astral light means all planes above the physical, except one. But again, you need to know none of this as yet. Just hold to the light. Realizing that we are indeed in a pathway of darkness, we grope our way towards an understanding of the meaning of life, the reason for death."

"So tell me how I join. Is there a book I should read?"

"The tests of true Initiation aren't just something you read in a book. They reach down and test you in every aspect of your life and soul. In fact, you are already being tested by the Guardian of the Threshold of the Mysteries."

~

So in November, she goes with him to the Isis Urania Temple of the Golden Dawn. She is robed and blindfolded and led into the hall of true Initiation by a rope around her waist. At the door she is met, for the act of purification, by a voice announcing: "Light beyond all light."

She is led by the rope three times round the hall, presented first at the Throne of Darkness, then the Throne of Light and then brought before the Altar. Her hands are taken and placed on the red cross and the triangle, while WB intones a notice of obligation of secrecy to which she gives her agreement.

Then the blindfold is removed from her eyes. As her eyes adjust to the candlelight, she sees an altar, on which there is a red cross, a wine and water vessel, some occult signs and a lamp. A number of other officers—should she call them priests?—are also present, decorated in their own peculiar way according to their particular office.

Around her a circle of people, all robed, begin to recite words and, reaching in unison above their heads with the right hand, touching themselves on the forehead. She joins in, being led by WB, who is officiating the ceremony, into drawing down from a sphere of light above a shaft into the middle of her head that creates a smaller center of light just between and behind the eyebrows.

As this light illuminates her cranium, in a loud voice, she together with the rest vibrates in two long, resonant, monotone syllables the Hebrew word *Atoh*, which means 'thine', then brings the right hand down to the solar plexus, to draw the light down to the earth beneath their feet, while vibrating the Hebrew word for kingdom, *Malkuth*.

Then they all touch the left shoulder and the right, saying "*Va Gavura* and *Va Gahula*"—the power and the glory—while visualizing the white shaft of light extending left and then right.

Finally, they press the palms together at the breast and vibrate the words "*Leh Ohalem, Ahmen.*" Forever and ever, amen.

This is the Kabbalistic sign of the cross.

Reaching out with the right hand, then, they make a pentagram starting at lower left point and drawing up and center, while saying "*Yod Heh Vau Heh.*" Turning to the South, they say "*A-do-neye*". Turning to the West, they say "*Eh-Heh-Yeh*".

Turning to the North, they say "*A-Gah-Lah*".

Then, extending their arms in the form of a cross, they say together: "Before me Raphael. Behind me Gabriel. On my right hand Michael. On my left hand Auriel. For about me flames the Pentagram, and within shineth the Six-rayed Star."

While Maud Gonne recites these words in the company of people who've clearly said them many a time before, she must visualize a hexagram floating in her torso. The uppermost triangle glows with red fire, the downward pointing triangle is blue and wavers like a reflection on water. Its uppermost angle touches her throat, its lowermost her groin.

Repeating after WB, she takes the Neophyte Oath, vowing to learn to read and write Hebrew, and to master the philosophy that cross-references the Hebrew alphabet with planets, gods and goddesses and the human body. And to internalize The Tree of Life of the cosmos.

She promises and swears that with Divine permission she will, from this day forward, apply herself to this great work, which is to purify and exalt her spiritual nature so that with Divine aid, she may at length attain to be more than human and gradually raise and unite herself to her higher genius.

And that, in this event, she will not abuse the great power entrusted unto her.

Upon these sacred and sublime symbols, she swears to observe the Order's rules without evasion, equivocation, mental reservation of any kind whatsoever. And, on violation of any of them, to being "expelled as a willfully perjured wretch, void of all moral worth and unfit for the society of all upright and true persons," intones WB.

She hesitates and he repeats the words.

"...Expelled from this order as a willfully perjured wretch, void of all moral worth and unfit for the society of all upright and true persons." She, in soft voice, repeats after him.

And so they go, his voice then hers, intoning the rest of the rite, her voice weakening through the final lines: "...and, in addition, the penalty of voluntarily submitting myself to a deadly and hostile current, set in motion by the Chief of the Order, from which I shall fall slain or paralyzed without visible weapon, as if blasted by a Lightning Flash."

Maud Gonne finds herself a member of the Order of The Golden Dawn, standing with a sword poised above her head and her own magical motto: "*Per Ignem Ad Lucem*," WB says.

"*Per Ignem Ad Lucem*," she repeats.

Through Fire to Light.

The Poor Woman's Struggle

WHENEVER YOU see a road running long and straight for miles, you know the Romans were likely in that place. Mrs. Wilson lives just off one such, the Edgware Road that runs, unusual for London, ten straight miles from Marble Arch.

In our time, that road was the first artery of Irish London. County Kilburn we called it, County Cricklewood, to make us feel a little more at home. Our teacher in the national school back in Ireland used to point at us and say: "You: Kilburn! You: Cricklewood!" meaning we'd be going to England as we were the ones with no money. The whole town knew what we were destined for and they thought they had it made, able to stay at home on their "big" farms—anything over fifty acres was considered big—or in their little shops, or entering the hierarchical arms of the church. Me, I was glad to get out.

In my town, how far you could cycle was the limit of your world. Ten miles out and ten miles back, that was your reach into another life. England offered freedom: boys, jobs, money. No one to look after you, right enough, but that meant no one looking over you either. There were things you could do in England that in Ireland you didn't even know could be done. Best day's work I ever did was taking the boat to England.

Same, I'd say, for Mrs. Wilson. London landed her a good husband, and all would have stayed well, only he died young. Then she became the mistress of Colonel Gonne, only he upped and died on her too. So now she was here, in her little flat, not at the southern, more well-to-do end of the Roman Road, where people known to Maud Gonne and WB might live, but near Kilburn Park, where poverty and comfort scrape along together, middle-class and artisans alongside cabmen, sweeps and ostlers.

A different London, all noise and bustle and smells and chatter and clamor, and not far from where I lived myself, when I lived in the great city. Maybe we were drawn there because, before the Romans came, it was Celtic, part of an ancient trackway between the towns now known as Canterbury and St. Albans. Before the Celts, no doubt some other peoples walked the track, but it was the Romans who straightened and paved it, so we now think of it as theirs.

"Ah Miss Gonne, thank you for coming," Mrs. Wilson says, welcoming her in.

She looks pretty, neat and contained and her house is the same as last time, spotless and ordered, everything in its place though it is the home of a young child, no small achievement, Maud Gonne knows.

The carpet is ugly and worn, despite her best efforts, and the paper of the kind that went up during the Regency, peeling in many places. She has cut off the peels with a scissors or knife, to tidy up no doubt, but it has left strange jags all over the wall.

As she makes tea she is clearly nervous, so Maud Gonne puts her focus on little Eileen, takes her into her lap, like last time. So much has happened since then. "Who's a pretty little lady? Yes you are."

The child laughs up into her face, a rich gurgle. "Oh yes you are. You shall break hearts in years to come, oh yes."

"You're very good with her," Mrs. Wilson says, laying out the cups and saucers.

"Unlike most people, I am not a lover of newborns. I cannot see beauty in fledglings until their feathers appear, or in kittens or puppies until their eyes open, or in babies until their eyes gain some expression and color. But once they get to this age... so delightful... utterly delightful."

Little Eileen plays with her bracelet.

"Mrs. Wilson, I have some very good news for you."

The spoon stops on its way to the teapot.

"Yes. I have secured a position for you."

"Oh Miss Gonne, it's very good of you, but who'd take care of Eileen?"

"I've thought of that too, never fear. I have what I believe is the perfect solution. I think I've mentioned her to you before, our own nurse, Mary Ann Meredith. We called her Bo. She has recently gone into retirement, but I have spoken to her, and she is prepared to care for Eileen, just as she cared for us. I do think it's rather marvelous."

"And who would fund all this?"

Maud Gonne gives her a beatific smile. Just like she is so proud of the money she gives to the porters and attendants who must fetch and carry for her animals and birds when she travels, she has no thought what it is like to be on the receiving end of charity. She was born to her place and we to ours.

Suddenly, with a whimper, Mrs. Wilson starts to cry.

"My dear Mrs. Wilson... Are these tears of relief?"

Mrs. Wilson gets up, and with vehemence, takes the child across onto her own knee, and bounces her up and down. Soothing the child distracts her from her own emotion, Maud Gonne can see, but it gives her nothing to do except to try not to look too hard at them, until equilibrium is regained.

Once the sobs ease, she says, "This is such an excellent opportunity for you and Eileen both. I know you wish to do what is best."

"What I wish..." She stops, thinks, starts again. "All I have ever wished for, Miss Gonne, is a secure home, where I can live together with my child."

"Indeed, the world is not kind to us women. But we must think now of Eileen, of ensuring a better fate for her. Brought up as a young lady, in time she will make a good marriage."

"And when did you become a spokeswoman for marriage?"

Maud Gonne recoils at the hostility. "I'm going to pretend you didn't say that, Mrs. Wilson."

"I'm sorry, I am, I shouldn't have." She hugs her child closer and speaks over her head. "I think you are a most marvelous woman, Miss Gonne, you know I do. So I know you won't hold to this. Thank you for the offer, but we'll scrape along as best we can."

Maud Gonne is careful not to look around the room, its mean furnishings, frayed and faded carpets and the sound of omnibuses and traffic outside the window.

"I have given us a great deal of thought and consulted with my sister and my cousin and friends who all feel Eileen must have the advantages that are her birthright."

This sets the woman off again.

"Oh Mrs. Wilson... Please..."

"You said you would never take her from me. You *said*. You *promised*. You *know* the colonel wouldn't want her taken from me."

Maud Gonne is determined not to react to provocation. "The colonel... my father... Tommy would have wanted what is best for Eileen. My dear Mrs. Wilson, I can see you are upset, perhaps I should have foreseen this. But when you have time to think, I believe you'll..." Maud Gonne is stopped by the expression on the other woman's face.

She takes a deep breath, tries again. "I have gone to the greatest personal effort to secure this arrangement. To be sure, Bo could never have been coaxed out of retirement for anybody else."

"This governess position... It is here in England or in Ireland?"

Maud Gonne hesitates before saying, heartily, "Oh, it is very much more exciting than that."

"Pray tell me where."

"My dear Mrs. Wilson, do not look alarmed. In a little while, when you have had time to think..."

"Where is it?"

"Please, try to..."

"Where?"

"Russia."

"Russia?" she says, aghast. "*Russia?*"

"St. Petersburg. Do you know it? It is such a beautiful city. I was there myself last year. Oh Mrs. Wilson, you are going to see the world. In a while, in a very little while, you will come to understand what a privilege that is."

Cauldron Of Regeneration

"THINK OF IT," Maud Gonne says to Millevoye. "A new human entity is about to be brought into existence upon the earthly plane."

They are in a carriage, by night, hurtling towards Samois, the little village on the Seine where Georges is buried. Millevoye rolls his eyes, returns to the reverie that has held him aloof since they left Paris.

"Don't you wonder where our boy is now?" she persists. "In these moments, before he is brought into our plane? I imagine his soul as a ghostly vapor, hovering somewhere in space out of time."

Again, that cynical upward flick of his eyes. Oh it's a naïve image she is describing, she knows as much, but she's holding it out as the symbol of a deeper truth. There was a time he would have understood.

She lifts the curtain. Through the darkness she can perceive that they have left the city and are now passing through the villages that line the Seine from here, all the way out to Samois, her favorite village in all of France, where they have been so happy.

And so unhappy.

But she must not think of that tonight.

It *is* wondrous that this child towards which they rush exists as yet only as thought and feeling, swirls of sensation in their bodies. In her: a clamminess of the hands, a churning of the stomach, a tightness of the neck and shoulders. And, in Millevoye, if nothing else, an anticipatory stirring in the groin.

She can count on that, and tonight, for once, his priapic constancy is welcome—though his failure to show equal interest in other aspects of their ritual is...

No.

Banish such thoughts.

In a short while, if all proceeds to her careful arrangement, she and he shall come together within the crypt at Samois cemetery, where Georges, her beloved little Georgie, lies embalmed. At stroke of midnight, their egg and seed will unite again, rekindling his dear baby soul back into being.

But if success is to be theirs, hers and Millevoye's, if her timing is not to be set awry, then the coachman needs to *hurry*. Midnight is—she checks again the Victorian pocket-watch that once belonged to Tommy—a mere forty-five minutes away.

Snapping the timepiece shut, Maud Gonne sits back in her seat, twisting her thoughts to Higher Things. To how far the act of reincarnation changes the alchemy of flesh and blood and spirit? To whether the essence of new Georges will be a replica of the old, having the same soul as before? Or, being of new flesh, possessed also of a different inner nature?

So many of her questions have no answers, and her Irish mages were unclear.

The coach takes a sudden swerve, almost throwing her on top of Millevoye. As she lifts her eyes to his, she sees that he is smiling at her. A small stretch of the lips under his mustache, but most certainly a smile. A coil of triumph turns within her. Without Georges, she has had nothing to hold him, nothing to set against his first, legal family, but once they have again a son, the issue of his stock and hers—fighting stock, not the milk-and-water blood of Madame Millevoye—then he would be truly hers again.

Truly.

Again she lifts the curtain, tries to peer through the blackness to check where they are. Trees flash past, dark denizens of the great forest of Fontainbleau, telling her nothing.

Samois—about six kilometers from the town of Fontainbleau—is one of those somnolent villages that line the Seine outside Paris, of the kind immortalized by the painter Sisley. Thirty minutes before, the village day ended with the return to home of the last customers to leave Lepotier's Taverne. It has been dark since five o'clock, with the sun not due to surface again for another eight hours, and cold. Cold with winter damp, the sort of cold that seeps marrow from bone. What else to do on such a night, but sleep, sleep...

But here comes the carriage, hooves and harness jangling open the night-quiet, all the way along the winding road until it reaches the cemetery, where it halts with a jerk. The horse whinnies then quiets, so that for half a moment all folds back into silence. Within the carriage, this half-moment communicates itself to Maud Gonne, and not being one to let such a moment pass, she says to Millevoye, "Do you not feel as if the world is waiting, holding its breath at what is to come?"

He shrugs.

And perhaps he is right. Where is the wonder in what is about to happen? What is more everyday on this earth than the coming, or going, of life? Yet it's undeniable, this sense of significance she feels. It's in the night sky above with its hammering of stars, in the broken road beneath the wheels of the carriage, in the breathing of the trees, and in the sly bulk of the gravestones waiting in the cemetery, frosted sentries of the dark...

Enough! No more imaginative indulgence. She pushes the carriage door and steps out into the night, one hand to the mantle that covers her distinctive auburn coiffure. They are traveling incognito, and one never knows who is about, even here, even at this hour.

Millevoye steps down behind her, his arms full of candles wrapped in a blanket. "À bientôt, Roger," he calls up to the driver, who has his instructions to return for them in an hour, at 12:30. Roger lifts his tall hat in assent, his face impassive. "Cimetière de Samois," Maud Gonne can imagine him saying to his friends later, at his avern. "Les petits fous de la petite noblesse." With a flick of his reins, he leaves them, and they stand, watching the carriage disappear around the bend, listening to its rumble and clatter fade across the fields.

One hour to change all. She shivers and takes Millevoye's arm, steers him towards the cemetery gates left unlocked by a bribe to the sexton. Oh but it is cold out here in open countryside. Together they walk a slow, curiously formal walk, side by side, step for step, as if she were a bride and he her father escorting her up the aisle. Wearing their evening clothes and each of a height, they make a handsome couple yet, even if there is nobody but the tombstones to see them.

At the furthest side of the cemetery, Millevoye lays down his bundle before the finest mausoleum. He tries the key but the lock on the vault is troublesome; after wrestling with it for a time, he begins throwing petulant looks back over his shoulder. *Tut*, clicks his tongue. And again: *tut*. Maud Gonne closes her eyes to shut him out. He wishes—she can hear his thoughts clear as if he spoke them aloud—to blame her. Why, he would like to ask, has she allocated to him the task of opening up when the difficult lock is so much more familiar to her.

Oh Millevoye, Millevoye...

She will not permit him to disturb her equilibrium. It is hardly her fault that he has visited his son's tomb so rarely that he doesn't know the knack of unclicking that bolt, really quite simple when you are used to it. And has she not agreed with him the timetable of this evening, the exact distribution of tasks and duties? Agreed it over and again during the past days, so often that he told her to desist, that he needed no more directives or instructions? So what is this huffing and tutting for now, this giving of himself over to pique?

She inhales deep, wrapping herself inside what is to come, so his vexation cannot infect her and the work they have to do. The key clicks, as she knew it would, and the door opens with what seems like a sigh, puffing stale, malodorous air into their faces. Maud Gonne gasps: that dead stench, so much more concentrated by night, holds all their early grief in it. It slides in under the rivets in her mind, freeing incarcerated memories, allowing them to pierce her again. Her fear of the Grey Lady who showed herself to be a child-killer...

Is all that passed her fault?

She wills these thoughts from her mind, as she has so often before. With her will, she can do anything. Anything. Tommy taught her that, and isn't she here tonight to prove it once more?

She extends her hand to Millevoye, a mute request for him to hand over what he carries so she can take it down into the crypt.

"I do not think you can manage alone," he says, aloud. "It is so dark down there."

He has spoken. Spoken!

She wants to slap him to silence but restricts herself to placing her index finger on his lips. Be quiet, this finger insists. You know what is agreed.

He pulls back. For one moment she thinks he might turn and march off, past the watching gravestones, out the cemetery gate, into the night. She sees him consider it, knowing the reluctance she has had to overcome to get him here tonight, for his parliamentary enemies would like nothing more than to have such a *scandale* to spread... His eyes lock with hers in one of their mute struggles. Always so vexatious with each other, now: it exhausts her. Such a waste of energy—and tonight, it cannot be permitted: it will corrupt the mood.

She pulls herself up to her full height so she can transfer to him her thoughts. *We seek a reunion of the spirits. Our task is sacred. Let us banish petty human aggravations. Let us lay ourselves open to the spark of fire of the soul. Let us cast ourselves down in humble surrender so that we may become instruments of rebirth.*

He drops her gaze, in what feels almost like a bow, and her heart shudders: he has made her a pledge, a most grave and solemn promise. With the act that is to come, all will be reprieved.

She takes the candles and blankets from him, enters the crypt. Some might fear to go into a vaulted tomb by night but not she. It is only Georges down there, nothing to fear. She closes her eyes. It's so dark in here, sight will not serve her. She must rely on other senses. Hugging her armload, she takes a step forward, the flat of one foot nudging, engaging the whole of the step. Then the next. She is glad she wore her flattest boots.

It is colder in the crypt and damp. She lays down her bundle, feels among the candles for the tallest, fattest pair, the two she will place on either side of the coffin. The touch of cold candle-wax recalls her son's embalmed limbs: the same unbending texture. Tonight the warmth of flame will soften the wax.

The rasp of a match never sounded so loud, the glare of its flame so bright. One wick, then another, and the little crypt is suddenly filled with light. She stretches out her arms to place one hand on each side of the tombstone and bends until her forehead touches stone.

O, great spirits, purify and strengthen us and seal our lips for the work. Titans of light, higher souls: make of us your instrument.

She recalls the swollen face that was Georges and not Georges, his tiny starfish hands laid one upon another and now always to be thus. Those fingers, reaching up to touch her face, the wonder in his eyes at the brush of her skin. *Spear of Lugh, pierce the night. Let the essence of God, the spark of fire of the soul, flow down into the cauldron of regeneration and rebirth.*

She takes up the smaller candles and places in as wide a circle as the walls permit, wide enough for two tall people to lie within. In the center of the tombstone she lays the two blankets—folded lengthways into two strips—at right angles to each other in the form of a cross. Then she briskly lights the rest of the candles, all forty-eight of them, before kneeling for a final, quick invocation.

She has to hurry now; it is almost time.

Tonight, they shall make amends.

Tonight, atonement and retribution would be theirs.

She stands and, trying not to shiver, begins to peel off her clothes.

~

Above, sheltering in the small space between the door and the top of the stairs, Millevoye smokes and waits, the base of his cigarette flattened between two frozen fingers. He can hear her moving about below, see the faint glow coming on at the end of the stairs. He knows she is lighting the candles: forty-eight small ones, two thick, large ones: fifty in all. Already the chill of night is seeping through to his bones. *Sacré bleu*, why the devil did he agree to this madness?

He blames her crazed Irish friends. It is they who are responsible for all her follies. Poets are always mad but the Celtic types are the worst. He said as much to her last week.

"But Millevoye, it was you, not Mr. Yeats or Mr. Russell, who gave me the idea," she replied, and reminded him of the time he tried to persuade her, she who wanted to conceive an Irish patriot hero, to make love before the altar of Jeanne D'Arc in Paris Cathedral. He remembered then: how he bribed the sacristan but it all came to naught. And now, years later, this eerie travesty of his intention. On her terms. She really is the very devil of a woman.

The way she looked him in the eye before she went below, her finger pressed to his lips, attempting to subdue him. *Hah!* Once such behavior would have delighted him, the challenge of breaking her, of turning hauteur to need. Once, he treasured that arrogant head of hers, but now he knows it for a sham. All her fire is surface, as is the beauty that once consumed him. Beneath, she is the same as the rest.

Women are at their best when barely known, Millevoye has concluded. Time always turns the outer charms transparent. One comes to see the snarl of complications beneath, the chaos that lies at the heart of all females. It is true what he said to Déroulède: a mistress held too long becomes another wife.

Slap-slap-slap: from the foot of the steps come three loud handclaps, his cue to go down. He drops his cigarette, sparks falling through the dark, and crushes it underfoot. She pretends to mastery and he to submission, but they both know the truth: it is pity that has hauled him here tonight.

Yet what power these women wield in their weakness.

In the crypt, all is light, giving an illusion of warmth. Two candles, tall pillars of light, stand sentry over the tomb. There she is, surrounded by the wide ring of candles, naked to the skin. Lying out like Christ on his crucifix, arms outstretched across two blankets. Around her neck she wears her father's timepiece while candlelight gleams on the pale mound of her belly, along the skin of her thighs, across the rise of her breasts and her erect nipples, standing to attention. Is it just the cold—or has this bizarre ritual injected the sex act with some excitement?

Impossible to know as she keeps her eyes closed, her face impassive. Her father's fob watch is open, reading nine minutes to midnight. What if he were to leave her here, naked and unfulfilled? Is that not what she has done to him so often, with her fastidious aversion? And not just since Georges' death, though that is what she likes to pretend. What if he were to leave her, to know for herself that humiliation? *Bah!* Why does he torment himself with this nonsense? He knows he will do as he has pledged.

All he has to do is squint his eyes a little so he can forget what festers between them. Limit his attention to her fine physique. She is, after all, the most beautiful woman in the world, and not just according to that idiot, Stead. So center on those two peaked breasts, those long thighs, the shadow of promise between them. Why think of saying no, what man would? See, already it is working.

Already, he feels the stirring he needs. He shrugs off his overcoat, lets it lie where it fell at the end of the steps. Removes his jacket and waistcoat, his trousers and shirt, his undergarments and his stockings until he is as naked as she. The chill air on his bare skin feels almost solid. The cement floor underfoot is not dry. Damp, he hopes, and not the secretions of some animal.

Stepping into the circle of candles, he kneels on the edge of the blanket in front of Maud Gonne. No response. He bends to kiss her lips, lying along the length of her. Her skin is ice; she is like a corpse, her lips rigid under his. Her body holds its crucified position. Is she to be unmoving throughout, a passive receptacle? In her little lectures about who was to do what, she never covered that detail.

He reaches for her hands, splaying his arms out along hers, but she holds them in two tight fists. The devil! He will make her open at least her hands to him. With his fingers he prizes hers apart. Something is clutched in her grasp.

Something suede. He holds it to the candle: a small shoe, one in each hand. Georges' bootees that they bought for him in San Raphael.

Her lips are moving but making no sound. He moves to close her murmurs with his mouth. Forget the bootees, forget the cof-

fin... the lace robe... the small, solid, half-pouting, baby mouth...
Forget, forget... He feels for her breasts, squeezes the mounds of
flesh, thinks to take one in his own mouth. Yes, yes, a surge of
strength swells in his veins. He is in command, a man again.

~

Maud Gonne is glad she has kept her eyes fastened. He is
quite, quite lost to her now, sunk into his own coarseness, almost hurting her. No matter—she anticipated as much. Tonight
is about more than male pleasure. Tonight, he is for her what
she has so often been to him, a means to an end.

This is what he has done to her, to them. She turns her head
and, without making it obvious, checks Tommy's watch. Almost
time. She opens her legs, guides Millevoye into place. As he breaks
her, she cries out, a small surprised shriek. Not her cry of old, but
he, with his thickening breath, shows no sign of understanding
that. Another glance at the time—one minute to go—and she
touches him on the buttocks, their signal, and he increases his
rhythm, plunging in and in again. She feels his moment approach,
the moment he wants to last forever, the moment that heralds its
own demise. She arches her hips to meet it, once... twice... thrice...

*May the spirits rise to meet us. May perpetual light shine upon us. May
the great Mother move to bring forth life. Life out of death, life out of death
eternally...*

As he climaxes (at—yes!—exactly midnight), as his seed
shudders through her, she is flooded with gratitude. Tears,
which since the death of Georges are always too ready to over-
run, rise, but she squeezes them back. No tears, no tears: they
have succeeded.

After a time, Millevoye lifts his head from her breast and tries
to shift, but she grips his shoulders, pins him with her eyes.
"This," she says, "is our greatest act together."

His eyes swivel from hers, unwilling to follow her thought.
Exasperating man. Then, almost to their own surprise, they
are drawn back. He stares at her, and wonder of this wondrous
night, through this staring intensity, she feels him submit. It is
as if he seeks to gaze into her soul, his expression is so intense,
so solid. He has need of her still.

"We have succeeded," she tells him with great, definite tenderness.

"How can you know this?"

"We have succeeded."

Life out of death. Light from the darkness. Unto us a child is born.

In truth, Millevoye is gazing not at her but at the reflection of fifty flames dancing in her eyes. Past the steaming fervor of Maud Gonne's certainty he stares, into the mystery of light.

Land Of
Heart's Desire

AND SO A NEW child begins, as we all began, in the channel of a woman.

One spark of time during which Maud Gonne's egg accepts one of Lucien's Millevoye's sperm and—*voilà!*—where a moment before there were two entities, now there is one. A bud of embodied potential.

When I think of the moment of conception, I always imagine the just fertilized egg pausing, as if overcome by what has just happened.

Then gathering itself for what's ahead, launching itself on its precarious way towards the womb, intent on implantation, and subdividing itself as it goes. From one cell to two, two to four, four to sixteen, 16 to 256, 256 to 65,536, 65,536 to... Well, on and on, in numberless number, the gradual firming of potential that takes nine months to complete. The process has hardly started for Maud Gonne before she is telling dear friend Ghénia that she knows, just knows, her endeavors have been successful: she is *enceinte*.

Ghénia lifts her head from among the hats. They are in the millinery department of Le Printemps.

"My dear, really? How wonderful. But are you sure?"

Dear Ghénia. Maud Gonne knows she is concerned. For two years now, since Georges' death, her friend has kindly endured what Maud Gonne knows herself has been, at times, almost an obsession for her.

"Oh yes, one just knows." She smiles at her friend, through the looking-glass, preens a hat. "Tell me, what do you think of this one?"

"I preferred the green."

"Yes. Simple lines are always best, are they not?"

"And that shade is more becoming to your hair."

She is glad today for the frivolity of hats. The knowledge of her condition has come trailing fronds of memory: recollections of little Georges' weight in her arm, the smoothness of his baby cheek touched to hers, the aroma of him, cleaner than lilac, softer than powder... Memories that, before Samois, were unbearable can now, she finds, be borne.

This pleases her. To be cowering from her own thoughts was something Maud Gonne hated. During that broken, incoherent autumn of 1891, each memory was a scalpel slicing into her wound. For a long time, too long a time, survival required denial.

"I think to give the good news to Lucien on Christmas Day," she says.

Ghénia frowns. "You are sure he will be pleased?"

"Of course. Think of the trouble we took. There is nothing he wants more. Nothing."

In the mirror, Ghénia opens her mouth as if to speak, then closes it again.

"Yes," Maud Gonne repeats. "What day could be more fitting than 25th of December to make the announcement that another significant son is about to born?" She ties the two long ribbons of her bonnet into a bow under her chin and turns her head this way and that in the mirror, taking care not to see how her friend is taking this blasphemy. "Yes, Christmas Day it shall be."

~

Christmas dinner at the Yeats house has descended into argument. It began harmless enough, with JB starting a Christmas speech on the state of the family, of how Jack was soon to marry and become a substantial man, with a cheerful kind-hearted wife and an open-handed welcome for his friends. This created the first awkwardness, as all in the room know that Jack and his fiancée are tying up her money so that JB won't be able to get his hands on any of it.

His father's self-serving cheerfulness wilts WB's spirits even before the ceremonial wineglass is turned on him. "And Willie will be famous and shed a bright light on us all, with sometimes a little money and sometimes not."

He drank and sat, signifying the end of the toast, whereupon Lolly's face began to redden. Lily reached over to pat her hand, a gesture that only doubled her sister's fury.

Papa noticed and hastily stood back up. "And Lolly will have a prosperous school and give away as prizes her eminent brother's volumes of poetry."

This, naturally, only enraged her the more. At that moment, Rose arrived in and plunked the plate of potatoes on the table. When Willie reached for one with his fork, it gives Lollly the outlet her angry hurt is seeking: "You might wait for grace before meals, Willie. You might wait until Mama is settled."

He looks at the potato sitting on the end of his fork, like a head on a spike, and says, "I think to go to Paris," taking them all, not least himself, by surprise.

"What?" Lolly replies. "You think to *what?*"

And she launches herself on a great oration about how *she* would like to go to Paris but there would never be money out of her wages by the time the household expenses were met. That there would never be enough time either, or permission from any of them to just take herself off, wash-day or some other female task would prevent it, blah de blah...

He is appalled to see in her again the same detestable excitability from which he suffers himself. He knows from his Order studies that she has Mars in square with Saturn while he has Moon in opposition to Mars. He determines again to exclude this irritability from his writing and speech, to escape it through adoption of a gracious style.

Is not one's art made out of the struggle in one's soul? His sister cannot understand that beauty is a victory over oneself.

JB congratulates him, asking about his intentions during the trip, and whether he has managed any letters of introduction.

"From York Powell to see Mallarmé, actually, and from Symons to Verlaine."

Which impresses Papa and surely must highlight to the misguided Lolly the difference between the needs of a poet and those of a kindergarten teacher.

But no. "This trip of yours," she says, "it has nothing to do with a certain Miss Maud Gonne, I suppose."

Papa interjects. "Now, now, Lolly."

"Like a little lapdog," she spits, her face burnt ugly red. "You should be ashamed."

Willie decides to be solicitous: "Are you tired, Lolly?"

"Tired?"

"Combined housekeeping and kindergarten anxieties too much for you, perhaps?"

Such elaborate courtesies always incense her. A while ago, when she complained of household tasks, he got up one morning to make her tea before she left for school, and the memory of her annoyance amused him for a week. Today his little gibe raised her rant some degrees higher, while her face grows red as a fishmonger's, but he draws no pleasure from this.

Mama sits, staring at them, in scowling oblivion.

He finds himself pushing away from the table, saying, "I am no longer hungry."

His father tells him to sit back down, and Lily says in her most plaintive voice, "Please Willie, it is Christmas," but he runs from the room, as if pursued.

~

Speechifying father, ravaged mother, clinging sisters, soon-to-be-married brother: he repudiates them all. He reaches his room and slams fast its door behind him. In the coming year, he must leave this house. He *must* escape this family of his, so drifting and useless. All this and also his drifting and hopeless love. He lies, face into his pillow, impaling himself upon his emotions. He loves! He loves! Five yearning years are surely reaching a crescendo. Either that, or the time has come to set it aside, this love that keeps him in unctuous celibacy.

She has abandoned him. Is it that vague desire of hers for some impossible life, some unvarying excitement, like the heroine of his play, *The Land of Heart's Desire*? The vague idealisms and impossible hopes which blow in upon us to the ruin of near and substantial ambitions?

Once he believed they would be together, he the poet-priest of a new age, she the human incarnation of female divinity, but for months, she has neglected their occult interests and freezes him with business letters.

And now she wishes to leave the Order. She has become suspicious, says she, of Golden Dawn links with the Freemasons. They hold initiation ceremonies in the Masons' Hall, and a friend has revealed that some of the order's passwords belong to the higher grades of freemasonry. In France and in Ireland, the Masons are pro-England, pro-Empire, and her mind, twisted by Boulangists, turns always on conspiracies.

He hears scandal about her all the time. The grosser scandal he knows to be untrue. He has heard untruths about his own relationship to her. And one persistent story he puts away with the thought that she would have told him. He holds always to the line of his poem: "their children's children will say: 'They lied'."

Despite what Lolly thinks—what they all think, except maybe Papa—it is not just for Maud Gonne that he makes this trip to the French capital. In February, Paris will see a performance of Villiers de l'Isle-Adman's *Axel*. Symbolists everywhere eagerly await this play: five hours of elevated drama where all the characters are symbols and all the events allegories. Only in France would a drama five hours long be tolerated.

Thinking of the Rosicrucian wisdom that inspired *Axel*'s creator restores his equilibrium a little. Perhaps he would never marry, but like those esoteric lovers, he would love his chosen woman unto death. Thinking such, he finds his hand journeying under his leg, towards the forbidden regions. He corrects himself, tucks them into two fists under his chest.

It is a torture to him, this enforced celibacy. He is not naturally chaste, and this continual struggle wears his nerves, but he knows of old that giving in to the impulse is worse. He turns determinedly, with a great sigh, to lie on his back.

A knock comes to the door, jerking him bolt upright on the bed. It is Rose, bearing a tray.

"Miss Lily said you'd better prefer to eat here, Sir."

His impulse is to wave it away, but he knows Lily would return with it herself. He waves the girl towards the table, and she thumps down the tray, thumps across the room and thumps the door closed behind her. He stares at the tray of food as if it presents him with a quandary. He has made of poverty a virtue. No matter how rich he might become in future, he also knows he will always walk to his work and eat little meat, for asceticism has become one of his ideals.

So what of this food, here, now? Should he, after his protest, eat it or leave it?

He gets off his bed, lifts the lid. Ham, which arrived anonymously on their doorstep two evenings ago from some tactful friend. Without such kindnesses, this household would fall apart. He never knows whether he considers his father courageous in this or negligent. A leg of the goose, sent from Sligo. Potatoes and buttered swede. On a smaller plate, brandy pudding and a slice of cake.

He pulls up a chair and begins to eat, mindlessly ingesting mouthful after mouthful, without pause, taking no drink. Thinking.

He shall ask Maud Gonne to accompany him to *Axel* and explain to her its importance. "The greatest work you can do for Ireland is to raise our literature," she has so often urged. "For the honor of our country, the world must recognize you as one the Great Poets of the century."

Was this not dew shining through a love decayed by slanderous tongues? Yes, yes, he thinks through his swede and potatoes, he shall go to her in Paris.

Dreams That Never Bend

ACROSS THE channel at exactly the same time as the poet is hurling himself up his father's stairs, Maud Gonne is tripping down the little steps that lead to her hallway, where Millevoye is hanging his cape and putting his umbrella in the stand. In Rue de la Tour, he was as her husband, coming and going as he pleased, but after their quarrel, she gave up those rooms, and here, as yet, he is a curious mixture of inhabitant and guest. After Christmas, she will take a more substantial apartment, for they shall have need of a nurse again.

He hands her a box of chocolates, and she gives him thanks most charming, though in truth she thinks little of such a thoughtless gift. In the drawing room, he stands before the fire, as is his way, rubbing his hands together.

"A drink?" she asks. Maud Gonne drinks little alcohol herself but she keeps a good cabinet.

"I shouldn't. I had too much last night, with Déroulède."

She waits.

"Perhaps a small glass of claret."

"How is our friend?" she asks, as she locates the decanter.

"Tolerable. As good as a man can be who has lost everything."

"Hardly *everything*, Millevoye. He still has family and friends, and he still has work to do." Her look as she hands him the crystal glass is pointed. "Just because he has lost his seat does not mean there is not work to be done."

A gust of rain bursts against the large window. "What a damnable day," he says, face scored with displeasure.

"We are well out of it."

She decides not to ask him whether she should heat the food, she'll get no good out of him for such a question in this mood. They shall have it as it is. She resolves to be tender. He is always unsettled by time with Madame. She must be charming, soothing, in contrast.

"So," she says, lifting her glass. "To a new year and a better one."

"It could hardly be worse."

"Oh come, *mon cher*. Do not take on so. We must fight back, so that in the next election, we regain what has been lost."

"Don't you ever tire, Maud, of the fight?"

"Certainly. And when I am tired, I rest. Thus I gather my strength for the next battle."

"I am forty-three. Too old for battles."

"Pouf! That is what you said after Boulanger's suicide. That you were finished."

"And maybe I should have finished then. Then this forgeries debacle should never have happened."

She had been in Manchester, on the speech trail, when she first heard of his humiliation. In the lobby of the Imperial Hotel, she had spotted the headline in the newspaper being read by a man at the breakfast table opposite. "*Deputy Millevoye's 'Revelations'??*" it squawked. Those hateful, ominous, question marks told her everything. Millevoye had been planning his revelation speech for months.

She sent the boy for a copy of *The Times* and read it with quailing heart, plate of kidney and bacon pushed aside.

"*...M. Millevoye stood before the deputies, lifting one by one the sheets and reading from them passages which were supposed to be incriminating of M. Clemenceau, but which were in fact quite devoid of serious interest. Hearing them greeted only by jeers or ironical laughter, he began to see the ridiculousness of his plight...*"

She wanted to dash immediately across the English Channel, to give him comfort. For all their differences these days, she agonized to see him humiliated.

Now, a six-month on, the unforgiving words remained to the

front of his life: "...M. Millevoye then pretended that there were some sentences which discretion forbade him to read but the Chamber saw through this. Each time he paused, they urged him with cries of 'go on, go on'. When he finally conceded to read the passages, they greeted them with long bursts of hilarity..."

Déroulède was forced to resign from the chamber that day, and when the papers proved to be forgeries, Millevoye forced to follow. He has since stuck to his story that it was all a set-up by Clemenceau, that he created the forgeries and drew them in, with spies and charlatans, all simply to undermine them. A piece of double-cross worthy of the Medicis. Maud Gonne almost believes him.

"I have a suggestion for you," she says. "Something that will help you fight back."

He groans and ducks his head down into his shoulders.

"But Millevoye, it is a fine idea. Don't you want to hear?"

"Why can you not just let me be?"

"Because, in reality, you do not want to be so let. Shall I tell you?"

"Can I stop you?"

"Jules Jaluzot is looking for an editor for his newspaper *La Patrie*."

Aha! There, she has surprised him. Jaluzot, director of the department store Le Printemps, is one of the richest men in Paris. And in Paris, every man who climbs to political or financial eminence shields himself with a newspaper.

"And what makes you think he would accept me?"

She and Jaluzot have already discussed the possibility, but Maud Gonne judges it untactful to tell him this, just yet.

She also resists the impulse to say: "Ah! So you are interested." saying instead: "Of course he would want you. What other writer of your caliber could he get?"

Really she is becoming quite the better person in this two-some.

He makes a modest face, to cover up his pleasure at this.

"You know it is true, Millevoye. Nobody uses words like you. How was it that Englishman described your writing: 'Sinewy'?"

"'Sinewy and mellifluous,'" he says with a little laugh.

"And he was right. He was right. You can make words dance like champagne."

"But *La Patrie*? Who reads it?"

"It is not worth reading now. But you are the very person to make that little-read paper the instrument with which we can rebuild our work."

He takes a long draught of wine. She refills his glass, enjoying how the cut glass makes the liquid shine like rubies in the glow of the fire. She tries not to push but when he doesn't speak, she says, "It would take time, yes, but with it you could regain your old influence a hundredfold."

"I don't know, Maud. Sometimes I think I might be best out of public life altogether. That the Boulangists, and all we stood for, have had our time. That we are a hangover from another, more noble age."

"Millevoye," she pauses for effect, "Our son will want a father whom he can admire."

But he doesn't hear. He is distracted, considering the proposal.

"Millevoye!" she calls him to attention, places her hand on her abdomen, and the words she just said reach their mark.

"Really?"

"Yes, our undertaking at Samois was successful."

"You are sure?"

"Quite, quite certain."

He drains his glass, the base of the crystal pointed at her, as he tilts back his head.

"And the stars are auspicious," she says. "I have checked."

He picks up the decanter and pours himself another.

"Though when he is born, I shall get Mr. Yeats to do a proper horoscope."

He swallows again, the sound loud.

To fill the gap he is leaving so wide, she says: "Did I ever tell you that I was born myself on a full moon at the exact moment of the winter solstice?"

"Yes."

"And what it means? According to Mr. Yeats, Mercury and Neptune both stopping their march across the sky like that is a moment associated with the birth of gods."

"Yes, Maud. You have told me this, many times."

"But wouldn't it be wonderful if such a sign were to be given to us at this birth."

He shrugs, his usual response to her astrology talk, to be sure. But...

"You do not seem happy, Millevoye."

"Happy? I am, I suppose, a trifle overwhelmed."

"Oh yes, that is natural. But it is wonderful, is it not? Truly, Millevoye, I believe that today represents—"

"When is the date? The summer?"

"Early August, I am told."

He nods, slowly and definitely then seems to give himself a shake. "I am sorry, *chérie*. Of course you are right. Of course this is good news." He picks up the decanter and his glass and comes across to sit beside her.

"Do you mean our child?" she asks. "Or the newspaper job?"

"Both."

"Oh Millevoye, truly?"

"Yes. Yes. Both."

"Oh darling, I am so pleased. And my plans to adopt Eileen also go well, so he shall have a big sister to look after him."

"Have you told anybody else?"

"About Eileen?"

"About the pregnancy."

"Only Ghénia."

He grimaces. He and her friend have had unending disputations of late.

"You should wait a while, I believe, before telling anybody else," he says, his voice holding a gentleness that recalls bygone times. "At least until you are beyond the three-month point." He takes one of her hands in his. "Remember what happened with Madame Millevoye."

"Millevoye!" What a thing to say. Does he not know how it hurts her to hear him so casually mention that? No, thoughts:

be gone! Center instead on the concerned timbres of his talk; she has not felt such concern from him in many a day. Recline back into this beautiful consideration, as Macha lies back into a warm shaft of sunshine. Yes, that is better. He places a hand on her knee. When she does not rebuff, he places the other on the dip of her waist and leans across to place his lips on hers.

"*Chérie*," he says, pulling back from the kiss to look in her eyes. "You must take greater care of yourself."

Something flutters in the base of her, like a repressed memory. She has created this new tenderness, so like the old, through sheer force of will. He kisses her again. A small flick of his tongue she allows. A little more, still permitted. He lets a sigh and she is surprised, as always, by the speed and intensity of his rising need. She does not halt the tentative brushing of her breasts through her clothing, the sliding of his other hand behind her back, his first fumblings with her neck buttons...

But by the time he has got through a quarter of them, her flickering ardor has dissolved. Her hip hurts. He is leaning too heavily, pushing a corner of her pelvis against a hard bar underpinning the upholstery. She shifts. Better.

She lets him proceed.

Why? Not because she fears him—she is not one of his chanteuses—but to stop him now would be to break the unspoken code they have evolved between them: that if she is not willing, she should turn aside or otherwise deflect his advances before or just after the mouth-on-mouth kiss. Now he drops soft kisses to her lips and eyes while he negotiates the detestable buttons and offers attentions that he thinks pleasing to her.

This will, she determines, be the final time until after their son is born. From now on, her condition will excuse her. He begins to draw patterns on the surface of her body.

It is when she feels his hand fumbling with the front of his trousers that she knows she can't go on. "Millevoye..."

"*Mmmmmm...*"

"I'm sorry. I—"

"*Chérie*, you are so beautiful. *Tu es si belle.*"

Faithless, false, meaningless. *His* need, *his* demand, patronizing her. Her beauty, or lack of it, is largely irrelevant. She puts her hands to his shoulders. "Truly Millevoye, I cannot. I feel a pain..."

He opens his eyes, perplexed, stops his hand so it wavers above her body.

"I am sorry, I do not feel well," she reiterates. "My condition."

"Oh, your condition. Pardon me." He snaps away from her, turns to fix his breeches.

Of course he is angry, he has a right to be angry. Maud Gonne must bring all her tact to bear now; if she doesn't soothe him, he might leave, and this she can't bear, not today. Not Christmas Day, not the day decreed for their joyous announcement.

"Thank you, Millevoye. I am..."

"Thank you." His voice is bitterly sarcastic. "Oh you are most welcome, Mme Gonne."

"Please, do not be vexed."

"Your vocabulary is poorly chosen, my dear."

"Millevoye, let us not fall out over this small thing when we have so many momentous things to be glad of today."

"It is true, what Déroulède said."

"Déroulède?"

"Every man who sees Maud Gonne wants her, but the sensible man soon sees that she is cold as the ocean bed."

"Millevoye, please..."

"You are frigid, Madame."

Frigid. What is that? A man's word for what he cannot have. "It was not always thus, Millevoye."

"I should have followed my friend's advice, beaten my retreat long ago. Cold, cold, cold..."

Enough. "If I *am* cold, you know well why."

"...as the ocean bed."

"It is not I who betrayed our love, Millevoye. It was you who did that when you asked me to sleep with de Rochefort to further your career."

This is the evil at the base of all their trouble: Boulanger's suicide, Parnell's heart attack, Georges' meningitis. The evidence is undeniable. All the horrors that followed are their punishment. Since she realised, she has been doing all she can to make amends. Taking across Eileen so that Georges might have a big sister and many other plans unfolding.

He has jumped to his feet. "Ah *non!*" he says. "*Non!* Not this, *again.*"

She stands too, tries to get him to look at her, to get beyond the hurt. "This pregnancy we have been given: it is a sign of forgiveness, Millevoye. Don't you see? We have been given another chance. We must protect it."

"By not making love?"

"Now that our love has resulted in a child, we should be content."

"*Pah!* Once could as easily say, now that our love has resulted in a child, we should love more often."

She takes his hand in both of hers; his fingers are bony. "Millevoye, this is no personal whim, it is what the gods demand. And not forever, just for now. We shall know when it is right again."

"Oh yes. When Maud Gonne deems it right." He slips his hands from her grasp. "We should never have come back together."

"Lucien!"

"Why reunite, if nothing is forgiven? I have apologized to you, Maud, over and again for what happened with de Rochefort. Explained my misunderstanding—"

"Don't use that word for it, *ever*. I have told you."

"Laid myself prostrate before you, but there is no forgiveness."

"It is not my forgiveness that counts, Millevoye, but that of the gods. Otherwise we are doomed. See what is happening to us right here." So long as he refuses to acknowledge his sins, she is forced to be a moral nature for two.

"Pay! We never have to worry about the gods' forgiveness for Maud Gonne's errors."

He turns away, towards the door. "I bid you good-day, Madame."

"Millevoye, don't go. We can—"

But he has already marched from the room with such purpose that to follow would be pure humiliation.

So she sits back down amid the remains of their day, the half-empty decanter, the candles and chocolates, listening to him retrieving his cape and slamming the door behind him. Oh, why didn't she just let him have his way? It wouldn't have taken long; by now, they would have been sitting happily together, talking.

That was the mental image she had clasped to herself for weeks: the pair of them reclining in togetherness on this chaise, she in the crook of his arm, exchanging gentle whispers about their darling new baby-to-be. She wants to suggest that they should name him for their dead son, and Millevoye's dead *général*. A tribute to their younger and happier selves, when they were full of what Willie Yeats calls the blossoming dreams that never bend.

Right now, she should have been explaining to Millevoye how this baby is the acknowledgement of all that went before and in that, their entrée into a new life together, a new way of being, wherein their hopes might rise again.

Instead...

Oh but it is the coming child who is the point of significance. What does another quarrel signify? They have quarreled before over similar sex rejections. He forgave then and would forgive again. He has to, does he not, now that she once again carries his child? A patriot son to redeem all their losses.

The Winds That Awaken The Stars

CALL ME IRISH, if you must. It's what they used to call me when I first went to England, not as a description, as a name. *Hey Irish, clean this! Hey Irish, fetch that! Lift your feet, Irish, do as you're bid!* And then in Paris too, when I worked for old Mrs. McAuley, for I told her about this, and how much it annoyed me, and it became her nickname for me, as a joke. *Tell me, Irish, what you're seeing in that picture—and don't speak too fast, now.* And then I never minded again.

Dear Mrs. McAuley, her eyes were very bad, but she could see things others couldn't.

She'd been born a FitzGerald of Johnstown but she married Hugh McAuley, a Fenian dynamitard who got himself locked up for eight in Pentonville prison and went to Paris on getting out. Paris—the city of light, the city of artists and occultists, the city of sin—was also the city of the exiled Irish, and Paris was always a better place to be Irish than London. *Les Irlandais sont une race bien sympathique*, the French say, but really it's the old saying. My enemy's enemy is my friend.

What a lot of thought we gave to all that back then. The French were dreaming of *revanche*, of getting to stride around Europe again, all Napoleonic, and we were dreaming a new country into being. In both countries, our nationalists kept harking back. To the old beliefs and ways and tales, to the great days before the Teuton Protestants—the Germans and English—came in and ruined everything.

The city suited old McAuley well and they stayed on, when others drifted back to Dublin or London. They had money, don't ask me how; I never learned in all my time with him. Maybe her family, maybe a nod-and-wink source from America.

My job for her was like that of a lady's companion. To read aloud for her and take her to the shops or the art galleries and talk to her. Listen to her, which I was glad to do. Be her eyes but also be an ear.

Listening and reading to Mme McAuley was my university. She gave me a sense of history, taught me how to locate the same characters across time, and how to look back and check first before laying out an opinion. Most people treat history, if they are aware of it at all, as their own personal backup file, rummaging through the centuries to pull out whatever inter-pretation of events they fancy. The devil can cite history for his purpose, Mme McAuley used to say, explaining how she despised argument and opinion.

People were what mattered to her, and like a true Republi-can, that meant all the people, rich and poor, black and white, men and women, French and German and English too. Instead of hating war, she loved peace. Instead of railing against men, she was all for women. Instead of running down England, she worked for Ireland. A proper understanding of history does away with hatred, she used to say, when talking about Maud Gonne. "Maudgonning" for Mrs. Mac was recklessly and flam-boyantly agitating for a cause.

I felt it differently for I felt, I believe, what Maud Gonne felt. For us, it was simple: until Ireland was free, her people could not be free. Until Ireland was prosperous, her people could not be prosperous. All who live in the free part of Ireland now need to be thankful, for wasn't it the minority that thought like that who willed our free Ireland into existence? It is for this, not her beau-ty, or its effect on the poet, or her incompetent conspiracies with French royalists, that some of us remember Maud Gonne yet.

Anyhow, all this is only by way of saying that I was in Paris in 1894, when WB paid her a visit. I saw him there one day, alone in the Luxembourg Gardens, smoking a cigarette.

~

He is only able to afford the trip because he stays with Mathers, who has moved to Paris with his new wife, Moina, to be closer to the Order's Secret Chiefs. At the time of WB's visit, Henri Bergson, Moina's brother, is also staying. The four play chess together in the evenings. If Bergson is not there—and as WB's visit goes on, he seems to spend more and more evenings away—WB partners Moina, while Mathers plays with a spirit partner. He covers his eyes with his hands, then moves his piece according to instructions from the empty chair across.

Their instructors have said that Mathers is now to be called McGregor Mathers, having divulged to him a Scottish ancestry. He styles himself The Comte de Glenstrae and is now regularly to be found in tartan, doing the highland fling, tossing silver daggers around his head. In a kilt, with daggers in his stockings he feels, he tells WB, "like a walking flame."

WB has a new costume too, in the style of Oscar Wilde and London's other aesthetes. A long, black cloak drops from his shoulders, a black silk tie voluminously overflows his collar, loose black trousers droop over his shoes, all topped with a soft black sombrero, and bottomed with an unfortunate pair of yellow shoes. It's the shoes that caught my attention in the garden, them and how he smokes. The cigarette, borne aloft, is part of the ensemble.

He stops to survey the damp flowers in the Luxembourg Gardens. Or maybe, more to be seen surveying, it's hard to tell. He is on his way to see the great symbolist poet, Paul Verlaine, something I find out later. I follow him, down-river from the honeycombs of the Parisian palaces near Mathers... pardon me!... McGregor Mathers' house.

Then away from the rows of identically shaped windows and doors, pillars and steps, so level and perfect, tier upon elegant tier, across the river to the Left Bank, towards the intricate lace of crooked streets behind the Boulevard San Michel. He stops there again for another cigarette, near a bench under the willow trees, too wet to sit on today, and spends a long time gazing into the grey rush of the Seine.

Then he is off again, down to where the cobblestones are damp from the recent shower; the air smells of dissolving horse dung. Narrow lanes of tilting hovels lean into each other, to stay standing. This is where he shall live if he moves to Paris, which he may well do.

He has never met Verlaine in person, having been in Ireland last year when his good friend Arthur Symons organized an English tour for the French poet. Symons has made it his life's work to introduce the French symbolists to the English-speaking world, and what WB has heard from him about Verlaine has made him avid for this meeting. Like Wilde, Verlaine has *lived*. He has known travel, marriage, fatherhood, infidelity, alcoholism, lust, violence, prison.

Married with a child, he had moved in his boy lover, Arthur Rimbaud, to live with his family, until his wife's family intervened and threw the boy out. Then husband and boy fought, passionately, drawing knives or razors, and in one such hotel brawl, Verlaine blasted his lover's hand with a revolver. He was arrested and subsequently imprisoned, officially for assault, though really for sodomy, while Rimbaud left Paris for a new life as a wandering trader in the deserts of Africa.

Rimbaud never wrote or discussed poetry again, dying of cancer aged thirty-seven, and Verlaine now lives on the Left Bank, telling everyone who will listen about Rimbaud's genius.

WB imagines Rimbaud lost in the dusky light of the desert, a fine gold dust settling on his skin, renouncing poetry and Verlaine in his attic room, with an aging mistress, clinging to it. They pose a question to him: for almost ten years now, he has slaved, never deviating from his determination to make poem and story. He has broken his life in a mortar and buried it and raised over it a cairn... of clouds.

In this cairn, he has buried his youth, his peace and all worldly hope. He has seen others enjoying life while he stood alone with himself, commenting, commenting. A mere dead mirror on which things reflect themselves.

McGregor Mathers is encouraging him to come and live in Paris, the cost of living is so very much cheaper than London.

Much depends, as always, on Maud Gonne. Since he arrived in Paris, she has been indisposed. The few times he has seen her, she looks pale and tired, and becomes breathless climbing stairs. A vexation of the spirits, he believes.

She has been friendly enough to him, but their old intimacy is withdrawn. He knows not why. They have gone about together, certainly, walked along the tree-lined boulevards, toured the *Opéra* and *Académie*, spent one long afternoon in The Louvre. She has come to visit the Mathers, and there she told them that she is determined to leave the Order.

She told Mathers that the rituals remind her of the fancy-dress frolics and frivolities of the *Association de Saint Patrick*, and WB thought Mathers would be offended—WB himself was—but Mathers only laughed. He adores Maud Gonne. Aside from present company, she smiled, and Florence Farr and a few others, she has found the members a little... what shall she say... middle-class drab?

WB knows her real word for people like this. Mediocre. She can bear anything in a person except that they be mediocre.

He is in danger of mediocrity himself. It is coming to obsess him, how his time on earth is passing into the composition of words. It is time for him, like Verlaine and Rimbaud, to cast poor poems away and be content to live.

~

She meets him at *Théâtre de la Gaîté*. She is friends with the Director, so they get a private box. The story centers on the life of Axel, a German nobleman who lives in his ancestral castle, deep in the Black Forest, attended only by a few ageing servants, and by the Kabbalist Rosicrucian, Master Janus.

Axel is tempted to leave his secluded life of mystical contemplation and head out into the world, a temptation that's made more acute by the arrival of Kaspar, a worldly courtier, who has heard about the great treasure which legend says is buried on Axel's estate.

Maud Gonne whispers English translations of the action into WB's left ear, and he translates back for her the Rosicrucian lore on which the play is based. The nearness of her as she leans towards his ear is unspeakably erotic. His lips burn for the skin of her bosom, which seems larger, more pronounced, than before, swelling above the folds of her dark green dress.

On stage, Kaspar continues to tempt Axel. If they find the treasure, they can go to the city and be boys about town together at court. Axel is mighty offended by all this and thinks he should challenge Kaspar to a duel, only it's against his morals and Master Janus' teachings. Eventually he gets over himself and kills Kaspar and a surge of diabolical emotion is unleashed by this evil, exciting his interest in the underworld.

Axel finds himself unable to finalize his initiation by Master Janus into the occult mysteries. Another temptation arrives in the form of a distant relation, Sarah, who had been training to be a nun but who has also fallen, and refused to take her final vows.

"You would be magnificent in this role," WB whispers to Maud Gonne as the first act draws towards interval.

"My stage is Ireland," she whispers back, a fleck of her saliva landing on his cheek. He feels it drying on him.

It is a night of overpowering sensuality for WB. He craves her more acutely than ever, a craving like the homesickness he used to have for Sligo, for its black earth and yellow sand, for a bowl of its blue sky overhead. He yearns for her skin and her hair, for her statuesque, overflowing curves, in just the same way: homesick for her, while she is right there in front of him, closer than ever. Yet not his, not his.

What does she really know of him and his longing? Does she realize that the skin on his fingers trembles at the ocean-wide inch of air that separates them from the curve of her neck? Does she feel how he longs to protect her? Her way of life in Paris and Dublin troubles him so. The government is against her and her associates in both places, she is dogged by spies and many clandestine enemies. Always she is hinting at menaces, conspiracy and unnamed betrayals.

Perhaps this play will show her the futility of such a life.

On stage, Sarah and Axel have found the hidden treasure, and are dreaming of traveling together around the world, of experiencing all that life has to offer. After a catalogue of exotic imaginings, Axel recovers his contempt for living and then, in a series of long—very long and very elaborate—arguments he tries to convince Sarah that any real life experience they might have would be vastly inferior to the dreams and imaginings they've just enjoyed. The only way to truth and beauty for them, he reckons, is to commit dual suicide.

She, for reasons unclear, agrees. It takes them over an hour and a quarter to finish themselves off.

~

WB is deeply affected. Afterwards, in the lobby, he waxes forth about the Rosicrucian wisdom, the symbology of the esoteric love-alliance, which can find peace only in death, and mostly by how the play validates his own inclinations towards symbolic drama and poetry.

Maud Gonne is finding it hard to exude the necessary responses. Though, yes, the play was uplifting, in a strange melancholic sort of way, she cannot quite connect with its meaning. She feels so tired, with an unnatural fatigue that is lining all her days, which is new to her. She did not experience this in her first pregnancy. Nothing but a play of Rosicrucian wisdom, where prose is elevated to poetry, could have induced her out this evening, but was it worth the effort?

"I'm not sure I understand it at all," she says.

"It is all the more profound and beautiful because it cannot be intellectually understood."

"Do you think it a masterpiece?"

"I do. Though perhaps it would be more accurate to call it a ceremony. A rite wherein our generation can be initiated."

"I believe the point could perhaps have been made in fewer hours?"

"Perhaps. But the imaginative drama must make mistakes before it can possess the stage again. It is so essentially different to the old melodrama and the new realism that it must learn its powers and limitations for itself. Then it will win all before it."

He shall win all before him, of that she is now certain: already much is being made of his genius. And she is his muse. Through him, she is being immortalized. This would be heady, except that she hardly recognizes herself in his depictions. That one he wrote of her dying in a strange land and the peasants nailing boards above her face: how offended he was when she laughed!

But she couldn't help it because it is so obviously not about her at all but about what he likes to call his "high, old way of love."

It's when his strange fervor merges with their desire to isolate and liberate the Irish national spirit that he writes his best work. This intricate weave has a power she can't begin to unravel, she doesn't even try. She never spends time analyzing such things. She knows only that it is profound and intensely beautiful, something of which she wants to be part.

The childlike, troubled soul that makes him so shy in his manner, gauche in his lovemaking and odd in his ways is also what makes him a great poet. Today he seems especially desperate. Perhaps she is wrong to treat his love so lightly. He is so in thrall to Axel and his notions of suicide. He wouldn't do anything foolish, would he? Sometimes he has a strange look of his mother, that poor woman.

How unforgettably poignant that visit to his home had been, the charming, talkative father offering his many opinions, the two polite sisters, and the silent, black-clad, downcast invalid, ignored by the intense, arm-waving son who looked most like her. Without that visit, she would not understand him as she does.

That word of Maud Gonne's, "weave," is a good word for WB's process, and yes, it's intricate indeed. For him, the self divides not into two but three. Two males: the living, bodily, sexual self and the daemonic, visionary, poetic self. The female is not a self but one of the conditions that contains the warring selves, upholding and feeding the daemon with her sexual allure.

Now, as they leave the theatre, he murmurs again the line from *Axel*. "'Live? The servants will do that for us.'"

"That's one of the lines I don't understand," Maud Gonne says.

"To agree to live is a sacrilege against ourselves, for only in dreams and death can perfection be had. Life is broken and weary. Miss Gonne, I would dearly wish to..."

"I have to confess, after so many hours of sitting, to a little weariness myself. I'm so tired, Mr. Yeats. Do you think we might go home now?"

Pearl-Pale, High-Born Ladies

ON WB's LAST night in Paris, Maud Gonne comes to the McGregor Mathers' house, and Moina performs the Rites of Isis for them, an enchantress in white chiffon, hair flowing loose and crowned by a paper lotus. Once she's finished, Mathers—looking a sight with his Golden Dawn robes on over his kilt, and over that a leopard-skin flung over his left shoulder—leads them in an evocation of the spirits.

Afterwards, when they are all opened by the experience, Maud Gonne and WB bring to the Mathers an idea that has always been live between them, but taking much of their conversation since the night they saw *Axel*. To establish a new Celtic Order, and the rites and rituals that would sustain it, along the lines of the Golden Dawn.

WB has long dreamed of creating an Irish writing school to rival the schools at Eleusis or Samothrace that the ancient Greeks wrote about, where initiates were taught the great religious mysteries and rites, secrets that have been passed down to initiates from generation to generation, and which have come down to them through the Middle Ages.

It has been an obsession with him, more constant than anything but his love for Maud Gonne, to found such a place, and now that she intends to leave the Order, he believes it is necessary to hold her interest and win her love. He says now to the Mathers: "We would go back from the medieval magic to the old Celtic Gods. Instead of thinking of Eleusis and Samothrace or Judea as holy, we must come to know our own Celtic lands as holy."

"And most holy where most beautiful," says Maud Gonne.

"By the writings of our school, Celtic art's secret symbolical relation to the religious mysteries would be reborn," says WB.

"We would create a Castle of the Heroes," Maud Gonne says, with breathy excitement. "An Irish Castle of the Heroes."

She doesn't want Mathers running off with this Celtic idea to Scotland. The point of harnessing the hidden forces of the land is to give strength to patriotic young men and women for the freeing of Ireland. Their new Order would be a counterweight to the Orange Order and Masonic Lodges that hold sway in unionist Ireland, especially in the North.

"Restore the ancient religion of the world to all people?" asks Mathers. "Through our own Celtic magic? Is that what you mean. By Jove."

"By Giobhniu!" laughs Maud Gonne, meaning the Celtic God of weaponry, and they all laugh and begin to speak excitedly. Mathers believes others from the Order can be recruited. Hunter could work them up a Celtic Tree of Life. Or maybe Miss Gyles.

"And Mr. Russell," says Maud Gonne.

All in the room believe that lonely and lovely places are crowded with invisible beings, and that, given the correct mystical rites of evocation and meditation, communication with them is possible. But she and AE and Mathers pass most easily into trance and see visions—figures such as Blake might have drawn, archetypal images of "that age-long memoried self— most distinctly."

WB says he will write stories that would be the signatures, to use the medieval term that is the most accurate he says, of things invisible and ideal. He has one or two stories already sketched out, and a title ready for the volume: *The Secret Rose.*

"Perfect," says Moina Mathers. "Just perfect."

And, says her husband, as if it has all been his idea, he and WB and Maud Gonne and others, where necessary, shall work together on explicating the rituals through which postulants might ascend.

"The Celtic Mysteries," says WB. And they all nod, suddenly a little overawed at their daring. They are talking of nothing less here than a resurrection of the Gods.

Such work shall not be easily done. Symbols and formulae are powers, which act in their own right and with little consideration for human intentions, however excellent. A ritual cannot be consciously developed; it must be obtained through letting the unconscious move of itself.

Does Maud Gonne fully understand this, WB wonders? Perhaps not. Women cannot understand ideas till they have succeeded to some extent, because their minds are practical rather than speculative. But she is excited by it, which is enough for now.

"There shall be great disturbances," says Mathers. "We shall see the streets run with blood."

The women shiver.

"Our rites must combine the best of paganism and Christianity," says WB. "In fifth century Ireland, a man just tonsured by the Druids could learn from his nearest Christian neighbor to sign himself with the cross, without any sense of incongruity. Our school shall be an act of integration, reuniting the radical truths of Christianity with those of a more ancient world, and the Divine with the natural beauty, to unleash the beauty of true freedom. A Castle of the Heroes, as Miss Gonne has said."

The hall door bangs. Henri, Moina's brother, has arrived back and is throwing open the door. "What's on the mystical menu tonight, then?" he asks, cheerily.

The spell is broken.

But hope lives again for WB. If he can only once get her to fully understand his purpose, he believes she would leave her futile struggle, leave all the world, for it. For him.

As she is leaving and he is seeing her to her carriage, she says to him, "When you are back in London, let us try to visit each other on the astral plane. At a fixed hour, send me a thought, and I shall send thought to you. And let us each note down on paper what thought comes to mind and compare, when next we meet."

I Will Not in Grey Hours

I will not in grey hours revoke
The gift I gave in hours of light

Before the breath of slander broke
The thread my folly had drawn tight

The little thread weak hope had made
To bind two lonely hearts in one
But loves of light must fade & fade
Till all the dooms of men are spun,

The gift I gave once more I give
For you may come to winter time
But you white flower of beauty live
In a poor foolish book of rhyme.

In October he goes to Ireland, first Dublin then to Sligo where now he must stay with his uncle and Mary Battle, in George's gloomy little house, Thornhill. They spend days and evenings in experimentation.

He spends a night sleeping out in Sleuth Wood, on the southern shore of Lough Gill, between the lake and the Ox Mountains. He hardly sleeps at all, not so much from the cold, or the hardness of the dry rock on which he makes his bed, as from his fear of the wood-ranger. But he gets to watch the sun rise over the lake and its islands, to note the order in which the birds waken the day, and to feel dawn wind blowing through the reeds and through his hair. It transports him, just as it did when he was a boy.

The wind in the reeds is the sound that partly fired his poem "Inishfree." The Japanese picture that he keeps in his room, of cranes flying through a blue sky, has the same effect. Also his favorite lines from Homer: *I'll tell you a secret... The Gods envy us. They envy us because we are mortal, because any moment might be our last. Everything is more beautiful because we're doomed. You will never be lovelier than you are now.* Now *Axel* is added to his list of transcendent things, as much as the bird-sung wind in the reeds at Lough Gill. And Axel's woman, Sarah, the reflections of blood and gold on her soul, is forever indelibly woven with the image of Maud Gonne in the playhouse and her sultry whispers in his ear.

This is the Secret Rose for which men have spent themselves in every era, to which he gladly dedicates himself. On his return to London from Paris, he walks through the city lights and night shadows, seeing it everywhere: in the parks, in the streets, in the carriages, in the rain, in violinists in tuxedos outside the Royal Opera House, in the white stick of a blind man tapping the wet pavement, in a heap of slack cornered outside the museum, in the owned and the owed, the old and the crass, the lost and the lurking. Everywhere, her face and what it represents, is there.

Axel has shown him what he wants to do in his own plays and poems and stories. He wants to place all the modern visionary sects before his reader and so he is writing more of his wild Irish stories that will explain himself to her.

Before he left, Oscar Wilde praised one of these, "The Crucifixion of the Outcast". "Your story in *The National Observer* was sublime," he said. "Wonderful, wonderful!" True, he had come late to the theatre for WB's play, *The Land of Heart's Desire*, and in apology laid on the compliments: But there was sincerity in it too, WB thinks.

These are the thoughts that fill his head during his sleepless night in Sleuth Wood. By the time he gets back to his uncle's house from Lough Gill, having walked some thirty miles, over rough and boggy ground, he is unimaginably tired. Mary Battle winks at him behind his uncle's back, when he is explaining where he has been, thinking he'd spent the night in a different fashion. "And haven't you good right to be fatigued?" she says, in fits of laughter, and he blushes, prudish as an old maid.

During this Sligo stay, he is invited for the first time to overnight at the austere mansion, Lissadell, the Gore-Booths' house. A house, which to him as a child growing up among Pollexfen traders, was the epitome of unattainable. In those days, he would glimpse, on clear days from the hill above his grandparents' house, or from the carriage if their drive was towards Ben Bulben, the grey stone walls of Lissadell among its trees. He loves these country houses with their gardens and trees, their life set among natural beauty, with servants and laborers who seem themselves natural, as bird and tree are natural.

His father's people were respected rectors, and his mother's merchant people of the town, in trade but no matter how many souls a Yeats parish had, no matter how many thousands a year Pollexfen mills or ships brought in, they could never be "county." Now he wins an invitation through his work. He has attained "gentleman" status not by birth, but by genius. His uncle George is very proud.

The somber grey of Lissadell is at odds with the Gore-Booth colorful family history, with descendants who had pressed for political reform and progressive farming and industry, who had behaved well towards the people during the great famine. He finds them very pleasant and kindly, ready to take up new ideas and new things.

The two daughters of the house, Constance and Eva, were both excited by his thoughts on folklore, and he arranges to lend them some books. These girls are small legends throughout Sligo, renowned for good looks and daring horsemanship, and he spends most of his time at Lissadell with them, especially with Eva, who is most sympathetic to the sad story of his unrequited love.

He always tells any new woman he meets about Maud Gonne. If he isn't attracted, it warns them off, and if he is, women being women, no harm done. Eva is comely as well as sympathetic. She is also lesbian, but WB is not worldly enough to know or suspect this.

On the last evening of his second visit, he is returning from a walk in the grounds, in one of those gentle, golden Irish days that come mid-winter, with all the surprise of a birth or any other unexpected great gift, when December rain and cloud clear, and the sun for an hour in the afternoon holds the sky with a low-lying, mellow, memory of summer. As he walks back across the lawn, he spies Eva and her sister, sitting by the great windows that open onto the south-facing lawns, in silk kimonos. Both are beautiful, but Eva has something more than beauty. She is like a fleeting animal, glimpsed through a forest of autumn leaf. A gazelle.

He begins to think if he cannot get the woman he loves, perhaps it would be a comfort, even for a little while, to devote himself to another? And then, with that ambivalence of his that is almost pathological, he berates himself. He has no money.

Literally, none. He has come to stay in Ireland largely because he could not survive in London; going forward, his uncle has promised him a supplement of a pound a week. Without this, he would starve.

How can he think he would have any chance with a daughter of Lissadell? And anyway, Maud Gonne.

Maud Gonne.

~

But something is changing. Pound a week from his uncle in pocket, he returns to London for more good financial news. A new literary magazine, sympathetic to aestheticism and symbolism and decadence and able, through the auspices of a patron, to pay. *The Yellow Book*. Aubrey Beardsley is art editor, and it is he who came up with the idea of the yellow cover, liking the association with illicit French fiction.

To launch it, more than fifty writers and artists gather at the Hotel d'Italia, a fancy name for what is actually a rather shabby hotel off the Charing Cross Road. WB and George Moore are there. Beardsley and his sister Mabel are there. WB's friends, Arthur Symons and Lionel Johnson are there, and Johnson has brought along his cousin, Olivia, Mrs. Shakespear. And Mrs. Shakespear is exquisitely dressed... and something about her suggests "incomparable distinction" to WB.

Her mother is sister to Johnson's father, the army officer who all but disowned his son for not growing taller than an inch or two above five feet, and preferring the literary life to the military, and she is clearly fond of Johnson, smiling indulgently at his drunken antics over dinner. Later he learns that she's the only member of the family to whom Johnson can disclose himself. By which he means, disclose the homosexual proclivities that fuel his self-loathing and his alcoholism on one side, his religion and poetry on the other.

For now, he knows only that her face is Greek in its regularity, that her lips are very full and sensuous; that her darkly soulful eyes give her the sensitive look of distinction he always admires, that she has that kind of beauty that holds within it the nobility of defeated things.

The dinner is a little riotous. Aubrey Beardsley, London's latest *enfant terrible*, is there, accompanied as always by his adored sister, Mabel. They are said to have had sexual relations with each other since childhood.

Mr. Beardsley is as striking as ever, in a modish dinner jacket and patent pumps, with hair parted down the middle into a fringe that falls, fetchingly, across his shockingly pale face. Oscar Wilde once described him as having a face like a silver hatchet, and grass green hair. It's only a slight exaggeration.

Grotesque as his looks and his behavior are, they're as nothing compared to his art. Serpentine art-nouveau lines caricaturing perversion, especially in the now infamous image of Salome about to kiss the severed, blood-dripping head of John the Baptist. His drawings flirt with outrage, but he is a true artist, and he and Harland have demanded that *The Yellow Book* be what WB wants for his own coming book of esoteric stories, *The Secret Rose*: that it be beautiful, not just in content, but as an artifact, beautiful to look at and convenient to handle.

That it declare itself a book to be read, and placed upon one's shelves, and read again. A book with style, a book with finish; a book that every book-lover will love at first sight and that will make book-lovers of many who are now indifferent to books.

Mrs. Shakespear and WB study each other, covertly, across the long table all evening and when it comes time to go, as she rises she looks at him directly and enquiringly, and he knows if he were to step forward...

But there is no one to introduce them, and she is a lady, so she turns and slowly leaves. The manager comes in to tell him that she asked who he was on her way out.

She too, like Eva Gore-Booth, is a pearl-pale, high-born lady. And he is so starved for the bosom of his faery bride. This love of his is breaking him. Nothing is his, not the streets nor the stars, not his body nor his heart. If he cannot get the woman he loves, it would be a comfort for a little while to devote himself to another

A few days later, an invitation arrives, through Johnson. Mrs. Shakespear would like him to come to tea in the family home in Kensington. The home she shares with her husband, fourteen years older than her, who Johnson has told him "ceased to pay court" to her from the day they married. Together they have one child, a daughter, born nine months after the wedding.

She has added in her own handwriting on the invitation card: "I shall be so glad to see you."

On The Edge Of A Lake

OLIVIA SHAKESPEAR is not the only woman to come nudging Maud Gonne out of place that year. Enter also Lady Isabella Augusta Gregory of Coole Park.

Lady G I like to call her. She was nearly as complicated as Maud Gonne and had plenty in common with her, if not the beauty: a passionate affair with a professional philanderer; a lifetime of rumors around the parentage of her only son, Robert; and the youth filled with romantic nationalism, taking up the cause of Egyptian rebels, writing a long essay defending Arabi Bey, and eventually, though more circumspectly by then, taking up the cause of Ireland.

She was the seventh daughter of a Galway county family, counting soldiers, churchmen and English government officials that are typical of such in her ancestry, all the way back to the first settlements in the 1600s. She'd made a great match, capturing Sir William Gregory in 1880, much to her older sisters' surprise and dismay. He was Governor of Ceylon, and she enjoyed her travels with him around Europe and Egypt and India, among ambassadors, aristocrats and men of achievement.

Ethically intense, her hero was Dorothea Brooks in *Middlemarch*, not least because her catch of a husband was elderly (and twice widowed) but unlike Dorothea's husband, he died after only a few years in, leaving her his estate in trust for their only son Robert.

Lady G was a woman, like many, molded more by widowhood than marriage. Not that she disliked her husband but, as she put it, the loneliness thrust upon her after his departures made her rich. As WB's hero, William Blake, liked to put it: "full." Self-sufficient.

Marriage had taken her to London, where she and her husband ran weekly salons frequented by many leading literary and artistic figures of the day, including Browning, Tennyson and Henry James. Widowhood took her back home to the estate in County Galway, where to edit and publish her husband's autobiography while establishing herself, in everyone's eyes, from the servants to the county to the artists and writers she liked to encourage, as mistress of Coole.

If she hadn't married, she wouldn't have learned what she called "the quick enrichment of sentences that one gets in conversation" with such men. If she hadn't been widowed, she wouldn't have found the detachment of mind to express another's character. And if she hadn't experienced all of the above, she might not have recognized, as readily as she did, the genius of the young Irish poet.

She was a widow of four years when she first read WB's book of folklore, *The Celtic Twilight*. Touched by the beauty of the rhythmic stories and by the moving contrast between the poverty of the tellers and the splendor of the tales, she decided she would embark on a similar project herself, making use of the people in her local parish of Kiltartan.

"As soon as her terrible eye fell upon him," his friend Arthur Symons was later to say of her meeting with WB, "I knew she would keep him."

Symons called her "La Strega," the witch. I've being called that name myself and it's always the same kind of man who puts that word on a woman. I'll take the moniker, though, and proudly. Call me witch, any time. For is there anything wiser in this world than a wise old woman?

~

When she hears WB is staying in Tillira, the house of her near-neighbor, Edward Martyn, she calls over with a gift. Lady G is a great gifter and she wants to meet the young poet that people are starting to talk about. She has read his Oisin and his poems and when she sees him, she is instantly delighted. He is everything she expected, all that she seeks: hushed, musical eerie voice, dark looks, dreamy haunted expression, an adventurer of the imagination. Words spill from him, as he waxes about the Middle Ages and visions and talks invocations like a sorcerer.

In some respects, he seems no more mature than Robert, her fifteen-year-old son, a vulnerability she finds utterly charming and disarming. He is someone she would not be afraid to ask for help, someone she can help herself.

Tullira has a little old tower that rises beside a great new Gothic hall and stair, and last night, he had Martyn to put out all the lights, except a little Roman lamp. And in that faint light, among great vague shadows blotting away the details of the day, he took them all "away."

"Away, Mr. Yeats?" she asks.

"To the plane of vision and romance, Lady Gregory."

She, a plainly dressed woman of forty-five years, without obvious good looks, is not swept away. She issues an invitation to lunch at Coole the following week.

At first, WB prefers the Gothic mediaeval of Tullira to the little Georgian mansion of Coole. He doesn't like the over-ornamented gold frames around the pictures in the drawing room. The grounds are instantly stirring, not the walled garden laid out with classical statues and rare trees, crimson and white hawthorn, purple lilac and laburnum but the woodland paths. Carpeted with wet brown leaves even in summer, they lead down through the woods to a mysterious lake, where wild swans paddle the water or climb the air.

As soon as he sees that lake, he knows it will be significant, that he has come to a place where he needs to be. He has for some time now been troubled about his work. He has written the story "Rosa Alchemica" and penned some slow-moving, elaborate poems, but the old Irish country emotion that fired *The Countess Cathleen* and the early poems is lost to him.

Olivia shares his occult interests and is very psychic. Before he left, he sought her advice, and she obtained information that "he is too much under solar influence. He is to live near water and to avoid woods, which concentrate the solar power." At Tullira he evokes the lunar power for nine evenings with no great result. Then on the ninth night, as he is going to sleep, he sees first a centaur and then a marvelous naked woman shooting an arrow at a star. Then, when he comes to Coole and sees the great woods on the edge of a lake, he remembers the injunction about avoiding woods and living near the water.

Later, he will wonder if she came into his life because of his invocation. Or had the saying, and the invocation, been a prevision?

Whichever, Lady G has him in the library at Coole for only a few minutes before she is asking him if he can set her to some work for the intellectual movement in Ireland.

Back in London, in the autumn, she follows up on their friendship, draws him closer with small gifts of money and by organizing dining opportunities for him. Little threesomes or foursomes, like she used to enjoy with her husband, where select great and good are invited to meet her "interesting Celt," as one of them, Henry James, dubs him.

When WB moves out of home into his friend, Arthur Symons's, flat she sends round champagne, the first night. She knows how he longs to escape his family. Afterwards she helps the boys out with port, pies, meats, Bovril.

Lady G learned the power of generosity from her dead husband, Sir William. At Coole, the tenants got gifts of firewood, medicine, clothes, advice and even money, and were brought on regular parties and outings, and this paid off when the Land War broke out. Her brothers on her family estate in County Mayo needed armed guards to protect them during the troubles, but negotiations at Coole were conducted peacefully. It was a great lesson in the subtle bonds of connection and obligation that generosity creates, and one she never forgot.

WB laps up these ministrations and even he, who could take so much from women without noticing a cost to the giver, was humbled to gratitude for her thoughtful generosity.

She is soon to teach him to understand again, and much more

perfectly than before, the true countenance of Irish country life. It will take some years, and he needs first to study and come to understand the earlier nineteenth, and the eighteenth century. Then he comes to love Coole above all other houses.

But first: back to Paris. The old lure, yes, but also a new fascination, that is tightening its tentacles, squeezing his soul.

~

He has received a note inviting him to "coffee and cigarettes plentifully," signed "Yours quite cheerfully, Paul Verlaine." Last time the old poet was a disappointment. Even in his youth, Verlaine was unattractive; his skull was enlarged compared to a squashed-in face, his eyes were uneven, his nose pug. Now he resembles the popular idea of Socrates without that philosopher's equanimity.

WB finds him sitting in an easy chair, his bad leg swaddled in many bandages. He asks if WB now knows Paris well, and adds, pointing, that it has scorched his leg for he knows it "well, too well," having "lived in it like a fly in a pot of marmalade."

Again, they share cigarettes over coffee in the little attic room on Rue Descartes, decorated with newspaper cartoons of Verlaine that depict him as a monkey, and WB brings the conversation round to the subject he has come to investigate: hashish. Verlaine says he thought at one time it fed his work, not now. WB has been introduced by the young mystics of Paris. He took a pellet an hour before dinner, another after, but found the experience largely disappointing, except for a moment where he felt suddenly that a cloud he was looking at floated in an immense space, and for an instant rushed him out, as it seemed, into that space.

"But I had no visions," he says. "Nothing but a sensation of some dark shadow which seemed to be telling me that some day I would go into a trance and go out of my body, but not yet."

Verlaine explains that with hashish, the first time is generally the least interesting.

Verlaine alternates between the two halves of his nature with so little apparent resistance that he seems like a bad child, though to read his sacred poems is to remember that the Holy Infant shared His first home with the beasts at Bethlehem.

Verlaine reminds WB of his friend, Lionel Johnson, also beset by the demon of alcoholism too. Does the spiritual ecstasy which these great souls touch at times heighten—as complementary colors heighten one another—not only the experience of evil but its fascination?

He has been considering Johnson and Mathers in depth while writing his final stories for *The Secret Rose* collection and has devoted a story in the collection to each: "The Tables of the Law" to Johnson, "Rosa Alchemica" to Mathers. Certainly Johnson's craving, a "craving that made every atom of his body cry out" for alcohol is corrupting this once sanctified soul, who now is saying one moment, "I don't want to be cured," and a moment after that, "In ten years, I shall be penniless and shabby, and borrow half-crowns from friends," and seeming, in the saying of that, to be contemplating a pleasure.

One day he told WB how Wilde got an increase of pleasure and excitement from the degradation of the group of beggars and blackmailers where he sought his pleasure and when WB was surprised, Johnson smiled so condescendingly, as though these were psychological depths he could never enter.

And Mathers too becomes increasingly eccentric, half-knavish. WB is here in Paris to seek his help again with the Celtic Rites but he senses that Mathers is not in control, that he is deceiving intellects with subtlety and flattering hearts with beauty. The fancy has begun to possess him that the man behind Mathers's face has dissolved away, like salt in water, and that it laughs and sighs, appears and denounces at the bidding of other beings. That the man he spent time with is not Mathers.

He fears for the Order, and sometimes for himself. But he is pleased to have access to this mind-altering drug, hashish. It will foster the work. He and Miss Gyles have been working on the cover to his *The Secret Rose*. Her art is full of abundant and passionate life. When he looks at the design she has done, the subtle tree of life with its serpentine branches and intertwined roots rising out of the pelvic bowl of a skeleton, a floored knight, its continuous interweaving of branches and roots, he thinks of Blake's cry, "Exuberance is beauty". Or Palmer's command to the artist, "Always seek to make excess more abundantly excessive."

But A Dream

MAUD IS looking at Millevoye with limpid, apologetic eyes.

"Nauseous again?"

"I'm afraid so," she says, hands on abdomen. "I cannot complain, if this suffering means we shall have a healthy boy. Ghénia says all-day sickness is a sign that the baby is healthy."

"It never happened thus for Madame Millevoye. Mornings only, and then only for a few weeks."

"Ghénia says carrying low in front like this confirms it is a boy."

"You were not too unwell to go about with your poet."

"Oh but I had to, he might have suspected..."

"Pshaw! That lily-liver? I don't suppose he even knows how it happens."

"Millevoye, you are cruel. Poor Mr. Yeats."

"Mr. Yeats!" he mimics. "Silly Willie! I am not so sure that being immortalized in his verses is worth the attention he demands."

"If I didn't know better, Millevoye, I'd say you were jealous."

He reaches for her. "Make me jealous, minx." He kisses her. "Tell me why you like to spend time with him."

She shivers but submits to the game. "He is a boy of special destiny."

He presses a kiss. "But you need a man to keep you in harness."

"His conversation is elevated."

Another kiss. "And mine is earthy."

"He makes me think of times when there was something worth doing in the world. When there were great and wise people living, the people one reads about in books, who are full of heroic beauty and noble virtue."

This stops the kisses. He lifts his head. "Yet you tell him nothing of import about yourself. Is not truth one of the noble virtues?"

"Ireland needs him to believe in the image he has made of me. He is to be Ireland's great poet."

"Ah I see," he said, again pressing hard kisses, half craving, half mocking kisses, onto her nose, her mouth, her eyes. "You do it... for Ireland." His grasp is too tight, and the kisses have turned insolent. She pushes him away, but he tightens his hold. "How wonderful... that what you want... coincides... with what's good... for Ireland."

The game has grown tiresome. With a great heave, she pushes him away.

~

In March, Maud Gonne makes her last public appearance and from there on, life hangs heavy. Summer arrives early; by May it is hot as August, and she moves out of Paris, renting a house with a large garden in Samois. There she takes a walk each day to visit Georges, or rather his embalmed body, and performs small rites that Mr. Russell has given her, to reinforce the migration of his baby soul.

She believes it is working; she can feel him now moving inside her.

And she is glad to be out of Paris and its discontents. Millevoye supports the expedition of laws that restrict the freedom of the press and facilitate the pursuit of anarchists. Socialists and radicals and pacifists argue that this is bad law that will, in time, be used against any group that has an argument with the government. Disputations rage, climaxing when President Carnot is assassinated by an anarchist.

Georges is due in early August, so in mid-July, she returns home, where the best medical attention awaits her lying-in. The city has slipped into torpor. In shop windows in every *quartier*, little paper cards announce that this or that patron is away until a date in late August or the beginning of September. This is the first year since she came to live in France that she has spent a summer in the city.

She longs for the cool of Samois or St. Raphael, where she and Lucien were once so happy, anywhere grass and trees cool the temperatures, and the air is free to blow. The air is so heavy along the streets and boulevards of Paris that some days, breathing feels almost like eating.

Perhaps once the baby is born, another escape might be possible. For now, time has slowed to the watching of one fat second slumping down onto another.

And then, finally, comes the day. She is taking her daily walk by the river when she feels her strength falter and sensations unfolding inside her, that make her clammy. She turns back.

Inside her hallway, as she lifts her arms to hang the wrap without which no respectable woman can walk around Paris, no matter how high the heat, she feels something shift in her lower abdomen, as if a band of muscle is opening out. "Like London Bridge," she says afterwards to Ghénia.

It is begun.

She calls Joséphine and sends her to alert the doctor and nurse. Last time, the baby took twenty-six hours to arrive from first contraction: the doctor is likely to go away again, as he did last time. Still, she would like him to come now and check that all is well.

~

The room is dark and full of sound, great gusts of Maud Gonne's breathing and crying, crying and breathing. Summer night is falling as the moment of birth approaches. Her revolutionary activity, her fine physique and physiognomy, her political passion, her strong will: none are of any use to her in here. Here she is nothing but source, vessel, channel. Mother.

The course of this birth is very different to the first. By the time the doctor and nurse arrive, it is well established. Now the nurse is mopping her brow, Joséphine is running hither and thither with jugs of water and cloths and glasses of iced tea, and the doctor is murmuring consolation. "Not long now. Not long." Maud Gonne is emitting the unmistakable, universal, female sounds. Whimpers have turned to cries; breaths have become gasps.

Now comes a long scream as her skin is stretched wider than skin can stretch, and the baby's head pushes through, then a rush and a slither and a cry, a small, faint sound. A wail for a lost world? Everyone in the room turns towards it.

"*Elle est parfaite*," says the nurse.

"*Elle?*" Maud gasps, as if a girl were some mysterious creature of whom she has only just heard.

The nurse holds up the baby and Maud gasps again at the reality of the child, no longer a notion inside her but a solid squirm of fleshy limbs, a squawk of throat and lungs. They stare at each other, the infant eyes still glazed with the fluids of her fetal world, the adult eyes riveted on the telltale genitals. A girl.

Maud's mouth widens into a dazzling smile, and the attendants around the bed let out a breath.

She holds up her arms and careful hands pass her the baby, and she pulls her daughter in close and sniffs her skin. She thinks of her man, so unfaithful and unreliable, of how a boy would have settled him better, but then she thinks of Ghénia, and the other women she is befriending. Think woman, she lectures herself through her disappointment, of your own work. Can't a daughter be a patriot just as well as a son?

She must ask Mr. Yeats, or better Mr. Russell, what it means when a male soul is reincarnated female. In the new dawn that is coming, perhaps it is appropriate.

Now she enfolds the miniature body close to hers, feels the little chest rising and falling in quick baby breaths. Her insides clench. Pray God this one will be stronger than her brother. She drops a kiss onto the baby's red, wrinkled forehead, inhales her scent. It is the scent of her own insides, a smell of blood and secrets.

She had no female name chosen. Georgina does not feel right, neither Georgie. In a rush of hormone-fueled emotion, she thinks of her favorite female name, one that carries in it all the sorrows and mysteries of womanhood, from her favorite work by her beloved Wagner, about an ancient Irish princess. She whispers it now in the child's tiny, curly conch of an ear. "Iseult."

After a time, while the doctor and nurse are doing what needs to be done, she turns to find Joséphine, who is rinsing a cloth in the corner.

"Joséphine, the letter on the bureau. Would you open it, please, and bring me my pen."

Joséphine does as asked and Maud Gonne removes the sheet of paper from its envelope. It has no salutation or signature, in case it should fall into the wrong hands. Just four stark words: "Your son is born." She scratches out "son," replaces it with "child." And adds two more truncated sentences: "A daughter. Iseult Germaine Lucille."

Then she holds it up and waves it in the air to dry.

Nestled in the crook of Maud Gonne's other arm, Iseult has no idea what her mother is writing or saying, or even that any-one is speaking. Her eardrums will take time to tune up to the full range of sounds in this new, noisy world. She barely feels the touch of her mother's lips and only a sliver of light from the candle, as yet, pierces her retina. She will be some weeks in this world before she is exposed to full sensory onslaught and some years before she takes up the rope of human sorrow.

For now, all she knows is the familiar timbres and touch of her mother, her vibrations and the taste of her milk. She lets her eyelids droop, and she drops into her first sleep in the breathing world.

Exalted Above
The Senses

ON THE DAY of Iseult Gonne's birth, across the English Channel, WB sits down at his desk to write a letter to Olivia Shakespear. She has asked him to read extracts from her impending novel, *Beauty's Hour*, and he has found it to be what it is: a slight piece, a love story with a wooden hero and without any compensating resonance.

He doesn't write her any of this. What he says is, he has never come upon any new work so full of this kind of tremulous delicacy, this fragile beauty. Then he offers the following: "I no more complain of your writing of love than I would complain of a portrait painter keeping to portraits. I would complain, however, if his backgrounds were too slightly imagined for the scheme of his art."

Which has almost no merits as literary criticism. What does one do with the advice that one's work is "too slightly imagined"? But WB never claimed to be a mentor, and people will keep showing him their cribbling, pretending to ask for honesty but actually seeking, craving, validation.

When the asker is a young and beautiful woman, it would take a better man than WB to resist the temptation to take advantage.

His only practical suggestion for Olivia is that she should reconstruct her anti-hero as "one of those vigorous, fair-haired men who are very positive and what is called 'manly' in external activities and energies, but wholly passive and plastic in emotional and intellectual things." That is, he should be the kind of man who is WB's opposite.

He signs off with the hope that they might meet when she returns from her holiday. She has shared with him a little about her marital difficulties; he has told her all about his love sorrow.

Olivia returns to London, fairly sure that WB has been writing her love letters. All that stuff about her protagonist: isn't it just a poet's convoluted way of saying her hero should be more like him. As soon as she gets home, she invites Cousin Lionel round.

This passion WB has for Maud Gonne—what does he know of it? It is arid, Johnson believes; the lady's not for turning. But if she, his dear cousin, is determined to set sail with Yeats, she needs to know that his friend has come to almost thirty years without yet putting out to sea.

Olivia is charmed, not deflected, by this knowledge.

Next time she meets her intended, on a day out to Kent, she makes her declaration. Her marriage is a sham, and so often she has taken refuge in attractions to other men who were not right for her. WB's love affair seems equally doomed. They have both been so unhappy. Are they not entitled to such happiness as they can create, together?

He leaves her, still troubled, and next time they meet, the troubling seems to have redoubled.

What's wrong? She asks.

Her cure for marital unhappiness, he believes, is flawed. Knowing her as he does, it is no doubt the sort of flaw that arises from fineness, the sort she shares with her cousin. It comes from having a soul so distinguished and contemplative that the common world seems empty, and so they choose the extremes: sanctity or dissipation.

In Johnson's case the Catholic Church. In hers... There he flounders, perhaps realizing how offensive he is being.

She says: He has it wrong, entirely. She is dismayed that he should have such thoughts of her. She has never voyaged with another, except in her imagination.

He (blushing) says: He is happy to know it.

She says: She is happy to know him, to have met him. Had any other man said what he has just said... But she knows it comes from a discriminating soul.

He says: This is all to the good. But what of their various diffi-culties: her husband, his lack of money, the scandal, her daughter Dorothy? Is it correct that for having an affair, her husband can immediately divorce her and will gain unquestioned custody of the child?

She says: They must make sure they are not found out.

He says: Can she give him some time? He needs to think about how this might be best managed.

She gives her assent. It takes him a fortnight to come back to her with the suggestion that when they are in a position to live together, he shall ask her to leave her husband. Until such time, their friendship should remain platonic.

She says: She too has had time to think. Though her husband would have grounds to sue them, and destroy both their reputa-tions, and keep her from Dorothy, she does not believe he would do so. He has a strong dislike of public scenes.

He says: Hmmmm.

He says: They should not be hasty. Next time they meet, per-haps they might take an outing and discuss the question some more? Leaving, he gives her a platonic kiss on the cheek.

Next time, in the railway carriage on their way to Kew Gar-dens, she praises him for the beautiful tact he showed last time, giving her but a brother's kiss at such a moment. He takes the praise.

He says: He was exalted above the senses. (Though truth is, he doesn't know any other way of kissing.)

She says... Actually, she has grown tired of talk. She leans in to kiss him, kiss him properly, opening his mouth with a gentle, probing tongue.

He is greatly startled.

She sees it and lets him lie.

At Kew Gardens, among the thousands of plants that Captain Cook's botanist brought from all over the world, the fashionable Kensington lady and the shabby, bespectacled bohemian walk and talk some more.

He says: They must move carefully. Perhaps she ought to seek a legal separation instead of a divorce. Would that spare her social ostracism and financial ruin? Perhaps they ought to wait until her mother has died? It is so hard to know what to do.

She says: Why don't they bring in somebody else for advice?

The chosen advisors are his friend, Florence Farr, and her dear friend, Valentine Fox, both older, experienced in love affairs, broadminded and sensible. They listen to the tales of woe, the complications and obstructions, the impediments and impossibilities and having heard it all have little more to say than fire ahead.

She says: They are right. She says: She is tired of these public meetings in the Reading Room and the railways, the parks and galleries. She says: Shouldn't she come round to his new flat next time?

Yes, WB finally has rooms of his own. He left home to much resentment from father and sisters. Now that "He thinks he can live on fifty pence a week," said Lily. Yes, Lily not Lolly. They were all hurt by his desertion. "Well, let him try."

~

First, he moved in with Arthur Symons, the friend who, more than any man he has ever known, can slip into his own mind. Symons, fluent in French, helps him read *Axel*. He has been going on with the book, slowly and with so much difficulty that certain passages have come to have an exaggerated importance, while the whole remains so obscure that he imagines it the Sacred Book he has longed for. Then after the summer, he gets his own place, in Woburn Buildings, near Euston station. The rooms—a large sitting room in front, a back kitchen and bedroom—are spartan, without electric light, papered with brown wallpaper and brown baize curtains. The table has to be lifted out to eat if he is dining with anyone else.

But he set up a shrine in his bedroom, an engraving of Blake's head and a print of his Ancient of Daysand a beautiful pencil drawing by Cecil French, of a woman holding a rose between her lips, and Beardsley's poster for the Florence Farr production of *The Land of Heart's Desire*.

Lady G lays in a supply of tall, white paschal candles. She interviews his housekeeper, Mrs. Old, whom she passed as having the correct brand of loyalty. The last thing one needs, when trying to write, is emotional trouble from the servants. Sometimes, after a visit from her, he finds discreet five and ten-pound notes under the clock.

Her generosity releases him from the grind of journalism undertaken to survive and from his family.

It is she who makes it possible for him to continue living alone. Just as necessarily, it validated his choice of life that he could attract such a patron. Thanks to her, he is able to live independently. She asks only one thing: he must work. And they must set each other to work. He begins to invite other artists and writers over for a regular Monday night at-home—tea and whiskey or Benedictine and no dress. At last, he is able to gain a purchase on literary London.

When Olivia arrives to the flat as agreed, chaperoned by Valentine Fox, the ladies find WB sitting on the step. He says: He has locked the key inside, locked them all out.

She says: Perhaps they two should repair to a hotel?

He says: Wait there a moment. He needs to find a locksmith, the lock must be sorted. By the time he returns with a neighbor, who crawls in the window, they are gone.

And a few days later, out of nowhere, he receives a letter from Maud Gonne, wondering why she has not heard from him in a while and telling him that he "appeared" to her in Dublin, in the hotel where she was sitting with friends. She saw him standing near a table on which lay his book, which she had been reading. Was he aware?

Those in the room with her knew nothing of occultism, so mentally she gave him a rendezvous for midnight. A little before twelve, she got into a half-waking half-sleeping state, then saw him again, and together they went to the cliffs at Howth. But the seabirds were all asleep, and it was dark and so cold, and the wind blew so.

What does it mean, he wonders, reading and rereading the letter, torturing himself about why this happened on the very day he locked Olivia out of his room?

If this were a play, the symbolism would be unmistakable. And he says (to himself), Olivia is like a mild heroine from one of his plays. She seems so much a part of himself, she is so friendly and unexacting, she understands him and demands nothing that he cannot give. This is what he needs.

And looks forward to having. But perhaps not now. When her husband agrees, perhaps. When her child is grown? When the time is right.

Olivia says, she asked her husband for separation, but he became so distressed. It may be kinder to deceive him. Let them proceed, now, not some unnamable time in the future.

She says: Now that WB has his own flat, there is nothing to stop them.

She says: They will need a double bed. She will go with him to buy it.

She says: Healy's Furniture Emporium. Tottenham Court Road. Next Tuesday afternoon.

~

And so they get as far as buying the bed, much to WB's embarrassment, not to mention anxiety about the expense, each additional inch adding to the cost. Olivia sets a date for the deed to be done and arrives promptly at the appointed time, and waits in the front room, patiently smoking, as he fusses about. He is nervous, she knows that.

And she's not wrong. He's working himself into a right old lather, imagining the taste of the tip of her tongue, the smoky scent of her hair unbound and falling over his breast, the beat of her heart over his heart. He is doing so much imagining that when they finally make it to the bedroom, and a sufficient state of undress (not an easy task in those days of intricate female clothing), he has fomented himself into a great nervous excitement that renders him impotent.

Horror of horrors. He shoots his bolt and cannot rise to the occasion again.

His embarrassment is excruciating. Disabling. He can never, ever, through all time see her again. Never, never, ever.

Yet he knows he has an appointment to see her the very next

day, at the Reading Room where they are researching the work of Nicholas Flamell. And though he thinks to stay at home, he knows the one place he cannot avoid, hardly for a day never mind forever, is the Reading Room. Sitting in his library seat, he trembles with shame as he sees her approach, anticipating, dreading her disdain. But the disdain he can live with, so long as she does not share it around. If she tells Johnson, or any other of their mutual friends, he shall have to move to Paris, or America, or the furthest ends of the earth.

She says: "Hello Willie."

She does not say anything untoward, whatsoever, just chats with just the same kind attention as always, and falls into conversation as open and free as ever.

Later, in private, she chooses only to understand, only to be troubled by his trouble.

So, a week later, they try again. And though once again he suffers a paroxysm of pain and nervousness, after another round of tea and talk, finally—six years after he first met Maud Gonne, almost two years after *The Yellow Book* inaugural dinner where he first had the thought of Olivia—finally, by the womanly virtues of kindness and patience WB's maiden voyage is launched.

He Bids His Beloved Be At Peace

I HEAR the Shadowy Horses, their long manes a-shake,
Their hooves heavy with tumult, their eyes glimmering white;
The North unfolds above them clinging, creeping night,
The East her hidden joy before the morning break,
The West weeps in pale dew and sighs passing away,
The South is pouring down roses of crimson fire:
O vanity of Sleep, Hope, Dream, endless Desire,
The Horses of Disaster plunge in the heavy clay:
Beloved, let your eyes half close, and your heart beat
Over my heart, and your hair fall over my breast,
Drowning love's lonely hour in deep twilight of rest,
And hiding their tossing manes and their tumultuous feet.

Part Three:
1895–1900

Dream Heavy Land

HE REMEMBERS FORGOTTEN BEAUTY

WHEN my arms wrap you round I press
My heart upon the loveliness
That has long faded from the world;
The jewelled crowns that kings have hurled
In shadowy pools, when armies fled;
The love-tales wrought with silken thread
By dreaming ladies upon cloth
That has made fat the murderous moth;
The roses that of old time were
Woven by ladies in their hair,
The dew-cold lilies ladies bore
Through many a sacred corridor
Where such grey clouds of incense rose
That only God's eyes did not close:
For that pale breast and lingering hand
Come from a more dream-heavy land,
A more dream-heavy hour than this;
And when you sigh from kiss to kiss
I hear white Beauty sighing, too,
For hours when all must fade like dew,
But flame on flame, and deep on deep,
Throne over throne where in half sleep,
Their swords upon their iron knees,
Brood her high lonely mysteries.

Ah, sweet mystery of love. I could cry dream-heavy tears my-self, and sigh a dew-dappled, deep-flame sigh when I think of him at this time, and all that Olivia brought him that had been so long delayed and he might have missed altogether, if he had gone for another less kindly woman. I know he was a bit odd, but then, which of us isn't? All wrapped up in his own advance-ment, but what young man is otherwise, except those who can't lift themselves above their misery? He was also a soft, under-loved boy, and she being a soft woman with an overload of love to give, they fitted together very nicely.

She was everything a mistress should be, graced with all the attendant virtues. Patient, accommodating, sensitive, focused on him and his needs. For her, it was like coaxing a child out of a corner, or an animal to eat out of your hand. She had to stay still, peddle tact, if she was to win his trust. He had to be brought to let down his guard and she had to take a great deal of time and a circuitous route to bring him. When he finally got going, though, there was no stopping him.

Oh those long, languorous afternoons at his flat. She would arrive to his door, having changed cabs in central London, as she could never order a direct cab to Woburn Buildings from her home. All the servants would wonder what on earth she could possibly be doing in such an outlandish location.

He ushers her in, each time, straight down the little corridor to his bedroom in the back, with the expensive bed. Their first challenge is the female dress and underwear of the nineteenth century. Then there is the messy question of contraception. Their choices are coitus interruptus or a nineteenth-century mechanical device. WB is none too easy to instruct in the in-tricacies of ladies dress and the people of the *Shee* never had to unlace a corset or dispose of a rubber.

Hats off to Olivia. It gets easier each time to get Mr. Romance beyond such botherments, over his impotence, and into his pleasure.

Afterwards, they have tea and bread in their underwear, their hands wrapped round his rough-and-ready cups, and blankets wrapped round their shoulders on cold days, for it got very cold in the old dark rooms. And many times, especially in the early days, after the tea they go again, for they are young, and hale, and compelled to making more good love by the astonishing joy of it all.

But soon, always too soon, it's time to leave and then she has to be carefully reassembled, to make sure she returns home buttoned and laced the same way she came out, without any discrepancies that might be noted by her lady's maid, and held to be evidence in a possible divorce court. And he is left to lie back into the bed and luxuriate over it all or go out or sit to his desk and make poetry from it.

He lays down a belief at this time which comes to rule his later life: that he needs sex to make poetry, to access the great Creative Spirit who is always slip-sliding so tantalizingly beyond the trembling veil.

~

As the weeks and months go on, they draw closer. Their love is founded on friendship and although he never becomes a great lover, being always over-focused on his own fulfillment, right from the start he is a good friend to her. Friendship is the kind of love WB does best, his whole life long. For his friends, he stands up, spends time, goes deep, helps out, shares knowledge, gives affection and does favors. All of this he brings now into his first love affair.

They bond over past rejections, by her unfeeling solicitor husband, Hope Shakespear, by his unfeeling muse and political colleague, Maud Gonne. He tells her how Maud Gonne laughed when he dreamt she had died, and sent her a poem that resulted from his fear, imagining a lonely funeral among unknown peasants who would have (he quotes) "left her to the indifferent stars above" until he "carved these words: She was more beautiful than thy first love, But now lies under boards."

Olivia is aghast. His poetic gifts are incomparable. And she laughed to receive a tribute such as this? She *laughed*?

She treasures the poems he writes for her almost as much as she treasures Dorothy, her daughter. She has them by heart and recites them over and again.

Beloved, let your eyes half close, and your heart beat.
Over my heart, and your hair fall over my breast...

Fasten your hair with a golden pin,
And bind up every wandering tress;
You need but lift a pearl-pale hand,
And bind up your long hair and sigh;
And all men's hearts must burn and beat;
And candle-like foam on the dim sand,
And stars climbing the dew-dropping sky,
Live but to light your passing feet

Oh, she thinks, if only they'd met when she was younger, and unmarried, and they could have been together properly, as man and wife, without all this subterfuge. Yet she knows her experience as a married woman, what it taught her about sex, and also about sex rejection, was essential to their connection now.

How unhappy Maud Gonne made him and how proud she is to be, now, the font of his happiness. Truly theirs is the most perfect happiness.

They bond over occult ideas and experiments, for Olivia too is a believer. They bond over their mutual care for Lionel Johnson, her cousin, whose alcohol addiction is now so pronounced, and such a worry to them both. They bond over the tribulations of families, especially of mothers, and the importance of literature and the Higher Things of life.

He helps her with her novels, which he sees are slight and under-developed. And for himself, the poems come pouring, new kinds of rhymes full of images that are more sensual and human and earthy than those inspired by Maud Gonne. The critics are forever arguing which poem came from what woman in this period. If the poem focuses on hair, especially hair unwound or unbound, it was born of those gilded afternoons with Olivia but if it's all about eyelids or immortal perfection, it came from Maud Gonne.

Such nonsense. Into his poems, into words and forms that came from who knows where, he puts all he knows and feels, all he is learning about love and all he knows without learning. You can't parse out love. Or poetry. Or sex either, come to that.

~

Life goes lolloping on, as it does. He goes home when he has to, but nothing there seems so bad now, even though since her last apoplectic fit, Mama has been paralyzed and immobile and is now entirely silent, oblivious to everything but the view of the sky from her window. Papa tried to have her write a note to him each day, he tells him, to keep her from complete isolation. But all she wrote about was the sky and the weather, which now comprise her whole existence, and the effort petered out.

Lily has given up work, Lolly is teaching and has published a book on brushwork and is at work on another. WB brings Lady G to Bedford Park one day and the girls are amazed at how she speaks to their brother, and how he lets her. Her tone and her pronouncements are both proprietal and motherly and he laps it up. She is a short woman, forty-five years old now, with a look of Queen Victoria about her. Like the queen, she is substantial in weight, and a widow, always dressed in severest black.

She has little time for women, she doesn't ask about Lily's embroidery or Lolly's books or artwork, but spends the afternoon making pronouncements, and trying to win over the men. She praises Papa and urges him to do more work. She praises Jack who's also home on a visit, but he wants nothing to do with patronage and manages to slide away. She praises Willie, who can't get enough of it, and practically begs for more like a needy puppy.

They see now where so many of his new opinions and actions are coming from, especially the developments of the Irish Literary Society in London, and a new Irish National theatre in Dublin. She has their brother looking more towards Ireland than England for his future, they see, and though they cannot say they warm to her, they all admit, after she and WB have departed, that there is much in what she says.

My dear Mr. Yeats

I got your letter just before leaving France. It was most interesting. I'm staying with my sister for a month, she is not well. I hope to be in Paris the end of October and I should be very glad to see you there. I wish Irishmen would come oftener to Paris. There is lots of interesting work to be done there. We want to have Ireland better known and her struggle for independence brought more prominently before the world.
  I won't write more now as I hope to see you soon.

With kindest regards
I remain
Dear Mr. Yeats
Very sincerely your friend
Maud Gonne

Olivia arrives to Woburn Buildings and is not led to the bedroom. He tells her he must go to Paris at the end of the year as August next year sees Queen Victoria's 60th Jubilee requiring organized protest in Ireland. While the year after is the centenary of the 1798 Rebellion, there will be much celebration and commemoration and he needs to ensure that the proper Irish line is presented.

"Shall we read a little poetry, to get into the mood?"

Since when did they need to get into the mood? She looks at him, askance, but he is already reading. Clarence Mangan, an Irish poet. She sits down opposite him and listens.

Beware Of Mars By Moon

NEW YEAR'S DAY 1887. Maud Gonne has called the Irish nationalists of Paris together to get organized around two upcoming events but when people arrive, they are surprised to find it is the poet Yeats at the door, ushering them in with a small bow that feels ironical, his long arm sweeping them in the direction of the drawing room.

"Come in, come in. Miss Gonne has had to go on an errand. She shall return shortly."

Behind the length of his back, they exchange small looks and smiles. His delight in playing host here, in her apartment, is so very evident. "Almost a statement, would you say?" whispers Miss Ryan.

An affectation, like his poet's apparel.

In the drawing room, he introduces a new man sitting in the corner chair by the window. A Mr. Synge (spelt S-y-n-g-e but, yes, pronounced "Sing"), who is also staying at the Hotel Corneille, a student of languages who is interested in the Irish literary revival. Mr. Synge is dark and so quiet that Miss Bell pronounces him, in another whispered aside, "dour enough to call sour." He is a friend of Mr. Stephen McKenna, the classicist. They say Mr. Synge lives on what he borrows from Mr. McKenna, and Mr. McKenna lives on what Mr. Synge repays him.

Nobody minds, at first, that Miss Gonne is absent. It gives them a chance, as the poet jumps to attend to the next arrivals, to engage the newcomer in small talk and to have a good look around at these rooms. What a lot to see. Just look at the elegant chaise longue, the colorful scatter rugs and plants, the airy decor that uses mirrors and lamps to emphasize the light from the two, floor-to-ceiling windows. See the way she has of placing an ornament just so: like that figurine on the presentation table by the door. Look at the antimacassars, made of the very finest lace. Carrickmacross perhaps? Limerick?

But what about the animals? How does she bear so many of them? That brutish hound taking up the best spot in front of the fire, the felines slinking between one's feet—how many are there? Three? Four? More?—and those caged birds whose twittering can been heard from the dining room whenever the talk goes into a lull. Is this pet craze of hers showy or charming? The company is divided.

And Mr. Yeats. Each time he jumps up to answer the bell, his long legs shoot him across the room in a rapid series of leaps. He is so strange, one might even say a little weird. Miss Duke has heard he is a diabolist. She hopes he won't put a spell on them.

All passes most pleasant for a while but then the second pot of tea is drunk, the fittings and furnishings offer no more conversation, the small talk begins to dwindle and the minutes to lengthen. An hour beyond their proposed starting time and she still has not arrived. Having seen them in, the poet has now abdicated all hosting responsibilities and is scribbling in a corner, his high shoulders pressed up as though he wishes them to cover his ears. Lost to them all or playing it so. Could it be a poem he is writing over there, among them all?

"I cannot understand it," says Miss Ryan aloud, addressing the entire ensemble from beneath an alarming bonnet. "She was so precise about the time."

"It is most unlike her," Miss Delaney says, not for the first time.

"Not good enough," grumbles Mr. Arthur Lynch, Paris correspondent for the *Daily Mail*. A busy man who is immensely fond of Maud Gonne, he is unaccustomed to being kept waiting.

"If she does not come soon, I shall have to leave anyway," Mr. O'Brien declares. "We are expected at the palace by eight o'clock prompt."

"So you said."

"And we have much to do before we leave. It's not every night one is invited to the palace of the Comte de Frisconne."

"We all have things to be going to," says Miss Ryan, patting her bonnet. "Given the night that's in it." It is *le premier de l'an*, the first day of the year, France's gayest holiday.

Stephen McKenna says, "It's my belief that we should make a start. At this rate, she may not be back at all."

"Certainly and indeed she'll be back!" Miss Delaney's indignation bulges in her prominent eyelids. "She's been delayed, that's the height of it."

If they could see though the protective arm crooked around the white sheet on his lap, they would find the letters shape nothing erudite or literary. It is not even a real word that he writes, but three letters over and over in a multitude of angles and sizes. WBY. WBY. WBY. The initials that henceforth shall be his moniker. WBY. With a blotting rag, he wipes the new nib of his new pen, trying not to notice the quality of the talk around him.

Why are the Irish always so unnecessarily avid? An eavesdropping Frenchman or Englishman would think these people adversaries, even enemies, but it is just the Irish way. The only escape from the tyranny of opinion, he has recently come to realize, is style. Personality, deliberately adopted, as a mask. During this meeting of Maud Gonne's, to avoid combat, he would say only fanciful things.

He turns a new page, unscrews his pen again. WBY. The letters have the air he is seeking. The appellation of his boyhood, the name by which his father and sisters and brother know him—Willie—has grown detestable to him. It is a boy's name, inappropriate now that he is thirty-one years old, living in his own rooms, with his own friends. His own mistress.

Dear Olivia. He should write to her. A whole stream of eloquent words flows through his mind, but he continues to doodle. WBY. WBY. He feels the talk falter and silence rise in the room. He suppresses the urge that rises in him to fill it. WBY, WBY...

He should be using this time to write a letter to Olivia. Why has he not yet written; she would be expecting a letter.

"Mr. Yeats!" The voice of Miss Delaney breaks his reverie. "You don't believe we should commence without Miss Gonne, I'm sure?"

He feels the faces turning his way, awaiting his answer but is unable to satisfy them. The ordinary folly of this very ordinary person, Miss Delaney, makes him lose all social presence of mind. It is his worst fault, rooted in Mars in opposition to Moon. He scratches a note on the paper: *Beware of Mars X moon. Record errors.*

Should he perhaps seek out people he dislikes until he has conquered this petulant combativeness of his? It is always inexcusable to lose one's self-possession, as he and his sister Lolly are so inclined to do. It comes from impatience, from a kind of spiritual fright at someone who is here and now more powerful, even if only from stupidity. He is never angry with those in his power. It is representatives of the collective opinion who make him rage stupidly and rudely, exaggerating what he feels and thinks. He will not succumb. He keeps his head lowered and pushes the nib so hard the paper tears, and he has to begin again at another point.

WBY, he writes. WBY of 18 Woburn Buildings, Euston Road, London. WBY, no longer of his father's house. WBY, poet. WBY, lover of Olivia Shakespear. There, it is done with pen and paper: old name, old life, old love, unseated. He should not be here today; he should be at the hotel working on proofs of his stories. He is coming to hate Maud Gonne's politics, though he no longer, thanks to Olivia, thinks of it as a rival, but he can never see sufficient gain for so much toil. A few more tenants restored to their lands, a few dynamite prisoners released: is it really worth it?

Women, perhaps because the main event of their lives is a giving of themselves and giving birth, gave all to an opinion, as if it were some terrible stone doll. Men take up an opinion lightly and are easily false to it or, even when faithful, keep the habit of many interests. Men see the world, if they are of strong mind and body, with considerate eyes, but to women, opinions become as their children or their sweethearts. The greater their emotional capacity, the more they forget all other things. Thus it is with Maud Gonne and Ireland.

He can no longer afford to let her absorb him in outer things, risking the loss of his inspiration....

The door in the hallway bangs shut, breaking his reverie.

"She is come," says Miss Delaney, and indeed, yes, here is Maud Gonne in the drawing room doorway, her hair the color of a summer sunset on the sea at Rosses Point, Parisian bonnet adding inches to her already great height, so that its top almost brushes the door lintel. That face, the complexion that always makes him think of apple blossoms through which light is falling. A coat of finest wool, cashmere probably, trimmed with velvet and carrying a basket topped by a blanket.

"Gentlemen!" Her face is a picture of apology. "Ladies! I am I, so terribly sorry. My lateness was..." She gives a tragic shrug "... unavoidable."

"No matter," says Arthur Lynch, smoothing his mustache with his index finger. "Here you are now, and isn't that the main thing."

"Funny that," says Stephen McKenna. "And there I was thinking the main thing was to get this association of ours off the ground."

"You are quite right, Mr. McKenna." She dips her head to one side. "It is unforgivable to keep you all waiting like this. I did not intend it so; believe me. I was most unavoidably detained."

She looks down at the basket. The blanket appears to move. At first WB thinks himself mistaken, but then it happens again: something live is there. A child? He doesn't know why, but he is suddenly gripped by alarm, as if an icy fist has taken his internal organs in his hand and was about to crush them.

"Please, everybody," Maud Gonne says, smiling around. "Know that the fault was not mine." She peeps into the blanket, which wriggles. "This is the being you must blame."

The corner of the blanket is thrown aside, and a small and a hairy paw comes into view. Then two skittering brown eyes in a jerking head.

"Ladies and Gentlemen," says Maud Gonne. "Allow me to introduce Chaperone."

It is a monkey, a marmoset.

"What the devil!" expostulates Lynch.

Maud Gonne's teeth glitter. "When I was younger, my aunts were always concerned about my tendency to go about alone. So I bought a small primate on a trip to Marseilles and called him Chaperone and told my aunts that I was no longer alone. The original Chaperone has gone to his reward, but this little fellow is named for him."

Yeats has heard her tell this tale before. A good show. Even taciturn Synge is entranced. The monkey stares round with a look of sadness and old age: they are degenerate men, monkeys, not man's ancestors.

"The poor dear is unwell," Maud Gonne says. "Hence my disappearance. I walked the streets of Passy and then Auteuil, seeking a vet who would see us on New Year's Day."

As if they are a double act in some music hall, the monkey lets a fit of small sneezes, one after another. Then a small cry.

"You see, poor darling. His eyes stream up with tears and need to be wiped." She takes a handkerchief from her purse, snaps it shut, wipes the monkey's eyes. "There, there my little one." She dabs at his eyes, and he tries to grab the handkerchief from her. Maud Gonne laughs, says to the company, "Do not worry, he shall not interfere with the work."

"If so, might we please proceed?" says Lynch, putting his watch back in his fob.

She moves to the chair that has been left empty for her and sits, the monkey curled on her lap. "Miss Delaney, you have the papers."

Miss Delaney nods, passes them across.

Miss Delaney holds up the pen and paper she has at the ready.

"Can you all see in this dark?" asks Richard Best, from behind his spectacles. "Because I'm damned if I can."

"We need the lamps lit," says Maud Gonne, stroking the monkey's curving spine. "Would you be so kind, Mr. Yeats? Thank you so much. So come, let us begin."

Observe, thinks WB. See how she can look at each man to whom she speaks as if he were the only man in all the world.

Her low, thrilling notes can charm even her most bitter enemy. For strange to say, she has enemies among this band of extremists whose opinion she shares.

He watches her pass from one of her guests to the next with smiling sympathy. Hears her speak English and French, both with a remarkable purity of phrase and accent. Notices how the subtle artifice of her beauty leaves each of them feeling elevated by association.

The meeting concludes once she has what she wanted from this day: her loose grouping of Irish nationalists is now molded into *L'Alliance Irlandaise*, committed to a centenary celebrating 1798. All her suggestions have been taken up. She will ensure a French presence at each of the gatherings and muster meetings to be held throughout the coming year in Ireland. They will help raise funds to erect Wolfe Tone monuments in the towns, and she will write notices for the press. And they need a sympathetic publication here in France, so she intends to fund and edit one *L'Irlande Libre*.

It is now time to go. Lynch takes and palpates her hand, as if it were the handle of a village pump.

"*Au revoir*, Mr. Lynch," she says, so charming. Handsome face, athletic figure. Cordial smile. Dark blue eyes. Quick eager clasp of his hand. Musical ring of his voice. A suggestion of Don Quixote in his manner. Does he interest her?

"And goodbye, Mr. Synge, thank you so much for coming. And Mr. McKenna," she inclines her head with grace. "Until we meet again."

Some more lifting of hats and buttoning of coats and tying of scarves against the winter air, and then they are all gone, all except Miss Delaney, now officially the Secretary of *L'Alliance Irlandais*, who is still in the dining room, stooped over the big red book, greatly conscious of her responsibilities.

Maud Gonne's mood is high and exalted. "I do believe that went just about as well as we could have hoped."

Her skin is flushed, her hair has come a little loose. He turns away from this excitement. It will take all his power to calm her for the real work of their day. He pats the pocket of his jacket, feels the reassuring swell within, the drug that will help them slip into the altered consciousness they need.

His interest in her now is purely in her seership. He cannot influence her outer actions, but he can dominate her inner being, guide her clairvoyance to produce forms that arise from both minds, though mainly seen by hers.

And he has such news for her. In August, while staying in Ireland, he found what they have so long been seeking: a site for their Castle of the Heroes. A tiny, uninhabited island in the center of Lough Key, with a ruined castle at its center. Castle Rock, the locals call it. The last man who lived there, apparently, was Douglas Hyde's father—when young he stayed there a few months—but it is not too dilapidated. The roof is sound, the windows intact, and there is even a stone platform for meditation. With a little money, it can easily be made habitable.

And so the work on the Celtic Mysteries has become urgent. Russell has been called in, also Uncle George and other members of the Golden Dawn: Dorothea and Edmund Hunter, Annie Horniman and, of course, McGregor Mathers. It is to further this work with Mathers and Maud Gonne that he is here in Paris, instead of in his rooms in London with Olivia. (Dear Olivia.)

"So, Mr. Yeats, nineteen months to create a triumph for Ireland."

"We shall see."

Miss Delaney is packing books into her bag in her self-conscious way, hoping to be invited to stay. WB is afraid to sit in case it should encourage her to remain. He hopes Maud Gonne won't ask him about her writing. Some months ago she gave him some stories of Miss Delaney's to read and, if possible, to place, but he has not even tried: he cannot afford to be associated with writing of such deficiency.

Miss Delaney perhaps feels his attention on her and turns his way. "How do you find Paris, Mr. Yeats?" she asks in her strong brogue. "Do you like it?"

Like? Like? What a word for the city where one can spend an entire day with Moreau's chimeras and demon lovers, where Mme Loie Fuller nightly tantalizes the theatre with her veils.

"Mr. Yeats thinks he might move here," says Maud Gonne. "He thinks only Paris is able for the advanced theatre."

"You'd make a grand addition to the place," says Miss Delaney. "We'd all be delighted."

He bows a small bow. "Nothing is settled."

He despises his own stiffness, that he can't give to this vulgar woman simple kindness, as Maud Gonne does so naturally. Her bag is packed. Still she lingers, but no invitation comes, and Maud Gonne sees her out.

Precious Amour

OUTSIDE, PARIS is winding down. Since morning, the toyshops, the flower shops and the four rival princes of the bonbon trade—Siraudin, Boissier, Guerre and Jullien—have been open for business, but now, as daylight begins to dim, their bustle is slowing. Darkness seeps from the unlit corners of streets and alleyways, and along the arc of the Seine, the breath of dusk rises, ruffling the blackening waters.

In *le parc zoologique*, the animals are being fed their evening meal, giving pause to visitors who were in the act of leaving. Near the Western exit, on the path in front of the aviary, a little girl is bent over the lawn. She knows nothing of feeding time. Whatever she sees among the blades of grass has all her attention.

"Iseult, please," her father says again, from twenty paces ahead, but she does not lift her head.

He knows that even if she did, her eyes would wear that dark expression he finds so unnerving. Do all children of this age look so cognizant? He does not remember it with Henri. Certainly not all two-and-a-half-year-olds are so stubborn. His son never was... but then, neither is his mother. The lengthiest days of provocative debate at the *Chambre* have not tried him as has this one day with his daughter.

When Maud brought the girl to him—a crisis provoked by some visitors from Ireland and Ghénia de St. Croix becoming suddenly unavailable—he had thought he should quite enjoy the experience of a day with her. He has been very busy of late and at first, yes, it was a pleasure, walking with her small hand in his, past the wine shops and the cab stands and tobacco bureau, accepting cheery good wishes: *Je vous la souhaite bonne et heureuse.* A beautiful child brings out the best in people, and she is an exceptionally beautiful child.

In the chocolatier's, as he lifted her into his arms so she could point out her choice of bonbon, the fat feel of her legs against his hands, and the excited beauty of her face, and the sweet smell in the shop, and her arms around his neck, all welled in him, taking him by surprise. So much so that when the shopkeeper said, "*Ah Monsieur, quelle adorable petite fille,*" with the sincerest admiration, he had to dip his head to hide his face in her hair.

(With every passing year, it seems, he grows more sentimental.)

Marrons glacés, she chose, and when she asked that Tassie too might have some—Tassie being that ridiculous rag-doll she insisted on carrying everywhere—he shared the shoptender's smiles and indulged her without wincing at the price (seven francs to the pound!). He set her gently to the floor, and when he handed her the two glazed-paper cornets and she looked up at him through her silky lashes with a gaze of unadulterated adoration, her arms full of her beloved Tassie and the bonbons, he felt himself well rewarded.

All most gratifying.

But then began the trouble. She wanted to eat them then and there instead of at the zoo, and when he declined his permission for this, she threw a tantrum as spectacular as the worst of her mother's!

"Tassie want bonbons *now!*"

He had to secrete the cornets into the inner pocket of his jacket, which very much ruined the line. She would not be calmed. Before they had gone a hundred paces, her outbursts were attracting such attention from passers-by, and he so feared a sticky mess on his best grey wool, that he ended by giving them to her after all.

It was the first of many such struggles throughout the day. Maud is too lax, that is the problem, and the result is that Iseult is a perfect little savage, giving in to every impulse.

Now, he takes out his watch to check the time. Almost 4:15. It seems as if he has been forever on this path, trying to leave this wretched place. He cannot stand this dawdling, it makes his legs ache, but she will not let him carry her.

He walks back towards her. "Iseult, we must hurry. The gates will be closed, and we shall be locked in. All night."

"Oh yes!" She claps her hands. "That is good, Papon."

"No, it is not, my dear. The night would be dark and cold, and the big bear would come out and eat us."

The darkness glows in her eyes. "Bear in cage."

"Not at night. At night all the animals come out. And if they find a little girl still left in here, they will eat her up. Now come on."

Once again, he turns and walks, but this time with only half a hope that she will follow. Sure enough, when he looks back, she is bent once again, rapt, over the grass. She calls him. "Look, Papon."

"We have no time."

"Papon, look."

"Truly Iseult, I must insist—"

"Papon! Loooooooook."

"Oh for goodness' sake, what? What is it?"

He returns to her and looks at what lies beyond the little pointing finger. He can only see a bug. Black. Hard shelled. *Un cafard*, a cockroach.

"Leave that, Iseult. It's not nice."

"Iseult look Papon."

What she means is that she has made him look. This afternoon he has become more accustomed to her lingo. "All right, Iseult. Very nice. Now let us please go."

"No."

No again. Must everything today be "No!" and "Look!" and "Don't want to!" in that bossy tone so reminiscent of her mother?

Now the cockroach is forgotten, and now an ordinary leaf on an ordinary bush has all her attention as she shows it to her rag of a doll, stroking its surface. All the monkeys, lions and giraffes put together are no more to her than this leaf she is caressing.

Millevoye stops in front of the caged tiger, lamenting magnificence confined. Even in the gathering gloom, the glory of the beast's striped limbs is manifest. This zoo in the *Jardin des Plantes*—the world's first to be opened to the public rather than kept as the private plaything of an aristocrat—was intended to be a zoological Louvre, stocked with creatures seized from Europe and beyond by the Revolutionary armies, its exhibits displayed in cages scattered among Rousseauesque parkland designed to imitate what Parisians call *la nature.*

In actuality, it is a disgrace, cramped and unclean. The terrarium smells like an open sewer, and far too many of the cages are too small. He counts the tiger's paces: one-two-three-four-five-six... Only seven paces before he has to turn to walk in the opposite direction. One more than the polar bear he observed earlier.

Millevoye is one of a group of reformers who has put pressure in the *Chambre* on the committee that runs the zoo to make improvements. It is why he thought to bring Iseult here today: to check on progress. True liberty is, of course, impossible to grant to the animals, but some of the buildings and parts of the park have been modified to give to visitors an impression of freedom. It is too little and for the wrong reasons—the managers are moved less by reforming instincts than by the falling levels of visitors to their facility—but it is a start, and would not have happened without their pressure group.

He looks back. His daughter has not moved one step, still focused on the grass, dark hair falling forward.

"Come *along* my dear."

How can she remain so unmoved by the sights around her? He had thought she would love it here, but he might as well have brought her to the local park. Is it that she is too young? Or too like her mother, who, though she claims to be such an animal lover, responded to his campaign by saying that many an Irish family—not to mention the denizens of the prisons—would be happy to be confined in quarters as roomy as the tiger pen at *le parc zoologique.*

"Come Iseult. Come now. We must go home."

~

Iseult doesn't want to walk. She's tired, though she doesn't yet know herself well enough to name the sticky feeling that's stopped her in her tracks. In her short and inward-pointing life, nothing has happened often enough or lasted long enough yet to be held and named. Fatigue, hunger, pain, pleasure are sensations that rise like winds through the grass.

So it's not she who cries, it's sadness itself; not she who stamps her foot and refuses to budge, but frustration.

The tacky drag of feeling won't let her walk. Her head is marshmallow, and all the animal names Papon gave her knock about inside it, making it hurt. If she had a tower of bricks in front of her now, she would kick them right over, without knowing why.

She holds up Tassie to show her a bush that looks like the bush outside the grove of wonder in Passy park. Tassie looks at the leaf, and Iseult takes it in her fingers to show her how it feels. "Furry," she whispers into her ear. The feel reminds her of Lulu, the cat. As she whispers, Tassie jerks, then flies up into the air, like an arrow from a bow.

"Tassie!"

"Stop that noise, silly girl. Look, dolly is leaving. Come along. Follow dolly."

"Tassiiiie!" Iseult screams, then screams again louder, and Tassie's face returns, looming large and close against Iseult's own, her stitch smile glad to be back. Iseult reaches for her, but again she jerks away.

"Dolly wants you to follow her, Iseult."

"No! Papon! Tassie!"

"Come and get her, here she is... Phew! I do believe the thing smells. Come... Here she is. She wants you."

Iseult cannot run after her. Gluey tiredness has her sealed in place. She starts to scream. "Noooooo!" The noise she makes frightens her, and she howls louder.

"Stop it at once, you naughty girl. Your dolly is here. You are to come to her."

"No!" Iseult screams again. "Meeeee want Tassieeeeeee!"

"Stop. Here is your stupid doll. Stop it at once!"

Tassie is back. Iseult clutches her tight. Poor Tassie is crying too.

Papon's face comes down to hers. "Iseult, please. You must come. For Papon."

Tassie says no. Tassie says Papon is bad.

"Iseult, I am warning you now. I shall have to smack you. I do not want to smack you."

He grabs her hand, begins to drag her along.

Tassie starts to scream, and Iseult copies her. "Aaaaaeeeeeek!"

"Stop it, you wicked child."

Her hand is being grasped, turned over. A smack lands, sharp and stinging. Pain and shock stops her scream. And then, the sharp slap of a hand on her bottom. And then another, harder. Her breath constricts. Again, another.

Iseult has never been smacked before.

Cradling her injured hand in her armpit, she finds her breath, and now she really starts to scream. "A...mour," she sobs.

"Enough," hisses Millevoye. The release of physical punishment has added shame to the cocktail of feelings that assails him.

"Amour... Iseult... want... Am...our." She starts to raise her voice again. "AMOUR! AHHH-MOUR!"

The girl is impossible. Maud has asked him to keep her for the entire evening, until Ghénia can return to collect her. Impossible.

She crouches, her face puckered up like a pug dog, theatrical sobs shaking her body. Very well then: he picks her up. "We shall see, my little *anarchiste*, who is the person in charge here."

She begins to kick. "AHHH-MOUR!"

He tightens his grasp.

"Papon, NO! My LEG! You hurt LEG."

"Why do you scream so, Iseult? Am I not doing what you asked? Am I not taking you to your precious Amour?"

A Torn Rose

On Maud Gonne's return to the room, she says: "You had no luck placing Delaney's writings?"

He doesn't tell her that he didn't even try, a decision that at the time seemed like the only one possible. Now, in her generous presence, he wonders how he could have failed to do this small thing for her friend.

"Oh I know she is not artistic," Maud says. "But I thought the sensational weirdness of some of them might suit a certain class of not very cultivated people. And it would be doing such a charity to the poor girl."

"Perhaps it might be kinder not to encourage."

"I cannot think it is our job to *discourage*. Why would the gods give Delaney the impulse to write if the world has no use for her writings? Who knows what may come if she is resolute?"

Her monkey peeps at him around the corner of her chair, then scurries behind the *pouffe*. "Come here, my little Chappie," says Maud Gonne, shrugging off Miss Delaney. She'd prefer an animal to a human any day, and her tones warm now to the affectionate voice she always uses with her menagerie. "This is for you, *mon petit. Oui*, for you." She cracks the shell and holds it out. "*Voilà*."

The monkey snatches it and runs with a mistrustful greed that makes them both laugh.

"Tell me—this news I hear of you from Dublin. Is it true?"

"What news?"

"Taken up, I am told, by the London papers."

"You speak in riddles."

"Come now, Mr. Yeats. Do not play coy with me."

"I assure you, I know not—"

"Is it true that you have lately married a widow?"

"Married! If such a thing were true, don't you think you might have heard it first from me?"

She smiles. "I did think that we were sufficiently friends for you to have told me. But then, on reflection, I thought: perhaps not. Marriage, after all, is only a little detail in life. I said to my-self: if he did marry, it would make no difference to his character or life or to our work together. So I began to think it quite possible that you had married and not thought it important enough to report."

Such bantering on such a topic. Surely this is a mask? She speaks as if he had never proposed that she should share the little kingdom he would make.

"You well know whom I would choose to marry."

"Come, Mr. Yeats, I was only—"

"Oh Miss Gonne, why do you not give up your tragic declamatory struggle, and come sit with me in the kingdom I am making and be its queen?"

"Are you not tired of asking me that question? How often have I told you that you and the world would not thank me for marrying you? You make such beautiful poetry out of what you call your love and your unhappiness. Marriage would be such a dull affair in comparison."

He shakes his head, vehemently. "If not for me, do it for Ireland. You have more to offer our country as symbol than as organizer or propagandist." He leans forward to persuade. "Ours is the voice of the renaissance that is coming, Miss Gonne. The renaissance of the soul against the intellect."

"Mr. Yeats, please..."

She squirms in her seat, but at least he has broken through the teasing mask. She is his again, the only woman who knows all the subtlety of his thought.

"Oh, we will make no more than a beginning, I know that," he says. "But centuries after we die, cities will be overthrown because of an anthem we once hummed, or a fabric full of meaning that we hung upon a wall. For that, you will accept me."

"If you begin to make love to me again, Mr. Yeats, I will not be able to see you, and that will distress me very much."

"For that, you will accept a penniless suitor. And for that I will relinquish pure devotion to my magic and to my poetry in order to further your political causes. That is the price we will pay for our happiness."

"I do not want you to give me such a place in your life."

"We shall be martyrs together. For pleasure seekers who pay no price are immoral. True lovers are united by their payment to Iseult and Brunhilde and all the saints of love."

"Are you listening to me, Mr. Yeats? If you find that an absolutely platonic friendship—which is all I can or ever will be able to give—unsettles you and spoils your work, then you must have the strength and courage at once to give up meeting me."

"Every desire, every joy, has its martyrdom. By that it is uplifted above the world and becomes part of revelation. Miss Gonne, I will do whatever you like, work for any cause you see fit, live as you tell me to live. I should die to serve you and think it happiness."

She stands. "Oh Mr. Yeats, I am only a commonplace woman," she says, as though she repeated words she knew by heart. "And you are, I think, a man of genius. Yet some day I know you will understand what I am telling you. This martyrdom of which you speak is the very opposite to that which you are called to make. It is not your work that you are called on to sacrifice, it is me."

The monkey makes little melancholy cries at the hearthrug.

When he does not answer her, she says in a gentler voice: "What is best for your genius, that is what must always be your first consideration. For the honor of our country, the world must recognize you as one of the great poets of the coming century. Your genius belongs to Ireland, and you have no right to allow anything to injure it. Not even our friendship."

Can it be so? If he could but prove himself to her by putting his hand in the fire until it burnt, would not that make her understand that devotion such as his was not to be wasted? The flames flicker and lick at the chimney, and he thinks to do it but does not, held back not by the fear of pain but the fear of being thought mad. *Is he mad?*

When he last stayed in Sligo with his uncle George, he called on his cousin, Henry Middleton, towards midnight and asked him to get his yacht out, for he wanted to find out what sea-birds began to stir before dawn. Henry was indignant and refused and the plan would have been scuppered, only Elizabeth, his elder sister, overheard and came to the head of the stairs and forbade Henry to stir. That so vexed him that he shouted to the kitchen for his sea boots.

He came in a great gloom, though. He himself had people's respect, he declared, and nobody so far said he was mad, as they said WB was. He didn't want them to start.

"Do you understand me, Mr. Yeats?"

Yes, he understands. Like Lancelot, he must love his queen to the last. "If you do not love me now," he says, "you will come to love me in time. A love as great as mine must have some meaning."

To his dismay, she laughs.

"Oh come," she says, crosses towards the cupboard with purpose. "Let us put talk of love aside for now. Let us begin the work."

~

Maud Gonne opens the double doors to the dining room, where she keeps the birds twittering in their cages, to let out the monkey and also the hound, who has been enjoying a sleep in front of the fire. Animal life dispatched for now, she draws the shutters.

From a cupboard she takes a large, wooden box and from it, swathes of blue chiffon, which she places over the lamps. The fabric makes the light in the room dim and violet. Light at the blue end of the spectrum is what you want, say those in the know, if you're in the business of coaxing out the spirits.

From the box, she takes a bottle of Newgrange river-water, and while WB lights up some incense, she sprinkles the consecrated water on the furniture and into the air. He brings the small armchair across, beside the chaise longue where she will lie. Then they distribute around the room the implements that will help them crystallize the astral plane: a mirror, Enochian squares, a pyramid, diagrams of the elemental forces they call Tattvas...

Room set, she takes down cigarette papers and tobacco from a box on a high shelf and places them on the coffee table, then hitches up her skirt to sit cross-legged and straight-backed, like an oriental, on the floor beside his chair. It makes her a little stiff, but she likes the careless feel of it. And she knows he likes her to sit beneath him, looking up.

Today she's happy to give him that small pleasure.

He is sifting the tobacco evenly along the length of the ciga-rette paper with his long fingers. His fingers are beautiful; she has noticed that before. He strikes the match, lighting a corner of the lump of resin, and her nostrils fill with the sweet hash-ish scent. Once the resin has cooled enough to touch, he breaks away some crumbs and scatters them through the tobacco. Carefully, he lifts the open paper and begins to roll it around the tobacco to form a cigarette. With small flicks of a pink tongue, he licks the edge, moistening the gum. A twist on top, a small piece of board to stiffen the base, and it is complete.

He hands it to her, strikes another match, and she leans into the flame. She draws deep to keep it alight: one inhalation, down into her lungs. A second, then a third, and she hands it back to him. He closes his eyes, and she sees he is wearing the precise ex-pression that her pious Aunt Judith makes at Holy Communion. That must be why he suggested they should smoke the drug this time. Not just because his friend Arthur Symons declared it a more efficient mode of getting the drug into the bloodstream, but so they might share it. Mouth upon vestige of mouth, the ecstasy of putting his lips where hers have been.

Sometimes, his adoration irritates her; sometimes, like ear-lier, it frightens her. Today, it makes her smile. He has always been a good friend to her. She wants to be a good friend to him. He knows what it is to suffer. Her thoughts are disintegrating. It is the effect of the drug. The flowers on the wallpaper appear to stand out from the wall as if one could go over and cup them in one's hands and smell a fragrance. Hashish is such a strange drug, making every object seem more complete in itself and si-multaneously more connected to all.

They don the black tau robes she's laid out for the purpose, then, standing side-by-side on the hearth, the fireplace behind them, East, they make the sign of the cross. Only it's not the Kabbalistic cross any more for them, but the Celtic.

They have researched Celtic spirits and omens, heroic deeds and wonder voyages, to draw on for their new rites, in echo of the sinuous patterns, potent symbols and shape-shifting figures of Celtic art. It is giving WB a new understanding of the liminal, the twilight of dawn and dusk that is both night and day; the plash of dew and mist that is both air and water; the dream-state that is both life and death.

Now, standing together, they visualize themselves expand-ing, until in their minds, they grow larger than the room, and they rise through the ceiling, to surround the building, then the city of Paris, the country of France, the continent of Europe, the whole world, the planet. On they continue to grow, until the solar system is a disk at their feet, until they rise above the spiral form of the Milky Way, and on they continue to grow until the galaxy is a speck of light at their feet, and the hundred billion or so other galaxies shine like tiny stars in the oval shaped auras they have imaginatively generated, their vast astral bodies.

Yet, even as they outgrow the galaxies and float in the whole universe, their feet remain firmly planted in the ritual room, in Maud Gonne's apartment.

Banishing ritual complete, Maud Gonne lies down on the chaise longue, and he takes his seat in the chair beside her, inch-es from her head. "You are disturbed?" he asks.

Her trances are often preceded by a moment of nausea or giddiness.

"No."

"Ready to proceed?"

She inclines her head. She feels ineffably well.

He places a fire wand in her hand to help focus her will and clarify their intention and holds up a black, painted square of card. She gazes at the card, concentrating on the symbol, transferring the vital effort from the optic nerve to the men-tal perception, from eye-seeing to thought-seeing, letting one form of apprehension glide into the other. Her every movement now has symbolic meaning, of which she is fully conscious. Now, while manipulating an object in the physical plane, her god-form may be manipulating an entirely different force in the astral plane.

He says, "Picture a square of yellow, perhaps it might be a door."

The picture comes easily to her. All is clear and radiant. "Walk through it," he says. "Tell me what you see beyond."

"I see a well, in a garden. Leaning over the well on the left is a mountain-ash tree, laden with red berries. They keep dropping, dropping into the water, like drops of blood reddening the pool."

"Are you alone?"

"No. Midir is here."

"How does he look?"

"He is calm. He shows me interlocking circles."

"How many are your circles?"

"Three of each. Three interlocking circles of Heaven, my way to peace. And three of Hell. Midir is telling me that I am in Hell now, but that some day, I will be able to enter the three heavenly circles, though now I cannot."

"And what do you see within them?"

"The first is a garden. The circle of almost fulfilled desire."

It is no effort now to see, as all is bathed in light. The garden is very beautiful, with butterflies and bees, exotic and elegant flowers. As she focuses upon it, already it is fading into the second circle. Midir leads her on, and she is his willing vassal.

"The second is a place in a wood with a fallen tree. It is quiet, the place of peace eternal. This, Midir says, is very brief for any human soul."

She can hear the scratching of Willie Yeats's pen on paper writing down what she sees. Near her ear but a long way off.

After a time he says: "And the third?"

"A mountain with a winding road and a cross." She pauses. "The circle of labor from Divine love."

"And what of the hellish circles?" he asks.

The moment he says this, the light switches to dark grey. It is not night but the kind of light that precedes a great thunderstorm. Water swells. "I see an ocean, a dark ocean, with hands of drowning men rising out of it."

Her voice has changed, and her body—she is still aware of it on the chaise while her soul takes this journey—begins to feel cold. "This is the circle of unfulfilled desire. I can see a great precipice with dragons trying in vain to climb it, a continual climbing and falling."

She would rather not go on. She knows she must go on.

"And again, the third circle?"

"A vast emptiness." She can hear anguish forming the words. She has an urge to cry. "The falling petals of a torn rose."

"What is this circle?"

"This is the circle of revenge."

Silence falls, except for the scraping of the pen.

Midir leaves the circle of revenge and takes her along a path, towards a sprinkling of lights. Along the way, he hands her over to another man, an old man with a long grey beard, who points the way to a castle on a hill. "There is a castle and a wizard who—"

Ring, ring! This is a sound from the outer world, not the inner. *Ring, ring!* Her doorbell. The mind picture vanishes as she is snapped back to the material plane. She knows that signature ring.

"Somebody..." she says, jumping up. "The door... Mr. Yeats!"

"Miss Gonne, please. Do not strain yourself... Cannot Joséphine take care of whoever it is?"

"No, quickly, get up..." She is throwing off her robe, rolling it into a ball, stuffing it under the chair. "Please... help me set this place to rights. I think it is... It could be some of our Irish friends returned."

She is almost running now to the door, snatching the blue cloth from the lamp as she goes.

A voice calls from the hallway. "Maud? *Est-ce que tu es là?*"

"Ple-e-e-ase," she hisses back, opening the door only wide enough to slip through. "Take off your robe. And get rid of what is on the table. Stick it into the box."

"But—"
"I beg of you."
The voice comes again: "Maud?"
"Who is it?" asks the poet, getting up but oh-so-slowly.
"I have no idea."
She is gone.

A Mouthful Of Air

LEFT ALONE, what can he do but to do her bidding, but he rises slowly. It is not good for her to throw off her trance so quickly. He himself feels to be so abruptly interrupted. He removes his robe, sweeps up the loose tobacco with his hands and throws it in the fire, puts the paraphernalia away in its box.

Voices in the hall. A male voice. Is that a child he hears? And now hers, a furious whisper.

By the time they come in, he has the room reverted to order. She and a tall Frenchman stand in the doorway, reflected in the mirror opposite, so that at first, to his dream-and-drug-befuddled mind, it is as if there are two couples, not one.

"Mr. Yeats," says Maud Gonne, leading the fellow in. "You remember Monsieur Millevoye?"

The Boulangist journalist. A sensationalist. His name is one of those linked to hers by malicious gossip, gossip that has stirred a poem in him. It is as yet unwritten, but one line keeps recurring: their children's children will say they lied.

"And you remember Mr. Yeats?"

"Indeed." The hand the Frenchman proffers is lax, almost greasy. He has the Gallic arrogance: his bow is conventional but somehow manages to be antagonistic, too.

Frustration burns. Their work shall not resume tonight. Is this to be his life always, this endless preparation for something that never happens?

"We are just about to take tea, Mr. Millevoye. You will join us?"

"Alas, I need to leave. I am here only to deliver Iseult."

Maud Gonne looks about her. "Where is Iseult?"

The Frenchman too looks behind. "She was here a moment ago."

Maud Gonne goes to the door. "Iseult..." calls Maud Gonne. "Are you there?"

A small bundle of energy comes charging in from the hallway and flings itself at Maud Gonne's legs. "Amour."

"There, my little one. Why all the fuss?" Maud Gonne crouches down, so she is level with the child's face. This is a new mask; it makes him feel queasy. Or is that the drug befuddlement? "Did you have a nice time?"

"*Moi voit singe.*"

"A monkey? You mean Chap?"

"*Grand singe. Beaucoup de singes.*"

"The zoological gardens," says M. Millevoye.

"How lovely. Now Iseult, where are your manners?" She pulls the folds of her skirt out of the child's grasp. "Come out of there, and say 'Bonjour' to our guest."

The girl peeps, suspicious. How should he address her? "How do you do?" he attempts, holding out his hand. She disappears back into the skirts.

"Don't be shy, darling. Mr. Yeats will think you most impolite."

"Oh I don't, I assure you. Assuredly not."

"She is tired, are you not, my sweet?"

Maud Gonne whispers a long string of words into the small ear. Whatever she says makes the girl disengage herself and walk across to him with hand outstretched. "*Bonsoir M. Yeats,*" she says.

"*Bonsoir, Mademoiselle,*" he replies, self-conscious of his deplorable accent.

Millevoye coughs. "I must leave, I am already late."

"Certainly, do not let us detain you," says Maud Gonne.

WB likes the tone in which she says this.

Goodbyes are made and she leads the interloper out. The child remains behind, looking up at him, as if for guidance. Her eyes seem almost too large for her small head to hold. From the hallway comes an animated exchange in French that is somehow depressing.

"What age are you?" he asks the girl, a poor attempt to be friendly.

"AMOUR!" she shrieks, turning towards the door.

Even he, with his atrocious French, understands that word. What a strange moniker for her to give Maud Gonne. She follows her amour out to the hall, leaving him with his shame, struck once again by his accursed timidity, this quality of his that is so painful to experience. Timid with a tiny child. Pitiful!

The hall door closes. Maud Gonne returns with the child in her arms. "Monsieur Millevoye let himself in with Ghénia's key," she says.

He feels an answer is required of him, but what?

The child squirms in Maud Gonne's arms, much as the monkey did earlier. "*Bonbon, Amour. Tu dis.*"

"Yes, my little one. You shall have your bonbon." She sets her down and puts her hand in her skirt pocket. "Now hold out your hands like a good girl."

Yeats watches. He has seen her gay beneficence with the urchins of Dublin and London for whom she always has coppers or some fruit or nuts, but this is something he must add to his imagery of her. All the child's self leans into those two greedy, grasping hands. Maud Gonne places a sweet in each: "*Un, deux...*" then another: "*trois... quatre.* Now, go across to the table, and when you have eaten them, you must go to bed as you promised."

The child nods, crosses to the table and climbs up onto the chair. She sits with her back to them, her dark hair hanging down. Maud Gonne returns to the chair opposite him, drops her voice to a whisper. "Her mother is a young girl to whom the world has not been kind."

"When is the world ever kind?"

"Ghénia and I have taken pity on her. I am thinking I might adopt her."

The suggestion alarms him. "A generous gesture."

She smiles one of her beatific smiles. Yes, he has pleased her. One never quite knows what will please her.

"But would you not be concerned that such an arrangement might limit your freedom?" he asks.

"I should hire a nursemaid. Or make use of one of the con-vents who are very willing to take in young girls for financial reimbursement."

He nods, slowly.

"I sense you do not approve. I hope it is not for any reasons of false morality. These things happen in life, do they not? Are we to waste our time in condemnations? Why should this little one suffer for the sins of her father?"

"And her mother."

"Her mother was only a young girl, too young to be con-demned. The man was a great deal older and married. But stop... Really, are you shocked, Mr. Yeats? You who are so indulgent of the far greater vices of your London friends."

"No, no. Not shocked."

"What then?"

"A little... concerned, perhaps." He waves his hands before him, helplessly. He is being tried and found wanting.

"Such double standards. Do you feel it is right that the wom-an should suffer so much more than the man in these matters, Mr. Yeats?"

"Miss Gonne, I assure you, I did not mean to be in any way... My concern is only that you should not encumber yourself with a situation that is detrimental to your work."

She knows he would, by the writings of this school that he hopes to found, forge a secret symbolical relation to the religious mysteries. It is work that needs great concentration. "You know my work will always come first, Mr. Yeats. It was unfortunate that we were interrupted tonight, but we can resume. Once Is-eult is in bed, she falls immediately to sleep and doesn't waken. She shall not disturb us."

He's appalled. Can she really think the force of their work will be unaffected by the child's presence? But she's turned from him. "Come my little one. Time for bed. You are tired, *ma petite chérie*, are you not? *Dis Bonne Nuit.*"

The child appraises him with dark eyes. "*Bonne Nuit.*"

"Good night, my dear."

Maud Gonne points to the sideboard, the decanter. "Help yourself to refreshments, I shall return."

As she is leaving the room, he calls her back. "Miss Gonne?"

She turns, the child's hand in hers, and the smaller head turns too, an eerie echo of Maud Gonne's expression. Still he refuses to see.

"Your vision... earlier... Did you see color?"

"Why yes."

"Good," he says, nodding. "Good. The visions that come in color are true."

Gone Weeping Away

Thank you so much for your letter. I have been meaning to write very often lately, but I have been so busy. I enclose an article for United Ireland. Let me know when it appears and send me a copy, as I don't always see it. I am very busy with the new paper, L'Irlande Libre.

I wanted often to write and tell you how much I love your book of wild and dreamy stories, The Secret Rose. I like it best of all your work. I have it by my bed, and I read a little every night. I have read it all through and go back and read some of it many times, especially "Rosa Alchemica." That is the one I think I like the best.

The language is so lovely, it is like some wonderful Eastern jewel. One never tires of it—it must be heavenly to be able to express one's thoughts like that...

...I hope you will be in Dublin for the meeting on the 22nd. We have fixed it for the 22nd as a protest against the Jubilee. Do come for it as you and I will be the only delegates from London, and I must have someone to support me.

I think both the 2 committees here & in London are really anxious for united action for the '98 movement, so our task will, I hope, be easy. Do come to Dublin for the meeting—it is necessary!

Then I have to thank you for the dream drug, which I have not tried as yet, being very busy and having need of all my energy and activity for the moment. But I mean to try it soon.

I saw Dr. Ryan yesterday. He told me you were again suffering from your eyes, have you been working too much? Or trying too much vision work? Do take care. Let me know how you are.

I will write no more today, as I am very busy getting off material for L'Irlande Libre.

With very kind regards
Always your very sincere friend
Maud Gonne

When Olivia arrives at Woburn Buildings, again WB is not in the small, draughty bedroom that looks out on St. Pancras Church with its caryatids and trees, as he used to wait in the early days of their affair. Now, as so often he sits at his desk, in the large, low front room that looks out onto the flagged pavement out front. Neither is he—as is his wont of late—reading love poetry to get himself in the mood. Instead, he is writing letters, and as she arrives, he barely looks up. He lets her sit in silence, looking at him, while he writes on.

After a time she says, "Will you not give off writing, Willie, and come and talk to me?"

"Just a moment." He continues, hardly knowing to whom he is writing, knowing only that he dreads to stop.

"Last time, you spent my entire visit reading."

He looks out the window, pen aloft. "It was a poor play. Yet I think I can read almost anything written in dramatic form."

"She is in London, isn't she?"

The pen hovers above the page.

"You have seen her?"

He puts down the pen.

"Answer me, Willie."

He removes his spectacles.

"Answer me!" she screams.

And he is so shocked to hear mild Olivia's voice so raised that he hurriedly replies. "We dined together, yes."

"You dined together."

"She has had much success with the release of her prisoners." And he begins a story of Maud Gonne visiting a gaol where there are many treason-felony prisoners, and being beset with a vision and seeing when each man would be released, and telling each of them when it would happen, though they were all serving life sentences, and the gaoler and others thought she was wrong. But thus it happened, every prophecy fulfilled to the letter.

Olivia lets a long silence pass, then says: "How do you know?"

"Know?"

"That every prophecy was fulfilled?"

"Maud Gonne told me so."

Over her face passes a look of ineffable sadness. "Why do you never ask me about Dorothy?" she asks

He is puzzled at the swerve of subject, acute even for a woman. Why does she bring up her daughter? And what should he ask of her? What has she to do with him? "Olivia..." he starts, but he cannot go on.

"What? What is it you have to say to me, Willie?"

What to say? The problems they had at the start are not resolved. This is an affair. An affair with a gentle and generous woman, yes, but an affair nonetheless: secret and a little squalid. Perhaps she is touching on something when she raises the question of family. He has known more writers and artists destroyed by the desire to have wife and child and to keep them in comfort than he has seen destroyed by harlots and drink.

Union with Maud Gonne would involve a conflagration of his whole being, not this sordid deception, this unseemly half-life.

He says: "She has overpowered my imagination."

Olivia shakes her head, creases her eyes against tears. She has forced the revelation she didn't want. "No, Willie. No, it is the other way around. Your imagination has placed her on a pedestal. 'Her beauty is an index to her soul,' you say. What happens if you find she does not possess the soul she never claimed to have, but which you insisted on crediting her with? And what happens to the others, as you deny them the soul that you have forced elsewhere?"

He looks down at the paper he had been writing on, hardly knowing whether he should speak.

"You have overpowered the living woman with your imagination, Willie, and now you are in a relationship with an image. If you do not become more like other people, you will have no rest in your life. You will always be unhappy."

He thinks of the story he has so recently written, "The Book of the Great Dhoul," in which Red Hanrahan rejects Cliona of the Wave, when she leaves the Shee and becomes mortal for him.

He had written: *She turned toward him a face so full of the tender substance of mortality, and smiled upon him with lips so full of red mortal blood, that he did not recognize the immortal of his dreams, and she said to him in a caressing voice: "You have always loved me better than your own soul, and you have sought for me everywhere, without knowing what you sought, and now I have come to you and taken on mortality that I may share your sorrow."*

She came over to him, and laying her hand upon his shoulder, said in a half whisper: "I will surround you with peace, and I will make your days calm, and I will grow old by your side. Do you not see I have always loved you?" And as she spoke, her voice was broken with tears.

And WB remembers what he had Hanrahan say to her: *"Woman, be gone out of this. I have had enough of women. I am weary of women. I am weary of life."*

He pre-wrote it and now here he is...

All our lives, we long, we long, thinking it is the moon we long for. So how, when we meet it in the shape of a most fair woman, can we do less than leave all others for her? Must we not seek our dissolution upon her lips?

For Maud Gonne he would endure the travail of passion, the scourge, the plaited thorns, the way crowded with bitter faces, the passionate dream.

"I have failed to be anything to you," Olivia says, still crying. Not even trying not to cry.

He continues to look down at his own writing on the paper, the blur of words on the page, and hears the snap of the clasp of her purse opening, as she takes out a handkerchief, the snap of it closing, the gathering up of her things.

Then he hears silence and knows she is standing at the door, waiting. He does not look up, what can he offer? After long silence, the door opens, slowly closes.

Remorse fights with relief. Poor, dear Olivia. It would always be a grief to him that he could not give her the love that is her beauty's right. He had taken her as mistress from the increasing intensity, the persecution of his bodily need. The satisfaction of the need ended its glamour.

Yet he knows this marks the end of his boyish hope that one can be wisest when happiest.

The old theme from *Axel* returns: The servants would do the living. Happiness was for ordinary people. His fate is to love the most beautiful woman in the world.

Five Songs

1. He Laments the Loss of Love

Pale brows, still hands and dim hair,
I had a beautiful friend
And dreamed that the old despair
Would end in love in the end:
She looked in my heart one day
And saw your image is there;
She has gone weeping away.

2. He Hears the Cry of the Sedge

I wander by the edge
Of this desolate lake
Where wind cries in the sedge,
Until the axle break
That keeps the stars in their round,
And hands hurl in the deep
The banners of East and West,
And the girdle of light is unbound,
Your breast will not lie on the breast
Of your beloved in sleep.

3. He Thinks of Those Who Have Spoken Evil of his Beloved

Half close your eyelids, loosen your hair,
And dream about the great and their pride,
They have spoken against you everywhere,
But weigh this song with the great and their pride;
I made it out of a mouthful of air;
Their children's children shall say they have lied.

4. He Tells of A Valley Full of Lovers

I dreamed that I stood in a valley, and amid sighs,
For happy lovers passed two by two where I stood;
And I dreamed my lost love came stealthily out of the wood
With her cloud-pale eyelids falling on dream-dimmed eyes:
I cried in my dream, O women, bid the young men lay
Their heads on your knees, and drown their eyes with your fair,
Or remembering hers they will find no other face fair
Till all the valleys of the world have been withered away.

Watered With Mothers' Tears

THE EARLY morning air in Dublin is damp and smells sulphuric. Smoke from the ships hangs heavy on the air, mingling with the slow-drifting, yellow fumes from the gasworks. It smells and tastes of fog, but Maud Gonne decides to walk nonetheless; she always prefers to walk when she has to think, and Dagda will keep her safe through the slums she needs to traverse.

The streets are mostly empty so early. Garlands entwine the railings of the wealthier houses of Harcourt Street, and the corporation has made a start on the bunting flags that soon will hang from every lamppost for Queen Victoria's 60th Jubilee.

Once she crosses the road at Kelly's Corner, the streets turn small and crooked, and she is soon in a different Dublin, where the sulphur smell fights with the smell of dung, where muffled drunken voices can be heard nearby, coming, she hopes, no closer. In this Dublin, cats and dogs are thin and hollow-eyed as their owners, if they have owners. Need breeds beggary, and villainy, and prostitution of body and soul. Here, life as it is lived by people like her is a dream as distant as the moon.

As she walks, street urchins gather and run behind her, alert to the possibility of money or amusement. One shouts, "Is that yer donkey, Missus?" meaning Dagda, who is taller than himself.

"You're a donkey," replies another, and they all fall about laughing, as if the comment were the height of wit. Now they have her attention, another is shouting a long line of patter, but his Dublin brogue is so strong that all she can understand is

"Yes missus?" Whatever he's saying gives great amusement to his friends.

She thinks of her own little Iseult, so beautiful, and so pro-tected in her convent. Thanks to the British Empire, the slums of Dublin are the worst in Europe, not limited to the back-streets, or to impoverished ghettos, but spilling into previously fashion-able streets and squares. The houses in this part of the city fell into disrepair after the Act of Union, absentee landlords failing to keep them up and now, as the wealthy move further out, the big red-brick buildings are abandoned to filth, overcrowding and poverty.

The houses look wounded and broken, like the excavations of a lost civilization, windows draped with rags, front walls and gardens slung with clothes lines, smattered with old iron piping, and wooden wheels and crates. At Charlemont Street, a person of indiscriminate age and sex is poking around the ash-bins. She turns to the urchins, asks if any know the house of James Connolly?

"The speecher? Yes'm, I do," says one, and he leads the way with a crippled walk that requires him to help himself along every ten steps or so with his hand, like one of the chimpanzees in the zoological gardens. She follows his puny, twisted lead through an archway and down a lane into a blackened hallway. Two derelicts are sprawled on the landing but her guide steps over them, and mounts the stairs by propelling himself along the bannisters.

"Mind yer step there, Missus, it's rottin."

He stops outside a closed door.

"This is it?" she asks.

He nods.

"Thank you so much." She hands him a coin. He stares at it a moment until she says, "Yes, it is yours, thank you for your help."

He snatches it and leaps up on the banister and slides down, hooting a loud laugh, his entourage in his wake, shouting after him: *Show, show us, give us, give...*

The door is opened by Connolly himself, a stocky man, only

five feet six, square-jawed, with bright intelligent eyes that always show humor. But not now. He is too surprised. "Madame Gonne!"

Pride and natural good manners quickly cover over. "This is a great honor," he says. "Come in, please. Come in."

The beds along two of the walls show that the whole family—he, his wife and four children—live in this single poky and dimly-lit room. Overcoats are folded across the beds, no doubt supplementing the blankets at night. But the place is clean. His wife must be a woman of pride.

There she is in the corner, stopped in the act of bathing her youngest child in a tub atop the table. "Madame Gonne, is it?" She cannot take her arms from the soapy water, or the child—too young to support itself—will fall.

Dagda chooses this moment to lunge forward to lick the cake of soap, thinking it a sweetmeat. The taste is quite horrid to him, and he pulls back, but not before the baby has taken fright.

"Dagda, come here! Sit!" He obeys at once, but it is too late. The child is screaming and started to bawl.

Mrs. Connolly has the child out of the water, clutched to her bosom, wetting her clothes.

"It's all right," she says to the child. "It's all right, now."

"Please tell her not to be afraid. Dagda is gentle as a lamb. He won't harm her."

Mrs. Connolly looks doubtful and opens a strong stare on her. The baby quiets a little, cries turning to whimper.

"Nothing to fear," says her mother. "See now, big doggie sits. See?"

The child settles. "I'm sorry for the alarm, Madame. She was caught unawares."

"Please... It is I... Mrs. Connolly, forgive me for calling unannounced."

"Not at all now,&rdquot; says James Connolly. &ldquot;You are very welcome." He has the rolling r's of the Scots accent. He is hanging the kettle over the fire with its fine marble surround, carved with fruit and leaves. This would have been a gentleman's drawing room, in the house's better days.

At least it gives the Connollys plenty of room for cooking. In one corner is what appears to be a coffin, standing upright, the lid standing beside it. Have they had a bereavement?

They take tea in cracked but clean mugs.

Maud Gonne likes how he speaks to his wife. He treats women as equals. His parents were Irish, he tells her, though he was born in Scotland.

"Cowgate," he says. "In Edinburgh. They called it Little Ireland."

"I do not know it."

"No, you would not," he says with grim smile, and she understands it is a slum. His father worked as a manure carter, removing dung from the streets at night, and his mother, a domestic servant, died young from bronchitis. He has educated and elevated himself.

"Oh I have seen in all sorts of places, Mr. Connolly."

"I know you have, Madame. I hope it's not too bold to ask your reason for being in this place now. I trust it does not mean you've changed your mind on the meeting?"

Maud puts down her cup. "Mr. Connolly, when I agreed to speak to a meeting of your party, I did not expect to arrive to Dublin the day before the event, to find the streets covered with posters announcing a socialist meeting, with me as principal speaker."

"I thought the bigger and more public the meeting, the better."

"I'm afraid I cannot speak for socialism."

Mrs. Connolly gets up, busies herself with another of the children, the eldest it looks, also a girl. "You wouldn't have to say much, Madame," he says. "Your presence alone would be enough."

"Do you think it right that you should so claim me for your cause?"

"I thought, Madame, given your work for prisoners, that you'd understand the need for *our* cause."

"My cause is a free Ireland."

"As is mine. A true Republic of the people. Not as in France, saving your presence, where a capitalist monarchy parodies the constitutional abortions of England, while flaunting its apostasy to the traditions of the French Revolution. Not as in the United States, where the power of the purse has established a new tyranny."

"You should have asked me, Mr. Connolly."

He looks sheepish. "I should. You're right... and I always will again."

"There can be no again, alas. And, I fear, no this time, either."

"Madame, while class privilege remains intact, you can remove the English Army tomorrow and hoist a green flag over Dublin Castle, but England will still rule, through her capitalists. Through her landlords. Through her financiers. The rule of Westminster is secondary to the rule of the commercial and industrial institutions she has planted here in Ireland. She is such an old miser, Victoria. This Jubilee is just another way for her to rake in the money."

"I think," Maud Gonne says, engaging despite herself, "that it is Irish soldiers in her army that most interests her. You know Irish soldiers have a reputation for bravery."

Mrs. Connolly speaks up from across the room. "None knows it better than James, Madame. Wasn't he in the army himself?"

"Och Lily..."

"He doesn't like to talk of it now."

"My father too served," says Maud Gonne.

"Of course, I know that, Madame. The Colonel."

"James has had many jobs, Madame," says Mrs. Connolly, into the silence that followed. "He has been baker and printer, among others. But now, it's nothing but working for the workers."

Maud Gonne feels the weight and size of their sacrifice. This man could be a success at anything; he chooses to work for the people.

"You are a great support to him, Mrs. Connolly."

She shrugs. "What can you do?"

"Army, Westminster, the Crown," says Connolly. "All have been watered with tears and sweat. The tears of our mothers and the sweat of our workers."

"But don't take too much notice of him, Madame," Mrs. Connolly snorts. "He does get a bit carried away b'times. Show Madame the coffin, James."

He gets up and turns the wooden casket around so she can see the lid, the carving on it that says: *British Empire, RIP*.

"Our march will be a funeral procession, to the sound of 'The Dead March'."

Maud Gonne, despite herself, breaks into a loud, natural laughing.

Lily reaches up onto a shelf. "We'll be holding these black flags."

"John Daly's suggestion," says Connolly.

Maud Gonne looks at them, thoughtfully. "I could get the ladies to embroider them with facts and figures about the star-vations and evictions, if you thought it appropriate. This is an opportunity to educate the people."

He looks excited. "A fine idea, Madame."

"And I have Pat O'Brien's slides of battering rams and evic-tion scenes. I use it in my lectures. Perhaps we could arrange for it to be put in a window somewhere? I thought to ask the National club in Rutland Square if perhaps we could set up a screen opposite."

"If they say yes," Connolly says, excitedly, "I'll have the work-ers interrupt the power supply at the appropriate time, so the festive lights will not compete with your slides."

Their eyes meet, kindred spirits.

Maud Gonne strokes Dagda's great neck. "In these ways I can help, but I cannot appear on your platform, I'm afraid."

"Madame, you know we are barred from participation in the Wolfe Tone Committee demonstrations because we are socialists?"

The same committee has refused her permission to go on a fundraising trip to America. She wants to go to America.

"That is precisely the difficulty you have created for me, Mr. Connolly," she says. "You know how conservative our national-ist politicians are. Association with socialism could well harm such influence as I have."

"Oh Madame, please. This once. If you don't do it, they'll all think I only made it up. And I'll never again be able to draw a crowd."

The Undecorated Dead

A CROWD IS assembled in Dame Street. James Connolly and WB
wait in the wings. "You are nervous," he says to her.

"I have never spoken to so many before. So many working
people. I do not know this audience."

Connolly steps out and introduces her, to cheers from the
crowd. He takes her hand and helps her up onto the chair that
must serve for a platform. She begins low, in conversational
tones, reminding them that Queen Victoria is having her Jubilee
and the Irish are being asked to celebrate.

> *Are we to forget the fact in this, the sixtieth year of the reign of Her*
> *Most Gracious Majesty, that during that reign the population of*
> *Ireland has fallen from eight million to four million and a half? That so*
> *many of our countrymen have perished from hunger and famine-fever*
> *in a land of plenty, which alien government has reduced and ruined,*
> *until the name of Ireland has become a by-word for poverty among the*
> *nations of the earth.*

She has them, they are all hers. WB watches closely, trying
to anatomize the source of her power. It is not just the effect of
her beauty. Her presence, backed by her great stature, moves
minds that are full of old Gaelic stories and poems. Some por-
tion comes from her ability, even when pushing a principle to
what might seem an absurdity (as today), to keep her mind and
spirit free.

> *Famine and hunger still live in thousands of memories, and every*
> *empty, abandoned home in Ireland repeats our tragic history. Every*
> *eviction during the 60 years of her reign has been carried out in her*

name. Yet, with the help of her 30,000 soldiers and her 17,000 police and the weakness of our political leaders, Victoria still reigns over Ireland.

An old woman waves a placard bearing a miniature of John Mitchel and heckles. "I was in it before Maud Gonne was even born."

Some of the crowd around her titter, but Maud Gonne holds up her hand for silence, speaks on, in the same quiet, relentless voice. To WB, she looks as though she has stepped out of an ancient civilization where all superiorities, whether of the mind or the body, were part of a public ceremonial, were in some way the crowd's creation. As the entrance of the Pope into Saint Peter's Basilica is the crowd's creation.

She drops her voice:

Today I attempted to visit the grave of our great martyr, Robert Emmet, at St. Michan's cemetery. The attendant denied me access. Nobody could enter the graveyard today, he explained. It is closed because of Victoria's Jubilee. My friends, I ask you...

She pauses. The crowd appears to lean forward to hear her question. They are under her spell, he realizes, because the nature of her beauty, of her person, of her pilgrim soul, suggests joy and freedom. She has them now; even the old woman is expectant.

I ask you: Must the graves of our dead go undecorated because Victoria has her Jubilee?

With a bow of her head, she steps backwards. Emotion clogs the crowd for a moment, and then the cheering erupts.

~

Next evening, Maud Gonne and WB attend the convention of the '98 Centenary Commemoration Committee at City Hall, under the leadership of John O'Leary. They both do their best to bring round some of their opponents to their way of thought. WB gives an inspiring speech, that well pleases Maud Gonne. Quite magnificent, she thinks, quite the best she ever heard him make.

Afterwards, they join the procession with Connolly behind a rickety handcart draped with black ribbons in the semblance of a hearse, pushed by two faux undertakers. She and Willie fall in with many of the other '98 delegates.

"Pray they do not lose control of the mob," says Mrs. Wyse-Power.

Maud Gonne hands out flags, and yes, as they move through, emotion is rising. A window is smashed, then another. At first it is the Unionist shops with the Jubilee regalia that are attacked, and some of the shops, fearing trouble, have refrained from announcing their loyalty to the queen. But then a looter attacks a small sweetshop, and now, anyone is fair game.

The police, beginning to wake up, call in mounted police from Dublin Castle. They arrive and advance with batons raised. Spectators are dispersed by baton charges. The fighting intensifies, and now everywhere, excited crowds are being dispersed by the police.

"Madame Gonne!" Connolly shouts. "We have to go to the National! Your magic lantern display is attracting the crowds up there."

Have they any chance, she wonders, of making it that far?

At O'Connell Bridge, Connolly realizes he can go no further, and the police are closing in. There will be a fight between mob and police for ownership of the coffin, and their brutality and determination to win will go hard on the people. He yells at the pretend pall-bearers, "We'll have to throw it into the Liffey!"

Maud Gonne holds up one of the flags. "We are going to drown the coffin of the British Empire," she roars, to the crowd.

"To Hell with the British Empire!" shouts Connolly, as it is tipped into the Liffey, and the crowd cheers, as the Royal Irish Constabulary close in to arrest him.

~

Maud Gonne and WB escape and continue along O'Connell Street towards Parnell Street. He has lost his voice from all the talk at the convention. He can only whisper and gesticulate, and so should be freed from responsibility able to share the emotion of the crowd, and maybe even feel as they feel when glass is broken and houses stoned, but no. They elude him.

She, on the other hand, is in her element, striding along the night streets joyous and exultant, her laughing head thrown back. By the time they reach the National Club, the mood of the crowd is wild. WB knocks on the door.

"We are friends," Maud Gonne says, knocking again, when they receive no response.

A voice comes through the door. "Who is it?"

"Is that you, Mr. Sherlock?"

"Madame Gonne?"

"Yes. Yes, it is me and Mr. Yeats."

They hear the sound of the bolt being undone then the caretaker puts his head round the door. "Madame, I fear you're going to get me in deep trouble. Did the committee know of this lantern show? Is permission given? I am told..."

"Oh Mr. Sherlock, please don't worry, all will be well. Just refer them to me."

They sweep in. Maud Gonne orders tea and WB, still voiceless, is silent and glum, with all manner of reservations about what's going on.

"Actually," she says, "I realize I don't want tea. I want to be outside."

As she speaks, there is a loud scream from outside the window, and somebody shouting out: "The police! The police! The police!"

She rushes to the window. "What's happening? We must go out. Mr. Yeats, look."

"They are battoning people outside," a man says from the other window.

She rushes from the room. WB runs behind, calling after her in his rasping voice. "Miss Gonne, no! We can do nothing now."

But she is gone, disappearing below around the turning in the stairs.

"Mr. Sherlock," he croaks. "Do not open those doors! If anything happens to her, you will be held responsible."

She turns back, faces him in full fury. "Mr. Yeats, you forget yourself! Mr. Sherlock, the door, please."

Sherlock dithers between them.

"I shall let him open the lock," whispers WB, "if you tell me what you intend to do."

"How do I know until I get out there?"

"No," he says, as firmly as a lost voice will allow. "I cannot permit it."

"Permit it? *Permit* it? You cannot prevent it."

"Let me go out and check what is happening. I shall check, if you promise not to slip out behind me."

"I make you *no* such promise."

She turns and strides down the corridor towards the back door, to try to get out the other way, as he follows, unable to call after her.

My dear Mr. Yeats

Many thanks for your very charming letter. Yes, we are friends; we will always remain so I hope. You have often been of great help to me when I was very unhappy. But our friendship must indeed be strong for me not to hate you, for you made me do the most cowardly thing I have ever done in my life.

It is quite absurd for you to say I should have reasoned and given explanations. Do you ask a soldier for explanations on the battlefield?

Of course it is only a very small thing, a riot and a police charge, but the same need for immediate action is there—there is no time to give explanations.

I don't ask for obedience from others, I am only answerable from my own acts.

I, less than any others, would be capable of giving lengthy explanations of what I want and what I intend to do, as my rule in life is to obey inspirations which come to me and which always guide me right.

For a long time, I have had a feeling that I should not encourage you to mix yourself in the outer side of politics. And you know I have never asked you to do so. I see now that I was wrong in not obeying this feeling more completely—and probably you were allowed to hinder me on that comparatively unimportant occasion to show me that it is necessary you should not mix in what is really not your line of action.

You have a higher work to do—with me it is different. I was born to be in the midst of a crowd.

To return to the unfortunate event in Rutland Square. Everyone who remained in the club and did not go out to the rescue of the people who were battoned by the police ought to be ashamed of themselves, owing to their action, or rather their inaction, as that poor old woman Mrs. FitzSimon was taken to hospital on a cart and allowed to fall from it by half drunken, wholly mad policemen.

This would not have happened if I had been able to do my duty.

Do you know that to be a coward for those we love is only a degree less bad than to be a coward for oneself? The latter I know well you are not, the former you know well you are. It is therefore impossible for us ever to do any work together where there is likely to be excitement or physical danger. And now let us never allude to this stupid subject again.

Your speech at the '98 centenary convention was quite the best I have ever heard you make; it was magnificent. You have done splendid work in this '98 movement...

With kindest regards dear Mr. Yeats and hoping you will not be very vexed or hurt by anything I have said in this letter.

My dear Mr. Connolly

"Bravo! All my congratulations to you! You were right, and I was wrong about this evening. You may have the satisfaction of knowing that you saved Dublin from the humiliation of an English Jubilee without a public meeting of protestation. You are the only man who has the courage to carry through in spite of all discouragement—even from friends..."

The Ropes Of Human Sorrow

THE SUMMER OF 1897 is WB's first deep dip into the sanctuary of Coole Park. Last year, he did little work while there and Lady G had made it clear what a disappointment this had been. So when he arrives at Coole this year, exhausted from his Jubilee adventures, he knows what is expected of him.

Lady G too is fresh from protesting the Jubilee, having refused to light a celebratory bon-fire for the event, and explaining to those who question her that it is on account of Queen Victoria's continuing neglect of the country. Not lighting a bonfire: it seems a small gesture compared to what went on in Dublin, but he knows how horrified her neighbors and friends must be. She is no Maud Gonne, but it takes as much courage for her to make this gesture in the tightly woven, beleaguered Unionist community where she has made her life.

He is shattered by anxiety and fatigue, and they agree a routine. He shall have her son Robert's room; it has the best aspect over the lawn down to the lake. He shall have cups of soup brought up when he's called in the morning. He shall have the best desk, currently in the morning room, put up there. He shall have clean nibs, paper and ink always ready.

In return, he must by day produce at least six satisfactory lines, and then she shall provide good food, and stimulating company in the evening.

Yes, six lines. Lady G understands, now, just how slow is his rate of poetic composition, that the creation of those five or six lines is hard labor to him, drafting and redrafting until it is so seamless, so perfect, it's as if it arrived fully formed, in an instant.

Such beauties emerge from his pen, though the poor boy is thinner and more brittle than ever, full of every sort of fear. That the committee work he has agreed to at Maud Gonne's instigation will take him away from poetry. That his writing seems to be moving away from the spiritualization of the Irish imagination he has set as his work in the world, becoming too full of those little jeweled thoughts that come from the sun, and have no nation.

That perhaps he is not destined, after all, to find his heaven in the place where he first crawled the floor. Perhaps his task is to write an elaborate mysticism without any special birthplace?

Lady G does not agree.

WB does his best to keep to her timetable, but often finds himself wandering the ground in a dejected haze, taking one of the hashish tablets he has had delivered from Paris, craving the dance of ecstatic escape. Often, he wishes he could scream aloud. When the agony of his desire becomes unendurable, he masturbates, but no matter how moderate he is, that always makes him sick with guilt, flat out, take-to-the-bed, physically ill.

He is awash in cravings: for goals and glory, for drugs and dreams, for magic and mystery and, of course, for Maud Gonne, Maud Gonne, Maud Gonne.

One evening on a walk through Coole Park after following the course of the river that runs through the estate, and seeing it disappear, he comes to the place where it surfaces again, and forms a shaded, deep pool hidden in the forest. In that spot, according to the tradition of the local people, the river is the abode of a spirit race, very like the Greek nymphs.

He sits by the pool, looking at his own reflection and sees again the immortal, august woman with the black lilies in her hair, whom he wrote about in *The Secret Rose*.

He feels again how her dreamy gestures are laden with wisdom more profound than the darkness that is between star and star. Then again, with some horror, he is swept over by the knowledge that this immortal female is drinking up his soul. More than one mortal, looking into this pool, has felt a sudden and powerful impulse to plunge in.

He feels himself being pulled towards the water. He imagines allowing himself to perish in the folds of her heavy hair, of letting the darkness of the lake pass over him. He cries out for the birth of that beauty which could alone uplift a soul such as his, weighted with so many dreams.

L'Irlande Libre
6 Rue des Martyrs, 6
Paris

My dear Mr. Yeats

I will write you at length from the ship, for I am terribly busy before starting for America! Such complications owing to party political differences! Then, great differences in the '98 committee. It is absurd making an open quarrel—which will harm the '98 movement. I have done what I can for now, things must take their chance.

I am glad you are in the country with Lady Gregory. I'm sure it is good for you to be with her, and you will do beautiful work. There is the peace and restful ease you need. I am in my whirlwind, but in the midst of it is dead quiet, which is peace too... But I envy you in the quiet of the country in the beautiful and faery West.

Always your friend
Maud Gonne

Lady G has no understanding how much of her protégé's paranoia and dejection is fed by hashish, but she knows what he needs. Folklore! Investigating the faery beliefs of the country people around Gort will sooth him, she prescribes. So out they go among the cottages, walking for miles, inviting the people to tell their stories, Lady G translating from the Irish.

And WB confirms his sense that the ancient belief in the Shee, the faery folk, is exactly the same thing as occult spiritualism, except that faery belief is very much more subtle and charming. Personages and emotions that are inseparable from their first, ancient, expression before the coming of St. Patrick have been passed on from generation to generation, to these people in their West of Ireland cottages. Only Greece could rival this Celtic mythology in exuberance and power.

Not all stories are of equal value and not all can be used. One day of hearing many tales they had heard many times before, of giant killers and little people and the like, delivered them only one story, but they couldn't use it, as it was of the mortal, not the immortal, world.

It was from a man who was tried in Sligo, for breaking open another man's skull in an argument, and his defense was that some heads are so thin, you couldn't be responsible for them. "I turned towards the solicitor who was prosecuting me and said, 'That small fellow's skull, now, if ye were to hit it, would go like an eggshell.' Then I turned to the judge and gave his skull great praise. 'A man might wallop away at yer lordship's for a fortnight,' I said."

"And that got you off?" Lady G asked.

"Indeed and it did, yer ladyship. He was well pleased with me."

They are tired by the time they reach Gort crossroads that evening, having walked more than twelve miles in the day, but at the crossroads, they find a group of country people singing in Irish, voices melting into the twilight, melding with the trees. They stop to listen, and WB is carried away with the music and the words, so far that he feels as though he has come to one of the four rivers, and followed it under the wall of Paradise, to the roots of the Tree of Life.

Many of the songs and stories handed down among the cottages have words and thoughts that carry one away like this. All his life, he has heard about banshees and fairies, as well as angels and saints: as a boy from his grandparents' servants in Sligo; from the fisherwomen his mother used to talk to, before she was silenced; from Mary Battle; and from his cousin's gardener, Paddy Flynn, who was a constant stream of the old tales.

But Lady G's understanding of the extravagant symbolism of the stories matches his own. She understands the literary value of the heroic passions and wildness of the songs, of the mythological and visionary dimensions of both, and how it is bringing him the ancient wisdom he has been seeking.

And, as she predicted, that together with the long walks in the fresh air and the simple grace of the country people, is giving him ease.

As for her, she has been learning Irish so that she might be closer to the people, and thinking to turn Catholic for the same motive. What working together in this way with WB is teaching her is that paganism can bring her closer still.

~

He is repaired. When the summer is over, and he returns to London, Lady G follows and dispenses order and ease into his London life, too. She measures up his rooms for furniture and curtains; sends over a big leather easy-chair and some painted antique furniture; helps him to acquire and hang new mystic prints and engravings by Blake, Rossetti and Beardsley, and paintings by his father and brother.

When he falls ill, in October, she turns up, morning and evening, to care for him. She brings a folk-remedy from Galway for his eyes: dog-violet, boiled in milk.

Alas, it does not work.

At one of her dinner parties, she invites the nationalist MP, Barry O'Brien, and Horace Plunkett, leader of the Irish cooperative movement to meet him. And for each of them she has one of her gifts: for Plunkett, extracts she's typed from Froude's *History of the English in Ireland in the Eighteenth Century*, background material for a speech he was planning. For O'Brien, a cooperative pamphlet by Plunkett. And for WB, a typescript of the folklore material they gathered around Coole together during the summer.

He thinks to give her what he knows would be the great gift of telling her that she has been more of a mother to him in the short time he's known her than his own mother ever was, but something holds his normally garrulous tongue on this. Perhaps the fear of being misunderstood. What he means is that it is she who has given him what a mother is charged to give: gifts and loans, yes, but even more precious, encouragement and moral support. Admiration and affection.

And why wouldn't she, if she liked him, and she had the need to give? Mother is a verb maybe more than a noun, a doing more than a person. Anyone, man or woman, who wants to mother anyone else, man or woman or child, surely can.

I myself had no biological children, but many a one was mothered by me, and I'd like to think, though it's lonely hereabouts these days, I might have the privilege of offering that to someone once more before I'm gone.

Actually, do you know what? It's just struck me that this story itself is one such offering.

Call me Mammy.

A Servant Of The Queen

ISN'T IT THE most splendid audience, the audience for opera? Any opera, but especially Paris Opera, before curtain up? The men look all alike, so many penguins in their black suits and stiff white collars, but the women...

Look at them tonight at the Palais Garnier, so splendidly, brightly colorful under Lenepveu's ceiling depicting The Muses. Snow-white arms and shoulders rising from laces and satins and velvets of green or violet and carmine, each dress cut to accentuate womanly curves. Hair piled and combed and smoothed away from the forehead, worn like a crown.

And the jewels! Diamonds and pearls, opals or rubies or garnets, in loops or stars or butterflies, trembling on wrists and throats and bosom corsages. Fans, purses and opera glasses held like garlands. Finery fine enough to rival the gilded stage and boxes and the arch of the vaulted ceiling.

Maud Gonne is one of the most splendid of all, in a low-cut gown of deepest jade-blue, the fabric catching the glow of the new electric lighting as she twists and turns. Beside her, in one of the largest viewing boxes, is her friend Ghénia in a frock of butter yellow, her lightest silk, for it's a warm night, the warmest of the summer so far. Together they observe and comment on the sea of people below, while to their left Millevoye leans over the balcony and calls down to his friend Romaine below. A coarse sound. They had to pull him away from the wine downstairs.

"I know a woman," he says, sitting back down, "who sings Brunnhilde's part far better than Breval."

Maud Gonne snorts. "Oh Millevoye, don't be an imbecile! Breval is the finest diva in all Europe."

"It is true, I assure you. But her talent will never be rewarded, because she will not sleep with the *Directeur*."

"They do not generally employ café *chanteuses* at Paris Opera, Lucien," Ghénia says, narrowing her eyes at him.

He ignores her, keeps the conversation pointed at Maud Gonne. "I shall bring her to see you, Maud. You would admire her, I am sure. She reminds me greatly of you, at that age."

Maud Gonne detects something. "You know I leave for Ireland soon, Lucien."

"When you return, then."

"I do not intend giving any parties in the near future."

"She is most anxious to meet you."

"I cannot wait to see Breval," Ghénia says, picking up her eye-glasses, changing the subject.

"Oh yes," says Maud Gonne. "It is such a pity our Irish friends missed this treat."

The lights dim, the orchestra begins the overture, and Wagner's driving rhythms sweep away talk.

They three were not supposed to be alone here tonight. Maud Gonne had arranged for the Paris Municipal Council to invite an Irish delegation to Paris for Bastille Day. A banquet was held in their honor at the Restaurant Vantler, where Maud Gonne sat to the right of the Depute Archdeacon, at the head of a long table of dignitaries, and heard him toast the day when French and Irish, bound by their Celtic heritage, would see the end of England's tyranny. Then the Secretary of the Opera invited them to a performance of *Les Valkyries* but, alas, they couldn't stay long enough to attend. So she has invited her, Ghénia, and Millevoye to share the box instead, though she so rarely mixes their company now.

It is not a bad arrangement, a way to go out together without having to be together.

Such great efforts Maud made for these visitors from Ireland. Ghénia was glad to finally meet them and they helped her to better understand her dear, complicated friend. Why she has not been invited to speak at the Dublin 1798 commemoration and why she feels it necessary to arrange her own ceremony in the West of Ireland.

Little Miss Wyse-Power contended it was because too many still believe Maud Gonne to be an English spy.

"Because she's English born and Protestant, they find it hard to believe that she is true," Miss Wyse-Power had whispered to Ghénia, in the tram on the way to the boat train that took them home. But Miss Wyse-Power must know that the native Irish have accepted Protestant Anglo-Irish as leaders before. Parnell. Robert Emmet. Wolfe Tone himself, the very man whose death they commemorate with this centenary.

No, it is not because Maud is Protestant, or because she is rich, that she had been rejected, but because she is a woman. A woman who has not lived by men's rules. Lucien Millevoye can sleep around and still hold his position as a deputy of parliament. A woman cannot be one shade less than virtuous without punishment.

It is mere waste of energy to rail against this double standard. One must always point it up, but one must then work within it, Ghénia believes.

After seeing the Irish delegates away, Ghénia had questioned Maud Gonne, delicately, carefully, and been given an explanation most convincing. It was not a matter of the committee failing to invite her to contribute, no, not at all. It was *she* who decided not to speak. The organizers had allowed parliamentarians—"milk-and-water fellows" who had previously denounced the more radical protestors—a place on the platform. People unworthy of her association.

The true soul of the Irish people was not to be found in the city of Dublin, no. This was why she was organizing her own event in the rural west, in out-of-the-way County Mayo.

The original French expedition of 1798 landed in Mayo, went to Ballina, won a battle at Castlebar. This is the itinerary she wishes to follow, not only for historical reasons, but also because it is in the west that Gaelic Ireland is still alive, where the Gaelic understanding of life is still honored.

All plausible but...

Ghénia knows how much sorrow her friend can hide. Look at her now, sparkling like the champagne they drank earlier, re-paying Lucien's provocations with pure charm. Her eyeglasses are up, her forehead has relaxed and she leans forward a little, smiling into the music. Is it real, this pleasure? Yes, Wagner is Maud Gonne's favorite composer and *Les Valkyries* her favorite of his works, but is she indulging in a distraction from her trou-bles? Is she acting, as her friend knows she so well can. Or is she as ignorant as she appears of the trouble she is in?

At the interval, Lucien leaves them to mingle and to enjoy another quaff of wine. Maud Gonne is lost in reverie, humming to herself. Ghénia lays a hand on her arm. "You are too much away, my dear."

Maud Gonne looks at her blank-eyed, her mind full of Brunnhilde. "I must go away. This is a most important year for Ireland," she says.

"Always, Maud, you put work first. But it is not good to leave a man like Lucien so much alone."

Maud Gonne pulls herself up to her highest height.

"No, my friend," says Ghénia. "Do not rebuke me. I do not speak so for my own interest or amusement."

Maud Gonne waves her hand. "We both know Lucien, my dear. He is not likely to change now."

"It is not of Lucien that I wish to speak, but of you."

"Oh Ghénia, you know I never like to talk of myself. And on such a night, with such exquisite music..."

Ghénia sighs. "It is not easy to speak frankly to you, my friend. You do not make it easy. But I shall speak. When you were young, you were unfeasibly beautiful, and every man who met you wanted to marry you. Now you are still beautiful but..."

"...not so young," Maud Gonne shrugs. "*Comme ci, comme ça.*"

"Pah! You are young enough. But you are compromised by your relationship with Lucien."

"I am proud of our alliance. Millevoye's political fortunes have improved. He has been re-elected and when the Irish del-egation was here, he wrote a most excellent editorial in *La Patrie*, welcoming them in the name of the French generals Hoche and Humbert, all the daring echoes of a French-Irish alliance a hundred years ago."

"Alliance may be how you like to think of you and Lucien, Maud. But to the unforgiving world, it is a dalliance." There! It is said!

Maud Gonne's jaw is up. "My friend, please..."

"Oh my dear, I heard what happened at Comtesse de Piedemont's salon last week."

"If we wanted to keep odious women from indulging in gossip, we should never stir from our firesides."

"Yet it cannot have been easy, to be so publicly treated."

"You know I care nothing for clacking tongues."

"My dear, are you not tired of being brave? Would you not like to lay down your armory?"

"I want only what I have always wanted. To control my own life. To follow my own pathway."

"As a married woman, you would not be such a target when you do."

"You know I consider marriage an abomination. As, my dear, did you," Maud Gonne smiles to take the sting out of her words, "until not very long ago."

"Marriage can be made to work, even for women such as us."

"But not with most men, alas. How many husbands are as accommodating as Monsieur Avril?"

"Paris is a cold place without male protection. Even for Maud Gonne."

"Is this my friend, la féministe?" She gives one of her tinkling laughs and flutters her fan.

"I am serious, my friend. I urge you to consider a marriage."

Maud Gonne flutters her ivory fan and sighs. "Ghénia, last time I was in Ireland, I was travelling back from Donegal on a train when I looked out the window across dark bog land. I saw a tall, beautiful woman with dark hair blown on the wind, and I knew it was *Cathleen ní Houlihan*. She was crossing the bog towards the hills, springing from stone to stone over the treacherous surface, and the little white stones shone, marking a path behind her, then fading into the darkness. As I watched, I heard a voice say: 'You are one of the little stones on which the feet of the Queen will rest on her way to Freedom.' I cried, Ghénia. It seemed so lonely to be one of those little stones left behind on the path. I wanted to be more than that."

"You are more than that. Much, much more."

"No, you misunderstand me. What I wanted to say is that afterwards, when I had time to ponder, I realized that I was happy to be a servant of my queen. It seems to me the finest thing I can do."

"Nobody is suggesting that marriage should be the end of your work, any more than it will be the end of mine. Thankfully, the days when a married woman had to give up her work are over."

"Marriage to another would break my alliance with Lucien, Ghénia. I thought you should have understood that."

Ghénia shifts in her chair. "How so, when he himself is married?" Her pulse skids: "And when he is no more faithful to you than he is to his wife."

Maud Gonne flinches, as if slapped.

Moments pass.

When she looks up, her face is the color of water just after sundown. Paler than dusk, darker than day. Remorse floods through Ghénia. "Oh *ma chérie*, forgive me."

"I have always thought these matters understood between us, Ghénia. I do not like to speak of such things, but let me explain and then let us put it away. Lucien's...indiscretions...they make my position awkward, but our alliance is useful to Ireland. I, whom you know to be proud, perhaps too proud, am willing to sacrifice even my pride for Ireland."

Ghénia speaks carefully, winnowing her words. "I can perhaps grant you that, Maud, though I should wish for more for you. But what of Iseult? She is now four years old. Soon she will be old enough to understand that she has no father."

"She has a father."

"Well then, that she is illegitimate in the eyes of law and of society."

"Oh society."

"Would you consider the Irish poet?"

"Ghénia!"

"His love is a true thing. He has so long adored you. If only you could allow yourself to be adored."

"He is only a boy," Maud Gonne says.

"The same age as you, is he not?"

"A little older. But nonetheless, a boy."

"That can be an advantage in a husband."

She shakes her head. "I could never be with Willie as a husband would expect."

"If he is so immature, he might accept that. Tell him you think the sex act is justified only by procreation."

Maud Gonne laughs, this time with real amusement. "What a conniver you are, Ghénia. Is that what you tell François?" Ghénia has recently engaged to marry her longtime admirer and lover, the engineer François Avril.

Ghénia shrugs. "It is a man's world, my dear, and men have constructed the institution of marriage to suit themselves entirely. They have women at their service in the kitchen, the drawing room and the bedroom. We must use what ploys we can."

"If I were to go to Willie, I should have to tell him about Iseult."

"You will have to do that, whomsoever you choose."

"It would shatter his view of the world and my place in it. You know I believe the Celtic literary movement is absolutely essential for the carrying out of our scheme for the liberation of Ireland, in fact, the most important. A great poet can give nobler and more precious gifts to his country than the greatest philanthropist or politician."

"I thought he saw himself as an Irish mage?" Ghénia is smiling, but kindly. "With you by his side, incarnation of some Gaelic goddess?"

"Mr. Yeats makes great poetry out of what he calls his unhappiness about me, and he is happy in that. In coming times, the world will thank me for not marrying him. Anyway, if he knew..." She pauses, imagining, and shudders. "No...our friendship means a great deal to me, he has helped me when I needed help, needed it more than he ever knew. For I never talk or even think of these things. We are doing wonderful work together, and the '98 commemoration is going to be even more wonderful. Oh my dear friend, I am so excited that you are coming across at this time. It is going to change everything."

Ghénia is one of a French contingent that Maud Gonne has inveigled to come to Ireland for the '98 commemorations. But her friend refuses to be diverted. "All right, if not the poet, then what about the Comte?"

"Oh Ghénia, don't be ridiculous."

"The poet, then. I am sure he would rather know about Iseult and marry you himself than hear you are to wed another. Perhaps I shall meet him when I come to Ireland?"

"No, Ghénia: stop. Marriage I consider a major impediment to any woman who wants to make a mark on the world. I shall speak to Millevoye. I shall make him see my position."

"*Pffff!* If you will not think of yourself, Maud, think of Iseult."

"Here he comes now. *Shhh!* Let us make idle talk. What did you think of the orchestra? And the divine Breval? Was she not divine?"

Out Of The Purple Deep

BALLINA, IRELAND

Report to The Inspector General, Co. Mayo Royal Irish Constabulary,

August 1898.

The '98 Centenary Association has shot its bolt, and the two meetings, so long talked of and from which such great things were expected, were held this month and (contrary to reports in the nationalist press) were failures. One was held in Ballina, the other at Castlebar, Miss Maud Gonne being the moving spirit behind both.

Having previously announced that she would be bringing over a contingent of some hundreds of French sympathisers, she succeeded in producing six unknown French delegates, an Italian named Capriani, a couple of Irish Americans, a few from Dublin and London and a man named Gillingham from South Africa...

The whole thing lacked enthusiasm.

The people's attendance was small, and from a financial point of view, it was a complete failure. To fill the half-empty hall, they allowed a large number of the roughs of the town to attend, free of charge.

In Samois, autumn has begun its slow creep of color through the trees. The day is crisp, pleasant in the mid-afternoon sun, though still cold. Frost glistens in patches where the sun's rays have not pierced. It is early in the year for such cold, and it will make the winter long. Too long.

Iseult knows nothing of days to come. Like all children, she is delightfully present. Look at her kicking the leaves with her boots, sending them up into the air. She loves the crackle they make and the crisp lightness of them as they separate out from each other and fall back to ground.

She stops, as if remembering something. "Brother, Amour?"

Maud Gonne stops too, squeezes Iseult's glove in hers. "Darling, please. Do not have me to tell you again."

"Sorry...Moura."

"Good girl. That wasn't so difficult, was it? So say it again: 'What about my brother, Moura?'"

"What about my brother, Moura?"

"That's it. I am your own Moura: I know it's hard, but please, please, try to remember. For me."

"Yes Moura," says Iseult, with her lovely smile, her little hand tugging as she trips into stepping forward. "And brother?"

"Yes, yes, soon you shall see your brother."

She smiles, content at the prospect and Maud Gonne reassures herself that yes, her daughter will be fine. And needs to know her brother. It is right and fitting for her to meet him now, while she is still young. Ghénia had worried her last night when she said, shuddering, that she thought it a mistake to bring her there. Ghoulish.

Ghoulish? The word made Maud Gonne want to slap her, a most unaccustomed feeling that she has started to have of late with Ghénia. What is ghoulish about death? Is it not merely the mirror of life? Iseult will have no more siblings—that much, if nothing else with Lucien, is certain—and if she is told of Georges now, at four years—old enough to understand, but too young to grasp the full implications—she will grow with the knowledge. The other way he would become a secret kept from her: a big revelation at some later, more aware point of life.

"You know what a secret is, Iseult?"

Iseult nods.

"Tell me a secret that you know."

"But Amour, if—"

Maud Gonne stops in her tracks again. "Moura, Iseult."

"Sorry. Moura."

"Please try to remember."

Iseult nods.

"So go on, tell me."

"But...if Iseult tells, it won't be secret."

"Excellent!" Maud Gonne smiles down. Truly this child is remarkable. What intelligence at only four years old. "Excellent. You have passed the test."

The child gives a little skip. Through the shadows of the branches above, winter sunlight splashes across her tilted-up face, adding to the beauty of her artless smile. She is a child whose loveliness never grows familiar: in different moods, under different lights, she can look startlingly altered, so that to catch sight of her is to experience all over again the shock of her beauty. Beauty like Iseult's *is* a kind of shock.

"Moura?" She is tilting her head to the side, her hair falling free of her ear.

"Yes."

"Iseult hates England."

This is something new. "You do, my darling? And why, pray?"

"England is..." The little face squints up over the words. "England is...a nation...of shopkeepers."

A loud laugh swoops through Maud Gonne's throat, before she has time to think. "Oh my sweet darling, did Papon teach you to say that?"

Iseult shrugs.

"You are delightful, truly you are."

"Moura."

Maud Gonne is still chuckling. "Yes Iseult."

"Why is it bad to keep a shop?"

"It is not the keeping of a shop in itself that is shameful. What is reprehensible is to care too much about the shop's profits to the exclusion of other, finer aspects of life."

Iseult nods slowly, digesting. Is this a message sent from Lucien through their child, an imaginative attempt at making amends? "Did Papon teach those words to you, Iseult? Did he ask you to say them to me?"

Iseult's face closes.

"Are you listening, Iseult? When Papon came to visit you the last time, at home...while Amour—I mean Moura—was away? Do you remember? Do you? Did he bring a lady with him?"

But the child turns her face blank as a pickpocket's.

Lucien has grown quarrelsome again and most fiercely and wretchedly so. He published in *La Patrie* a detestable editorial, a sentimental and exaggerated appeal for Alsace-Lorraine, pointing to Germany as the one and only enemy of France. Nothing about England. It was a clear betrayal of their alliance, but when she called his attention to it, he mumbled something about only having signed it, not written it.

It was obvious that its flowery and sloppy language was not his. She had known as soon as she read it whose work it was. Hers. That singer he had wanted her to meet.

When he saw the knowledge in her, he began to bluster about her Irish friends, as if the shortcomings were theirs: "Those absurd Irish Revolutionists of yours, they lead you astray, their schemes will come to nothing. I have seen them and judged them, they will never do anything. You should go work with the Home Rule party; outside parliament you won't be able to do anything for Ireland..."

"So, our alliance is at an end," she had said to him.

"Don't be absurd, Maud. You know I will always help you."

"How can you when we have different enemies?"

"England is not the threat to France that Germany is. Surely you must see—"

"And different friends."

A chorus girl. He would be taking them off the streets next and asking her to favor them but what she really wants to know is what else he is daring to do.

"Please Iseult, even if it is a secret. Moura needs to know. Did Papon bring a lady with him? He did, did he not?"

Nothing.

"Oh my darling, I am sorry. Perhaps you are right. Perhaps it is not fair to press you. Let us go in and see your brother."

~

The funeral director she'd hired, the best in all Paris, had told her that having the body embalmed would maintain Georges's body for decades. That he would be restored from the trauma of the horrible disease that had taken him, the spots removed, the face corrected, to look just like himself again—and be preserved that way for a quarter century or more.

He had lied.

Georges had looked better than he had in the hospital, yes, the horrible, pained expression of shock had been removed, and the shadows round his eyes and the pinched thinness that had invaded his mouth were gone. But no, he did not look like himself. And today, as each time she visits, he is a little more dried-up and desiccated.

She went back to the funeral director about it last time. He said, "Madame, I do not create museum pieces. What I create is a lasting memory."

Which was so far from what he'd said when she'd first approached him, grief-stricken, in the time of death, that she could have sued him for false claims, but it would be unthinkable to argue so over the body of her dear Georges.

So she had gone, weeping, away.

Each visit now, though, is preceded with tortuous anticipation. It's another reason she wants Iseult to see him, before further deterioration sets in. There will come a time when she shall have to have him interred.

She removes the lid. The blue mold that was on his forehead last time is spreading. It's no longer his face at all, but becoming the face of an ancient, little monkey child. She takes Iseult's hand, draws her in close to see.

As soon as they come out, Maud Gonne crouches down among the autumn leaves, reaches for her daughter, pulls her in tight. "Your brother would have grown up to be a great hero, and would have freed Ireland, if only he had not been taken by meningitis."

"Men..i..?"

"Meningitis. You have never heard of it, of course. It is the most ghastly disease."

"Men-in-"

"Yes, yes, there's no need to keep saying it, dear. Listen to me. You know the bootees you found in my drawer that I didn't want you playing with? That is the reason why. Those bootees were his. Georges's. You see?"

It appears not. Her face is blank. "He passed away when he was only two years old. Younger than you are now, darling. It was all so sudden. I hurried from Ireland, the moment I heard. I hired a hansom cab to take me immediately to the next boat. I didn't even take my belongings from the hotel. I came as quick as I could, as quick as ever I could. I couldn't have been any quicker."

She sinks her nose in Iseult's lovely hair and inhales deep. "Oh, the smell of the outdoors on you, *ma chérie*. It is divine. So clean. *Ma belle*. You are so good with your secrets. But Moura would like it if you could only tell her this one thing. Do you think you can?"

Iseult's hand slips away, and she looks up at the branches of the trees as if they are the ones who speak loudest to her. Maud Gonne grips her shoulders. "Iseult, I *know* Papon had the lady there, so you don't have to keep the secret any more. Because I know. So it's not a secret, do you see?"

"You're hurting my shoulders, Am...Moura."

"Oh my dear. Am I? What is wrong with me? What am I saying? Look at your little hands, blue with cold. I told you to wear your gloves. Where are they? Here in your pockets. And look, look at your fingernails. *Mon Dieu*, you have an entire field buried in here! Stand still, my little fidget, and let me wipe those grubby, grubby fingers with my handkerchief. Oh dear child don't look at me so. Moura does not mean to cry, truly she doesn't. Come closer to me again, Iseult, please. Come close. Here, let me hold you. Oh yes, that is better. Hug me. Hug me tight with your little arms. There, yes, I knew it, see? You have made Moura feel so much...so much better, yes you have, you clever thing. Yes. I will stop now...in a-a moment... Just give me a moment. How silly. How... Oh Iseult..."

~

Meningitis. That is what Iseult remembers of that day. To her childish imagination, meningitis is an angular, shadow-man who springs, out of the purple deep, with long, sharp-nailed, unclean fingers and evil intent. He stalks her house, an ever-present, invisible menace, lurking behind what's there. A shadow within the shadows thrown by candlelight, especially in her bedroom, at night, just before the moment of sleep.

Iseult forgets that her mother once buried a weeping face in her neck. She remembers her childhood fear of meningitis, a black and intractable monster, who took in her mind the shape of a giant cockroach. She remembers the sight of the embalmed boy in his coffin. And she remembers the smell of the vault, which she thinks of as the smell of the illness that made him. The smell of meningitis.

My dear friend,

How nice you are writing to me when I have been so lazy about answering, that is what I like so much about you, I am always sure of finding you the same—no matter what happens! I have been going through a state of mind I don't quite understand, for the last month, I have been incapable of any sort of work; each time I tried, something seemed to stop me.

It was not that I had my mind full of other things, quite the contrary; my mind was blank and stupid. I thought it must be some of the forces that work for England that were paralyzing my will, so I have been imagining Celtic things with the water of the west & the earth from New Grange & suddenly feel as if the stupefying weight has disappeared, & I can be active & useful again.

Just when I got your letter about Maeve I had been invoking Maeve...

I cross to London on the 24th Nov. and go to Manchester for a meeting on the 27th, and shall be in Ireland by the end of this month. Write & let me know where you will be & where we can see each other & talk over the things which interest us.

In haste
I remain
Always your friend
Maud Gonne

The Labyrinth
Of Another

So to Dublin, where the poet awaits his muse. He arrives to her hotel, the Crown in Nassau Street, for breakfast as soon as he knows she is here. They eat together in the morning room, which has an agreeable view northwards over the cricket greens of Trinity College. Over eggs and toast, with crumbs falling unheeded onto WB's waistcoat front, they discuss their occult interests, careful throughout to keep their voices low so as not to shock the respectables at the tables nearby.

After breakfast, they stroll together up Kildare Street to be at the new National Library of Ireland when it opens at ten. Under the round dome, modeled on the larger Reading Room at the British Museum, they pore for several hours over ancient tomes and recent research, progressing their work on their Castle of the Heroes and the Celtic Mysteries that will sustain it.

Mr. Lyster, the Librarian, is a friend of Willie's father and permits them to work in rooms that are off-limits to others. Thus they have privacy behind their library stacks. Both agree that these Celtic rituals must, in their main outline, be the work of invisible hands, brought into being not by conscious thought but through invocation and meditation and a holding open of the soul. What the library research provides is the details: names of gods and goddesses, objects and symbols that confirm their direction and will add substance to their rites.

Now, instead of invoking Raphael or Gabriel or Michael or Auriel, they call up Deirdre and Maeve, Cuchulain and Fergus,

Midir and Lugh, her special guardian. That it can seem so hard to invest Irish words with the same solemnity as the Hebrew is a measure of how the English have degraded the Irish language, how the modern has degraded the ancient.

This Celtic mythology gives Mr. Yeats an orderly background against which to write his poetry and plays—he felt the need of it badly when writing *The Shadowy Waters*, he said.

Their work shall give dignity again to the timeless avatars and symbols. To Midir, master of the fairies, clearer of the stone out of Meath, builder of the way in the bog. To Lugh, caster of stone, thrower of flame. To Cathleen ní Houlihan, the defeated and dispossessed old woman who needs the blood of young men willing to fight and die for her, to make her walk again with the walk of a queen.

Red Hanrahan's Song About Ireland

The old brown thorn-trees break in two high over Cummen Strand,
Under a bitter black wind that blows from the left hand;
Our courage breaks like an old tree in a black wind and dies,
But we have hidden in our hearts the flame out of the eyes
Of Cathleen, the daughter of Houlihan.

The wind has bundled up the clouds high over Knocknarea,
And thrown the thunder on the stones for all that Maeve can say.
Angers that are like noisy clouds have set our hearts abeat;
But we have all bent low and low and kissed the quiet feet
Of Cathleen, the daughter of Houlihan.

The yellow pool has overflowed high up on Clooth-na-Bare,
For the wet winds are blowing out of the clinging air;
Like heavy flooded waters our bodies and our blood;
But purer than a tall candle before the Holy Rood
Is Cathleen, the daughter of Houlihan.

On the ninth morning of her visit, Maud Gonne sits to her bureau before breakfast, but instead of writing, she sits staring out the window, the cap of her fountain pen in her mouth, recalling the previous day when, in handing him a book, she allowed her hand to gently graze his. The touch reached its mark, for he blushed like a girl, but all he did was open the book at the desired page and point her towards what to read.

Contrary boy. So often she has discouraged him; now that she wishes him to speak: nothing. He has been refused so often, he no longer even asks. She is beginning to think she'll have to take matters into her own hands.

She turns to the letters before her: quite a pile, forwarded from France. A bill for the house at Samois (she really should let it go, they never use it anymore), a request to speak at a rally in Manchester and a selection of other dispatches, all as yet unopened except for Ghénia's, which contained a dear little missive from Iseult. A picture fashioned in blue crayon of a tall lady and a little girl, *maman et fille*. They are hand-in-hand beside a bushy green tree with red apples. Underneath she has written in her dear, unformed hand: *Chère Moura, Je t'aime. Xxx Iseult.*

Clever girl.

Maud Gonne has begun her reply—a sketch of the seashore at Howth Head where she went walking on Sunday, complete with fish and seagulls—when a knock comes to her hotel room door. At this hour it can only be him. Opening it, she sees immediately that he is greatly excited. Only one thing could bring about such fervor at this hour. "I went to you last night," she says, ushering him in. "Did you find me in your dreams?"

"Yes, yes, that is what I have come to tell you." His eyes flash, his fingers clutch each other, and he looks more than ever like a skinny, disheveled demon. "I woke with the fading vision of your face bending over mine. With the knowledge that you had just..."

"Just what? Oh do go on, Mr. Yeats."

"That you had just...kissed me."

She moves a step closer, but still he talks, in his volatile, overexcitable fashion, of how he has often dreamt of kissing her hands, of how once, only once, her spirit came to him at Coole and, bent over him for a fleeting moment, she kissed him in a dream. This kissing, he says, blushing but determined, was of quite a different order. This kissing was mutual.

She lets him talk and lets him finish and lets the ensuing silence grow as she feeds him a look, with eyes open and limpid, for as long as is seemly. Until such a look can surely be borne no longer.

Nothing.

She tries again. "And did you not say that our natal horoscopes, Venus and Mars, are in close trine, mirroring each other?"

He knows as does she that this juxtaposition suggests a conjunction of marriage.

Again nothing.

The moment passes. And in any case, it is too early in the morning to talk of marriage. "Come," she says, a little weary. "Let us go down for breakfast."

~

They spend that morning as they have spent every other morning, in the library, and in the afternoon, they visit the old Fenian leader, James Stephens. All day she is at her most charming and affectionate to him. That evening, when dinner is finished, and they are in her room, she moves to try again.

"Let me tell you now what happened last night," she says. "It was not so much a dream as a vision. At first it was quite foolish. Something about Noah, but all at once everything got very full of light, and I began to see forms and colors more distinctly than I had ever seen them with my ordinary eyes."

"I think I am beginning to understand." The excitement that occult matters always evince in him is alive in his eyes. "We have been sent the same dream."

"I believe so. More vision than dream. When I fell asleep, I saw standing at my bedside a great spirit. He took me to a great throng of spirits, and you were among them. My hand was put into yours and..."

"Pray, continue."

"I was told that we were married."

She leans forward in her chair, close enough to see the hairs on his face, a small tuft on the underside of his chin that he missed in his morning shave. At least he has stopped wearing that ill-judged beard.

"Go on," he says, with vehemence.

"Well, that is it. I saw enormous multitudes of birds, and in the midst was one very beautiful bird wearing a crown, a bird like a great white eagle. By now I was aware that I was out of my body, seeing my body from outside itself. My hand was put in your hand, and I was told that we were married. Then I kissed you..."

He still looks at her, expectant. What else does he expect?

"...I kissed you, and all became dark."

"And after that?"

"After that I remember nothing. I think we went away together to do some work."

He assumes the air he always assumes in their most secret, symbolical dealings. "What were you wearing in this vision?"

"Wearing?"

"Yes, when you came to me?"

"A white dress."

He frowns. "In my dream, you wore the red dress with the skirt of yellow flowers."

"I don't attribute much importance to this, do you?"

"In my dream, the flowers gradually grew and grew until all else was blotted out." What a boy he is, she thinks. So shy.

Every man Maud Gonne has had, she has approached in the same way. She tells them she has known them in another life. Indeed, she believes she has. Millevoye responded as expected, he hadn't needed to be asked twice. She shivers, as if the Royat rain still dampened her skin, and shakes away the memory of that balcony, the aroma of crushed roses.

So be it. This is the very attraction of the boy-poet who has loved her for so many years. She loves him too, as a sister loves a brother, which she presumes will be a more stable love in the end. What hideous deformity the sex act puts on everything. They do far better to rise above it.

She leans a little further out of her seat, stretches forward to place her lips on his. There!

There, Mr. Yeats.

Your dream come true.

She strengthens the kiss, makes it full and unmistakable in intent. His lips are cool under hers, unmoving. How much she has to teach him, about private and public ease. He makes life so difficult for himself and all around him.

She finishes the kiss with a delicate touch of the lips, once, twice, then sits back and opens her eyes to him.

But his mouth hangs, shocked and slack, his eyebrows are frozen on a face that bears an unmistakable expression of alarm. Has she misjudged the move?

"You had better leave, Mr. Yeats," she says.

"Miss Gonne...Please..."

"I beg of you, do not speak. Go from here." Of course, she had been planning for days. He will need time to understand, to switch his thoughts. For so long she has been unattainable.

"I must—"

"Please Mr. Yeats, I entreat you. Put all thoughts of me from you. If you care at all for me, go. Go now."

Their Children's Children

WB IS NO stranger to sleeplessness, but that night he welcomes the turning over and over in his bed, like one on a spit over a fire. He burns, he yearns...and the burning and yearning has its familiar, half-delicious sorrow. And yet...

When she kissed him with her bodily mouth, he was afraid. That much he knows. He longs to tell her...what? That his body contains his steady, unwavering heart but also something else, something even he can't find words or images to hold, something porous that shifts and breathes through his urges and haunts his memories, that is speckled with brightness like the night sky is speckled with stars but is also blank as the spaces between.

It was wrong of her, that kiss. Of that he is certain. But why? His thoughts go round and round as miserable thoughts do, without reaching a conclusion.

Next day, he returns to her room and finds her sitting, with folded hands in her lap, staring gloomily into the fire. "I should never have spoken to you in that way," she says. "For I can never be your wife in reality."

"Why?"

"Mr. Yeats, I have something to tell you."

"I think I know it."

"Do you?"

"You are betrothed to another?" He has always denied it as scandal, calumny, but now, it seems the only explanation. Her periodic cold spells, her physical reserve, the obscure look in her eye, the meaning of which he has so often wondered at. Some journalist once said it contained the shadow of battles yet to come, but he has always thought it points to a more intimate struggle.

"Not betrothed. There is another, but..." Her voice quails under the intensity of his stare. "It is not...not as you think."

But it is. He sees that it is, that this is what has been between them, always. The most banal of explanations: another man. He cannot sit, he rises, begins to stride around the room.

Should he move toward her? It seems not: as he does so, she holds up her hand.

"It is not as you think," she repeats. "I do not love him...but I am forced to be the moral nature for us both."

"You speak in riddles."

"I know. I have something to tell you which is very painful for me. Before I speak, I want you to know that I do love you. That I have loved you for a very long time. That for years now, your love has been the only beautiful thing in my life."

He is at a loss to hear these words from her lips. Should he move towards her? It seems not, she is holding up her hand. "No, please. Hear me out. I have kept you close while keeping a wall of glass between us. You have felt this, and it has been most selfish of me. When you know all, you will understand all, and you will love me no more."

"I assure you..."

"...and that is as I deserve. Please, I beg you, do not move. You must hear me first."

He sits back down, and she begins her story, her face all the while turned towards the fire. "I have told you of when I was a young girl, how desperate I was to be free and how I told Satan he could have my soul if I could have my freedom."

He nods.

"You know how I suffered from the outcome. I have not shared the details, wishing to spare us both. Though you were privy to my suffering and your kindness then..."

She falters. The flickering of the fire is loud in the silence that grows.

"Shortly after Tommy died, a Frenchman came into my life. I fell in love with this man. After some months, I became his...his mistress."

Now her narration speeds up. She was often away from Millevoye, for yes, it is him, that nauseating sensationalist he once met at her apartment in Paris. Sexual love soon began to repel her, but for all that, she was much in love. A little boy was born, the child she had once told him about, saying he was adopted. Her lover failed her in various ways, and then the boy died—otherwise she would have broken with her Frenchman altogether and lived in Ireland.

She had thought of breaking with him and had engaged herself to someone else, but had broken it off after a week.

He thinks: I might have had that poor betrothal for my reward.

She goes over and over the details of the death of the child. Here, her account becomes incoherent, and she clenches and unclenches her hands and, when he asks some questions, she says it would not go well for them to speak of it. The most horrendous time of her life. Her *annus horribilis*, 1891. She had suffered nervous collapse, had lost the ability to speak French. She had built a memorial chapel in a village outside Paris, using some of her capital, "for what did money matter now?" She had the body embalmed.

He knows all this, he wrote about it in his poem for her. Does she even remember?

Still, having said they should not speak of it, she speaks on. She had gone back to Millevoye in the vault under the memorial chapel where they buried the boy and had relations with him there.

Seeing his horror, she says: "But, Mr. Yeats, it was you who made me return," and she tells him how he and Russell convinced her that the lost child might be reborn. Except it was a girl who ensued. The child he had met that day in Paris with...

"So now," she says, finally ceasing, raising her eyes to his. "You know all."

It is his turn to speak, but he cannot, he is as one paralyzed.

"Now you know why, despite my love for you, I can never be your wife."

He can think only of the poem he published so recently, the one defending her: *Their children's children shall say they have lied.*

"You understand now why marriage seems impossible," she repeats.

He is saturated with that feeling he most dreads: the knowledge that his energy, his will, his transforming power, is stopped by what feels like a blank wall, a vast emptiness... Something one must either submit to, or rage against helplessly. It frightens him. Is this how his mother feels? He has seen it settle on his sister, and it was uppermost in Aunt Agnes, Mama's sister, the night she escaped from the asylum and arrived at their door in Bedford Park, wild and unable to sleep, and incessantly talking, talking, talking against it.

He has to leave. He rises to his feet, careful not to touch Maud Gonne. Oh, how all who know must laugh at him. And he can see, as he thinks back over the years of his long devotion, that many know.

Maud Gonne, his Rose of the World, for whom his reverent hands wrought passionate rhymes of beauty and despair, is the mistress of that greasy French politician.

Maud Gonne, who used to gather herbs in a great wood under full moon and burn them in the temple, now speaks of a repugnance for sex while making pathetic sexual overtures.

Maud Gonne, who was once a priestess in a temple of the moon in Syria, who used to sit upon a throne and prophesy, now sits, a fallen woman by a hotel fire. Offering herself for love and marriage, but in the offering, taking full love, full marriage away.

He fears that all he holds dear, all that binds him to spiritual and social order, is being cut loose by the winds that blow beyond this world, and from beyond the stars, leaving his soul naked and shivering. "You are not Maud Gonne," he says, at the door, hardly knowing what he says, still fearing to touch her.

"Maud Gonne is a creation," she whispers. "And I am partly her but... Willie... I am also a mother."

Willie. She uses his first name, for the first time, to *say* that. He fears he *will* go mad.

~

Next day could be embarrassing but they are both experts by now in the unsaid. She's giving him time to get used to the new landscape, he's putting foot in front of foot, word in front of word, without knowing what he does. Staying one step ahead of collapse.

They still go around Dublin very much as a couple, still do their book and occult research for their Celtic Mysteries, still dine and sometimes breakfast together. On 17th December, the night before she leaves to return to Paris, tension is taut between them as they sit alone together again in her hotel room, preparing to do their final vision work.

"I wonder, shall we be sent a sign?" she asked, the first mention made since the night of the revelations that he has a decision to make. It is the last night, it is truly now or never.

She suddenly sits upright. "I hear a voice saying, 'You are about to receive the initiation of the spear.'"

Her voice is distant and tremulous, as it always is during visions.

He says, "I am with you," reaching for the notebook and ink.

And they both fall silent.

Maud Gonne sees the Celtic God, Lugh, behind an altar, in dazzling light so great that it seemed to emanate from him and makes it hard to see details. Morfessi, the red-haired Druid, takes both her hands and gazes into her eyes and tells her this was how they knew who is fit to take the initiation. Morfessi says: "She is not pure enough, is not strong enough, she is not silent enough."

But then she sees two dark shadow forms standing behind her. A voice on the right hand of the altar cries, "We need her, purify her, strengthen her and seal her lips for the work."

And after a few moments, she feels a fire fountain rising within her, coming up through her chest like a flame and playing above her head.

Lugh from the other side of the altar holds his great spear over her and says, "She is purified; she is strengthened, and her lips are sealed for our service."

Afterwards, she says to WB, "What do you think?"

He says, while she was undergoing this vision, he felt himself becoming flame, mounting up a great stone Minerva, then looking out of its eyes.

She says, "It seems clear." And turns significant eyes on him. The eyes of which he wrote: *My world was fallen and over, for your dark soft eyes on it shone; A thousand years it had waited and now it is gone, it is gone.*

He says, "Could it really be? Are the beings which stand behind human life trying to unite us?"

She says she believes so. She says it seems very clear. She says, woe to whomever turns back from the service of the Gods.

After long silence, he says, "But perhaps we wrought the vision ourselves, by our own dreams and longings?"

She stands. She says, "As you say, perhaps."

She says, In any case, marriage seems to her impossible. She has a horror and terror of physical love.

And he and she say a great many other things, just as they had before that night and after, but that's the sentence that becomes famous, taken up and thrown around by so many to explain their relationship and the poor poet's long unrequited love.

Call her coquette. Call her frigid. Call her tease. A woman's place is in the wrong.

Epilogue
The Blossom
Of The Dust

Two YEARS later. on the evening of 2nd January 1900, JB and WB spend the evening with their friend, George Moore, at his house. As they leave, father seems to son a little lonely. Jack is down in Devon, and the girls are away: Lolly in Germany on a short holiday, Lily in Ireland. Moore has been uncommonly entertaining, so WB finds himself in good mood. Instead of walking the five miles back to Woburn Buildings, he says he shall bed down for the night in Bedford Park.

In the middle of the night, Maria, the girl who cares for Mrs. Yeats and sleeps in her room, wakens to the sound of breathing that, as she would tell everyone afterwards, is all wrong. Rough and weak, both at the same time and taking more effort that it should ever take just to get air into a body and back out.

Alarmed, she goes to knock on her master's door, and JB, as soon as he perceives the situation, calls his son. And so it is that Susan Yeats's departure from this world is overseen not by the daughters, who have given her the care that kept her going in this world for as long as she did. Nor by her younger son, the child who seemed to love her most. It is her husband and her eldest boy, the two members of her family least able to reach her, who witness her last, coarse, dissonant breath.

As in life, so in death: it doesn't matter to her who's there. She never wakens again, and before the doctor arrives, it's all over. The daughter of the great Sligo merchant family is laid to rest in the new, large London cemetery in the raw, emerging suburb of Acton. Her children club together with their father to pay the £38 for the grave plot. Afterwards, at the gathering in the house that he said would be small but winds up involving most of Bedford Park and a great deal of artistic London, JB gives a great oration about how, by marrying his wife, he had given voice to the sea cliffs.

And he drinks a little too much Irish whiskey and afterwards, when everyone is gone, and it is only the five of them together, he speaks of how, when he and Susan were first married, he would no sooner be in the house than he would have to listen to such dreadful complaints of everybody and everything. As he says this, he glances at his son and glances quickly away again, and the other three, to whom he'd often told this story before, when Willie wasn't there, remembered how he'd always said: "Especially of Willie. It was always Willie."

"Sometimes," he says now instead, "I would beg of her to wait till after supper."

But WB knew, without it ever having been said, and they knew he knew, with that knowing given only to those who grow up in the same house together, as they all valiantly pretend not to know what they know.

Tonight it is JB, usually the most valiant of them all, who is felled. "Do you think," he asks, of no one in particular, "it is possible that she was not as unhappy as she seemed?"

And tonight not even kindly Lily can say, Yes Papa. That is possible.

~

"I think Lily and I feel it worst for our father," WB says to Lady G, who has invited him to tea at her apartment the next day. "But it is such a great blow to Jack."

"How interesting that the youngest should be so devoted."

"With his first earnings, he hired a medical specialist for her, though by then she was beyond all help. To the end, he wrote her a long weekly letter, all news and amusement, as though she were of a mind to read them. Now, he cannot paint...or even sketch."

"The poor boy."

"The same happened to Maud Gonne after her...after a bereavement. She lost the ability to speak French."

He doesn't say that the same has happened to him. Since that night in the Crown Hotel with Maud Gonne two years ago, his gift has deserted him. He can find nothing worth making a song about, except helmets, and swords, and half-forgotten things, that are like memories of her. This is a trouble that cannot be admitted, lest he give it more power than it already has.

"Let's hope his coming exhibition will cheer him," says Lady G, not wanting to go down the Maud Gonne track, not today. Her ladyship's generosity now extends to all the males of the Yeats family. She has bought some of Jack's work and is organizing a show in Dublin for him, and soon she will do the same for JB.

"Jack wishes to pay for a plaque to be erected in the church in Sligo, but only from us."

"Not your father?"

"Jack does not forgive our father."

Lady G can understand why but a father's life is rarely as simple as a son would have it.

That marriage that devastated them all: you could see it, as Lady G did, from the perspective of tall, handsome, eloquent Johnny Yeats, who fell in love with his friend's sister and married her without knowing her, as was the way in those days, and was hit with nothing but complaints on the wedding night and never heard an affectionate word from her thereafter. Daughter of the crossest family he ever met, who withdrew ever further into depression, until illness put her beyond reach.

Or could see it from the perspective of sweet Susan Yeats, who married a barrister but then found herself hitched to an artist, hauled off to bohemian penury in London, where no notice was taken of her needs or wants.

You'd only be part right, either way, and even the two versions, side by side, didn't make up the whole of it.

"I always see her talking over a cup of tea in the kitchen," says her son now. "She was happiest there, with our servant, the fisherman's wife. Talking on the only themes outside our house that seemed of interest to her, the fishing people... They would tell each other stories that Homer might have told, pleased with the plot turns... laughing together over the satires."

"This was in Ireland?"

"At Sligo and Howth. She was never happy in London. From the time we came back, in '87, she took herself away into her own mind."

"Or was taken," says Lady G. "Do you remember, Willie, that woman we saw when collecting folklore from the London Irish, talking about the faeries taking people away? The old Kildare woman who knew the girl who didn't like to go."

"But she had to go away with them, when they called her."

"Away," Lady G says again, wistfully. "It is such a strange belief."

"It is a belief of the emotions, not the intellect. The Irish country people, as we know, make it easy to believe."

And they both know each other is recalling that night at Coole in '97, when they were out collecting stories, and the Irish singing at the crossroads, the voices melting into the twilight and the trees, carried them both so far away.

"It is a belief with which you have comforted so many," she says. "Your poem, 'The Stolen Child' expresses the belief so beautifully. Can you offer the same consolation, now, to yourself?"

"You think...Mama was..." But he can't go on. He is struggling to swallow back a sob that is trying to convulse him.

It's always hard to see a man cry but Lady G doesn't mind. Indeed, she's glad. She believes his mismanagement of Maud Gonne is all tied up with his mother. Once, his sister Lily told her that when they were children, he used to pray to die and then, after frightening himself half way to death, frantically pray that he might live. Lily told her this so lightly, so amused, but Lady G had been horrified for the poor sensitive child and his paroxysms of terror.

The sister must have seen her horror, because she went on to tell of how, whenever she or Lolly laughed at him, he would cry, not with anger but so very sorrowfully, that they would be filled with remorse. And that is how he begins to cry before her now, with a sorrow of a different kind to his conspicuous love sorrow. "I remember... so little... of childhood. Only..." He struggles to say something that must be said. "Only its pain."

The last time she saw him like this was in that terrible period back in December '98, when Maud Gonne almost sent him into madness. He had turned to her then, as now. She was in Venice when his incoherent letter arrived, out of which she could make neither rhyme nor reason. How, if Maud Gonne had finally offered him hope of a future, was it not happening?

That was before she grasped the strange complexity of their relationship. She'd set out from Venice immediately and diverted all other arrangements to go to him in Dublin, and after a long conversation, she'd understood even less. She tried to talk sense to him. If Maud Gonne had told him, "with every circumstance of deep emotion" that she loved him, why was he not now seizing his opportunity. Never mind the Parisian lover, the child, the mystical obstacles. If they were together, they would smooth all out in time, or learn to live with the rough.

"That's what marriage *is*, holding together through the challenges of life," she'd insisted. She knew what she was talking about. She'd overcome all sorts to make a success of her own marriage to a man thirty-five years her senior. "If you commit to each other, nothing else matters. Everything doesn't have to be sorted up front."

He answered in riddles. Maud Gonne's war had been in part the war of fantasy and blinded idealism against eternal law. It was too monstrous a thing, this offer of returned but unrequited love. And in any case, his entire imagination had shifted on its foundations. Who *was* Maud Gonne? He no longer knew her.

Who, indeed? Seeing the floundering depths of his confusion, Lady G arranged to meet the lady herself, to see if she might use her influence.

She was shocked by the drawn and haggard woman who came to meet her and saw no beauty there, only a death's head.

Once they settled in over scones and jam, she got straight to the point and asked Maud Gonne about her intentions.

"I think you have misunderstood, Lady Gregory," Maud Gonne said, manners impeccable but implacable. "Neither Mr. Yeats nor I are the marrying kind."

"You must know he has thought of nothing but marrying you for years."

"Neither of us is the marrying kind," Maud Gonne repeated, smiling her ghoulish smile. "We have other things which interest us more."

Tea didn't last long, and Lady G left, feeling Maud Gonne was only playing with him, out of vanity. "I do not wish her ill," she'd written to a friend later that evening. "But God is unjust if she dies a quiet death."

Even so, when Maud Gonne returned to Paris, she had offered him the funds to go after her, follow her over there and not leave her side until he had her promise.

He'd said, No.

"No," he said. "I am too exhausted. I can do no more."

And though he did follow her six weeks later, it was too late. It was all over, killed by his favorite word: perhaps.

Now finally, on this day of his mother's death, she understands. Having been in thrall, since childhood, to a woman who disliked or hardly noticed him, who became ever more unavailable, he could only fasten his love onto the unobtainable. A married woman like Mrs. Shakespear or a Gorgon like Maud Gonne.

Yes, she was a Gorgon, a Medusa. If he persists in his perplexed wooing of her, he shall have no happiness, ever. He must be brought to understanding. Yes, Lady G is glad to see the tears come. She has never felt closer to him than now. They shall always be bonded by this.

~

You could blame Tommy Gonne, I suppose, for making a consort of his daughter, something a father should never do. Or Susan Yeats for how she rejected her son, something a mother should never do. Or you could, as I did for a long time, blame

WB. He blamed himself, too, years later, writing of how, for many nights after he turned away from her and "her great labyrinth, out of pride", he lay awake, accusing himself of having done wrong. His thoughts going round and round, as do miserable thoughts, coming to no solution.

"Perhaps when one loves, one is not quite sane," is what he said of it all, when he came to write it up in his memoir. "I have often wondered if I did great evil."

That's the bit Lady G, and the critics, don't seem to see. Bedazzled by his gifts, and dismissive of his beliefs, they are blind to how he wronged Maud Gonne.

Evil. It's a big word but it's the right word. Daemonic evil. The fluttering women, like Miss Ryan in Paris and Mrs. Ellis in Bedford Park, who quaked when they saw him and feared he might put a spell on them, were not so wrong. He asked a question about spiritual ecstasy: whether it heightens not only the vision of evil, but also its fascination? He asked it of Johnson, and of Mathers, and of increasing numbers of people in the Golden Dawn, until eventually he came to ask it of himself.

But he came to no answer, of course, except perhaps.

Wrong answer because it was the wrong question. Addiction to the high of ecstasy is not spiritual. In a truer time, he said so himself, with his *Secret Rose* stories. Where there is nothing, there is God is a simultaneous equation: where there is God, there is nothing.

Angus and Lugh, like Jesus and Buddha, and the Great Father and the Great Mother, and the Holy Spirit and the people of the Shee: they are only symbols, they are not the thing itself. And if you're manipulating any of them, or anything in the God realm for your own advantage, you're not just seeing evil, or fascinated by evil. You're doing evil.

When we look at it that way, we see that he did it to many: his uncle George; others in the Order; the many women who fed him tea and sympathy, whom he put to work on his projects, and pulled into his web of mystery and wizardry; Olivia, of course. But none more than Maud Gonne.

In her, his three great interests came together: occultism,

poetry and plans for Ireland. He gave her to believe that together the two of them could control the gods and alter the
course of history. I call him evil in that.

Yes, it was easy to blame him, and for years I did, only I got
older and wiser and had to admit that she was at it too, in her
way. He wronged her and she wronged him and when I think of
the pair of them, facing each other all a-tremble on that December night, on the rim of love's great welling pool, half-clothed
and shivering, so cold but so afraid to jump, I still find it hard
not to blame them both.

Her, for not trusting enough in life, in love, in herself, to say
to him: "Help me to know that, although love is earthy, it is also
sacred and should never be traded for power or glory. Help me
put down my pride, and lie before you naked, and love you as a
man should be loved."

Him, for not trusting enough in life, in love, in himself, to say
to her: "Help me to know that, although love is ethereal, it is
also of this earth and shows its true face around cradle and coin.
Help me put down my pride, and lie before you naked, and love
you as a woman should be loved."

I could shake the pair of them; only I know, when I'm thinking right, that blame doesn't come into it. Which of us doesn't
howl for the moon through the light of day, and cry for the sun
while darkness seeks to soothe?

Who among us has never let pride defeat love? And who
wouldn't leap out of pride into love's welling waters, if we only
could? First, we have to know how.

I went deep looking for them, I wanted to know their true
story, for I knew they couldn't be as magnificent as they made
themselves out to be, or as foolish as others said. And I found
they were magnificent all right, with the magnificence that can
only grow in the ground of great foolishness. Call me satisfied.

And so it is that two years on from that fateful December
night with Maud Gonne, WB is comforted on the loss of his
mother not by her, or by any other lady love, but by his friend,
Lady Gregory.

And so it is that, just as Lady G pours the final cup from the teapot, over in Paris Maud Gonne is dropping her daughter off with her friend Ghénia, and getting ready to set off again, bound for another funds-and-profile-raising trip to America. She thinks she doesn't want to go; she dreads the journey, and the nationalist quarrels and disputations that are even worse than at home over there. She believes she does it for Ireland and has yet to realize that she is so desirous of love but unable for intimacy, that she needs her work, and the Irish people, now more than ever.

She went from WB and he turned from her but where there's life, there's learning, and the truth is always calling us out of our pride. If we don't harken, it will call louder, and throw a situation at us. A pebble at first. If we still don't listen, we'll get a stone. Then a rock. Then a great crashing boulder. We must learn, or die.

WB is learning, thinks Lady G as she sits among the used cups and the remains of their tea, watching the light fade from the London winter's day. She is loathe to call the servant and disturb their melancholy harmony. Poor boy, dear boy, he shall, now more than ever, have need of a mother.

"It is time for peace, Willie," she says, wondering if she should reach across and touch her hand to his hand. "I believe suffering has done all it can for your soul. Peace and happiness will be best for both body and soul now."

He runs his handkerchief across his eyes. "I'm sorry. To keep happy seems like walking on stilts. When one is tired, one falls off."

"Never fear, your friends are here to catch you, to help you back up. I want you now to have all you want."

So while Maud Gonne kisses Iseult and Ghénia goodbye and heads off waving and smiling, smiling and waving, these two sit on together, the portly, motherly, middle-aged woman, the lanky, bereaved young man, their silhouettes hardening in the gathering dark, so still in their companionable silence that the flickering fire in the grate seems the only thing alive in the room.

The Stolen Child

Where dips the rocky highland
Of Sleuth Wood in the lake,
There lies a leafy island
Where flapping herons wake
The drowsy water rats;
There we've hid our faery vats,
Full of berry
And of reddest stolen cherries.
Come away, O human child!
To the waters and the wild
With a faery, hand in hand,
For the world's more full of weeping than you can understand.

Where the wave of moonlight glosses
The dim gray sands with light,
Far off by furthest Rosses
We foot it all the night,
Weaving olden dances
Mingling hands and mingling glances
Till the moon has taken flight;
To and fro we leap
And chase the frothy bubbles,
While the world is full of troubles
And anxious in its sleep.
Come away, O human child!
To the waters and the wild
With a faery, hand in hand,
For the world's more full of weeping than you can understand.

Where the wandering water gushes
From the hills above Glen-Car,
In pools among the rushes
That scarce could bathe a star,
We seek for slumbering trout

And whispering in their ears
Give them unquiet dreams;
Leaning softly out
From ferns that drop their tears
Over the young streams.
Come away, O human child!
To the waters and the wild
With a faery, hand in hand,
For the world's more full of weeping than you can understand.

Away with us he's going,
The solemn-eyed:
He'll hear no more the lowing
Of the calves on the warm hillside
Or the kettle on the hob
Sing peace into his breast,
Or see the brown mice bob
Round and round the oatmeal chest.
For he comes, the human child,
To the waters and the wild
With a faery, hand in hand,
For the world's more full of weeping than he can understand.

A BRASS PLAQUE IN ST. JOHN'S CHURCH SLIGO

TO THE MEMORY OF SUSAN MARY, WIFE OF JOHN BUTLER
YEATS AND ELDEST DAUGHTER OF THE LATE WILLIAM AND
ELIZABETH POLLEXFEN OF THIS TOWN.

BORN JULY 13TH 1841, DIED JANUARY 3RD 1900.

ERECTED BY HER FOUR CHILDREN.

THE END

Publication Note

Her Secret Rose is the first book in Orna Ross's *Between The Words* trilogy, about the relationship between WB Yeats and the Gonnes, mother and daughter, Maud and Iseult.

In Book Two, *A Child Dancing*, Eileen Wilson comes to live with the Gonnes, and Maud finally gives birth to her patriot son. As England and France go to war with Germany, WB's astrological indicators seem to point to marriage. Will Maud Gonne say yes this time? Or ought he to consider Iseult, who is growing up to be as beautiful as her mother?

When Iseult's young adult rebellion is echoed by an independence rising in Ireland, WB Yeats and Maud Gonne are brought face-to-face with the terrible beauty they've created.

You can purchase *A Child Dancing* through Amazon, Apple iBooks, Kobo and other retailers. Full details on the *A Child Dancing* page on the author's website. www.ornaross.com

Sign Up For A Free Book

Would you like to receive *After the Rising*
my first novel (ebook), FREE?

You can sign up at www.ornaross.com
You'll also receive my newsletter.
No spam ever
&
you can unsubscribe any time.

Acknowledgements

My thanks to: the editorial duo, mother and daughter Joni and Jerusha Rogers and proofreader Helen Baggot; designer Jane Dixon Smith; assistant Yen Ooi; publicists Jay Artale and Valerie Shanley; and formatter Amie McCracken. To the library staff at The British Library and the National Library of Ireland. And, as always, to Philip, Ornagh and Ross.

Other Books By Orna Ross Published And Forthcoming

GO CREATIVE! BOOKS
Go Creative! It's Your Native State
How To Create Anything: A Creativist Guide
Creating Money, Creating Meaning: Getting Into Financial Flow
F-R-E-E-Writing; How To Do It & Why You Should
F-R-E-E-Writing Notebook
Inspiration Meditation
Inspiration Meditation Audio
How To Write Haiku: Moments of Creative Presence

NOVELS
The Irish Trilogy I: After The Rising
The Irish Trilogy II: Before The Fall
The Irish Trilogy III: In The Hour
The Yeats Trilogy II: A Child Dancing
The Yeats Trilogy III: But A Dream
Blue Mercy

POEMS
Ten Thoughts About Love I, II, III
Poetry For Christmas
Selected Poetry 2012-2014

AUTHOR GUIDES
Opening Up To Indie Authors (Editor)
How To Choose A Self Publishing Service (Editor)
How I Self-Publish My Books
How Authors Sell Publishing Rights (Editor)

More information at: www.ornaross.com

Made in the USA
San Bernardino, CA
01 November 2017